RETURN

to

ARCADIA

A Novel

H NIGEL THOMAS

We acknowledge the support of
the Canada Council for the Arts for our publishing program.

 Canada Council   Conseil des Arts    ONTARIO ARTS COUNCIL
for the Arts   du Canada   CONSEIL DES ARTS DE L'ONTARIO

We also acknowledge support from
the Government of Ontario through the Ontario Arts Council.

Cover design by David Drummond

Library and Archives Canada Cataloguing in Publication

Thomas, H. Nigel, 1947-
    Return to Arcadia : novel / H. Nigel Thomas.

ISBN 978-1-894770-38-5

    I. Title.

PS8589.H4578R48 2007   C813'.54   C2007-902735-0

Printed in Canada by Coach House Printing

TSAR Publications
P. O. Box 6996, Station A
Toronto, Ontario M5W 1X7
Canada

www.tsarbooks.com

[Genealogy's] task is to expose a body totally imprinted by history.

MICHEL FOUCAULT

BOOK ONE

Names! Damn Names!

1

H E GRIPS THE EDGE of the windowsill with his left hand, steadies himself, places the cane in his right hand onto the mattress, and eases himself into a sitting position on the edge of the bed. He stares out the window at a pale blue sky and a flat, sunlit, glimmering white, almost treeless land-scape. It's bounded in the distance by a street where there's swift traffic. To his left, the land is vast with icy patches. In places the wind stirs the snow and mists the surrounding air. A strong wind whistles over and around the building. Each gust rattles the glass in the window.

It's the first time he notices the landscape around this mysterious build-ing. He tries to remember the name of another place that is flat for miles around, that's sometimes green and sometimes brown, that's bounded, he's sure, by a snarling, pounding sea on one side, and on the other side by smoke-grey mountains.

He gazes upwards, at fangs of ice hanging from the cornice, reflecting the sun's light. For a moment it's as if he has been half-swallowed by a dragon, and the window is a transparent glottis through which he sees the dragon's diamond fangs.

The Saint Lawrence is near here, he vaguely remembers Dr Stein telling him some time ago, after asking him whether the Saint Lawrence was "a lake, a river, a sea, or a country." "A river—a river in Canada," he'd replied as he would have done in his high school geography class, in a past that's now reduced to grey billowing smoke. Stein said his identity was returning. His palms began to sweat.

He turns his head slightly to the right and looks at a spot where there are trees. Their bare, grey twigs hide nothing, except when they're bundled by the gusting wind. There are redbrick apartment buildings some three hundred feet away, outside a chain-link fence with a gate that's now open. To the far right, about 150 feet from the window, a long, oxblood, rectangular four-storey brick building hides the view.

"How are you today, Mr Cock Robin?" he hears Dr Stein asking from the doorway at his back.

"Fine, but Cock Robin's not my name. That much I can tell you." He doesn't turn to face Doctor Stein, keeps his eyes focused on a rime-patterned part of the window.

"What's it, then?"

He doesn't answer.

"How's your foot feeling?"

"Like a painful foot. Pain's necessary."

"When it isn't pleasure." Now it's Dr Defoe speaking.

Cock Robin turns his head. The usual trio is there. Gladys Knights, in her baggy, drab, bark-brown clothes, her bulk taking up more than half the space inside the doorway, faithfully holds the tape recorder.

"What were you staring at?" Defoe continues. The light from the window transforms his eyes into glowing blond marbles. His glossy black, mixed-race curls and oak-coloured forehead glisten.

"Just wondering why this place looks both strange and familiar."

Stein says, "You are in . . .?"

"Montreal. And you are not Sparrow. I know that now. How did I get to Montreal and then to . . . ?"

"Douglas Hospital."

"A . . . ?"

"Psychiatric hospital."

"Psychiatric. I've been here before."

"Not according to our records," Stein says.

"How do you know that? You don't know my name."

Stein starts to say something but checks himself.

There's a long pause.

"Which letter will we be working on today, folks?"

"J," Stein replies and begins putting on his glasses. They are suspended from a copper chain. They magnify the wrinkles below and at the corners of his eyes and make his bulbous nose seem larger. It's usually Gladys who reads, and Cock Robin is supposed to stop her if the name she mentions means anything to him. So far the names they've called are not his, unless he has forgotten his name.

But today it's Stein who reads from the thick, worn, blue-black book. "Jack, Jacob, Jake, James, Japheth, Jarred, Jason, Jasper, Jemmoth, Jethro,

Jim, Job, Joel, John." After each name Stein lifts his head to see Cock Robin's reactions. Gladys's and Defoe's eyes are spotlighted on Cock Robin.

Cock Robin returns to staring out the window.

"Jonathan, Joseph . . . "

"*Joseph and Jonathan,*" he interrupts Stein and pauses for a while. "But they're not my real names." His hands begin to sweat and his skin tightens the way it does when he's in a dusty place.

"Pseudonyms?"

"Yes, pseudonyms."

"Why *pseudonyms?*"

"If I knew would I be trapped here?"

"You mean this has happened to you before?"

"I'm sure it has. Maybe even here."

"In London? Paris? Madrid?"

He doesn't answer.

"In your confused state, you told us you've lived in those cities. Did you?"

"*Sí. Sí. Es verdad. Pero no me acuerdo mucho.*"

"What did you study in school?"

"Don't remember."

"You think someone might've hit you over the head and stolen your wallet before the police found you? You had a contusion on the back of your head."

"More likely hit from inside my head."

"Now you're speaking in riddles."

"Riddle me! Riddle me!" He giggles. *I don't have to be hit over the head to have welts.* "May I rest now? Oh, and may I go for a walk later? I'd like to see what's behind that four-storey brick building."

"To the south?"

"Yes." The word south orients him, and he remembers east, west, north, and how to find them.

"I'll get an aid to accompany you after lunch. But go easy on your left foot. Before I leave, though, I want to ask you one more question: Who is Sparrow?"

"He kept the accounts. Was supposed to. He pronounced his nickname Sparrer."

"Is he alive?"

"Yes and no. That's two questions, Doctor Stein. He is more alive now than before he died. You would be too, depending on the life you lead."

"Do you see his ghost?"

"His ghost!"

"You said you used to see your sister's."

"Yes. That's certainly true." He pauses. "Maybe I dreamed it. I've told you: gales howl in my head when I try to remember some things."

"Do you see Sparrow's ghost?"

"No. It's in me."

"You mean his ghost possesses you?"

"No, *I* possess *it*." He shakes his head with a can-you-believe-it gesture. "'*Each man kills the thing he loves/ but each man does not die.*' '*Greater love hath no man than to lay down his life for his friends,*'" he quotes in a drone. "Ever loved anyone that deeply, Doctor Stein?"

"I guess not: I'm still alive."

"You, Dr Defoe? You're so silent."

Defoe doesn't answer.

"Dr Stein, I used to think you were Sparrow come back from the dead to haunt me." He knows he's jesting. "Have you ever been a fundamentalist preacher?"

Stein says nothing.

"Well, it's one with fundament."

Stein looks puzzled.

"The arse, Doctor. That organ that processes shit? '*Fair and foul are next of kin.*'" He pauses, concentrates. "'*Love has pitched his mansion in the place of excrement.*' There's someone who knew a thing or two about shit."

"More important to spot it," Defoe says.

"Some hoard it."

"What are you running away from?" Stein asks.

They're provoking me so I'd blurt out something useful to them. "Now, *you* are full of shit, Dr Stein. You're paid to give your patients shit, right? Just leave me alone. Go analyze your own shit. If it doesn't poison you, you'll be old before there's time for mine."

He hopes they leave now.

"Do you know why you're here?" Stein continues.

He sighs, exasperated. "Because the police brought me here. You told me so. And you've kept me here." He pauses. His jaws are clamping; he has to force to get the words out. "Because I'm poisoned."

"So you haven't been disposing of your own shit, then," Defoe says.

"Stop being so vulgar, Dr Defoe! You're black so I know you've been taught to respect your elders."

"There's enough spunk in you to make two people well. Keep it up," Defoe says.

"Where do you live?" Stein asks.

He rolls his eyes. "Montreal. You've told me so several times, Dr Stein."

"Where in Montreal?"

He's a while answering. "I'd love to know. But the rent is paid. I pay my rent a year ahead of time. That much I remember."

"That's unusual."

"Not really. Why can't I remember anything?" He deliberately turns away from them and returns to looking out the window, at the trees. Eventually he says, "Doctors, you've already asked me ten questions, not one! Didn't you learn to count in med school?"

Now he knows what will make them leave. "Weren't you a Rhodes scholar?" he asks, turning to stare at Stein.

"In fact I was. How did you know that?"

Cock Robin smiles but doesn't know how he knows.

"Were you?" Stein's pupils have dilated and some of his facial wrinkles have vanished.

"No."

"Why did you ask?" His wrinkles have returned.

"Doctor Stein, if you, a Rhodes scholar, don't know, it's pointless my telling you."

"Am I on trial?"

"Certainly. Unless you're spiritually dead. I see now. You're part of my illness. Bye-bye." He lifts his right hand and wiggles his fingers in a contemptuous bye-bye gesture.

Stein and his retinue leave, and Cock Robin-Joseph-Jonathan (who knows he is not altogether Cock Robin-Joseph-Jonathan) picks up the cane he uses to ease the pressure on his left foot when he moves around. He leans on it, gets up from the edge of the bed where he's been sitting, walks around the foot of the bed and goes to sit in the armchair on the other side, near the head of his bed.

He's in the isolation room. He knows he has money. Knows too that unless he can remember where it is, they'll put him in the public ward, and that would be a live burial. If he wanders out onto the street, would he find the bank? What would he say his name was? Perhaps someone would recognize him and call out to him. The question of his leaving the isolation room didn't come up today. He appreciates the privacy of this room, especially when he hears the howls and yells of the patients in the large communal room that he goes through whenever he takes the short indoor walks he has been prescribed. He would bully the staff in whatever way he could to avoid being sent there.

Thinking these thoughts he dozes.

His sister Bita sits on the armrest of the chair and takes his face in her hand the way she used to in the hallucinations he had during his first wipeout at age sixteen.

"Bita, you no longer come to see me."

"Hush."

"You've come to get me?"

"Hush."

"Why'd you go without me?"

"Hush."

"Sing me one of your songs."

"Be quiet, Joshua!"

"Joshua! That's my name."

"Bita! Bita!" he shouts, half-awake.

Leroy, the orderly, comes running.

"Joshua Éclair! Don't forget it. Tell Dr Stein. Joshua Éclair! Her name was Averill Éclair. Joshua Éclair." Something dissolves in him, like a frozen river melting, releasing torrents of water; outside his body, it literally feels like the cutting loose of a tightly wound rope—and he sobs, loud, hiccupping sobs.

Stein arrives, followed by Defoe and Gladys.

They look away from him, uncomfortably.

"It's all right. It's all right," he tells them. He takes a tissue from the box on the night table on his right, wipes his eyes and blows his nostrils. "What would you like to know?"

"You don't have to talk now," Defoe says. "We could come back."

"No. Stay."

"How many names do you use?" Stein asks.

"I don't know."

"Why so many?"

"Joshua Éclair is a borrowed name. Joshua Éclair pays the bills. Please write down my adopted mother's name: Averill Éclair. Dead but not buried."

They stay on a few more minutes, and when they leave they post Leroy to his room. Joshua gets into bed, lies on his back and closes his eyes.

"Who're you talking to? Your lips are moving." It's Dr Stein. He's alone. Joshua didn't hear him reenter the room.

"My sister."

"What're you telling her?"

"None of your business."

"Where's your sister?"

"In the Atlantic."

"How did you come by all this money?"

"I got it from Averill Éclair. She got it from Cecil Rhodes or her husband—same thing. Rhodes was the archetype. Before him Prospero." He stares hard at the doctor, expecting a reaction.

None comes.

"The immediate problem is solved." He takes a deep, audible breath. "I can now have my own private room. Tomorrow you will have my bank account, my social insurance number and my health insurance number. You and your damn hospital will be paid."

"You are angry."

"You are lucky not to be. We can't control what history does. A puppeteer we perform for until our strings break or we're thrown onto the rubbish heap. We eat its fruits—are its fruits—are the spokes in its wheel; we nurse its wounds, wear its crutches, repeat its lies, enact its horrors." He wants to stop, but the stuff, like water heading down a cataract, just rushes out.

"Would you like a sedative?"

"Yes. Shut me up. It's all you can do for me, Doctor: write prescriptions!" He's shouting. He wants to stop but is unable to. "Damn Joshua Éclair! Damn all Éclairs! Damn history! Damn humanity! Damn you, too, Doctor! Where's that sedative?"

"Gladys will bring it shortly," Stein says softly.

"Let her bring cyanide too."

2

THE SUPPER TRAY IS STILL sitting on the trolley it was wheeled in on. The radio is on and playing "Help Me Make it Through the Night"—Gladys Knights's rendition, the real Gladys Knights. And day too, Joshua thinks. He brought it, the radio, a small short wave he uses to get the BBC, back from his apartment earlier that day.

He is tired and anxious despite earlier willing himself to be calm. The trips to the bank and to his apartment this morning have thrown him back into the world he'd run from. As things stand, he doesn't need to pay the hospital any money. At the bank, they gave him a comfortable armchair, gave Leroy a plastic one, and brought them coffee, while they searched and found out that he had medical insurance to cover private hospital care, including his personal nurse. He doesn't remember having the policy, though he remembers some talk of insurance while he was in England. It has probably been following him around since Isabella Island. There must have been a time when he paid attention to such things.

Accompanied by Leroy, he headed from the bank to his apartment—on Saint-Marc, about fifty feet in from Ste-Catherine.

Leroy is Jamaican. Tamarind brown—and tamarind tart—with an open, oval, unpretentious face; flat nose and moderately thick lips. There are natural gaps between his upper incisors. Has all his teeth. No signs of fillings. Is irritating sometimes, but Joshua likes him.

Hates silence. During the fifteen minutes it took them to get from the hospital to the bank, he learned that Leroy has eight children, because his religion forbids birth control. *Sparrow did not need to practice birth control. His religion was also against it. What did Sparrow call his church? People named it Pastor Sparrow Chu'ch (swallowing the r, moulding the name to fit their tongue or acknowledging that it lacked something: righteousness perhaps).* Leroy does not drink and attends church three times per week. Leroy even had time to propose a cure for him: "When you come out o' the hospital, you must come join in worship with we, Mister Éclair. We have a woman in the congregation. She did sick plenty more worse than you. Yes, man, sick can't done. And is 'bout ten years now she better, stop taking her pills and everything. God mercy and grace straighten her head out. Straighten it out good-good."

Leroy's Pastor is called Blassingame, and Joshua teased Leroy, saying it was a heavy name; was he a Blessinggame? Could he preach? How good were his games? His eyes gleaming, excitement in his voice, Leroy said no dry eyes are in the church after Blassingame's sermons, and when "the holy spirit full him so, him drip sweat. Sumpen for behold. That church does rock. Rock, I tell you. Brothers and sisters jump, roll 'pon the floor full o'

God's praise and the Holy Ghost. Him does be like Michael blowing that trumpet and fulling us up with the holy spirit."

"Do you all rip off your clothes?" He was remembering the sexually inflamed Dionysian women who hurled themselves onto bulls' horns and a hilarious novel: *Lord of Dark Places.*

"Your mind in the gutter, Mr Éclair."

Joshua envies his simple faith. He thinks of the members of Sparrow's church counting their blessings and forgetting their curses without a Blassingame, making do with a Sparrow, but prancing just the same.

The janitor had to let them into the apartment because Joshua didn't know where his keys were. He found the keys where he usually keeps them, on a hook inside the door. The apartment smelt like a rotting corpse. It's one large room, about twenty-five by fifteen feet, with a tiny alcove that serves as a kitchenette and a separate room that is the bathroom. All the furniture in it are a sofa-bed (which was open, the sheets tousled), a recliner, a small oak table for two with matching chairs, a single floor lamp, and several book shelves lining the two walls where there are no windows. Weeks of newspapers lay heaped in a corner. In front of the bookshelves, books were strewn about the floor. Several of the shelves were empty.

A whirring sound in the kitchenette distracted him. Leroy was already heading there. It came from the exhaust fan above the stove. His wallet was on the counter, along with decayed food, dried out and coated with green and grey furry moss in the supermarket styrofoam trays.

"Is a good thing you forget your fan on," Leroy said.

Joshua was thinking how vital a wallet is and how different things might've been if he'd had it on him.

"I say," Leroy repeated loud, "is a good thing you forget your fan on."

"What do you mean?"

"People would o' have to leave this building. It would o' been stinking is what I mean. This is meat," he indicated with a heave of his chin, "that been on the counter here a long long time. See? It rotten first and afterwards it dry out."

"I should get this place cleaned up. Into a rubbish bin you keep dumping rubbish. Wouldn't you say so, Leroy?"

"Longst you empty it when it full up."

"And what if you yourself are bin?"

"You get somebody for empty it."

Literal Leroy. A simple—or is it cunning?—soul. Leave Leroy alone, he tells himself now.

"Mr Éclair, you going need somebody for help you put this place here back in order and somebody for keep it in order after you get discharge. I know a trustworthy church sister who will do it for you for a good price."

"That will have to wait, Leroy, until I am discharged."

"I know, but a nice, trustworthy, honest sister ask me for keep me eye out if me see a chance for she make couple o' dollars."

"Is she your mistress, Leroy?"

"Me is a save, born-again man, Mr Éclair. What devilish thing you asking me?"

"But you are a man just the same. With eight children as proof."

"He-he-he. You is embarrassing me, Mr Éclair. The Bible say not for yield to temptation, Mr Éclair."

"Leroy, I also need somebody who can put my books in alphabetical order. This sister, or mistress, can she read and write?"

"She read the Bible good-good, pronounce good-good like a school teacher, Mr Éclair."

"Does she obey it?"

"We all does."

"Be serious!"

"By the grace of God, we does. Don't forget your keys-them. Me going out 'pon Sainte-Catherine for flag down a taxi. You not going run 'way on me for get me in trouble?" he asked, staring at Joshua pleadingly.

"No, Leroy."

"You sure? Me have eight pickney and a wife for feed, you know. Job like thisya one, when you lose it, you not getting it back at all."

"Why don't the two of us just walk to Ste-Catherine and flag down a taxi there?"

Leroy reminds him of Henry, the yardboy at Arcadia during his youth. Something about Leroy's naivety and transparent guile.

Quite a morning, Joshua tells himself. Amnesia has its advantages. A great anaesthetic. You get better. To do what? Watch the days go by? Read about the world's calamities? He no longer owns a TV. He got rid of it during the Ethiopian famine. Human misery is live, scripted, and unscripted theatre. Obscene. The Six O'clock Calamity Hour. In the US, The Crime and Disaster Report.

In the doorway of Union United Church in Montreal, he'd observed an altercation between an antiapartheid advocate and a woman reporter covering Bishop Tutu's Montreal visit. Signing a petition for sanctions against South Africa would put her in conflict of interest, she told the advocate.

"And conflict is your principal and interest," the advocate countered.

The reporter's face reddened and her knuckles whitened from the ferocity with which she held her professionalism and her microphone.

Enough "objective coverage" of sorrow and depravity. Must he get well just to battle his way through the labyrinth of human foolishness?

The thoughts he had when he rented the St-Marc apartment return to him: *sometimes we need the tower—of brick, not ivory; sometimes the cavern—dry with an egress.* He never quite decided whether the apartment had been one or the other. But there he'd managed, until a few weeks ago, to give his *me* definite shape and weight; had pared it down to a thing he could at last carry, a thing he'd encapsulated deep in his innards. Even if, in his pellucid moments, a me/it split was there: the carrier and the carried. In fuzzier, dreary moments me/it interlaced. On the worse occasions clarity went altogether and returned only after some unnameable force in him sorted out and reassembled the displaced chunks, and cleansed each chunk of the other's debris. A confounding that came suddenly, seismically or quietly, and took two to three days to repair, during which he was barely functional. Other than one time when he'd had no awareness of his existence for two days, the blanks rarely exceeded half a day; and oftentimes he knew one had occurred because he was unable to tell, for example, what happened between washing his breakfast plate and CBC Radio's *The World at Six*.

Whatever brought it on had its own will. And the experience though paralyzing was cleansing, like leeches fed by the festering they relieve, and left him with the sort of peace he'd felt as a child on his Union Island holiday jaunts.

When he had classes on his recuperating days, if he made it there, the lecture drifted past him like a noisy vapour, and it was the noise the students made while getting up that let him know they were over.

About five years after he moved to Montreal, one fall Friday atop Mount Royal, while he contemplated the leaves carpeting the ground under the bare trees, the thought occurred to him that he should try his hand at writing. It would be a good way to preserve his solitude while making his life useful. What would he write about? How does one write? Obviously having a desire to write was a good way to start. The sky in the direction of Côtes-des-Neiges was a dense grey, so he headed down the steps and home as quickly as he could before the rain began falling. Perhaps he should write children's books. He walked over to his bookshelves and fingered the spines of the books, then to his window from which he looked onto Ste-Catherine Street and up at Mount Royal, now a grey blur, for the rain had begun to fall. People, leaving work early, moved briskly under their black umbrellas along Ste-Catherine Street. His mind went back to his years at Queen Mary College, to his lecturer for eighteenth- and nineteenth-century British fiction. In his introductory lecture, the lecturer, something of a misogynist, had asked them if they remembered Pope's line about women turning bottles and calling out for corks (They'd certainly remembered. The males had changed the wording in various ways right there in class—one version he remembered: "women turn bottles beg to be uncorked"—and the lecturer had laughed). "Some of the women writers we'll be looking at were spinsters, some wives, and writing was their way to uncork—they had no other. They gave to characters desires they weren't allowed to have, and some of what they wrote was exquisite." (His comment did not apply to George Eliot but none of them knew enough to tell him so.)

Gazing at the Ste-Catherine traffic, it struck Joshua that writing might be his way to uncork. But what came out could very well undo him. He thought of writers who'd been insane: Roethke, Lowell, Woolf, Nelligan. No, he mustn't write, couldn't write, shouldn't write, about himself. His books, if he ever wrote them, would be for children. *How did one write? Even for children? Especially for children?* It had to be entertaining and full of fantasy. Like Lewis Carroll's Alice. He became afraid, thought of Virgina Woolf: *journeying into fantasy was a sure way to lose one's sanity.* He knew the pen name he would write under: Prufrock, the name his classmates had given him in high school after Mr Morrison, their literature teacher, had taught them "The Lovesong of J. Alfred Prufrock." Later they'd shortened the nickname to Proufy. This was before he'd had his breakdown. After his illness they returned to calling him Joshua, and he'd wondered why.

He got no further with writing. Mostly his days brimmed with boredom. And now, here at the hospital, they are a thorny shrub reaching over and around him, hemming him in; and he wishes for an axe, a scythe, something to cut a liberating path. Not to be had. And time, lead-weighted, nets him in its heavy greyness.

A straightened-out head. Joshua laughs as he recalls Leroy's prescribed cure. Well, he hopes the sister doesn't have same-sex needs or Leroy's ilk would not care whether insanity swallows up the rest of her life. Fundamentalist cruelty. Or cruel fundament that's a fundamentalist's necessity. Leroy's Levitical life.

An hour after lunch, Nurse Knights entered with clipboard and pen. Now that parts of his memory have returned, they're desperate to know everything about him, urgently, as if lucidity is brief: an *Exodus* breach in Cecil B De Mille's Red Sea.

She eyed the armchair beside his bed, decided it couldn't hold her and remained standing at the foot of his bed. "What's your occupation, Mr Éclair?" pen pressed against clipboard, clipboard pressed like a lover's head against her copious breasts.

"Nothing," he told her.

"What did you use to do before you became unemployed?" she insisted, the clipboard now in her left hand and level with her thigh, the pen in the right, a weapon clasped by four fingers, that she flicks off-on, on-off nonstop, as she stared, frowning; her eyes slanting and getting smaller and threatening to disappear in their sockets; her perfume strong, rose-scented.

"I was never employed."

"You've *never* had a job!" Incredulity in her voice; a slanting of the head, an askance widening of the eyes furrowing her facial flesh.

"No. Never."

"Well, I have never met anyone fifty-one years of age who has never worked.

"You'll find *many* on *other* wards."

But she didn't understand because she replied, "Even the Royal family works."

"I daresay it does. In any event it gets paid."

"So how do you live?"

"Better than the Royal family: better than the lilies of the field, gloriously and better clad than Solomon but barely wise." After a short silence, he added, "It's not important, Nurse Knights."

"Call me Gladys."

"Okay, Gladys. I have a job in an employment category Employment Canada does not recognize, so I'm afraid to tell you."

"Not even a hint?"

"Not even a hint, because my hints would become your howls."

Yesterday, Leroy had taken him for a walk on the hospital grounds, and he'd asked Leroy if he'd ever paid for sex. Leroy seemed shocked, had stood still for a good fifteen seconds. Later Dr Stein asked him whether there was someone in his life. He said no. And Dr Stein wanted to know whether he bought affection. He'd told Stein it was none of his business and had fumed for a long time over the fact that his idle question had been reported to Dr Stein.

"Well, then I'll have to speculate," Gladys Knights interrupted his thinking, relaxed, her tone jovial—the way he likes to see her, when humour veils the etchings of her own suffering.

"Do that. If it's good you could publish it, and maybe die famous. Don't you want to be famous, like your namesake?"

"Why are you giving me a hard time?" She was giving him an under-the-eyelids look. Quite seductive.

"You look seductive, Gladys. Are you always this charming?"

"Stop flirting with me. I have no illusions about how I look."

"All right. Let's make a deal: you won't ask me anymore questions and I won't flirt with you."

"I can't."

"Well, I can."

"You're impossible."

"That's because you're well and I'm sick. Have you a boyfriend?"

"That's none of your business."

"Have you a girlfriend?"

"You are weird."

"I know what it is: you have a boyfriend and a girlfriend. The three of you live in the same gingerbread house in the middle of a forest and sleep in the same four-poster king-size bed that has a red counterpane. And your boyfriend sleeps in the middle always with his clothes on. And your girlfriend whips you to make you come."

Her eyes grew large and her face and ears turned lilac. Even the colossal half-formed drop under her chin came alive. "I think I'd better leave you alone."

"I think so too."

Silently, quickly, her hips fully cooperating, she left the room.

He thinks he needs a sedative. He doesn't know the evening nurse well. She's Bonita Ramon, a Filipino, and she's not particularly friendly. He presses the call button and waits for her to come and give him whatever's been prescribed to turn his thoughts off.

3

NOW HE IS FULLY ABLE to remember his past.

The woman came into the yard. The sun was shining directly on her. Her eyes were two tiny pools of deep water. They frightened him. Her hair looked like the sun before it set behind *El Tigre*. Her nose was like a sharp ridge. Her lips were thin as paper. There were tiny wrinkles that ran in curved lines at the corners of her mouth. She smelt different from everyone he'd ever met—like jasmine after sunset, as if she were a flower. Her toenails showed through the sandals she was wearing and looked as if they were bleeding. Her fingernails bled too. She stared at him often, and each time she did he looked away. She was wearing dark glasses, and when she took them off to wipe them, he saw that there were tiny lines at the outer corners of her eyes too.

She was wearing a sleeveless cream bodice and short khaki pants. Her arms from halfway above her elbow all the way down to her hands were darker than the parts above it. The upper parts of her thighs were paler too. He could hear her breathing and he watched her chest—with its breasts upright, not hanging down like Mammy's—rise and fall like fields of ready-to-cut, ripe sugar cane when the wind gusted over them. When she breathed out, her nostrils shook slightly. When she turned around, he saw that her back was straight and that there were no mounds where she should have a bottom. He wanted her to leave so he could ask Bita why this woman did not have a bottom. But just as he was expecting her to leave, Mammy took him inside and put clean clothes on him, and told him the woman was going to take him for a ride in her car. He said he wasn't going unless Bita came with him. Mammy said Bita couldn't go. Bita had to remain with her. He held on to Bita. He kicked the White woman on her shin when she tried to put her arm around him. The White woman went a little distance away from them, beckoned to his mother to come where she was, and spoke to his mother in a whisper. Next his mother pulled Bita aside and spoke with her. Then the woman said Bita could come too.

The woman sat in the front seat beside the driver. He sat on the back seat with Bita. In her hand Bita held her box, which contained shells and pieces of coloured glass, coloured thread, and needles. She handed him the box.

She used to spank him whenever he played with it. Now she told him he could keep it. He did not want it. He only wanted to be allowed to play with it. But Bita insisted that she was giving it to him.

The car went into a big gate and they went into a house that was big and frightening. The room in which he and Bita sat had lots of windows (the same ones he would break twelve years later) with what he later knew were silk burgundy drapes. They were drawn and the room was dark (to keep the house cool, he found out later). The floor was of dark wood. The furniture strange. It was, they told him long after, Louis XVI, upholstered in silk brocade that featured old country roses on a pale grey field. There were paintings—ships half-buried under waves, men on galloping horses, armies facing each other with long spears—in large frames all over the walls. In the centre of the room hung a gigantic crystal chandelier whose rainbow light caught his attention momentarily. It all frightened him. The biggest building he'd been in was the Camden clinic and that was about half the size of this house. He stayed close to Bita.

He and Bita were taken into the kitchen and given food, but he did not eat his. Worms, like the ones that came out of his bottom when Mammy forced castor oil down his throat, were on their plates. Strange, people eating worms! Strange too, Bita ate hers and said it wasn't worms, it was macaroni. But he knew they were lying.

With Bita looking on, Marie, a po-po, yaller woman with long straight hair on which she wore a white bonnet, bathed him and lathered his body with cream, then dressed him in perfumed new pyjamas. Wearing a nightgown that swallowed her and dragged on the floor, Bita crept into the same bed with him. She cried a long time but she did not tell him why.

When he woke up next morning, Bita was gone. The box she'd offered him the day before was on the side of the bed where she'd slept. He rushed out of the room screaming her name. Marie came running and told him to stop screaming, that good little boys didn't scream.

"Where Bita?"

"She gone home."

"No. She won' go an' leave me."

"Come, let we go see Mistress. She can answer your question-them."

Marie took him into a room where the White woman was sitting on a pale blue sofa, reading.

"Good morning, Joshua. Did you sleep well last night?"

He did not answer.

"You've lost your tongue, Joshua. Open your mouth and let me see if you have a tongue."

Joshua pressed his lips close and clenched his teeth.

"See? I have a tongue." She stretched out her tongue. "You don't have one. Open your mouth, let's see."

But Joshua kept his mouth clamped.

"Mistress, he want for know where his sister is."

"Now, Joshua, you no longer have a sister. You are my son and I don't have a daughter."

He became afraid and began to cry. He remembered stories Bita had told him about people who ate children that misbehaved. Now he was sure he would be eaten because sometimes Bita said he was bad. Bita was bad sometimes. That was when Mammy beat her. This woman probably ate Bita during the night and it would be his turn next. He stared into her blue eyes and wondered when she would eat him. "I want Bita! I want Bita!" he hiccupped through his sobs.

"Leave him with me, Marie."

But Joshua clung to Marie and began to scream louder. He was not going to let this woman eat him the way she had eaten Bita.

"Carry me home. Me want for go home." But the thought crossed his mind that with Bita eaten, there would be no one there to protect him. Now he knew he would be eaten for sure by this White woman who talked funny.

Later that day he gave Marie the slip, got past the porch and lay flat on his belly intending to crawl all the way to the gate in the hope that someone had left it open. But Booges began to growl at him and to bare his fangs. As Booges moved towards him, he screamed. Booges moved away with his head almost touching the ground. But it was too late. Marie and another servant had heard his scream and had come running.

"When you get 'way from me?" Marie asked him.

He did not answer.

"That will teach you not for wander away from me like that. Booges, come here."

Booges came with his head hanging and his tongue lolling. Joshua's heart battered his ribs.

Marie told Booges to take care of Joshua, if Joshua was a nice boy. She then made Joshua promise that he would be a nice boy. By then Booges began to wag his tail and to sidle up to him.

"Pat his head," Marie said. "He like you; he telling you he want for be your friend." She took Joshua's hand and put it on Booges's head.

Joshua patted Booges and pushed his fingers into his black and white fur (he was part collie). They became friends. Whenever Joshua came down the porch steps Booges would run to him and wag his tail, and rub his snout against Joshua's hand, and would hint that he wanted them to walk. He would walk ahead of Joshua, as if he felt he had to show him the premises. He would walk ahead, stop and look at Joshua, as if saying, "Aren't you coming? Hurry up! Slow-coach." The first time, Booges took him to the orchard, which was behind the chicken coop. But the gate leading into it was closed, and he imagined he heard Booges saying, "That damn Henry!" There was every fruit tree in it: breadfruit, plumrose, avocado, orange, grapefruit, tangerine, cashew, golden apple, mango, coconut, sapodilla, guava, sugar apple, soursop, hog plum. Through the chain-link fence he could see several mangoes and avocados rotting on the ground. Every day he and Booges explored the grounds. Sometimes they'd sit down on the grass or on the porch and Booges would snuggle up to him and take whichever hand was close to him and put it on his fur.

As for Marie, her arms were as thin as rope and her fingers looked like twigs. The evening after she'd made Booges befriend him, he watched her arms closely while she was bathing him. He'd never seen anybody *po-po* so. And Bita was no longer there to tell him why Marie was *po-po* so. Marie's legs resembled a girl's who'd cussed with Bita and whom Bita had called "goat foot gal"—someone whose legs and knees angled forward and whose shin bones curved outward and looked bent, so that when the person hop-walked, her bottom was up in the air, sort of like a goat's. "Marie, what make you so *po-po*?" he asked her.

"That is how God make me," she snapped. "What else you want for know?"

He wanted to tell her she walked like a goat, but knew it wasn't a nice thing to say, because the girl whom Bita had called goat foot had picked up a stick and said she would beat Bita with it until she turned porridge; and he didn't want Marie to get vexed with him.

For a few nights Marie stayed with him until he fell asleep. He was always surprised when he woke up to find that she was not there and that he had not been eaten.

Then other than the memory of peeing his bed and sleepwalking, a blank space replaced those first few weeks. He would wake up walking in the living room and not know where he was.

Marie placed a piece of plastic over the mattress and told him that Mistress would not like it if she found out he was peeing his bed. "Try."

"I try, Marie. I say I will get up and then like I in the toilet and peeing and in the morning I see I peed my bed," and he would cry. And Marie would say, "Don't cry. I not going to tell Mistress but you must try harder."

"I will try harder."

Then suddenly it stopped.

There was a time when he began speaking to the White woman, would even go to her room, sometimes with Marie and sometimes alone, and the White woman, who told him to call her mommy, would tease him and he would laugh. He was no longer afraid of her but he still wondered if she had eaten Bita, and one day he started to ask her but he could not finish the question. What if she said yes. And he became aware that he had a big room that started to fill up with toys. He sat at table to eat, and someone, maybe Marie, pushed a napkin into his shirt and stopped him from eating with his fingers, and there was always a lot to eat. And he was no longer sure whether Bita had been eaten.

Then he was allowed to go outside on his own and move about and watch Henry, the yardboy, mowing the lawn and tending the flowers and taking care of the chickens and turkeys. Henry always wore a green cap and dungarees that were discoloured at the knees. His clothes had a faint smell of horse manure. When it rained, he wore rubber boots that reached to his knees. They made a loud sshwoo-sshwoo sound whenever he moved, as if they were passing wind. Whenever he was looking after the flowers, he wore a second belt to which was attached a pair of pruning shears that he used to clip the dead flowers. When the sun was hot, he scooped the sweat off his forehead with his fingers, shook his fingers, and then wiped them on his dungaree trousers. Sometimes he untucked his shirt and used the tails to wipe the sweat off his face. He had a narrow face, and when he smiled he showed small even teeth, and his chin, on which there were scattered tufts of beard, would raise slightly, his flesh pull back to his ears, and his eyes would brighten.

One day Joshua snuggled up close to him and felt his beard and was surprised that it felt rough, like a grater. Henry wrinkled his brow and looked displeased. He dropped his tools, picked Joshua up and put him on the front porch and said, "Stay up there. You keeping me back from finishing my work." But Joshua went back onto the grounds and stayed a few feet away and taunted Henry with, "See, you can' catch me? You can' catch me."

But Henry said, "Master Joshua, you is more than all right. I have for get my work done," and thereafter ignored him. Dawn was cleaning the bedrooms. Marie was busy in the kitchen with Rose, who, whenever he was in the kitchen, always told him to stay quiet, her voice angry as if she was going to spank him or hit him with anything she got her hands on. Her reddish, teary eyes, the flesh under them darkish and swollen, made her look evil. When Dawn was in the kitchen, she would hug him, stroke his face, put him on her lap and sing for him. If he did not smile for her, she'd tickle him, and he would resist until he could no longer hold back his giggling. And if Rose shouted at him, Dawn would say, "Don't mind Rose; she can't control she mouth. She vexatious no end 'cause she don't got chick nor child. She wouldo' like for have one that look just like you, Joshua." Dawn shook with laughter then. Rose would cut her eye at Dawn and say, "Tell me something, the devil riding you today?" Then Rose would start shouting orders at Dawn, at which time Joshua knew he was in the way. Even in later years, when he understood that he had power and she did not, he never ventured close to Rose whenever she was alone.

That day, alone on the porch, he felt sad and bored, and he missed Bita and Miss Bessie, the woman who took care of him when Bita was at school. Eventually he played with Booges.

Once a week, usually on a Wednesday, Henry churned ice cream on the back steps outside the kitchen, periodically adding ice cubes and salt. Rose always reminded the milkman that Wednesday was ice cream day and he had to bring extra milk. It was the estate's own milk, and Marie let him drink as much as he could drink. Once Joshua wanted to churn the ice cream maker, but Henry said his arms weren't strong enough. Joshua insisted. Henry told him that people with his colour didn't churn ice cream makers.

The chickens and turkeys were in a coop in a fenced-off area behind a line of willow trees about a hundred yards from the house. Often he went with Henry to watch him collect the eggs in a basket. The roosters here were three or four times the size of those that wandered around his mother's hut. The biggest one—a white one with a scarlet comb and spurs the size of Joshua's thumbs—was placed among several hens. It would flap its wings, stirring up dust and twigs, rear on its legs and crow whenever Joshua approached the section of the coop where it was. One day he went to the coop with Booges. Henry was at the back painting the latticework enclosing the rear porch that gave off the bedrooms. Joshua did not know that

Henry had let the chickens out of the roost. The rooster that loved to flap its wings came towards Joshua with its head bowed close to the ground and its wings outstretched, and before Joshua knew what was happening it leaped at him. Booges growled and jumped at it, causing it to veer away and run for cover. Joshua could hear his heart pounding his ribcage. Booges sidled up to him, wagged his tail, and whimpered, until Joshua patted him and assured him that he was all right. Together they returned to the house.

Whenever Henry collected guavas, with which Dawn and Rose made jam, he allowed Joshua to eat as many as he wanted, and Marie or Dawn or Rose would quarrel with Henry, saying that all those guavas spoiled Joshua's appetite. Henry called him Master Joshua always. The women servants did so only when Mommy was around. Joshua loved to be with Henry, whenever his work allowed it, and would ask him questions, which sometimes he didn't answer.

At some point he began wondering if Mammy was dead. "Do you know my Mammy?" he one day asked Henry.

Henry stared at the ground and said nothing.

"Do you know my Mammy?" he asked again.

"I not too sure, Master Joshua. What is your Mammy name?"

Joshua had to think. "Rosalinda Johnson."

"Yes. I know her. You satisfy now?"

"Is she alive?"

"Yes, Master Joshua. Up till this morning, yes. If she did dead the news would o' spread."

Sometime during this period something happened to him, which afterwards he could only remember as if it had been a dream. A little boy is with a White woman in a speeding car. They have travelled a long distance. The car stops in front of a big white building. Behind it is the sea; the boy is fascinated by the yachts at anchor behind the building. He has never been on a boat and would like to go on one. The sea here is calm and close.

The woman holds the boy's hand and they mount the steps leading up to the building. There is flowering bougainvillea everywhere. They form a canopy over the arch they pass under.

They come to a door, where a black woman, dressed in blue, and wearing a hat like a policeman's, says, "He can't come in here."

"Lady, what do you mean, *he can't come in here?*" the woman holding the boy's hand shouts.

"Lady, don't bawl at me. I ain't no dog. You know the rules. He can't come in here." The little boy and the lady in blue stare at each other.

"Sonny, I ain't the one that make the rules."

"Call the manager!" the lady holding the boy's hand orders.

"He don't like for me to bother him with picky matters," the woman in blue replies.

"Take your black ass up from that stool and tell the manager *I* want to see him! Do you hear me?" the White woman says through clenched teeth. She's holding the boy's hand so hard, it hurts.

The lady in blue opens her mouth wide, doesn't close it at all, gets up and returns with a brown-skinned man.

"Molly," he says to the lady in blue. "He's all right. Just at the limit. You're doing a fine job."

The woman and the boy enter a large room that opens onto a porch that overhangs the sea. Briefly the boy watches the waves, less than a foot high, roll under it. There are lots of people, mostly women and children, all White, in the room. In a corner far off, children are listening to a storyteller.

"Go sit with them," the woman tells the boy.

He shakes his head. "I don't want to."

Later two black women in royal blue dresses, white aprons, and white caps serve drinks and sandwiches. The boy doesn't eat any. The boy doesn't remember much more.

The boy thinks he remembers the woman asking him to go back there with her and the boy saying, no, he did not want to go.

He kept wanting to think that it was a story he'd been told, that the little boy was not him. But it was him. It couldn't have been someone else and it couldn't have been a dream.

Then Elizabeth came to the house, and he could no longer spend time with Henry, or walk the grounds with Booges, or spend time with Dawn and Marie in the kitchen. She wore flowery dresses, had very black skin and a smooth round face that dimpled whenever she smiled. He liked her perfume. She said it was Khus-khus. He did not like her voice. It was as if she had a sore throat that never got better. She tried to teach him to read and write and to count, and she read stories to him, which she asked him to repeat to her. They were different from the stories Bita used to tell him. Bita's stories were about a tricky spider, about ghosts who took the spirits of little bad boys, women who took off their skins at night and turned people into bulls and rode them, and White men who cut open the chests of bad little boys and fed their hearts and livers to their dogs and horses. He used to be able to interrupt Bita and say it was the liver of bad little girls that the dogs and horses liked best. Bita would say "boys," and he would say "girls," and they went on like this until one of them gave up. But Elizabeth did not allow him to interrupt her. Big boys did not interrupt; they listened attentively and could repeat everything they had heard. Once, when he interrupted her, she spanked him, and he threatened to tell Mommy, and she begged him not to. After that he interrupted her all the time. One day he was so bad, he made her cry, and it was she who threatened to tell Mommy and he who begged her not to. Her stories were about Chicken Little—"Why Chicken Little and not Little Chicken?" Elizabeth pretended not to hear him—"Hansel and Gretel," "The Three Little Pigs," and "The Little Mermaid." Elizabeth cried the first time she told "The Little Mermaid."

Then late one afternoon, after Elizabeth had gone home, he was near the fence and he heard Booges growling, and he looked across the fence and saw Bita waving to him. She came to the fence and Booges tried to bite her, and he shouted at Booges, and Booges moved away with his head bowed and his tail between his legs.

"Bita, you're not dead? I thought Mistress ate you."

"I alive. I think you did done forget me. 'Cause now you live in big house and have servant and pretty clothes and all sorts o' things that poor people like me don't got. Tell Marie I out here to see you. Don't tell she if anybody else there."

Marie took him outside the gate and into the nearest cane field and then whistled, and Bita came. She left them there and said she would come back.

Bita visited him weekly in the cane field, and afterward, when he started going to school, at recess. During this time Mrs Éclair, whom he still had trouble calling Mommy like she wanted him to, told him, and kept reminding him, that he should forget about Bita and his mother, because now he was a new person. One time, she placed a dirty copper penny in the palm of her hand and told him, "See how this penny is?" He stared at the penny in her hand. "Now watch what will happen." She poured brasso onto it, and rubbed it with a rag until it was gleaming. "See, that's how you are now, shining and new. Before you were like the dirty penny, now you are shining and new so I want you to have a new mother: me. Don't you like me, Joshua?"

He said nothing.

"Answer me, Joshua. I want to be your Mommy, your only Mommy. You are my son."

But Joshua knew he was not and felt he should not say so unless Bita said it was all right.

"And if you are my mommy, where is my pappy?" he asked her.

Her eyes grew big and bluer than usual, and her face got pink, and for a while she did not speak. "How do you expect me to know," she answered, " I don't know *everything*."

"Are you sure?" he insisted, cocking his head to one side. "I thought you did."

"My! My! You're quite a little lawyer—and sassy too. I want you to grow up exactly like that."

Eventually he began calling her Mommy not to hurt her feelings and because Bita told him he could. Besides, she was kind to him, and he no longer feared that she would eat him, for she hadn't eaten Bita.

4

HE WAS NOW EIGHT and in standard three. The school was in Camden, not far from Arcadia. At first Marie took him there and would come to get him at lunch. But after a while he told her she did not need to. The boys wore blue shirts and khaki trousers and the girls wore blue skirts and beige blouses. Few children wore shoes, but he always wore shoes and socks. His only chore then was to shine his shoes. Two of the teachers called him Master Joshua.

In standard three they had to memorize poetry at home. Mommy loved to hear him recite poetry. By this time she had long been spending the time after supper right up to bedtime with him, unless there were guests or she had to go out. They played Snakes and Ladders, and a memory card game at which he sometimes beat her, but mostly they read.

When he learned

Piping down the valleys Wild,
Piping songs of pleasant glee,
On a cloud I saw a child
And he, laughing, said to me,

"Pipe a song about a lamb" . . .

She made him say it over and over again so that it would sound like real people were talking. She always loved it when there was poetry to memorize. She recited poetry too. Her favourite poet, she said, was Robert Frost. Robert Frost had lived in New England where she went to school. He had read once at the college she attended. Robert Frost made her sad. She cried more than once when she recited his poems. In one poem, she used to repeat *"and I have promises to keep."* Then her face would go blank and she would say to herself with a sigh, "promises."

"What promises?" he once asked her.

She pulled him close to her, tousled his hair and said, "Seeing you grow up to be a respectable young man."

Once, after she had recited "The Road Not Taken," he told her, "You can always turn back."

"If you haven't gone too far."

"Then use a car."

"No, you can't. You have to do it on foot, and always alone."

"Even when it's dark?"

"Especially when it's dark. And sometimes you do it sitting or lying down."

He stopped because he didn't know what she was talking about, and it was making him afraid.

The poem that made her cry most was "Nothing Gold Can Stay." He had thought it odd because gold was the colour of Mrs Manley's hair.

"Mrs Manley's hair is always there and it is gold?"

"It's not real."

She saw that he was puzzled. "It's a wig. It's made from false hair."

"You mean her hair does not grow out from her scalp?"

"Yes. That's what I mean. She is bald. She puts on her false hair just like you would put on a cap."

"Suppose somebody pulls it off?"

"Her brother would kill him. You must not mention what I told you to anybody. Mrs Manley would not like it and I won't either."

Eventually he told her, "I don't know why you like Robert Frost."

"Why'd you say that?"

"He makes you cry."

Her eyes squinted and she forced a smile. It came out as two deep lines in her cheeks and was full of sadness. "Yes, he makes me cry. I won't like him then." They were silent for a long while before she said, "Sometimes, I'm foolish. People who complain a lot end up talking to themselves."

Sometimes he saw her lips mumbling.

"Do you complain a lot, Mommy?"

"Why do you ask?"

"Because sometimes you talk to yourself."

She hugged him, caressed his face in her hand. "That's not what I meant. I mean that people don't like to be friends with people who complain. People don't like to hear their friends' problems. There is a saying like this: 'Smile, and the whole world smiles with you; weep, and you weep alone.' Do you understand?"

He nodded.

Thereafter she would help him to memorize his poems and ask him to tell her the stories in the books she gave him to read, but she stopped reciting poetry.

At school some of the children did not play with him. And Pauline would say, "Black is costly, White is nasty."

And Maurice said, "Joshua, you taking that from a girl? Box her in her big mouth!"

And Brenda, "If you all don' stop troubling Joshua, Mistress Éclair going send the devil fo' get all o' you."

"Me no' 'fraid she and me no' 'fraid the devil. Me will beat the two o' them with my little finger," Pauline replied, displaying her little finger, her long bottom pushed out behind her, her brown eyes glassy, the two braids that emerged from behind her ears and rested on her shoulders shaking. She was *dougla*.

"How you know Mistress Éclair dealing with devil?" Maurice asked.

"Just take one look at she eyes-them." Brenda replied. "You can read it there. People with eyes what blue like that always deal with the devil. Them treacherous just like the sea. And anybody what not blind can see hell fire inside o' Joshua eyes."

Joshua was uneasy but everyone else seemed convinced, even Fred, who had green eyes, chalk-white skin, "fowl bones," and rotten teeth.

Joshua never boxed anyone in school even though they sometimes mocked his bow-legged walk and his high-pitched voice.

Once, when Pauline was teasing him, Maurice said, "Joshua, hit her with your pistle and make her whistle."

Some of the students standing around laughed.

"Mammy say White man no' got pistle," Pauline stated.

"Well how them does make pickney?" Maurice asked.

Stumped, Pauline looked away, but not for long. "Them does go by the hospital and the doctor does make the pickney for them."

Everyone laughed.

"You *coonoomoonoo!*"

"*Boom-boom-ber,* who you calling *coo-noo-moo-noo*?" Her fists were balled and she advanced towards Maurice.

"All you hold her back before she kill me," Maurice said, laughing.

"All you better hold me back before I send him flying over the moon with me fist."

Laughter.

"And you going turn dish and run 'way without your spoon."

Pauline turned to her left, where Fred was standing and bopped him one on the forehead.

"What you hit me for?" Fred asked. "I don' trouble you."

At that point they saw a teacher nearby and pretended that nothing had happened.

All the boys brought tops to school that they themselves had made, and spun them outside at recess. Maurice's top would spin for as long as five minutes. Sometimes, while the girls played hopscotch, the boys played a game in which they tried to split one another's tops; if the top didn't spin after it struck the opponent's top the person had to put his top in the ring, and if he was lucky he would retrieve it unsplit. Maurice let Joshua spin his top a few times, but Joshua could never get it right, and the other top spinners said he couldn't spin top because he was White. Fred said it was because Joshua was better suited to play hopscotch with the girls. Maurice told Fred, "White boy, watch your mouth."

Fred was one of the best top spinners. So whenever they told Joshua he couldn't spin a top because he was White, he would point to Fred.

On another occasion when they were stating what White people couldn't do, Pauline said, "Fred only look White. Inside he Black just like we."

Fred's shoes contained pieces of cardboard to replace the worn-out soles. They'd laughed at him one day when a piece of the cardboard fell out. Fred had a lot of trouble reading and was flogged often for unfinished homework. His father was a baker. Fred's mornings, late afternoons, and early evenings were spent delivering bread on a three-wheel bicycle.

Joshua wanted to become a good top spinner. He tried to buy a top from Fred. Fred said they spun for you only if you'd made them yourself. When you made them yourself, you got to know them and they got to know you, and so when you spun them you could talk to them silently. Joshua laughed at him.

Joshua told Mommy that he would like to be able to spin a top like the other boys. "I'll get you one," she said.

Two months later she summoned him to her bedroom, and her face was happy: her eyes a bright blue, her cheeks a bright pink. She picked up a small carton, handed it to Joshua and told him to open it. He did and pulled out an object the diameter of a saucer and shaped like a huge egg that had been flattened at one end. The object mystified him. "What is it?" he finally asked.

"The top you wanted."

"A top! That's not how a top looks. The ones my schoolmates spin are smaller—the size of a large egg; they're made of wood and have a nail as a—"

"Pivot?"

"What's a pivot?"

"The point on which a spinning object spins."

" . . . as a pivot." He examined the object a bit more; the cold feel of the tin, painted strawberry, repelled him. He replaced the wrapping and pushed the top back into the box. He looked up and saw Mommy watching him. "Thanks, but it wasn't what I wanted."

"You can't say I didn't try."

"Yes, you did."

Somewhere around this time—it must have been during school holidays—he heard Rose telling Dawn what a wonderful son Henry had. He asked Henry, and Henry said yes, "But André a lot younger than you, Master Joshua."

"Bring him to play with me. Please, Henry? Please?"

"He too small, Master Joshua. André only three."

Joshua was eight, nearly nine, and he remembered how Bita used to care for him, and he had no doubt that he could care for André in the same way. And there were Dawn, Rose, and Marie who could help him. Each day

Henry gave him a different excuse for not bringing André. Joshua told Mommy about it, and she said, "That's because Henry doesn't want André to interfere with his work, and you should stop pestering him. You're making him fall behind in his work."

The day after he returned to school in September and began in standard four, Maurice brought two horse mangoes to school and gave him one. "That's 'cause we is now buddies," he told Joshua.

Mommy often told Joshua he was not acting the way a buddy should when he was with the children and grandchildren of the other plantation owners. He did not tell her that it was because one of them had called him a mongrel, and all the others had laughed, and afterwards whenever they wanted to tease him they called him *mongrel*. He hated being with them. One was called Boris, a baby-fat-covered, blond, green-eyed boy about Joshua's age from the Leeward side of the island; he was visiting his cousins, the Kevins. Boris had asked him if it was true that his "real" mother was a nigger.

"What are niggers like?" Joshua asked.

"Evil, black, dirty, stupid, and they stink," Boris replied, grinning.

He never told Mommy because that would have been complaining, and he remembered the dirty penny she had cleaned with Brasso.

That September evening Joshua asked for two helpings of dessert. It was bread pudding. When Mommy was not watching, he slipped a piece under the table and managed to go to the kitchen and hide it. Dawn caught him, and he told her the truth. She smiled and opened her eyes wide. He took it for Maurice next day.

A few days later when the school day ended, he and Maurice walked in the opposite direction from Arcadia to a village where the houses were mostly two-room wooden shacks built on land that belonged to the Kevins. Maurice lived in one of them. "Here is where I live."

He called out to the neighbour, telling her he was home.

The neighbour came to the door of her house and told him, "Behave yourself, now. I leave two fry-bakes and a piece o' saltfish fo' you."

Joshua saw that she was staring at him.

"Who is your friend?" she asked Maurice.

"Joshua."

"Hi," he said to her.

"All you don't make no mischief over there now, you know," she warned, and returned inside her house.

They went up the three pieces of rough wood that formed the step. The door was not locked. Maurice pulled it open. It was dark inside. The windows were all of wood. There were two in that room. Maurice opened one. He looked at Joshua and smiled. "You like where I live?"

"Yes. It's nice." Mommy had told him never to say anything was bad when he went to other people's houses. In one corner of the room there was a small dining table with two chairs. In another corner was a small china closet containing plates and glasses. Along one wall was a wooden cot with a mattress. The bed had not been made up. The floor was covered with a piece of brown linoleum with lots of roses printed in it.

"You have brothers and sisters?"

Maurice shook his head. "You?"

Joshua hesitated. "Yes. No."

"You had one but it died?"

Joshua said nothing.

"I thought the girl that does come see you sometimes at recess is your sister."

Joshua did not answer.

Maurice gave Joshua one of his fry-bakes and a piece of the saltfish. They ate. Joshua noted that Maurice did not wash his hands before eating, although they ate with their fingers.

Next they went outside to a bamboo hut: the kitchen. A counter made of split bamboo supported by sapling stakes took up one end of the hut. Maurice lifted a piece of plastic from a tin bucket on the counter, and with a cup that still had the Ovaltine pattern on it, dipped a cup of water and drank. He wiped his lips on his shirtsleeve. "You want water?" he asked Joshua, who shook his head. Between the bucket and a few turned-down dishes and calabashes there was a calabash of mangoes. Fruitflies rose from them as Maurice took two, wiped them on his shirt, and gave Joshua one. Then Maurice took him via a shortcut through the village of Compton, which belonged to the Manchesters' Estate, and back to Arcadia.

Maurice waited with him until Marie came to open the gate.

"Who you is?" she asked Maurice. She sounded cross.

"He's my buddy," Joshua answered before Maurice could. "Maurice meet Marie. She is the sweetest person in the world."

Marie smiled and screwed up her forehead.

"Thanks for everything," he told Maurice before Marie closed and locked the gate.

"You late," Marie scowled.

"That's 'cause I was with my buddy."

"You should ask permission from your Mommy."

"What? To have a buddy!"

"Suit yourself. You lucky your Mommy don't find out that you come home late."

"She won't mind."

Marie stopped walking, turned, and stared at him as if he was crazy.

After supper Joshua put a battery-powered car that Mrs Langley had given him for his birthday in a paper bag, climbed the fence near the chicken house and dropped it over the fence in a clump of weeds that grew there. Next morning he doubled back when he knew Marie was out of sight and retrieved it. But when he came onto the main road he saw that his socks and trousers were covered with burrs and sweetheart grass.

Maurice was already at school. His mother was the Anglican priest's housekeeper. The neighbour saw him off to school, and he was usually one of the first to be at school. Maurice laughed when he saw the state of Joshua's clothes. Together they picked off the burrs and the sweetheart grass.

"Now you look decent!" Maurice exclaimed.

"I have a surprise for you." He was about to say that was how he got covered with burrs and sweetheart grass but knew he shouldn't. He handed Maurice the bag and watched his pupils grow as he became aware of what was in it. But the smile turned to fright. His eyes became smaller, and his narrow face seemed narrower. Joshua always thought he was good-looking.

"Thanks, Joshua. You's truly my buddy. You know that? But my mammy not going lemme keep it." Seeing Joshua's disappointment, he added, looking away, "that's 'cause it run with batteries, and, and . . ."

"I will give you batteries."

"Mammy going think I steal it."

"Take me where she works. I'll tell her I gave it to you."

Maurice shook his head. He kept the car, however, and Joshua hoped his mammy would not object.

The next afternoon Joshua went straight home. When he rang the bell, Mommy came to open the gate. It was the servants' duty to answer the bell and to decide whether the person was worth or not worth letting onto the premises. Her eyes looked small and icy blue. She did not return his greeting. When they got onto the porch, she said, "Go change from your school uniform and then come to see me in my bedroom right after."

"Sit over there where I can see you," she told him as soon as he entered the anteroom. She pointed to the blue armchair that was directly facing the sofa on which she was seated.

The paper bag containing the car he had given Maurice was on the sofa, on her left. A book she had been reading was open page-down on her right. She picked up the paper bag and took out the toy car and dangled it. "I need an explanation, Joshua."

He hung his head.

"Look at me, Joshua."

He refused.

She got up, came to where he was seated, stood over him, lifted his chin, and forced him to look up into her face.

He closed his eyes.

She spanked him.

"It's *my* car. Mrs Langley gave it to me and I have the right to do what I want with it." He sensed the closeness of tears but was determined to hold them back, because "Big boys don't cry."

She returned to her seat and sat down.

"Joshua?" Her voice was soft, pleading. "Do you love me?"

"I don't know."

"Please, look at me."

"First, promise to let me give my car to Maurice. He stands up for me in school when others pick on me. He took me to his house and shared his supper with me. He is not mean like you."

"You are angry with me?"

"Yes!"

"I'm not angry with you."

"Then why did you hit me?"

"Can I say I am sorry?"

"Only if you mean it."

"I mean it. Now come and give me a big kiss."

He did and noticed tears welling up in her eyes.

"You do not know how much you mean to me, Joshua, and there is so much, oh so much, you cannot yet understand."

He began to feel ashamed.

They never mentioned the car anymore nor why she had summoned him to her room. He left the car on the couch when he left her room that afternoon.

The next day at school Maurice explained that his mother did not want him and Joshua to be friends. "She say that when nigger people step out o' they place and start for rub shoulders with *Bacra*, trouble just 'round the corner. She say oil and water don't mix, and she going beat me if I keep company with you." He looked away as he told Joshua this.

Joshua knew he was going to cry, so he left, saying he had to go to the toilet, telling himself as he headed there, "Big boys don't cry. Big boys don't cry. Don't cry, Joshua, you are a big boy." But he cried. And after that he hated Maurice, and he hated Mommy, and he hated Maurice's mother, and hoped that when they all died they would go to hell. For a moment he had visions of flames engulfing them the way he had seen flames swallow up a house in Petit-Bordel and reduce it to ashes, before he had gone to live at Arcadia. And he knew then why Henry was not bringing André there.

He wonders what became of Maurice. Those Isabellans able to have all emigrated. He'd like to see him again. What would they say to each other?

That same year Marie got married and gave up her job at Arcadia, and one lunch hour Joshua came in and met Bita sitting in the parlour. "Bita, it isn't carnival." She was wearing a black wig and had big tits. She was still flat-chested.

"Sh, Sh!" she whispered and put a finger over her lips. "Pretend you don' know me."

As Joshua left to go to the kitchen, Mommy entered the parlour. Joshua hung back in the passageway to overhear the conversation.

"I come 'bout the job what you have, Mistress Éclair."

"What job? What did you say your name is?" There was skepticism in Mommy's voice.

"Millicent. The job. The job that . . ."

"There are no vacancies. There are too many servants already."

Joshua backtracked to see what was taking place in the parlour. Mommy approached Bita, pinned her against her powerful body and pulled off Bita's wig. Bita struggled to get out of her clasp, but Mommy easily pushed her hands into Bita's chest and pulled out the rags she had stuffed into a bra.

"Don't ever come back here. I told you never to return here. I don't want Joshua keeping your company. If you ever return here I will put the dog on you."

Joshua moved out of the way, knowing he was not to hear this.

That evening when he came home from school Dawn took him to Mommy's room. Mommy sat him down on the couch beside her.

"How is school, Joshua?"

"Fine."

"Do you like your teachers?"

"Yes."

There was a long silence.

"Who is your mother, Joshua?" She asked and took a deep breath.

"You are." He gave her the answer she wanted.

"I am glad to hear you say it. Do you love me, Joshua?"

"Yes." He could not look at her.

"Do you always stare at the floor when you are speaking, Joshua?"

He looked up at her.

"I am glad you love me, Joshua. I want you to feel you are my son. My late husband Mr Éclair would like that."

"Is he my father?"

"What in the world would make you ask such a question?"

"I was just wondering."

"If he were your father, I would be your biological mother instead of your adopted mother."

Joshua smiled knowing that there was something foolish in what Mommy said.

"Do you remember your other home, Joshua?"

"No." Of course, he did. He realized he was staring at the floor. He looked up.

"Sometimes I think you are unhappy."

"I miss my sister." That came out before he could hold it back.

"I know." She sighed. "There are things you are too young to know, Joshua." She looked away and was silent for a while. "I might go back to the US one day and I would like you to live with me and become an American. Would you like that?"

He nodded.

She leaned over, pulled him against her, and held him with one arm while she examined his hair with the other. "You have sable, beautiful big curls, and lovely ivory skin, like shelled almonds. Beautiful. Michelangelo would have done wonders with you as his model. Yes, I think you will pass easily for an Italian."

"What's an Italian?"

"People from a country called Italy. Beautiful people. You look like them."

He was pleased.

"Do you think you could love me a lot, Joshua?"

He nodded.

"A whole, whole lot?"

He nodded.

"Can you love me enough to forget your sister?"

Joshua was silent.

"See, you don't love me a lot. I want you to love me, and me alone, Joshua. I want you to stop loving your sister and your other mother."

"Can't I love Bita and love you too?"

"No."

The next day Joshua went to school. That morning, he got all his sums wrong and he stumbled when he read. His mind was on Bita. He was anxious for recess to come. It was her visiting day. He held on to her. They were sitting on a tombstone in the cemetery adjoining the school grounds. "She wants me to stop loving you, Bita."

"You will soon do it too. Soon as you get big and have White friends. Mammy say you all do it."

He shook his head. "No, Bita."

"You will do it. Take my word; you will do it. All the pretty thing-them and the servant-them will turn your head. And you will stop liking me 'cause my skin black and my hair knotty; you White and your hair straight; and you wear shoes and socks and I barefoot."

He shook his head. "Don't say so, Bita. You will make me cry."

She pulled him close to her and hugged him tightly.

They saw each other at recess the week later for the last time at Campden School. School was getting ready to close for the July-August holidays. Bita must have sensed something. She told him why she'd tried to get the job. She wanted to be near to him, to be his servant like the story in the Bible. He laughed, remembering how Mommy had pushed her hand into Bita's chest and pulled the stuffing out of her bra.

"Why you laughing?"

"Nothing."

"Well, don't laugh, 'cause I is who save your life when you born."

"How?"

"I don' know if I should tell you." But she told him. Two days after he was born, Mammy took him down to the river and threw him into the water and left him there and went home. In his imagination he saw the river, its banks lined with gru-gru palms, vast, green fields of sugar cane stretching from the banks to where the slopes of the mountains began. Bita had bathed him in it many times. Women washed clothes and dishes and bathed children in it. Once they had run after and thrown stones at a man who'd defecated in the water. To get away, the man had to run barefoot over the fallen gru-gru fronds full of thorns. A woman shouted at him, "Me hope gru-gru *cashee* bruk in your foot and poison your blood—you godforsaken sonofabitch!"

"You're telling story, Bita," he told her, in the language he used when he was three-four and still living with Mammy and Bita.

"You remember Mammy used for say that you is a cross?"

He didn't remember.

"Well that was 'cause you was in a hurry to born. You born before the midwife reach. Aunt Stacey is who cut and tie your navel string. And she had to slap your backside for make you bawl."

"What's a navel string?"

"I don' know. Is probably something like the afterbirth that goat does pass after they birth their kids. I know where mine bury though, and where yours bury too."

He had never seen a goat or any animal give birth so he didn't understand what she meant.

"So what happened to me after she threw me in the river?"

"You too impatient. Lemme finish.

"When you born, Aunt Stacey tell me that Mammy was out of her head and liable for harm you. She tell me for watch for see if Mammy nursing you, and if I see she leave with you for go anywhere, for follow she; and if I see she do anything bad to you, for come and get she right away. So when Mammy throw you in the water—she didn' know I been following she; I stay at a distance 'cause she would o' beat me if she did know—I didn' go call Aunt Stacey. I know that you would o' drownded in the water before I get to Aunt Stacey house, so I take you out o' the water soon as Mammy leave, and I carry you straight to Aunt Stacey place."

"So that is why Mammy used to always beat you?"

"No. Is not because o' that. And Mammy did refuse to nurse you. Aunt Stacey use to bring milk in a nursing bottle and take you 'way from Mammy and nurse you. And Aunt Stacey use for leave a bottle o' milk with me. I use for hide it under the bed. When Mammy outside in the kitchen cooking, I use for feed you. When she find out she didn't do anything; she leave me alone, and afterward she start to feed you herself. One day she say to me, "Like Joshua is your child? You want him? Take him 'cause I don' want him. Carry him give Stacey. You-all is his mother."

"So that is why you used for put yourself between she and me when she start hitting me?"

Bita nodded.

"Where Aunt Stacey is?"

"She go 'way overseas before you could o' remember she. I did beg she for send for me, else for come back and get me, and she promised for do it, God willing."

She stopped talking, grew thoughtful.

"Mammy don't really hate me," she said, looking out over the tomb-stones and at the blue-grey mountains in the distance, talking as if to herself. "She hate my father though. He run 'way and leave she for look after me all by she self. One time she say to me, 'you always in the way, always in the way. I can't even kill myself 'cause I have for think 'bout who will take care o' you after I done dead. Your father! Help me, God! Don't make me say anything for damn my soul. Men! They blight! Blight!'" Then Bita focused her gaze on him and said, in a slow deliberate way, "But she really did *hate* you."

"Because I'm a boy?"

"No. A time I ask she who your father is and she slap me. Pow! Without warning. I see stars in bright daylight. That slap did leave four fingerprints on me face for two days, and it pain me for more than a week."

"Who my father is, Bita?"

"How you expect me for know?"

For a while neither said anything. The wind was strong. It raised clouds of dust and whistled through the willows that lined the road and bundled their leaves together and blew them forward, turning them into giant girls with their hair streaming out in front of their faces. Bita bundled the front of her skirt together and pulled it close to her body to keep the wind from blowing it over her head. She broke the silence.

"Mammy glad Miss Éclair take you from she. She always saying one pick-ney more than 'nough for wear out she soul case; two would o' kill she outright, and now she always thanking God she don' ha' for worry how for feed you. But a night I did hear she bawling out in she sleep, 'Mr Judge, I didn't want for kill Joshua. God know I didn't want for kill him,' so I know she does have bad dreams 'bout you. But you is not to mind, 'cause I love you, and Aunt Stacey love you, and sometimes I think even Mammy love you." She reached over and hugged him. It was time for him to return to class.

It was the last time they hugged each other.

A week later Mommy told him that she knew Bita was visiting him at school during recess, and that in September she would send him to a board-ing school in Hanovertown. He would come home only on weekends and holidays, and he would be with the kind of people she wanted him to be with. And she did not want him in a school where children were beaten.

In school they were beaten for spelling mistakes, giving wrong answers, inattention, bad behaviour, forgetting to do homework, and getting to class late. He was flogged twice for inattention. Mommy complained to the headteacher about it, and the headteacher told her that if she didn't like how the school was run, she should remove Joshua. Mommy told Joshua, "I don't want you growing up believing it's right to flog people. It's not. It's bestial. Cruelty on this island is shocking. Everybody is always searching out somebody to brutalize." She paused thoughtfully. "In my country too, but that doesn't make it right."

5

THAT JULY THE ACCOUNTANT for Éclair Estate Ltd. went away to the United States, and Sparrow, Mommy's cousin from Florida, came to do his job. He was thirty-eight (she was forty-five at the time), short and square, with the beginnings of a bulging belly, thick dark-brown hair he was already dyeing, and eyes that shone like two corn-grain electric bulbs. A glance from some-one was enough for him to turn on his buck-toothed grin. The way he spoke was amusing: everything was "mighty" that, "right" this, a "whole heap" that; "I reckon that," "the way I figure this," as if he did not know the word *think*.

He and Mommy were like people from different countries. Joshua asked her why one evening while they were playing scrabble. His father was poor, Mommy said; she didn't talk that way because she and Sparrow were brought up differently. Besides, she had gone to school in the North, in Massachusetts, at a college called Smith. She disliked the way Sparrow talked. "But family is family and blood is thicker than water." She said if Joshua got all his sums right and came first in his classes, he too would go to school overseas, maybe to Oxford or Cambridge or Harvard or Princeton, and he would be rich and have everything he wanted and would be well-educated. She would see to it.

Not everything, he remembers thinking, wondering if he would be forced to forget Bita.

Her cousin's real name was Astor Mann. Mommy called him Sparrow, (he pronounced it Sparrer) and he told Joshua to call him Uncle Sparrow. He really was different from her. He went into the villages, met people. He couldn't shut up and loved to make jokes. He often asked people if they liked him. When someone didn't answer loud enough to his "How you be doing today, Ma'am (Aunty, Uncle)," he'd exclaim, "Ma poor heart's done broke in twen'y pieces."

"What make so, Missah Sparrow?"

"'Cause you don't lak me, tha's how come." He pronounced it *kurmm*.

The listener would usually laugh. One man, lanky, shirtless, had scratched his head, puzzled.

"If you lak me, how come you be greetin' me so po'ly? You hear 'bout the church Ahm a-plannin'?"

The man nodded, a little more at ease.

"I'm o-be wantin' yer 'n yer fam'ly to be the first ones in it a-singin' 'n a-shoutin' hallelujah to the Lamb that was slain."

At the first reception Mommy organized after his arrival, fifteen minutes before the guests came, Sparrow came into the parlour wearing a sky-blue jacket, burgundy shirt, and mustard trousers.

"You forgot your pink shoes," Mommy told him.

"Ah could oblige some with a pink shirt, but pink shoes 'n pink socks Ah ain't got none of." He winked at Joshua.

"What are you: some liveried doorman in front of a Paris hotel?" She made no attempt to hide her disgust.

Sparrow grinned. "Guess then Ah knows ma place."

"Never mind that. I don't want you looking like a parrot—or a courting peacock—when you meet these people."

Sparrow left the parlour, went to his room, and stayed there until the guests arrived, and joined them exactly as he had been dressed.

The men in the party stared at him stone-faced. Most wore three-piece suits, a couple of them safari suits. The women glared at him and raised their eyebrows at one another. "So Averill" (tonight they placed extra emphasis on her name), "this is your dear cousin," and did their best not to snicker.

"Pleased to meet you, Mr Mann." (They certainly were.)

"Ma pleasure, Ma'am."

As soon as the last guest left, Mommy announced that she intended to burn every piece of clothing that Sparrow had brought from the States. He laughed at her, told her it was too late. She gave a loud sigh, shook her head slowly, and disappeared into her room.

The next day they resumed, he telling her, "This here's the Caribbean, 'n the people Ah sees 'bout here loves they bright colours, 'n Ah too, Ah sure loves 'em, Averill."

She said nothing.

"Truth is, Averill, Ah don' care none for yer planter friends. They's yer folks, not mine. They's rich folks, Averill. 'N rich folks looks at poor folks lak they smell. 'N Ah is poor, Averill. Livin' in yer house 'n off yer charity don't change ma poverty."

Thereafter he never attended any of the socials, and Mommy did not seem to mind.

Soon after Sparrow arrived, Joshua overheard Rose telling Dawn, "That Sparrow is a antipympym sure as I born. He better don't try to bull no nobody 'round here; they will chop off his balls, sure as sun rise . . ."

"Rose! Sparrow is a White man and cousin to Averill Éclair!"

"Yes, you right 'bout that. But I sure to God wish you was wrong."

When Sparrow told Mommy that he wanted to start a church she became alarmed. One evening after supper while Joshua was in the recreation room doing schoolwork, he heard them arguing about it on the front porch (she sat out there only when the wind was strong enough to keep the mosquitoes quiet).

"Fancy that. You a preacher!" Mommy said, laughing

"N why not, Averill?"

"You never studied theology."

"A body don' need no theology ter bring lost souls ter Christ. All a body got ter do is get called."

"Lord, help us! When did this foolishness enter your head?"

"Ah always wanted ter preach the word o' God. Ah always knew Ah had the gift. 'N Ah don' appreciate yer callin' it foolishness. Ain't nutten foolish 'bout it."

"The *gift*?"

"Sure. The spirit o' God revealin' thangs to me. Thangs Ah won' unner-stan' oth'wise."

Mommy's sigh was audible in spite of the wind.

There was a long silence.

"Ah always wanted ter bring souls ter redemption. 'N this is ma last chance."

"*Redemption*. I see. *Whose* redemption?"

"Lost souls'."

"Gimme a break, Sparrow. Whatever you do, don't lose *your senses*. Right now I'm none too worried about your soul. What's come over you? How come you never got to preaching in the States?"

"The taym weren't raat, Averill. There's a taym for ev'thang under the sun. Ya knows that, Averill. A raat taym 'n a wrong taym."

"A time for madness and con games too, I suppose."

"Well, Ah told the Lord that if he cured me o' that lil problem what you know Ah had, Ah gon' give ma laf to His service. 'N, Averill, the Lord done cure me. He sure did. It ain't been botherin' me none since. 'N now it's ma taym ter fulfill ma promise."

Mommy chuckled. "Well, I'm relieved about that, cousin. I sure am." They only called each other that when they were being sarcastic. "If that's the case, I need to stop doubting there's a God."

"If you'd a' been saved lak you ought ter, washed clean by the blood o' Chraise, you won' o-be mockin' me, Averill," he replied, reproof in his voice.

"It's a bloody business all right. Has always been, in more ways than I—never mind you—can even begin to understand." She paused. "So you're a changed man," she said with skeptical emphasis. "It's something I've been hesitating to talk to you about, to tell you to be careful about such things here. Isabella Island isn't Florida. You need to know that just in case you're only in remission." She chuckled.

And Joshua wondered what the problem was but knew he couldn't ask.

It wasn't long before people began referring to Joshua as Sparrow's son. Sparrow never said Joshua wasn't. Sometimes he said he wished Joshua were, and afterwards he said he was, "problem solved."

In September Joshua started school in town. Sparrow picked him up most Friday afternoons. If he couldn't, Mrs Manchester did. Her husband owned the plantation adjoining Éclair Estates. She and several of the planters' wives sometimes came to play bridge at Arcadia. Sometimes one or more of them dropped in without warning, and this often left Mommy wondering why they never phoned ahead to say that they were coming. "It's one thing I'll never get used to in this place. Everybody thinks you should drop what you're doing to serve their every whim."

School in town was good. His teacher was a Eurafrican woman. (Mommy had taught him the word Eurafrican, saying that mulatto was for mules, not people; at first he'd had trouble pronouncing it.) Most of the teachers in the school were. Half of the school's population looked like him, a few whiter, a few darker. Many of their parents were working temporarily on Isabella Island. There were about two hundred students in the school but only about forty of them stayed in the dormitory.

He had met the headmistress before. She was Aunt Mathilda, but in school he had to call her Mrs Templeton. She was from Birmingham, England. She came along with several people to the functions Mommy gave three or four times per year at Arcadia. Whenever Aunt Mathilda came she'd bring Joshua a gift. It was she who'd insisted he call her Aunt Mathilda, and she insisted always that he kiss her. Her husband was a physician. She took them to matins at the Anglican Cathedral every morning. Afterwards they exercised on the grass outside when it was dry, or, if it was raining, in the cafeteria. They'd push the chairs and tables aside and spread their towels on the floor and do pushups and sit-ups and touch their toes. Her mantra was: "A quick mind is quickest in an agile body." She did the exercises along with them. After exercises she went home and returned to the school after lunch.

Mommy was right: at Templeton's Academy children weren't flogged. When they didn't pay attention they wrote one hundred times, "I must be attentive always." And if they forgot to dot one 'i' or cross a 't' or left out a period, they had to do the lines over. If they were surly or if they failed their courses, they were expelled. Aunt Mathilda said, and said often, that she was not in the business of wasting time. It was rumoured that she had told a male student who had asked a teacher to kiss his arse that her school provided no such service and he would be happier in one that did.

One of the teachers, Miss Kevin, whose hateful mother sometimes visited at Arcadia, wrote plays and liked to stage them, and she was always busy about some play or other in which she wanted Joshua to act. One time he was a little Chinese orphan boy wearing a loincloth and holding a begging bowl, and his role was to pull at a White man's coat and say, "Sah, Massa, gi'e me nyam. Me belly got wind. Gi'e me nyam, Massa. Me belly him got wind."

The audience laughed whenever he said his lines, and Joshua thought they were laughing at him. The White man was Hans Frietag, the biggest boy in the school (he went back to Germany with his parents soon after the play ended). Hans wore a painted moustache and beard. All he had to do was stand on stage dressed in a suit that was too big for him and shake his head while Joshua begged for *nyam*. The White man was supposed to be rich and kind, and so he adopted the Chinese beggar boy and took him back to England with him. The voice of the playwright from behind the curtain told the audience this. The play ended at this point and the audience— parents, grandparents, aunts and uncles of the students—applauded.

By then Joshua no longer missed Bita.

By the August holidays a year later, Joshua had got to like Sparrow a lot. Sparrow had his own car and he was often driving all over the place, invit- ing people to come to his church, and he never missed a chance to carry Joshua along. He was comfortable with people; sometimes he'd stand beside them cooking in the open, with the smoke blowing in his face, and tell them their food smelt good, and he'd even ask to taste it. They'd hang their heads and say it was poor people's food and he would not like it. Once he'd insisted and a woman served him boiled breadfruit and roasted smoke herring flavoured with pepper sauce. He turned pink, his eyes bulged and watered, and his nostrils dripped. Joshua laughed, but the woman's face got all wrinkled from fright when she realized that Sparrow wanted to speak but couldn't. Only when he brought his hand up to his mouth with a drink- ing gesture did she understand that he needed water to cool the fire in his mouth.

There was another White American Pastor with a church in the area. He was living in a house the Manchesters had vacated. His church was in the house too. Sometimes the planters joked about him. Mrs Kevin said he was

"Bishop of the posterior persuasion." Later Joshua asked Mommy what Mrs Kevin had meant, and she said it was because everyone's nickname for the minister was Pastor O'bum, and he did not mind. Seeing Joshua's frown, she slapped her buttocks and said, "Bum. Like your bum and mine."

Sparrow often said he liked Isabella Island, that it was the last thing God made after he'd had "plenny o' practice ; 'n he been mighty pleased 'n, says he, he says, 'I ain't gon' wore me out with nutten else.' 'N Ahm sure glad he didn't."

Sparrow was supposed to be the estate's accountant and oversee the office operations, but most of the time he was doing something else. The Estate office, a barracks-like, grey-stone building with iron bars in the windows, was a quarter of a mile away from Arcadia. It had a front office with a dark wood counter and a back office where the vault and the account books were kept. The yellow paint was cracked and scaling. In places it had fallen off, showing an earlier coat of pale green. It always smelt of damp paper and dust. Its pitch pine wood floor was unvarnished. Everywhere behind the counter there were stacks of paper under football-size stones for paperweights. A large, rusty iron vault was fitted into a wall in the back room. It was where the money to pay the labourers was kept. It squealed like a hungry pig when it was opened. It had to be kicked for it to close properly. Three persons worked in the office. Mr Atwell—an amber-coloured man with straight, fox-coloured hair and grey eyes, who was an elder in the Presbyterian Church, and who, according to Rose, was an "outside" first cousin of Mommy's late husband—was the bookkeeper and overall manager of the drivers, who supervised the field labourers. Mommy said Mr Atwell was the most honest person she'd ever known, usually after the accounts had been audited by a man who came from Hanovertown once a year to do so. A White woman was Mr Atwell's secretary. A black woman, who was always dressed in a white bodice and a navy blue skirt, did general clerical work. Mommy went to the office on occasion, probably to sign cheques. She did not involve herself with the day-to-day running of the estate. Usually Mr Atwell would drive to the house to get her whenever she was needed. Occasionally they would have tea together at Arcadia, and once he'd been there at supper time and Mommy had to plead with him to sit at the table and eat with them. He'd sat stiffly and took extra time chewing and swallowing his food, half of which he left on his plate. But he was never invited to the house when the planters were there. Joshua doubts that Sparrow ever did any work at the office. Later, when he learnt the word "sinecure," he realized that was what Sparrow had been given.

Sparrow had his church ready for the New Year after his arrival. For the purpose he rented a wooden house, twenty feet by fourteen, on wooden stilts, with a galvanized gable roof and a partition down the middle. He removed the partition. A year later he bought the land and built a cement structure on it. Eventually he got an organ, but could never find anyone to play it. He even wanted Joshua to learn music so he could play the organ. But Mommy was firm about Joshua not becoming involved with what she called "Sparrow's mad enterprise."

Even so, for a couple of years during the school holidays, Joshua attended the weekday evening services. During the school year he was usually back in Hanovertown before the Sunday evening service at Sparrow's church started.

One of the first persons to join was a woman in her sixties, Sister Mavis. One Wednesday while Sparrow preached that "To them folks what done turn away from Gawd's word, saying how he don't exist none, that world he done make in seven days—"

"Six!" Mavis interrupted (it was the beginning of their constant battle). "He rested on the seventh."

"You catch me there, Sister. Thanks uh million. Ah see you ain't been dozin' none. Yeah, Gawd, he sure made the world in six days. Them people talkin' 'bout that ev'lution stuff, ain't know what they be talkin' 'bout. The fires o' hell be waitin' to roast 'em, lessen they be humble 'n repent. Don't you be lissenin' to 'em."

On Sunday mornings, Joshua went with Mommy to the Presbyterian Church. Most of the members were Black; a few were Eurafrican. The few Whites who attended, Mrs Manchester and Mrs Kevin among them, sat in pews close to the altar. Reverend Simmons was Eurafrican, the same complexion as Mr Atwell (who picked up the collection) but younger. "Fresh out of training," Mrs Manchester said. "Best time to catch them is when they're on probation and the congregation holds the reins." Mrs Manchester often repeated how he was hired. One such occasion was when Mommy suggested that Reverend Simmons be invited to the planters' receptions. The Anglican planters on the Leeward side had invited their minister.

"Averill, Father Brewster is a blue-blooded Englishman!" Mrs Manchester rebuked her.

"Start hobnobbing with that nigger and you can count me out," Mrs Kevin said. "It's bad enough I'm forced to mingle with you-know-who."

"No problem there, Eloise," Mrs Manchester interjected. "Ours knows his place, and knows the size of the collection depends on keeping it. When we interviewed him—you-all know I chaired the hiring committee—I told him the facts: how our last minister meddled in affairs that didn't concern him, like saying he supported workers' rights to unionize, and Caribbean Presbyterianism was outdated. And as for the minister before him, well we couldn't keep him out of the rumshops and off Black women. And to think both were from Scotland! The least we expected was that they would preach and live a pure form of Presbyterianism. Naturally, I told him, we stopped going to church and stopped giving. 'Reverend, you should know that six families here pay 95 percent of the minister's salary and the church's upkeep.'

"The committee wanted to hire another Scot. A young blade who'd already passed his probation; dangerously good looking, too. I told them no. Enough of those. See, I know our mulattoes well. It's not for nothing I'm from Bermuda. Daddy had a mulatto bookkeeper that worked for the same pay for fifteen years. Never grumbled a day. He told Daddy—I was there when he said it—'I love working for you Mr MacLaughlin. It's an honour and a privilege.' A damn fool, Daddy thought, but more faithful than a jackass. Of course, I'm not saying all mulattoes are this good. Back to Reverend Simmons, so I said to the committee, let's bring them back in for a second round of questioning. And I asked Simmons: 'Reverend,' I said, 'what are your views on traditional Presbyterian doctrines, and how do you feel about all the social agitation going on here and in the States?'

"He answered, 'I fully support the doctrines laid down by John Calvin and John Knox. And I oppose all social agitation. It's as the verse in the hymn "All Things Bright and Beautiful" says:

The rich man in his castle,
The poor man at his gate,
God made the high and lowly
And ordered their estate.'

"I tested him further. 'But Reverend, that verse is no longer printed with the rest.' And that mulatto lackey answered, 'It shouldn't have been removed.' Just what I wanted to hear." Mrs Manchester guffawed. "I knew that barring his death, we would not have to look for a minister for a long time."

"Believe me, Eloise, Simmons knows his place. He has a car that's road-worthy, a presbytery that doesn't leak. He even has a housekeeper. It's our collection that pays for it, not his wife's schoolteacher salary. In matters of this sort, I will choose the right mulatto any day. What is his favourite statement?"

"'Who are we to tinker with the divine plan?'" Eloise Kevin responded.

"Exactly! Can we ask for more? Now, Averill, don't go inviting him here when we aren't around. Don't spoil a good thing. Don't you tempt Simmons into stepping out of his place."

Joshua was surprised during the Christmas holidays to find Bita dressed in white sitting on a bench in Sparrow's church. Sparrow always insisted that the converts to his church wear white to symbolize their purity. (Sister Mavis never did.) During those weeks Bita came early so they could talk.

"You not close to me like before," she told him.

"That's not true," he protested, staring at the floor. He rarely thought of Bita then and he had almost completely forgotten his mother.

Bita stayed only a short time with the congregation. "She couldn' control she nature," Sister "Runmouth" Mavis said.

Joshua knew it wasn't a compliment.

"You, Mr Joshua, you better take a leaf from your Uncle Pastor Mann book."

Bita had left the church to go live with Skeeter. He never did visit Bita at Skeeter's place. Skeeter lived in a village some distance in from the main road. Joshua never had any reason to go into that village. Occasionally he glimpsed Bita in town. Rarely was he close enough for them to talk.

When at thirteen his voice changed and he began to desire sex, he understood why Bita had moved in with Skeeter. And she became common—like sluts held fast to bulldogs that children coming from school occasionally discovered in ditches by the side of the road and stoned.

Thinking about it now, after his own tormenting experiences, he's ashamed of those reactions.

The next day it's one of the issues he discusses with Dr Defoe.

"I should have defied my adopted mother. Doctor, why didn't I defy her?

Do you think Bita died knowing I loved her? Did I betray her? I never visited her at Skeeter's place. He lived in a village away from the main road, but it was no excuse. Sparrow would have carried me. Then he couldn't say no to anything I asked him. It's important for me to know that Bita died knowing I loved her."

"We can't undo the past. We can only try to understand it."

"But the past may undo us."

"Yes, if we let it."

"And even when we don't." *Yes, and even when we don't.*

They are silent. Both thinking.

"With prolonged psychotherapy," Defoe says, "you'll be able to put most of that behind you."

"Really, Doctor? Are you telling me to 'look on the broight soide o' loife?'"

Defoe laughs.

"You think there's enough line and sinker here to plumb these depths?"

"Looking at your back, I wonder. *Why* do you do it?"

"Do what, Doctor?"

"We're beyond the word games now, Joshua. I want you to think about why you do it. No kidding, I want you to reflect seriously on why you do it, and to tell me, as early as tomorrow."

"'*Need a bear, wolf, or sheep?*'" He laughs.

"I don't understand parables."

"Why state the obvious? If you want me to pin words to futility and foolishness, and—er—feelings—yes feelings, when I can feel—you'll have to work quickly." He stares at Defoe hard. Their gazes lock. "No tasers. Not even a blowtorch to my balls will get a sound out of me."

Defoe winces.

"I'm serious. As certain as a corpse. My stutter returns and then I talk only when I deem it necessary. You've been hinting that I love pain. Torture. Yes, it's my sanity. Sanity comes in many forms. Did you know that?"

6

WHEN DR DEFOE LEAVES, Joshua returns to recalling his childhood, and centres on the day he became Joshua Éclair. It was around the time that he was becoming politically aware, when class and race conflicts were beginning to have meaning.

It was six weeks before his twelfth birthday, and he was on the northern porch at Arcadia, his elbows supported by the porch railing, looking out over the landscape. A beautiful late afternoon in August. The canefields stretched for miles to the north and west. The strong breeze blowing over them created the illusion of moving water and turned them into vast sheets of undulating jade.

He thought of the trips he and Mommy used to make four or five times per year to Union Island. They'd always spent August there. The trips had started almost as soon as he went to live at Arcadia. Four months ago Mommy had sold the property to a hotel developer and said she would buy one on Isabella Island. It would cut down on the fifty-plus miles they had to travel to get there from Hanovertown. They'd had to clear immigration every time. Never more than, "Hope you have a pleasant holiday, Mrs Éclair. Master Joshua, don't eat all the fish. Leave some for the locals," from the immigration officer. Most times they'd go in a rented yacht. When Mommy's husband was alive he'd owned a yacht, but Mommy had sold it soon after his death. Mommy sometimes planned the trip to coincide with the Manchesters'; they too owned a beach property there and had a yacht, a twenty-five-foot one.

One of the servants, usually Dawn, or Marie when she still worked for them, went with them. Rose was left to manage Arcadia. The beach house was of wood perched on concrete stilts so that things could be stored underneath it. It had three bedrooms, and was in Clifton. When there he spent his daylight hours either in the water or on the beach watching the conch harvesters, Black men bare to the waist. With a single stroke they'd crack a hole with a hatchet into the head of the conch shell, push a flat screwdriver into the hole, and hold the pink-lip part of the shell over a bucket into which the conch meat would fall, then they'd toss the empty shell onto a hillock of similar shells. It was like music—the cracking tap of the hatchet, the soft thud of the conch flesh, followed by the sound of the conch shell hitting the pile of other shells like bone hitting bone. There was always a faint stink where the conch shells, smooth pink on the inside, rough, stucco-white on the outside, the bottom ones green with mildew, were piled in mounds on the golden sand.

The first time he visited Union Island he'd eaten conch, and before the meal was over he'd developed throat spasms and an itchy skin. The district medical officer gave him a shot of adrenaline, and said he was allergic to shellfish and should never eat it or any preparation containing it. It made eating difficult on Union Island for there were few preparations that didn't contain seafood.

Sometimes when Mommy's friends and acquaintances with yachts visited, he'd go with them on day trips to the Tobago Cays and be spellbound by the magical shades of the water: azure, turquoise, emerald. Sometimes he'd just stare at the beauty of the water, at the foam churned by the propeller, and imagine that it was whipped cream on a gargantuan mass of emerald jelly. Other times he closed his eyes and let his body sway to the yacht's undulating rock. On occasions when the day was very hot and the water almost still, flying fish darted from it, like aquatic meteors reflecting the sun's rays. Time itself stopped; he'd be just there, mesmerized by the emerald below, the azure above and the transparence between. On the Tobago Cays the beaches were a dazzling coral and silent, except for the birds, the wind through the trees, and the gentlest of lapping waves.

On Union Island Mommy never fussed about his mixing with the local Black children. They taught him to swim and to fish. Sometimes they'd build a fire on the beach at Big Sand, at the far end of the valley from Clifton, and roast the fish they'd caught. Once, while they were gathering wood to make the fire, he had picked up a manchineel fruit thinking it was a guava. They had laughed and asked him if he was tired of living. Sometimes they'd take the road beside the Clifton dump, where there were always untethered cattle feeding, climb the steep hill up to the fort, and look out at neighbouring Mayreau and the steep rocky slopes of Union itself, covered with leafless trees in dry years. In some places they grew cotton. It was he, each time he returned, who had to seek his friends out, as if they wanted to make sure that during his absence he hadn't forgotten them or changed his mind about associating with them. Mommy always made sure he had a bag of toffees for them.

On some days, Mr Stewart, the caretaker of the cottage, would take him on foot to Ashton in the heart of the island, where people farmed in a valley walled in by steep, grey cliffs. Occasionally Mr Stewart did the trip by canoe and he would let Joshua steer.

On the calmest of days Joshua and a few of his island pals would paddle the canoe over to Prune Island. One time over there they'd explored one another's genitals. Alvin, a Eurafrican boy who was bigger than all of them, had masturbated for them—to show them the pleasure of sex, he said. His semen looked like snot. Yuk! They exclaimed in disgust. The grimace, contortions, breathlessness, and scream that accompanied Alvin's orgasm made Joshua think he was in pain. Alvin had caught the semen in his hand and chased them along the beach, intent, he said, on making them taste it.

He always looked forward to being with them. He laughed freely with them, did not watch what he said. They did not say cruel things to him.

Now standing on the porch at Arcadia he thought of all this. He hoped somehow that he would be able to go back there and visit them. He wished he'd known their last names. He would have written to them. If he'd known Mommy would sell the beach house, he'd have gotten their addresses.

A passing shower, typical of August, had fallen about thirty minutes earlier but the sky was all blue again—a deep azure, as if the rain had washed it of all impurities—and the sun, orange, at its largest and low on the horizon, was getting ready to disappear behind the mountains over which it now hung and was tinting pale yellow. Its rays were in the lingering drops of water on the leaves of the distant trees. A few times he'd ridden his bike to the edge of the cane fields where the coconut groves began. The last time he'd not ventured into the coconuts because he'd seen Hitler—a mahogany bull everyone said you should keep far from—in his path a few feet away.

To his right, in the distance, from roughly the same direction as the 5:30 chimes of the Camden Presbyterian Church bell, the Atlantic tossed, made and unmade its many heads. Its blows to the shore—a wet, sucking whoosh between a snort and a grunt—fell within the familiar. Earlier it had been all silent and still, almost like a painting, the sea and sky violet sheets distinguishable from each other only by angle and surface ruffles. But a quick, fierce shower from the Atlantic had changed all that.

Flocks of martins flitted from one cherry tree to another, before escaping to the nearby blooming flame and poinciana trees or the more distant fruit trees in the orchard, where they twitted contentedly as they devoured their booty. The ground doves, their eyes warily angled in Joshua's direction, gobbled up those earthworms the rain had flushed out of their burrows, or picked blades of grass no one would miss from the emerald lawn—kept perennially green by the truckloads of cattle and horse manure Henry spread on it twice yearly. The dry weather never affected the grass, for Éclair's estate had its own reservoir that provided a superabundance of pipe-borne water. In the dry season the lawn spigots were turned on morning and evening. Now the lawn effused the smell of rich, wet earth that he later came to associate with naturalness and an easy life. He remembered Sparrow's statement that after God created Isabella Island he was so satisfied he refused to try his hand at anything else.

Just as suddenly he remembered reading in *The Isabellan* that on September 1 wages for labourers would go up: men to earn thirty-six cents a day and women twenty-four. A pound of beef cost sixty cents, as did a dozen eggs; he'd heard Dawn telling Rose this as they complained that for the third year Mrs Éclair had not raised their pay. He wondered how people lived on such wages. He alone ate two eggs each day and a lot more than a pound of beef in a week. He remembered that it was as a seasonal labourer on Éclair Estate that Mammy earned her living.

The cane field that came up to the chain-link fence about two hundred feet from the porch where he stood had been harvested in April while he was home on a two-week school break. Standing at the fence he'd watched the cane cutters. They wore long-sleeve shirts to protect their arms against the cane prickles and blade-sharp leaves. Sweat poured off their foreheads. They wiped it with washrags stuck in their belts. Some of them supported their backs with broad belts. The sharp blades of their machetes flashed in the sun as they swung them. They worked to a rhythm: first holding a cane stalk, then bending to chop it at the root, then straightening to lop off the top that contained the leaves, and with a few strokes remove any dry leaves clinging to the stalk, before throwing the cane stalk behind them and the leaves on the side. Women, their heads looking like bouquets from the colourful headwraps they wore, their bodies bent and looking like blooming poinsettas or queen of flowers, created a floral, horizontal line the width of the field, which stretched for almost a mile; they gathered the cane stalks into bundles, which they then carried to a trailer a short distance away. The sky was a cloudless blue. The April sun at its zenith poured down heat, which in the far distance looked like zigzagging lines of fluid zinc. When the trailer was full, a tractor pulled it away and brought an empty one. Mammy would have been among the workers, her body indistinct from theirs, invisible to him.

The workers called often for water, which a woman brought in a plastic bucket. There were two tin cups: one for dipping and one for drinking. A drinker drank then passed the cup to another, and the woman dipped water from the bucket and filled the cup. On the first day he could hear the cutters nearest the fence swallowing the water.

They'd work like this from sunrise to just before sunset. *For twenty-four and thirty-six cents a day!* Bita had told him that Mammy used to steal peas from the estate around sunset, and that one time Mr Éclair had caught her. But Bita never told him what Mr Éclair had done, because, she said, he was too young to understand. Did she go to prison for it? Was she therefore a "jailbird"? He shuddered at the thought.

The planters were opposed to the wage increase. They'd signed a petition demanding that it be rescinded. Two weeks earlier, eight of them from the northeast constituency had met in the parlour at Arcadia to vent their anger. If the Legislative Council did not withdraw the increase they would reduce the workforce by a quarter, and lengthen the workday by two hours, they'd threatened. "Tough," said "Pine Knot" Kevin (Joshua had picked up their nicknames from eavesdropping on Rose and Dawn's conversations), twisted and gnarled like a century-old oak, his dead left eye a green olive, brimstone threatening to erupt from the clear-green, living one onto anyone who'd dare to disagree with him. "We own the land, goddamit! We are more important than the Legco. To hell with the Administrator! He don't like our decision, let the bloody fool board the boat back to London and commence drawing his pension." Unlike the others, who mostly wore sport shirts on such occasions, he always wore khaki shirts and shorts and his cork hat, the uniform of the planter class.

Manchester stopped pulling on his pipe, removed it from his mouth and interrupted him. Deep lines like valleys linked to shallow inlets indented the circular bony ridge on both sides of his face and flattened out in shallow depressions below his cheekbones. His Adam's apple, the size of a small fist, was fascinating to watch as it rose and fell. He was tall and gaunt, rakelike and a rake. Rosé called him Bamboo Pole. Dawn called him Polecat. "We don't elect anything anymore," he declaimed with a boom, and droplets of his spit glistened in the light. "Every nigger and half-wit has the vote. We handed our destiny to them when we gave them the vote. We're still lucky we have our throats. I told you all we had to oppose this, with our lives if it came to that. But you all fought for four years and then suddenly gave up. Sat back like sheep. Went to sleep. You let Westminster wipe out our God-given rights." Now his voice was loud and there was wheezing with each intake of breath and a slight rattling of phlegm. "We made this colony what it is: with our sweat, our blood, and our brains. Damn it!" His fists were balled, but he was too far from the table to hit it, so he struck the air instead. "And in the twinkling of an eye, Westminster hands it all over to niggers. Turned it over to the niggers!" He shook his head slowly in disbelief.

"Where was Westminster when we were building this colony? And you"—he slowly turned his head to look at all seven of them sitting around the dining table; Mommy was in the recreation room with their wives—"who should have fought to the bitter end, you gave in. And now you are surprised that they are increasing wages while sugar prices are going through the floor! You should be glad you still have your throats." He lowered his voice almost to a whisper and resumed shaking his head, his face incandescently pink, his breath rasping. "Civil servants, their asses spreading from too much sitting, that nap whole days behind their desks, that never saw a cane blade, let alone get cut by one, civil servants nourished by *our* toil"—here he gave his chest a sonorous blow—"*they* tell us what our labourers' work is worth. Don't get me started. It's bad enough we're taxed almost to bankruptcy to send their pickaninnies to sit down in school all day and hear 'See Dick run,' when they should be pulling up weeds in the fields. Don't get me started, please." Breathing heavily, he put his pipe back into his mouth. He had to relight it. Usually when he got this excited he needed nitroglycerine, but he didn't take any this time.

"Flingfoot" Robinson took over then. When walking he steadied himself with his right leg, which was straight, and flung forward the left one, which was bent and shorter—a war injury, it was said. The action had caused his left shoulder to be out of alignment with the right, and whether walking, standing, or sitting he always looked unbalanced. "Coddling niggers is now the rage," he said with detachment. "It will pass," he added with lowered volume, "except, of course, we're in the last days, which from the look o' things is probably so." He paused and his tone became nostalgic. "Time was when you went somewhere and saw the Union Jack, you knew it had an army and navy behind it and no upstart would trifle with you. With a British passport in your pocket you could call the shots and no brown-faced monkey the world over dared to disrespect you. In them days the only coddling a nigger got was rawhide on his ass. Now there's a motion in the Legco to banish flogging."

"Somebody should flog sense into those monkeys in the Legco, beginning with the one that got elected from around here"—Pine Knot interrupted.

"Horse Jaw" Langley blinking his eyes rapidly to cover up the twitching below his right eye, took over. "That's what happens when niggers that can't read and write—don't even know to figure on their fingers, let alone the meaning of property—get the vote. I tell you some nights I tremble in my bed to think what this colony has come to." He broke into song: *"Crawl, Britannia. Britannia, crawl like crabs . . ."* He got up at that point, probably to ease the pressure on his bad back, and completed his song standing.

"You're so damn right! Our navy's a pisspot. We're one step from wiping nigger's asses," Manchester agreed, barely removing his pipe.

Blacks without property voting for the first time. Those elections. Curfews. Demonstrations. Arrests. Deaths. Police had stood guard around the clock at Arcadia. 1955 had been the worst year. The planters had tried to stop the election, and the Administrator was ordered to employ the militia against them. The planters in the Legco withheld the salaries of all public servants, and the Black political candidates had got the labourers on the estates to riot. Before it ended, fifteen people—fourteen laborers and one political candidate—had lost their lives, two of them killed by Pine Knot, who claimed he caught them trying to set fire to his greathouse. Every planter was turfed out of the Legco.

That had been two years before. At the height of the tension Joshua was forced to stay in Hanovertown on weekends. During the crisis White people did not venture far from home without police or privately hired protection, and never without loaded guns.

"Ichabod Crane"—that was Mommy's nickname for him—used to be a regular guest to the house then. His real name was Arnold Robinson. He was "Flingfoot's" younger brother, and he ran the Robinson and Co. Hardware and Grocery in Hanovertown, in which Mommy owned shares. He was nearly seven feet tall and had a narrow, bony, kidney-shaped face, slitlike brown eyes sunk deep in their sockets. His nose seemed to take up the centre of his face and flared as if he were always sniffing. His light-brown short hair was always slicked back. His upper body was tilted forward as if his back couldn't fully support it. His clothes seemed to be swallowing him, perhaps because his arms and legs were so stringy. He said he was in love with Mommy, and so his brother "Flingfoot" often brought him a-courting, and sometimes he came alone. He was twelve years Mommy's junior. Mommy said she would not marry him, and when Joshua asked her why, she said he was too young to understand such things. But Joshua had on occasion overheard their conversations in the parlour. Ichabod insisted that Mommy had womanly needs that weren't being met, and it wasn't normal for a woman to be running a plantation. Another time he told her, "They say you're one woman not to be trifled with."

Mommy chuckled. "That never stopped any of you from treating me like a trifle."

She'd yawned then, summoned Rose with her bell and told her to give Mr Robinson whatever he wanted to drink, and excused herself, saying she had to help Joshua with his homework, which was true.

Yesterday Mommy told Ichabod in a loud voice that if he could not come to her place without constantly proposing marriage, he was no longer welcome. He got up right away and said he would only return if she asked him to.

A woman not to be trifled with. He'd wished he could ask her why Ichabod had said so, but she'd know that he often eavesdropped on her conversations. It wasn't something he could ask the servants about. He recalled all this vividly years later when he read the documents given to him after her death.

He was still standing on the porch looking out at the landscape that was now yellow, as if coated with pollen, when the supper bell rang. He washed his hands and took his place at table, on Mommy's right, between her and Sparrow. There was a bottle of wine on the table. Alcohol was never served unless Mommy had company. Sparrow's religion forbade drinking alcohol and Mommy's favourite uncle—*on her mother's side, the side she loved*—had died of cirrhosis of the liver, and she had vowed, she'd say, to be a teetotaller. But on special occasions she took her drop, and when Pine Knot, Flingfoot, Horse Jaw, Polecat, and the lot came by, the whisky flowed. Joshua wondered now what the occasion was. The first course was kingfish soup made with coconut milk. It was one of Joshua's favourite dishes. Something special was happening, he knew, and from the way Mommy looked at him—her eyes a bright blue, her face as if she was doing her best not to tell a secret—he knew it concerned him. Rose brought in a platter of sliced stuffed roast pork and a bowl of plantain cou-cou. The rosemary in the stuffing perfumed the dining room and got his salivary glands going.

"Call the servants, Rose, and bring six wine glasses," Mommy said.

"Henry can't come, Mistress. He cleaning out the chicken house this very minute."

"Let Dawn come then."

They came, in their aprons and caps, probably annoyed. This elaborate meal on a Wednesday. It would mean getting home to their families at least an hour and a half later than usual. Mommy had razed the servants' quarters, but left the adjoining unused stables the year after Joshua went to live at Arcadia. She said she didn't want servants living on the place. They got to know too much of your business. Rose and Marie, who lived in the rooms then, had grumbled about it, especially when they found out they weren't going to have pay increases. Now when she gave her evening receptions she made Rose and Dawn work evenings, gave them large packages of left-over food to take home, and let them come to work at ten the next day and leave around four.

Mommy beamed, then got up. "I want to make a toast to Joshua." She poured a half-inch of wine into Joshua's glass, filled Sparrow's and her own, and then poured the bulk of what remained into Dawn's and Rose's glasses. "This is to Joshua. He passed the entrance exams to *Expatriates Academy* with flying colours. He almost won a scholarship. To your success, Joshua."

Everyone drank the toast, and Dawn and Rose smiled. Dawn teased and joked with him whenever Mommy wasn't around, and Rose was no longer as diffident with him as she used to. He understood their code. When they knew he was overhearing them, one would tell the other, "Little jackass got big ears," meaning he was nearby and they should watch what they say. But he never repeated anything they said.

After Dawn and Rose had left the dining room, Mommy said, "And there is something else. For a month now the formal adoption papers have been ready for signing but I had been putting it off. Yesterday when I got your results, I had the lawyer bring them here and I signed them. Joshua"—he stared at her attentively, she at him with equal intensity—"You are now my son, formally."

Sparrow yodelled and drained his glass. "This here occasion calls for another bottle o' that there wine. Missis Éclair will yer do me the honour . . . ," He stopped short, a big grin on his face. "Pour me that lil tas'e you got in that there bottle."

Joshua felt he should say something. Emotions he couldn't define rushed through him. He was overjoyed and yet something about it didn't feel right. Bita should be here. Mammy too. There should be some sort of handing over. He remembered Bita's accusation that he'd forget her. He became aware that Sparrow and Mommy were looking at him, were waiting for him to say something. "Thanks," he said. "I am glad to be your son, Mommy. I am very glad." He knew that was what she wanted to hear, and he truly did not mind, was aware of the privilege and prestige he enjoyed. The coming of Sparrow had filled a void in the household. But even so he wondered when and how he would tell Bita and how she would react. Would she accuse him of no longer loving her? Had he stopped loving her?

Nowadays, he admitted, he rarely thought of her. At that moment he looked down at his plate and saw that it was full. He hadn't even seen when Mommy took it. And she hadn't noticed that he hadn't said thanks.

He decided it would be better not to let Bita know he'd been formally adopted.

There is power, power
Wonder working power
In the blood of the lamb.
There is power, power
Wonder working power
In the precious blood of the lamb

The saints militant (Sparrow's name for his followers, who after death became saints triumphant) sang. With deep sadness in his voice, Sparrow would say, "Can't give 'em food; Lord knows they could use some. Can't give 'em medical care, and they need it som'n awful. Can't pay for their chillun ter go ter school. Can't offer 'em justice; Lord knows they ain't never had none. All Ah can offer 'em is hope in the life ter come."

That August they were up to thirty in spite of the frequent backsliding. "No matter what a body tells 'em they's constantly a-fallin' 'n a-stumblin' into the traps o' the flesh," he'd say, shaking his head and wrinkling his brow. "Jesus promised ter send the holy sperrit ter guide 'n uphol' 'em, but they's so randy, it can't get nary a hol' on 'em. Makes a body wonder if they's ever been saved 'n sanctified. Never know. Baable says many be called, ain't but few chosen.

"'N I got ter admit there be tayms Ah'm a whole heap discouraged 'cause Ah wants ter see ma flock increase. There's times Ah be downrat disheartened 'n Ah gets ter doubtin'. But this ain't never been no race fer the fainthearted. 'N is mah determination fer ter win."

There were never more than four or five men in the congregation. Those women snagged by the flesh withdrew quietly when their pelvises began to bulge. Sparrow's bigger battles were with those who stayed, older women mostly, over the paying of tithes. He would read the Old Testament passages that sanction tithing. In vain. A guilty plantation hand would on occasion give twelve cents (ten percent) of her week's pay, or a housemaid sixty cents, ten percent of her month's wage; but it was never more than a one-shot deal. The best Joshua heard on the subject was from "Runmouth" Mavis, who lived off remittances her daughter, a nurse in the US, sent her (everyone knew her business because she stated it all in her prayers, bragging perhaps): "God didn' mean for we to interpret the things in the Bible like He say them." (Of course, Sister Mavis chose what to interpret literally and what to interpret figuratively or not all.) She and Sparrow differed over the meaning of wealth in Christianity. Giving Job as his example, Sparrow suggested that eventually wealth came to those whom God tried and did not find wanting. Her examples were Dives and the rich man who'd caused Jesus to say that it was easier for a camel to pass through the eye of a needle than for a rich man to enter into the kingdom of heaven. That would leave Sparrow without a comeback. It then became his turn to tell her the Bible shouldn't always be interpreted literally. Sister "Runmouth" Mavis was a firm believer in the good works that others did.

Their quarrels see-sawed, sometimes going into remission, at which times they would be laughing and talking, and sometimes suddenly erupting, scalding, her voice an ice pick piercing the ears of those who hadn't fled—usually after a sermon she didn't like, or after Sparrow's reading of Paul's ordinances to silence women.

The final incident happened one Wednesday. Sparrow was at the pulpit holding forth: "Sin, brothers 'n sisters, makes a body feel good. Good lak a newborn calf be feeling when the mother cow's a-lickin' him."

Sister Mavis laughed.

"Can't yer be quiet!" Sparrow shouted at her and pounded the lectern.

The congregation of about a dozen turned their stares on her. Joshua, a seat ahead of her, turned too. Her eyes were like pink stones in a leathery, dull brown face encircled in a parrot-blue headkerchief.

"Sparrow, it take more than you to quiet me. You ain't no brother o' mine. Let me tell me you something: I not no pit latrine. These others in here can't smell. You been . . . on us ever since you start this chu'ch. Chu'ch!" She laughed, one long peal of sneering scorn. "I can smell . . . even when you wrap it in God's word. One more thing, you always trying to heft thoughts that's too heavy for your brains. You say the Holy Ghost enlightening you! Benighting is more like it. I have a important question to ask you: Is what you run away from in America? What sort of penance you doing here? I got part o' the answer last night in a dream: a White man in police uniform ask me if I know you. He say he got a warrant for your arrest." She stopped talking. The congregation stared at Sparrow. The church had become a court room. Sparrow clutched the lectern with both hands, his head bowed as if praying.

"Let us pray," someone in the congregation said, to break the tension.

He did not remember the prayer, and he and Sparrow walked the quarter of a mile back to Arcadia in complete silence, Joshua recalling the conversation on the porch between Sparrow and Mommy. Joshua developed something of a grudging admiration for Sister Mavis. But she never returned to Sparrow's church, and shortly afterwards Mommy stopped him too from going.

Half of Sparrow's sermons were on sexual continence. Now Joshua wonders if the sins a preacher flays point to the temptations he has trouble resisting.

Before the end of that same August, Mommy sought to purge him of any love he had for Bita. It was clear she wasn't reassured by the answers he gave. She would be seated on the couch in the antechamber of her bedroom, he on the armchair; beside her a magazine rack and a shelf of books, a reading lamp, and a foot-high crystal vase of freshly-cut gerbras and asparagus fern; her khaki-coloured clothing constrasting with the azure couch, her eyes like the Caribbean sea when unplacid. "Joshua," she'd say, rubbing her hands as if creaming them. "Lord, this is so difficult to say," and she'd stop speaking and stare fiercely at him. "You are now old enough to understand these things. Do you know the story of the Flood?"

He would not answer and she would insist on an answer.

"What about it?"

"Well you know how . . . how—"

"God drowned the world?"

"Yes that. That, and what followed?" she goaded.

"He put a rainbow in the sky and promised he would destroy the world with fire next time. Even God couldn't deal with the stench of all those corpses," he taunted her because his taunting made her blush and left her embarrassed to the point where she would usually drop the subject. But in this session it didn't work.

"Why are you avoiding the subject?"

"I am not."

"Yes, you are."

"Then why don't *you* state what the subject is?"

"The subject is how Black people came to be on this earth."

There she goes again, he told himself, raising his eyes to the ceiling.

"Don't look up at the ceiling."

"'I will lift up mine eyes to the hills from whence cometh my help,'" he said mockingly.

"You are avoiding the subject."

"*You* are afraid to say what the subject is."

"No, I'm not."

"Then, what is it?"

"It's about Blackness."

"No, it's not." But it was. He had to oppose her, frustrate her into not discussing it, because Bita was Black and Mommy could not convince him that Bita was cursed into being a servant for White people for the rest of her life, and that he should stop loving her.

"Will you send me to an early grave, Joshua?"

That one was new and it threw him momentarily off guard. He wanted to say, no—provocatively—not before I reach manhood and "you keep your promises," and tell me who my father is—although he'd begun to think she did not know, that maybe his mother had slept with several White men and did not know which one she had conceived for. Of late the thought had made him loathe to inquire about his father.

"You haven't answered me."

"What do you want me to say: that I *don't want you to go to an early grave?* Mommy, I don't want you to go to an early grave."

"You're being sarcastic, Joshua. And what's worse, you know it."

"Mommy, you are asking me to disown my sister, to believe that she was born cursed. But I cannot disown my sister. It is not her fault that she was born Black."

"And your biological mother?"

He did not answer, for she did not matter.

"I'm waiting for an answer, Joshua."

He thought then of how she'd snipped his beginning friendship with Maurice. Just like that, as if it had been an out-of-place, embarrassing thread. They told him he could not be friends with Black people. And stupidly he did not put up a fight. This time he would. "I cannot forget Bita. I *will not forget* Bita. Ask me to give up anything else, but don't ask me to forget Bita." He was pleased by the finality with which he said it.

"You have to, Joshua."

He did not answer, largely because he was afraid he'd get angry. A knock on the door from Rose followed by the announcement that supper would be on the table in a short while broke the impasse.

"Please, Joshua, please, for my own peace of mind, try. Will you try? Promise me you will try."

"All right, I *will* try but I'm making no promises." He had nothing to lose by saying so. She didn't have to know he didn't mean it. In his bed, later, he wondered about saying this, and tried to imagine that Bita wasn't his sister, that his memories were all a dream, that Mommy was his mother and that Mommy's husband was his father, that by some curious mix-up he'd ended up being the child of Bita's mother. But it never lasted for more than a few seconds, for once Bita's name came into his thoughts a tender feeling filled him, and he wished she had one of the rooms at Arcadia, ate the food served there, and benefited from all that could be had there. But Mommy must not know he harboured such thoughts.

7

THE WEEK BEFORE HE STARTED attending Expatriates Academy Mommy told him she no longer wanted him attending Sparrow's church. He'd have to spend more time on his schoolwork, which he'd soon be having a lot of.

Two days later, a Saturday night, she and Sparrow quarrelled over it. It began quietly. At first it was about how embarrassed she was by the barbarity of his language. He exaggerated his southern speech just to see her wince when there was company, she said. She didn't want Joshua associating too closely with him anymore, to pick up his speech "and God knows what other habits." She chuckled. "All that frothing-at-the-mouth foolishness you're spouting, that drives these illiterate plantation hands wild, the nonsense you call religion, would put Joshua's brain to sleep."

Sparrow replied slowly—Joshua could tell he was restraining himself—"Joshua is yer son. I ain't no ways responsible fer how yer raise him. Ah guess too Ah ain't so well placed to go ergainst yer wishes. Ah depends a whole heap on yer charity, 'n Ah 'preciates it, 'cause Ah sees som'n awful the slave treatment a body gets here. Ah knows 'bout the starvation wages yer pay yer workers, Averill, 'n it ain't raat."

"You know a lot and there's a lot you don't know. Dawn, Henry, and Rose eat the same food we eat, and I let them serve themselves. So I don't starve anybody."

"What 'bout them that workin' in the fields? Them that earns less'n a dollar and a half a week? Is a crime, Ah say, a crime that cries out to Gawd a'mighty for justice."

Mommy did not reply.

Their voices, with a wild energy of their own, rose as the quarrel progressed despite their pleas to each other to stop. He accused her of being like her father, who had stuffed himself like a fattening goose with his grandfather's wealth and had married a rich Jewess to double it. She countered that his father was a "fatuous fool, but you won't know what the word means." He said her father had bankrupted his.

Joshua pieced together that Sparrow's father was called Walter and was the younger of two brothers. In revolt against his father, who had been a member of the Klan, Walter had run off at nineteen to live with a Native American woman. In the meantime his father died and dispossessed him. At twenty-five Walter returned, contrite, and joined the local Klan, got married and tried to run a chicken business. But his devotion to Klan activities and a poultry virus wiped out his chicken business. He went to work in one of his brother's hardware stores and got more and more bitter with the years. By the time Sparrow was ten and his sister fourteen their father was an alcoholic and a wife- and child-abuser. A bomb he was planting in a Black community centre had exploded prematurely and severed his right arm.

According to Sparrow, "Papa would o' been a whole heap happier if he'd o' stayed with that Indian woman. He turn his back on her 'cause o' society, 'n what he got for it? Spite 'n proverty 'n a broken heart."

"You're the son of a bigot and a criminal and you have a double dose of both in you," was how Mommy summed it up.

"And yer the granddaughter o' one bigger'n him," Sparrow rejoined.

"I am responsible for my actions, not those of my father or my grandfather."

"Then yer oughter pay yer workers decently."

"Butt out of things you know nothing about."

Sparrow, who had been a regular delinquent throughout his school years, and his sister Marjorie were constantly sheltered by their Uncle Gladstone, Mommy's father, and they would have lost their house if Uncle Gladstone had not taken over the mortgage. "You forget that your skin used to look like liver—you smelled like it too. Once you came to us with two of your back teeth missing. I cried when I saw how bashed up you looked, bruises all over your face. I've always felt sorry for you, and I've always paid—I'm still paying—for it."

According to Sparrow, Uncle Gladstone had helped to disinherit his father. The charity he gave them was "Just him givin' back a lil' o' what he done stole 'n killed for. Eve'body that wanted ter know knowed he was in with the Tallahassee Mafia. There been a lotta fires in Tallahassee them days. Eve'y last one of 'em businesses sellin' somethin' Uncle Gladstone thank was his sole God-given rait ter sell. 'N as fer that JAP, yer mother, she take off her Jewry lak was a pair o' earrings. Treat us lak we been stray dogs. Other times like we been slaves. Had me totin' groceries, washin' windows, cuttin' grass. Only thang she ain't had me doing was pleasurin' her. I more'n earned ma keep when I was at yall. 'N she livin' off the fat o' ma grandfather's sweat. 'Course Ah ain't sayin' she come to yer father a pauper. Why, Uncle Gladstone, he should o' marry her fore Grampa died. 'N you, her only chile, she turned yer inter a Presbyterian praincess, 'n since then yer been expectin' ev'one ter wipe yer ass. I ain't gonna be doin' it jus' 'cause yer never learn ter do it yerself."

"Lay off my mother, you ungrateful dog! She sent your sister to college. And would have sent you too, but you couldn't learn. Talk about your own mother. You'd think she'd stepped straight out of *Tobacco Road*."

By midnight they were at white heat.

"When the police arrested you on charges of gross indecency, it was Daddy—you hear me?—who got your perverted ass out of their custody. And it was Daddy who prevented it from getting into the local papers. You were—I don't have to remind you what they caught you doing in the park. Daddy rescued you, 'cause, low as you'd sunk, he still saw you as family. We've always had to rescue you. Always. First Daddy, then me. You ingrate! Preacher! Only here you can pull that one off. *Inspired!* By guile and perversion! These poor, ignorant folks think you're somebody because you're White."

"Rescue me! Yer got ter be kiddin', Coz. And whad 'bout ya ownself? Seems lak Ah remember me comin' inter a room and hearin' a woman a-groanin' som'n fit ter make a rock holler and seen her lyin' in a pool o' her own blood, 'cause she done had a certain operation to haide her shame. Coz, seems to me that woman was yer ownself."

"You have no shame! You dare to mention that!"

"We's a-mentionin' ev'thang tonight, Ah reckon."

"Why don't you talk about running and leaving your trousers with those boys who caught you in the woods doing things with, with—"

"You're alive today, Coz, 'cause they did. That's how come Ah fled ter New York and got there on time ter save yer laf."

That observation ended the quarrel. Within seconds Joshua heard Mommy's footsteps going in the direction of her bedroom.

Next morning she did not come to his room to tell him to get ready for the 7 A.M. service at the Presbyterian Church. That day she had her meals brought to her room although there was never more than one servant in the house on Sunday. When she emerged on Monday morning her face was puffy. She made discreet inquiries to find out if Joshua had heard their quarrel.

"What quarrel? Who was quarreling? I slept like a brick," he told her.

"Sparrow and I. We had a nasty quarrel."

"What about?"

"Old family rivalries. Those things that have a way of staying quiet, then flaring up, and attacking virulently. Like shingles. We've made up, like civilized people should. It's all behind us now."

She said it with feeling. Her facial muscles sagged, her eyes were misty, and Joshua felt a deep tenderness for her. She looked vulnerable, and he did not like to see her that way. But he knew she would not want him to know the facts he'd gleaned from the quarrel. He wondered later how she'd met her husband, and told himself that one day, when he was older, he'd ask her. But somehow the opportunity never presented itself. And she never volunteered the information while she was still alive.

He would have preferred to be allowed to choose whether or not to attend Sparrow's church. He missed the colourful preaching, in which Adam argued with God and Jonah cursed God in his thoughts, "Where does this . . . get off? Brothers and Sisters that-there word's just too vile. Don't do no good fer me ter repeat it. 'N all the time he was a-cussin' he ain't know God was a-hearin' him and he just went right 'long a-cussin' God merrily with them-there filthy thoughts."

And he missed the babble of prayers and the tambourine-slapping as they sang and even danced:

My father is rich in houses and lands:
He holdeth the wealth of the world in his hands
Of rubies and diamonds, of silver and gold,
His coffers are full; he has riches untold.

I'm a child of the king, a child of the king.
With Jesus my Savior, I'm a child of the king.

They looked as if they'd swoon each time they sang this; their eyes got glassy, and Sparrow's interrupting *hallelujahs* and *praise-the-Lords* made it unearthly. Crude but delightful theatre, he now thinks.

Him on the pulpit crying, "Holy, holy, holy, Lord God Almighty . . . ," his golden eyes on fire, the fire in an actor's eye, everyone, including me, thinking he's filled with the holy ghost. I lying in my bed years later with these sounds echoing in my head when I should have been studying, knowing what's likely to happen later that night.

They're probably wondering why a White man whose cousin owns a thousand-acre plantation, who could be her heir, has built them a church and is their preacher, is interested in their spiritual welfare; and it inspires them to shout all the more. And he saying God in his unfathomable mercy and mystery had sent him to save their lost benighted souls.

From Greenland's icy mountains,
From India's coral strands,
Where Africa's sunny fountains
Roll down their golden sands . . .

Can we to men benighted
The lamp of life deny?

Jesus shall reign where'er the sun
Doth his successive journeys run,
His kingdom stretch from shore to shore
Till moons shall wax and wane no more . . .

None of the scandals of the brothers and sisters, none of that backsliding filth, ever soils him. He himself is like Paul, he implies. To the "burning" brothers he says, "It's better to be married than to burn."

And Sister Mavis taunting him: "Brother Mann don't does burn at all. Brother Mann not scorchable. Brother Mann get all his loving from the Lord. O what a holy man is our beloved pastor, Brother Mann!"

Some of the sisters and brothers laughing, but Brother Mann never gets the joke, refuses to get the joke, is above getting the joke.

Seriously, Sister "Runmouth" Mavis would say to me, her eyes garnet-red, a skin fold dangling from her chin like a lizard jowl, always in Sparrow's presence, "See what a God-fearing man your Uncle Pastor Mann is? Joshua, you must follow in his footsteps."

Did she know the size of his shoes? He wouldn't have put them under her bed. And she was beyond the age where he needed to wear "socks." But neither Joshua nor she knew that at the time.

He was around eleven when Mavis first asked him, "How come you don' done give your heart to Jesus yet?" But Joshua needed his heart. Wanted absolute certitude that no one but he owned it. Jesus owned Sister Mavis's and it hadn't stopped her mouth from running. Enough people had liens on him as it were.

GawdFAYring! That was how she pronounced it. And God, when all was said and done, was Sparrow's fare, which, Joshua now knows, went through him undigested and came out foul-smelling. If "The fear of the Lord is the beginning of wisdom," Sparrow had none, so he couldn't have feared God. *Lead head.* But that he was sincere in his belief that he was doing God's work, Joshua now has absolutely no doubt.

And the backslidden brother not able to hold out against the allures of the flesh is told, "You should take a leaf out o' Brother Mann book." Trouble most never opened it, and even if they could, had no Rosetta Stone for its hieroglyphs. Only Mavis suspected there was something sinister beneath it.

By then, Bita had already run off to live with Skeeter.

Once he went off to Expatriates Academy he hadn't much time to think about many things. He returned home every day. A taxi took him, Randolph Kevin (Pine Knot's grandson), and Alexander and Vincent Manchester (Polecat's sons) to school in the morning and returned for them in the afternoon. If one or the other of them was in detention, the driver waited. The driver called them all "master," and whenever he spoke to them he raised his hand to his head as if to touch his cap—he didn't wear one. Whenever he stood in front of them, he arched forward and bowed his head and stared at the ground, reminding Joshua of Booges's behaviour when-ever Joshua was angry with him. Randolph, Alexander, and Vincent—they were grades ahead of Joshua and had been travelling with this driver for at least three years—called the taxi driver by his nickname: Shilling. In time

Joshua did too.

In October, one month after he began at Expatriates, Mommy made him join the Boy Scouts. And because she could pay his passage to the various Caribbean islands, Joshua got chosen along with the Manchester boys to represent the scouts of Camden and, occasionally, the scouts of Isabella Island, except during the July-August holidays; in those months he had to practise his French and Spanish. Some years he had to go to Martinique and other years to Puerto Rico, but always in schools run like detention camps by Roman Catholic monks.

Outside in the dormitories things are quiet. He looks at his watch. Defoe and Stein should be here any minute now. He wonders what they will try to pry out of him today. When they've stripped away your memories and leave you bleeding, aching and empty, what follows? Well, he won't take off his clothes for Defoe to finger his warts and scars, and he won't let Defoe probe his entrails to examine his shit. They'd asked for permission to hypnotize him. And he said no. He observed them, frustrated by their futile efforts to get him to talk. "I don't like to go naked among strangers," he told them. "That sort of thing died out after the sixties. We're not exactly a 'Living Theater' troupe."

"We're here to help you."

"You're here to earn a living. And a damned good living it is."

"The labourer is worthy of his hire," Defoe interjected.

"Cut out the Pauline scriptures. How, Dr Defoe, will this hypnosis—or is it cyanosis—allow you to finger my psyche?"

Defoe did not answer, so Joshua continued. "What do an id, an ego, and a superego look like, Dr Defoe?"

Defoe remained silent.

"See? How will you know you've found what you're looking for if you don't know what it is? Let alone whether it's diseased. You must believe in ghosts. They're a lot more real than the psyche. At least some people claim to see them."

Defoe smiled.

"Yeah, my psyche is diseased. But you and I don't know what the psyche is, so I don't see how you and your colleagues can heal it. You'll get further with characters in a novel. Perhaps you've already turned me into a character."

But Defoe quietly placed his hand on Joshua's and slowly said, with utmost humility, "We are trying and we want you to try too." He did not remove his hand immediately. That touch. It told him that whatever happened afterwards, as long as Defoe was there, his humanity would not be compromised.

He squeezed Defoe's hand, looked straight into his eyes and nodded thanks.

"Things will turn out all right," Defoe responded.

Dr Defoe enters the room. He's holding the folding chair he's brought with him. Joshua knows that he must get out of the bed and sit in the armchair. More and more he realizes how much he likes Defoe. He doesn't mind Stein, but with Defoe it's different; it's brotherly mostly, and it embarrasses him a trifle. He wonders if there's anything sexual in it. There's at least twenty years' difference between them.

"Dr Defoe, where will you be probing today?" he asks in a playful tone.

"Where'd you think?" Defoe's response is equally playful. When Stein's absent, he slips into a folksier, more relaxed tone.

"Everywhere, Dr Defoe. But you won't be able to see much for the simple reason that it isn't seeable."

"Try me."

Joshua smiles. "Be humble, Dr Defoe. Even when we're most fully awake, there are parts of us that must remain asleep. Of course, if they awaken we end up here."

"You are right. But unless we examine our fears they hinder us. Since you are already *here* you might as well let every part of you awaken."

When this session with Defoe ends, the emotions their conversation has stirred up take Joshua back to the year following his thirteenth birthday.

He was wondering why the boy in his line of vision was looking with consternation at his fly, only to realize that it was because he Joshua had been staring at it. He vowed he'd stop doing it, and when he remembered, he did, but more often than not it was instinctual. His classmates caught on and asked him often if he was funny.

"Prufrock, you undress us with your eyes. Do you like men?"

"Do you let men push their peckers into you?"

"He wants to blow our flutes."

"We don't play your kind of music."

"See, he's blushing. He's funny."

"I'm not," he countered feebly.

"Well, why are you always staring at our flies?"

"Simple: he wants to play our instruments." This from Percival, who was bigger than all his classmates. His hazel eyes shone with uncommon brightness in a cinnamon face graced with generous, smiling lips.

"Prouffy, people like you get sent to prison."

"It's in the papers sometimes that one of your kind's been beaten. Have you ever been beaten, Prouffy?"

"He prefers to be eaten."

Eventually he chose silence and gave them his best impenetrable marble stare. But for a few months their barbs ulcerated his gut, turned his shit black and his soul into a tangled web that kept him night after night contemplating nooses, manchineel, and other ways to die.

The following May, one Saturday, Alexander Manchester persuaded him to go fishing with him. Alexander drove his father's jeep about two miles up into the hills of his father's plantation. Their fishing poles were in the stream, and Joshua was focusing on a fish he thought was biting when he felt Alexander's body leaning against his own and Alexander's erect penis pulsing against his bum. He froze where he stood on the bank of the stream, listening to Alexander's heightened breathing and pounding heartbeat, as Alexander ejaculated in his pants.

On their way home, Alexander told him that if he ever mentioned what happened, he'll say that it was Joshua who did what he'd done. "And Prouffy, trust me. They'll believe me."

One recess, two weeks later he was walking towards the willows and cedars at the school entrance. His classmates gathered there to joke about their real and imaginary exploits. He overheard Bull Breton exclaiming among them, "And you just let him! Imagine! Pressing up against you and coming!"

"Why'dn't you cut off his prick?" Percival asked.

He couldn't face them. He turned to head back to class.

"There he is, the pervert!" Bull Breton shouted. "Come down here! You pervert!" Joshua walked hurriedly back into the building, went into one of the classrooms and sat down. He felt cold. Sweat streamed from his armpits. How would he endure this? It would be his word against Alexander's. And he knew, for reasons of race, they would believe Alexander. Besides, it was he, not Alexander, they'd already tagged homosexual. Alexander had already implied this. For weeks he continued to avoid them at lunchtime and recess. But he couldn't in class. Every question he answered, whatever he did, they commented on under their breath and ended with the word *pervert*. Once when Miss Blunt left the class, someone slipped him a note. It read: "My mother says you're so because you're a mongrel. Interbreeding makes people funny. When are you going to start wearing dresses?" Miss Blunt returned just as they were getting ready to assail him. School became torture. His hands shook when he encountered them during the day, and at night, they chased him with flashing brandished butcher knives, and he could not run. He woke from these nightmares bathed in sweat.

A couple of months after this, Sparrow began to tell him smutty stories about men's penises. The telling continued for weeks. Why, Joshua wondered—why a preacher, a servant of God, would talk like this? He remembered the quarrel he'd had with Mommy and their earlier conversation on the porch. But he was sure that religion had changed Sparrow. Joshua believed that the Holy Spirit had cleansed Sparrow of sexual desire; Sparrow himself said so when he harangued his congregation to sanctify themselves. He had done so "for the greater glory o' God. Thangs we be slaves to, that grip us in a vise, just crack 'n fall to pieces when we's free 'n our souls is pure. Brothers 'n sisters, sin's lak manure, 'n our nature is lak roots that the holy sperrit burn out when we be sanctified, we ain't able to take in that there filth no more. Ma life's a testament to what it be lak before 'n after God's grace." In those days Joshua was certain that sex was evil and dirty, something dogs did coupled helplessly to each other in ditches and at the roadside; something cats snarled, caterwauled, and fought for in back-yards and alleys. Sex turned you into an animal. Nothing in his upbringing made him want to see any links between himself and animals. On the contrary. It made him want to flee those people linked to animals, through sex, powerlessness, and poverty; and race of course; race most certainly. He felt terribly sad for all the women and men who came to Sparrow's church but later abandoned it because of needs they held in common with cater-wauling cats and coupled dogs, and wished they would conquer their sexu-ality as Sparrow and Mommy had conquered theirs. He rarely admitted it but he despised Mammy and later Bita, when she went off to live with Skeeter, and himself, when he couldn't keep his eyes away from men's flies.

One evening, exactly a month after the smutty stories began—it was Mrs Manchester's turn to host the bridge party, so Mommy was at her house—Joshua was having his shower, and Sparrow came into the bathroom naked. Joshua hurried to get out of the shower stall, but Sparrow told him to stay, and he obeyed.

His hands are perspiring. *I ought to forget, not remember, my life.* He gets up and paces the length of the room. Gladys finds him pacing. She calls Defoe.

"Would you like something to calm you down?" Defoe asks him as soon as he comes into the room.

Joshua does not answer.

"You seem bothered by something. What is it?"

Joshua is silent. He sits down in the armchair. *It's my stench; it's not for the public's nostrils. I won't have my fears and frustrations, the wounds I've inflicted and received written down in doctors' charts, and later in textbooks. That would be the ultimate in nakedness.*

"You're so silent. What's causing the deep frowns in your face?"

"Nothing."

"Why do you constantly lie? The ridges in your brow form and unform like waves on the shore. Before that you were pacing. And you want me to believe you've been experiencing a blank! We watch you and we hear you pacing in this room, sometimes for over half an hour."

"Try another time, Dr Defoe. I'm tired," he feebly replies.

"Then you should lie down!"

"I'm tired nonetheless."

8

DEFOE LEAVES. JOSHUA FEELS a trifle guilty. Why's he giving Defoe such a hard time? Besides he likes him. That's part of the problem.

Gladys Knights brings him phenobarb. He dozes off and has a nightmare about Bita's death. When he wakes up he relives the actual experience and sweats profusely throughout.

He is sixteen. A student at Expatriates Academy. It's lunch hour and he is strolling in town. He's at the Market Quadrangle. All around him, women haggle, selling fruits and vegetables.

"Young man. Yo! You don't hear me callin' you?"

He turns to see a market mammy staring at him. She beckons to him. He doesn't feel like going. Mommy doesn't want him to mingle with people like her. The woman's eyes are bold and seem to be getting bigger by the heartbeat. She's wearing bright red earrings and a brilliant red headtie. Both contrast vividly against her coal-black skin. Barbarous clothing, screaming colours, Mommy would say.

He approaches. Stands before her. She scrutinizes him for a full ten seconds.

"Your mother is my sister-in-law," she says. "I hear your adopted mother teaching you not for mix with people like me." She stops talking and her eyes are burning. Joshua drops his gaze periodically.

"You hear about your sister?"

He shakes his head.

"She jump in the sea this morning. She drownded. They still didn' find the body when I leave. The rocks off there is dangerous. That place is a haunt for sharks."

Joshua feels his eyes growing dark. When he comes to, his head is on the woman's lap. Someone is bending over him, fanning him. It's not a dream.

"Bita?"

"Not Bita, Lita." She nods, then lifts her apron and wipes her eyes.

He stands. "I'm okay now."

He walks to the bus park, boards a bus and continues on it beyond Arcadia for about two miles, to a place he hasn't set foot in for twelve years. He has no trouble finding the hut. He goes to it. Opens the door. There's no one inside. He has forgotten how small it is. A single room slightly bigger than his and Sparrow's bathroom.

He leaves, moves to the road. There's a strong breeze. The dust is choking, it enters his throat, cakes it, and he sneezes. An April drought is on. He walks the two miles back to Arcadia. Dawn comes to the gate. She embraces him. Presses him to her. "I know you love her. We all know. You used for hide and meet her in the cane field. We hide it from Mistress." She is unable to hold back her grief.

She presses him even closer and begins to sing—in deep, haunting tones—"'We shall meet beyond the river . . .' You will see her in the next life and her spirit will guide you and keep you from harm in this one." They stay like that for he does not know how long.

"Joshua, what are you doing here at this time day? Dawn, what is going on under my roof? And you, Joshua, haven't I told you repeatedly not to fraternize with the servants? Dawn, get back to your work. I will deal with you later." She waves a finger at Joshua, "Come with me." Her voice is blade-edged.

He does not move. She comes up to him, grabs his shirt collar.

He follows her passively into the house.

She pushes him into an armchair and sits in another. "Now please enlighten me. What is going on under my roof?"

"My sister . . ."

"Sister! What sister? I thought we'd resolved that a long time ago."

Joshua gets up and looks as if he's about to spring on her. She stares at him, open-mouthed. He picks up a brass floor lamp on his left and moves towards her menacingly. She screams. He backs away and begins striking the windows. He breaks four windows before they immobilize him. Then a dense murk engulfs him. He disappears into it, and for three months he remembers nothing, except the occasional presence of Bita's form beside him and his asking her, "Bita, is Mammy a bad woman? Bita, why everyone's afraid to tell me who's my father?" But she never answers. And when the murkiness recedes and he emerges from his daze, he finds that he has a bad stutter and there are gaps in his memory.

The recall ends and he begins to cry, in heaving spasms.

"You are healing? What were you remembering?"

Throughout the reverie he'd been unaware that there was anyone in the room. "I've never forgiven myself, Dr Defoe, for Bita's death."

"Were you in anyway responsible?"

"No. She took her own life." He reflects on this and adds, "but we die many times before our death. There's something to that cliché, Doctor. There are many ways to kill a person, Doctor. Have I contributed to her death? I know I'm responsible for the murder and maiming of many." He falls silent for a while, wondering if he's making sense, even to himself. "While I was slipping in and out of lucidity here, I was convinced for a long time that I was dead. Sometimes there's no difference between life and death."

Dr Defoe taps him on the shoulder. "You're healing. Now you must begin to trust us, tell us what you're remembering." He looks at his watch.

Trust! Trust? Why should I trust anybody? I don't even know you. "Are you leaving, Doctor?"

"Yes. What's the point of staying? You're not sharing your memories with me."

"Stay with me a few more minutes. I'll be all right afterwards."

"I—"

Joshua lifts his arm, palm facing forward, a plea for silence and understanding.

Both remain silent for about five minutes.

"You can leave me alone now, Doctor. I'll be all right."

"I'll ask Nurse Knights to give you another sedative."

Joshua nods.

He'd come out of that first breakdown on July 15, feeling as if he'd been lost in a forest for several days and hadn't eaten all that time. But even so he barely had an appetite, and found he no longer liked the taste of sugar. For the first few days, brusque movements left him feeling dizzy. His stutter bothered him. He was not altogether sure he knew himself. He knew Mommy, Sparrow, Dawn, Rose, Henry, knew who they were and through them figured out that he had to be the person he was supposed to be. It was his first clue that something very serious had happened to him. Because of his stutter, he avoided talking whenever he could. He had trouble sleeping. He'd awaken around one and toss in bed and break out in a sweat as anxiety overpowered him. After a week of this he would put on a dressing gown and go to sit on the northern porch, and look out at the landscape silvered by the moon, when there was a moon, or up into the heavens at the stars. The Atlantic sounded different then, muted, probably because at night the wind came down from the mountain. The night breeze rustled the leaves of the cherry trees, and further on it made the willows dance, and turned the trees in the orchard into dark, abstract shapes. Sometimes it brought the smell of ripe mangoes from the orchard behind the chicken coop. Nearby or in the distance owls hooted and frogs croaked in a swamp a short distance off. The occasional bat flew under the porch roof. Sitting out there for a couple of hours relaxed him, made him sufficiently peaceful to return to bed around three and again waken around five.

Soon he felt an urge to get out of bed promptly and go walking on the beach. The early sunrise in late July and August suited him. He arrived on the beach just as the sun, still behind the horizon, seemed to be gathering in its darker colours leaving only gold. On the shore the sooty light and crashing waves, which looked like a shore-length fringe of white lace tossing back and forth between the dark-grey water and the black sand, held an indefinable something that daylight hid. Then dawn: day diaphanous, draped in spectral grey slowly transmuting into silver, then gold. He stood there until the sun had pulled all the darkness into itself. It was as if he and each day were reborn together.

For some three weeks they knew nothing of these visits to the sea. The visits alarmed Mommy when she found out. She asked him in all sorts of ways without actually saying it, if one morning he would walk into the Atlantic. His stutter worsened as he tried to reply and it embarrassed her. Finally she suggested that if he had to go she would ask Sparrow to accompany him. Joshua laughed and said, "In that case, we both might hold hands and walk in together." Her eyes contracted; her hands moved nervously;

she compressed and pulled in her lips and stared ahead of her thoughtfully. She never again brought up the subject.

The doctors felt that he should return to school that September. In class he stopped volunteering to answer the teachers' questions. He noted that his classmates stopped calling him Prouffy, returned to calling him Joshua. He wanted to know why, but didn't dare to ask them. At first he felt more tired than he should have, but eventually he no longer noted the difference and by the end of the first term his ability to concentrate was close to normal. He noted that Brent Lockwood, who used to sit in front of him, was not among the students and found out that Brent had killed himself in May. He learned too that Jerome Quashee, a quiet fellow whose mother was half-White and whose parents were squatters on the Manchester plantation, had been expelled because Miss Blunt, their English teacher from the US, a dunce whom everyone laughed at, had caught him making obscene gestures at her bottom. But Jerome had gone on to pass his O level exams and was now a clerk in the civil service. There was a story too about Jerome burning a bible in Pastor O'Bum's Church, which was in a house rented from the Manchesters. Seems Joshua wasn't the only person who'd had a breakdown. In November he had to stay at home for two days under sedation because Horton, a classmate, went berserk one morning in algebra class and had to be taken to the Good Shepherd Mental Asylum. But the rest of the year was uneventful, and in January he wrote the G.C.E. O level exams his breakdown had prevented him from writing the previous June.

The following July Mommy took him to the US. Part of their stay was in New York so he could see a psychologist who, she hoped, would get to the bottom of what had caused the breakdown. They spent six weeks in a small hotel on 35th Street, less than a block from Macy's, directly behind the Empire State Building. She took him to the museums on days he didn't have appointments with the psychologist. They visited the Metropolitan Museum over several days, and she tried to explain to him the symbolism behind colours. On his own he visited the Museum of Natural History and appreciated what he was able to learn about animals and their habitats and the opportunity to see them life-sized; but seeing various ores and minerals in their natural state was a very special treat. On evenings they sometimes went to the theatre and sometimes to the cinema. It was a silent closeness, the feeling that they had only each other. He was certain then that she loved him.

The psychologist wasn't much help. Joshua saw him in his Park Avenue clinic on Monday and Thursday. There were ten sessions in all. The psychologist seemed affable enough. He had grey eyes, black (probably dyed) hair, big rabbitlike ears out of which tufts of hair grew, and a stub of a nose; he spoke as if he had something up his nose. He told Joshua to talk about anything that was worrying him. Joshua told him nothing was. The psychologist never said more than three or four sentences in any of the sessions, except once when he seemed frustrated, after the sessions had moved well beyond the half-way point.

"So nothing is bothering you?"

"Baadring" was how he pronounced it, and his pronunciation was more interesting to Joshua than any of the questions he asked him.

"Would you say that you're normal?"

"I don't know."

"Your mother tells me you're adopted and that your birth mother is Black. Do you harbour any resentment against anybody because of this?"

Joshua shook his head and thought about Mommy's pressure on him to stifle his love for Bita.

"None!"

The psychologist was clearly frustrated.

Joshua stared at him.

"Do you have a girlfriend?"

Joshua shook his head.

"Is that part of the problem?"

Joshua shook his head.

Joshua wondered what would the psychologist say if he were to tell him he doesn't know who his father was and was afraid to ask his birth mother for fear that she herself would not know. But it was a fear he could not confess, not even to a psychologist.

The psychologist rapped his fingers on his desk. The third and final rap was loud and violent. He swallowed audibly.

Joshua wasn't intimidated. He wondered what you studied to become a psychologist. That was one occupation that wouldn't interest him.

While on the train to Tallahassee, where Mommy was headed to visit her relatives, she asked him if she had been a good mother to him.

"Yes," he told her in total sincerity.

"Did anything come of the sessions?"

"Not really."

"Why?"

"I don't know. I guess, I don't feel anything's wrong with me."

"I always felt that what I did was wrong."

"It's all right," he told her largely because he didn't want to hear about it. "It's because you've been worried about me. I listen to the news too. I know the strife around race. I hear what the planters say about Black people." And he hoped she would not continue.

"Yes, that's the greater part of it."

After that statement she grew tensely silent and he was relieved.

She'd chosen to go by train because he had never ridden on a train and wanted to see the landscape. They had roomettes because they had to overnight on the train. Somebody was going to meet them in Atlanta and drive them to Tallahassee. Joshua watched her face as the train chugged speedily over the land, greeting each hamlet with a blast of its whistle, or as she picked at her food and left most of it uneaten in the dining car. She did not even try to hide her emotions. She was in her fifties, and the double chin, loose, sagging facial flesh, and the dark spidery lines around her eyes and mouth were stark. Her skin too had taken on a creamish, unhealthy look. The deep blue her eyes had when he went to live at Arcadia had dulled; the intensity and liveliness in them gone, like bluing to which too much water had been added. She seemed a sagging bundle of weariness. For a long while she fidgeted and kept looking at the items in her purse over and over, and when she wasn't doing so she scrutinized the all-White passengers in the half-empty car they were in.

The nearest passengers were two rows behind them, and crowded together a few seats away from them to the front was a group of about fifteen girl guides and their three middle-aged chaperones. At one point she broke her silence and whispered to him, "I think I have failed you, Joshua. In my ignorance I did some horrible things. But my desire was to protect you from the cruelty of the world and to steel you to face what I won't be able to protect you from. You'll soon be seeing some of it."

He placed his hand on hers and squeezed it to reassure her, and she allowed the silence to close in again.

Just as the train entered the outskirts of Atlanta, she said, "God, I'm nervous. Feel my hand." He did. There was a tremor in them and her palms were sweaty. It was 5:47 A.M., and the sun was already up, trying to pierce a blanket of haze. He doubted whether she'd slept the entire night. At any rate when he awakened she was already dressed.

"I'm always nervous when I return to Tallahassee, and the closer I get the more nervous I become."

They were scheduled to spend two weeks with Mrs Marjorie Springer, Sparrow's sister—she was divorced but kept her married name. Mommy told Joshua he must call Marjorie Springer Aunt Marge. She met them in Atlanta. After she and Mommy hugged, they eyed each other like two people meeting for the first time after a quarrel. Hastily they had breakfast at a food counter in the train station. Mommy attempted to buy snacks for the journey, but Aunt Marge stopped her, saying that she had a cooler in the trunk with food. In the end Mommy bought three chocolate bars. Aunt Marge drove them in her white, air-conditioned Cadillac to Tallahassee. Mommy sat beside her in the front seat, yawned constantly, and excused herself. Marjorie Springer spoke nonstop from the time she left Atlanta— about who had married whom and had or hadn't children, or left their husbands or wives and for what reasons; who'd moved up in the world, and down, or out, penniless or with a fortune. Occasionally she forgot their names, at which point she tried to get Mommy into the conversation. "Averill, you sho' remember him. He had eyes fer that gal who been in private school wid yer. She went up No'th to study 'bout round the same taym you did. Now what's her name? Ah swear Ah be losing ma mem'ry. Lord have mercy." . . . "You must know him, Averill. He had the hots fer you." . . . "You useter date her brother." . . . "That gal—yer know who I mean—her brother 'n you was good as married."

Marjorie Springer was an elementary school principal. Joshua remembered that Mommy's mother had put her through college. They never once mentioned Sparrow in Joshua's presence.

Her house was small and covered on the outside with asphalt shingles. The kitchen was added on, and took up half of the little land space she had at the back. It had windows on two sides, and from the third side a door that led on to her balcony. At the back, along a half rotten wood fence with most of the paint already peeled off, some fifteen or so feet from the balcony, pea vines grew. The lawn was mostly weeds, through which there was a foot-path that led to her peas. She or the previous owner had planted flowers on the sides. He recognized a few rhododendron and azalea shrubs and some rose bushes whose few leaves were either yellowing or covered with black spots. Everything else in the garden was competing with tall weeds.

He went to bed early, leaving Mommy on the balcony and Aunt Marge in the living room. On the second day Mommy proposed that they go walking around the neighbourhood. Aunt Marge screwed up her face and shook her head. "Ah ain't none fer walkin'. 'N I think it's too hot fer yer to be traipsin' 'round in this-here Florida heat. 'Sides I don't think 'tis safe. You ain't proposing takin' Joshua wid yer?" she asked alarmed. He should have known why she was alarmed, but he'd paid no mind to it. He certainly wanted to walk. Yet at some level, he must have known, for he never went walking by himself or asked to be taken anywhere. On mornings after breakfast he sat on the balcony and read some of the fifty-odd books Mommy had bought in New York. In the afternoon he did the same. Once in a while, he and Mommy accompanied Aunt Marge when she went shopping. On one such outing Mommy bought a television set and arranged for the vendor to ship it to Isabella Island. That was the sum total of what they did together.

On the third morning at Aunt Marge's she said to Mommy, "Averill, ain't it kind o' odd that the Lord ain't never seen fit to bless you 'n me with chil'ren? 'N it was'n 'cause Ah did nutten wrong in ma youth. Ah sure did keep ma legs closed. Not lak these younguns now'days. It bothered ma husband som'n awful. Sure contributed some to ma divorce. Like the Manns they been blight or som'n. Ah tell you, it's been on ma conscience som'n awful these-here years." She was seated at the white formica table in her kitchen, her arms resting on it, her hands cupped (to keep them from moving around uncontrollably). He and Mommy and were at the sink: he washing the breakfast dishes and she drying and putting them in the cupboard.

Mommy put down the towel and stared ahead of her, then balled her fists and opened them as if she'd lost and wanted to regain the circulation in them. She told Joshua to leave the dishes alone and come along with her. They'd showered and dressed in the only bathroom, which was upstairs, while Aunt Marge was preparing breakfast. Having thrown her bait, Aunt Marge stared at them in silence, her jowls pendulous; yellowish baggy pouches below her eyes, which, at that moment, glowed with mischief.

He and Mommy spent the rest of the morning walking towards the city core, pausing every now and again to window-shop. They ate lunch in a Woolworth cafeteria. They returned to Aunt Marge in a taxi around four and found her puttering in the few square feet of ground in front of her house, where she grew pink and white petunias and a rosemary shrub, beside the strip of asphalt on which she parked her Cadillac. Mommy told her hello and she responded as if nothing had happened. But at supper,

Mommy, saying that she'd had a large late lunch, ate none of the potato salad, reheated fried chicken, and kale flavoured with ham skin that Aunt Marge served. Mommy stared sternly at Joshua while she spoke, for they'd eaten around one and all she'd had was a ham sandwich, a glass of milk, and a small bowl of fruit salad.

While in Tallahassee, they drove through police check lines several times. It was 1963 and Blacks were holding demonstrations and sit-ins in several places. One afternoon the three of them were on North Munro heading towards downtown, where Aunt Marge was going to check out some specials she'd seen advertised on TV, when they came upon a roadblock. FAMU students, helmeted police officers with guns in their holsters told them, were occupying a cinema up ahead, and the police were trying to route them. Marjorie Springer looked up to heaven (the roof of her car) and said, while turning the car around in the driveway of a hotel to head back home, "Ah swear this country is a-comin' upside down. Niggers a-keepin' me from gettin' where Ah'm a-goin'. Well ain't that sum'n! Ah do declare. Why Ah pay taxes God he alone knows. That's what we get fer puttin' a Catholic in the White House. Ah always vote the Democratic ticket. But Ah didn' vote last election. No sir, Ah didn' want no Catholic fer pres'dent, 'n Ah sure was right. Wasn't I, Averill? Say something." There was a long pause, for Mommy to respond. When she didn't, Marjorie Springer resumed, "If things ain't to the niggers likin' whyn't they go to Africa? I always remember Judge Terrell. He wasn't lak them jackleg judges we got now'days, that lettin' common criminals trample on ma God-given raats. I remember what he says when he opposed that desegregation o' schools law. He says God hisself favours segr'ation. He sure does. Don't he, Averill? Why else would he put the White man in Europe, the Yellow man in Asia, the Black man in Africa, and the Red man in America?"

"There are very few *Red men* left in North America," Mommy told her.

"That's their own fault, Averill. If they'd o' served the Almighty lak he wanted 'em to, he wouldn't o' upped and turned their lands over to us. He'd o' protected 'em lak he did the Israelites. It ain't ma fault. Ah serve the true and livin' Gawd 'n he blesses me for it."

Mommy responded with an ironic smile and turned her head sideways so Aunt Marge wouldn't see.

"Say som'n, Averill. Ah don' lak it when you're quiet lak that."

"You already have your answers, Marjorie. Your true and living God already gave you the answers."

"Yer bein' sarcastic, ain't yer?"

But Mommy did not answer, and when they got home Mommy said she had a headache and disappeared into the bedroom she and Joshua occupied.

On some days, usually after the news item about picketing Blacks or after some White official came on TV to reassure the White population that the police were keeping the protesters "firmly under control," Marjorie Springer would say, leaving a long space between each statement, that she felt sorry for "nigras," they were treated unjustly and "ev'thang," but she "laks thangs the way they're. . . . Ah gon lose ma appetite if they be eatin' in the same restaurants with me. . . . Have 'er chillun a-mixin' with ther'n! Lawd, whad a calam'ty! . . . 'N Ah sure don' want 'em in ma neighbourhood. Ah won' feel safe. . . . Ah take care o' ma trash; they don't. . . . Ah'll say one thang though: the guv'ment owes 'em som'n, them that's honest, Ah mean. They've been treated unfairly some. . . . Longst they ain't raise ma taxes, 'cause Ah can barely make do on what Ah make."

Mommy never filled the spaces Marjorie Springer gave her whenever she started on the "Race Question." It came up every day, sometimes twice, as if, caged and dangerous, it had to be inspected regularly.

So that she could intersperse her talking with snippets of TV watching, she held these monologues mostly in the living room, which showed various signs that it had been enlarged, probably to incorporate what was once the kitchen. The carpenter had not bothered to match the original floor lattes, and where he'd removed the wall the roughness was visible under the paint. She sat directly facing the television on a wicker couch whose cushions displayed large red hibiscuses on a black field; she looking like an over-filled, upholstered spilling laundry basket. She'd told them that she'd had the furniture changed in honour of their coming. "What with yer bein' rich an' ev'thang, Averill, Ah couldn' let yer come stay in ma shabbinness. Ah sure couldn't. This is all Ah could afford from the money Ah got after ma husban' 'n me sell our big house when we got divorced, where you visited us when you been here in '46. It ain't been much. 'N Ah decide Ah ain't going to put maself in debt."

"If I'd known it was so much trouble . . ."

"No troubl'atall. Not aft'rall yer fam'ly durn do fer me."

She made it clear that the couch was *her* seat. Sometimes she sat on it with her arms spread like wings stripped of their feathers against the back-rest, as if she needed to relieve pressure on her back or prevent anyone from sitting beside her. Once Mommy made the mistake of sitting on the couch, probably so that Joshua could sit beside her because the only other seats in the living room were two wicker armchairs placed in two corners of the living room. Marjorie Springer came into the living room, looked at them seated on the couch and wrinkled her brow. Next she glanced at both armchairs but remained standing.

"Is something wrong, Marjorie?"

"No, Averill." Her voice was tremulous and pitched higher than usual.

"Oh!" Mommy said, shock in her voice, and got up, tugging Joshua as she did so. With a toss of her head she indicated one of the armchairs. They went to sit in them.

Her health troubles intrigued Joshua. Once she burped, creating a minor detonation at the breakfast table, and said, "Now yall 'scuse me. It gotter come out somehow. Now Ah wish all this was happening down yonder. Ah feel so blowed up, lak if ma bowels is in chains." Joshua saw the faintest trace of a smile on Mommy's face. At other times she'd talk about "all the troubles that come 'cause o' the change o' life. Every woman ma age has 'em." She'd stare at Mommy with expectation, but Mommy would say nothing.

Once Joshua caught her scrutinizing him with her forehead all screwed up, and her lips moving in silent conversation with herself, and he wondered whether she knew that his curls and shelled-almond complexion had nothing to do with Italy, and whether that was why she never spoke to him except to ask him if he wanted something to eat or if he'd had enough.

The last evening they spent there, a Friday evening, she asked, "Averill, you still the *lib'ral* woman you once was?"

"Marjorie, what are you insinuating?"

Marjorie Springer smiled. "Nutten, honey. Just you never was opposed to anythang."

"Marjorie, why don't you say what you mean?"

"Ah don' mean nutten'. Ah see lak Ah hurt yer feelin's. Wasn't ma intentions."

They were silent for a long while, then Marjorie Springer began to laugh. She was wearing a pink, satiny floor-length housedress that smelt of camphor—her entire house did—and for all its glow, she might as well have been doing the sitting shimmy to music she alone heard. Mommy stared at her, alarmed. When she stopped laughing, she said, "Ah'll tell you what Ah been thinkin'. Don't you go gittin' mad at me now. Ah know you, Averill. You got a ernion skin. Ah was just wonderin' wha' happens when yer dye a blue stockin' red." This time she laughed so loud that she farted.

Later that evening, Mommy told Joshua they'd be moving into a hotel the next day.

The next morning Mommy left early, taking a cab, and returned an hour later. Marjorie Springer was out getting groceries to feed some fifty guests she'd invited to a "home-coming do" she'd planned for Mommy that Saturday evening. Her "coloured woman that sets thangs raat when Ah fall bahin' in ma house cleanin' 'n stuff" was "spozed to come by to help me clean 'n cook 'n serve."

Mommy shouted to him to pack his things quickly; they had to be at the airport in Miami for 1 P.M., and she wanted to be out of the house before Marjorie Springer returned.

"What will Aunt Marge think?" Joshua asked.

"Whatever she's capable of thinking." It came out sounding like a snarl.

"What will she do with all that food?"

"Feed it to her guests. Give it to the coloured woman. Eat it all herself— I don't care. Stop talking and let's get out of here."

Mommy called a cab, and while they waited for it she scribbled a note, which she put along with some fifty-dollar bills in an envelope and left on the kitchen counter. At 10:30 they were in the cab heading towards the Tallahassee airport.

He felt relieved when they were on board the small plane that took them to Miami, where they caught the plane that took them to Barbados. From there a small plane took them to Isabella Island—six days earlier than planned.

9

A MONTH AGO HE WOULDN'T have been able to remember any of this. His consciousness had come back in snatches, snatches that went out like a weak flame in a strong breeze. Sometimes he struggled to hold on when it began to flicker; other times he was too tired and would let it go out without a fight. He'd thought Dr Stein was Sparrow. He vaguely remembers that he'd tried to lift himself up once and couldn't and had wondered whether he was trapped in a bog.

Consciousness came back in what seemed like a dream about somebody else. In any event, what he remembers seems like dreamlets in a large dream, chapters in a novel, and he's uncertain what parts are true and what parts imaginary.

The man in the bed is observing a scene with two children. One's a girl of about ten: a malnourished Caribbean ten-year-old. She wears a red calico dress that's too big for her. The other's a boy; he's totally naked. They are sitting on jute sacks spread on a dirt floor of a mud hut. The ground outside is golden, and the air is dusty: the dry season. He is sure he's seen these children before. He can predict every line of dialogue, every image, as if he were the projector out of which all this was coming.

"*You is my doll baby,*" *the girl says.* "*Your eyes not blue though, but they pretty, like golden apple skin. Your hair black. Your daddy is a White man. My daddy Black.*"

"*Where my daddy is?*"

"*Mammy don' want me for know and she don' want you for know.*"

"*You telling story. I going tell Mammy.*"

"*And if you tell she I going run 'way an' leave you alone with she. And nobody going prevent she from killing you.*"

"*Don' run 'way without me,*" *the little boy pleads.* "*Carry me with you, please? I will give you some o' me food.*"

"*When you run 'way you have for go by yourself. You not going tell her what I tell you?*"

"*No, I no' will tell she.*"

"*I will stay then and I won' run 'way without you.*"

"*Promise?*"

"*Me promise.*"

"*Why she always beating you?*"

"*I don' know.*"

"*Why you all the time cover me when she try for hit me?*"

"*'Cause I make a promise for protect you, and 'cause your skin white and when you get hit it make welt on your skin and it make me feel bad, just for see it. You see my skin?*" *She points to her hand.* "*It black. So it don' show.*"

"*But it hurt. And sometime it swell. I see where it does swell and make welt too.*"

"*Don' mind that; you is like my doll baby and I don' will make her hurt you, when I can help it. You want a piece of golden apple? I have a sweet one, sweet like you, when you is a good boy. You is a good boy now?*"

The boy nods.

"First, I have to bathe you." She stands.

The boy pulls his penis. The girl spanks his hand, then takes it in hers, leads him out of the hut, and they move to a basin of water in the sun in the open yard. The girl tests it with her elbow. "It not warm enough. We'll go have we golden apple. When we finish I going give you your bath."

The little boy smiles. He likes it when the girl bathes him. The woman always quarrels with him when she does it. He has to stay still when it's the woman. When it's the girl he splashes the water sometimes in the girl's face and watches her lift her dress hem to wipe the water out of her eyes. Sometimes she threatens to slap him like the woman does if he doesn't stop.

The man experiencing this opens his eyes. "Where am I?" he asks. He feels as if he's floating. He senses the presence of others.

"Do you have sisters and brothers?" a male voice asks. The words seem to be coming out of a tunnel. He cannot see the questioner.

The man tries to sit up but finds that he can't lift his head. "Estelita," he answered. "I have a sister named Estelita. Folks call her Lita. For me alone she's Bita. Beat her. My beatingest Bita. My mother used to beat her. I love her. At sixteen she ran off with fifty-year-old Skeeter. He too beat her, and at twenty-two Neptune took her. O weep for Bita, she is dead. And in a grave without a tombstone at her head. That was the beginning of an elegy I wrote for her. Bad poetry.

Skeeter was a hunter.
Took his prey to bed.
Estelita emptied his rifle full of lead
into what she thought was Skeeter's head.
Filled him full of his own lead.

"Pow! Pow!" He extends his right forefinger and clasps the others to suggest a gun. "'Thought him dead, then fled.' The moral of the story? Beware of lead unless you're already dead."

He stops speaking and tries to focus and discerns the male figure who asked the question. Something in his memory clicks into place. "It's Sparrow!" he shouts. "You, Sparrow, you know a lot about lead. It filled your head. So Mommy said. You're too full of lead to know you're a lead-head.

After Bita leaped
it was only she who was dead.

That was the end of Sister Estelita
who for me and me alone was Bita.

It's an elegy. It's not a limerick. But you won't know the difference. Is she here? Bita,
I mean. No, she was good. In heaven or still with Neptune."

"*I am not Sparrow. I am Dr Stein. And my assistant here is Nurse Knights. Get*
that?"

The man in the bed is silent.

"*So you have a sister named Estelita?"*

"*Estelita, my dear, dear sister, who thought she'd pumped lead into Skeeter. For*
sure she ran to the rocks at Point Peter. People ran behind her.

Down below,
Neptune's basso profondo
trilling the rocks and churning the water
mesmerized her and drowned out the voices
and footsteps pursuing her.

I know she's happy in Neptune's bedchamber where the sharks took her. Estelita's
Leap. Look before, when, and after you leap. Lita the leaper, who sometimes left
Neptune's bed to comfort me. But she couldn't protect me from you, Sparrow."

"*Where's Estelita's Leap?"*

"*It's a metaphor."*

"*Is your name Cock Robin?"*

"*Maybe it is and then again maybe it isn't. Have you read the Royal Readers?*
Regal shit! Beware of it. It stinks worse than commoners'—"

"*Do you have a sister?"*

"*Yes. I've told you so already. Yes. A sister who was my mother. I hope Neptune's*
treating her kindly . . . Had/has?" he says, becoming fully aware of the question. "*She*
hasn't visited me lately. She's probably angry with me for . . ." He stops.

"*For what?"*

"*Doing what you taught me."*

"*What did I teach you?"*

"*Where's your shame?"*

"*Where did your sister live?"*

"*I don't remember."*

"*Who's your next of kin?"*

He giggles. "*Humanity. I despise them. I prefer my relatives at the zoo." He sighs.*

"*Sparrow, I am tired. I'm no longer afraid of you. Now I can say no.*"

Sparrow looks at the woman. The woman returns the look. They communicate with their eyes. Sparrow nods.

"*Tomorrow I'll be back to see you,*" *Sparrow says. With increased volume, like a TV commercial, he adds very slowly,* "*WE'RE TRYING A FEW E.C.T.-S ON YOU TO SEE WHETHER THEY'LL RESTORE YOUR MEMORY FULLY. WE DON'T HAVE A NAME FOR YOU. ARE YOU A LANDED IMMIGRANT? WE DON'T HAVE A HEALTH INSURANCE CARD FOR YOU. WE MUST FIND OUT WHO YOU ARE. AND THIS IS THE ISOLATION ROOM YOU'RE IN. WE'RE KEEPING YOU IN IT TO MINIMIZE YOUR CONTACT WITH OTHERS, WHAT WITH YOUR HAVING TO RECOVER FROM FOOT SURGERY AND ALL THAT, YOU KNOW. YOU TOLD US IN YOUR CONFUSED STATE THAT YOU HAVE LOTS OF MONEY. IS THAT TRUE?*"

"Yes," *he answers, amused by Sparrow's tone.* "Lots. *I'm stuffed with ill-gotten gain. Fancy needing it here. On earth, yes. To get to the head of the line, make people disown themselves, shred their identities . . .* 'All this Whiteness going to waste. Child, you need for raise by a White somebody.'"

"*Focus, Mr Cock Robin. Try and remember who you are.*" *This from the woman.* "*The curse of money notwithstanding, we got to pay our bills and be paid for our services.*"

"Services? Whose? Yours? I don't need your services. *Sparrow, you need her services? What sort of services you're offering?*" *Cock Robin stares at her and laughs.*

She turns a pinker pink. Tries to laugh. It chokes her. Her pink purples and she becomes breathless.

"*Oh dear! You saw the cow jump over the moon, didn't you? And, the dish, what a way it ran with the spoon!*"

"*What spoon? What dish?*"

"*As long as your name isn't Diddle and the cat doesn't play the fiddle, or Sparrow doesn't fiddle your cat.*" *He laughs.*

"*It's good to see you laughing.*"

"*Life is a laughing matter. Life is no laughing matter. It's a poisoned dish. Laugh, cry! Cry, laugh! Have your pick and eat it, in little doses, like relish, or you'll get sick.*"

"*You talk a lot.*"

"*Yes. I'm foolish. A still tongue keeps a wise head. An empty head is a drum head.*"

"*The police brought you here six days ago. They found you on Mount Royal half-buried in snow.*"

"What happened to my foot?"

"The left one was severely frost-bitten," he says slowly, deliberately, as if he doubts Cock Robin's ability to fully grasp the meaning of his words. *"We amputated—amputated: you understand what that means?"*

Cock Robin stares at him, amused, refusing to indicate one way or other whether he understands what that means.

"We amputated two of your toes." Sparrow holds up his right forefinger and his middle finger and wiggles them. *"Couldn't save 'em. You understand? It's healing all right, though. If you're lucky, the nerves won't bother you."* Sparrow pauses. Cock Robin says nothing, so he continues, *"You didn't have any papers on you. You were speaking in several languages, some of which we couldn't figure out. We thought you were Italian—you told us you're Italian—"*

"I was," Cock Robin interrupts him.

"—and sent out a public announcement to that effect, but no one came to claim you. You said you were Finnegan Joyce and your father's name was James. We announced that too and were told that's the name of a character, not a person."

"There, you have it. I'm a character in somebody's fiction. You're now an editor? Give me a break! You better leave me alone. I'm no Pirandello character. This is too funny. Watch out you don't get put in your own Dunciad.*"*

"Will you stop saying I am Sparrow!" Sparrow says with loud impatience. *"I am Dr Stein and this woman here is Nurse Knights, Gladys Knights."* He frowns. *"Why are you shading your eyes, Mr Cock Robin?"*

"Because I'm either mad or not seeing right."

"What are you not seeing right? Why are you laughing?"

"Gladys Knights turned white. Have you lost your Pips? It was that midnight train to Georgia, right? Well music is one thing and love's another. This is proof that without love we're in trouble. Her proof that no love can turn a Black body White."

"That last ECT, Gladys. In some ways they're working," he says in a whisper. *"Give him a shot of phenobarb. Let him sleep. He needs to sleep."*

There's a moment of silence during which Gladys leaves the room and returns with a syringe.

"What're you going to do with that syringe?"

"It's a sedative—to calm you."

"If you have to stick syringes in me, let a real Gladys Knights do it. I never let White people stick things into me."

"What colour is Bita?"

"Like the real Gladys Knights."

"Forget the phenobarb, Gladys. Give him 30 mg of mellaril instead. Tomorrow we'll do another ECT."

"I read somewhere that healthy people reinvent themselves every day—" but before he can finish the statement Sparrow leaves.

Gladys gives him the pill and changes his dressings.

"Mr Cock Robin, how are you feeling?"

He's been dozing and has trouble adjusting his sight to the bright light from the fluorescent lamp over the head of his bed. His vision is blurry but he sees that there are three persons in the room. "What is 'feeling'?" he mutters.

"This is Dr Defoe. He's a new member of the team. Nurse Knights?" He points to Gladys. "Do you remember her?"

"No. Who are you?"

"Dr Stein."

"Your voice is familiar but I don't remember you."

"Do you remember your name?"

"No."

"Who is Estelita?"

"My sister. I called her Bita. She made it up herself and told me to call her that. It was a joke between us. She used to get beaten at home and in school all the time. Sometimes she took my beatings. She was the only person who ever loved me unconditionally. She said it seemed as if everyone had the right to beat her, and she decided it wouldn't be so.

"I used to hide in the cane fields to be with her. Bita. Lita. Estelita. My Sister. My mother."

"Why are you crying?"

"I don't know."

"Where did all this happen?"

"I don't know. Maybe it's a story I invented, the plot of some novel I'll never write. "

"Where do you live? In which city do you live?"

"I don't know."

"Name some of the places where you've lived?"

"London, Madrid, Paris."

"Montreal? Have you lived in Montreal?"

"I'm not sure."

"You have a Caribbean accent. Are you from the Caribbean?"

"Probably."

"Jamaica? Trinidad? Barbados? Were you born on any of those?"
"No."
"Which one were you born on?"
"I can't remember. "
"But you are sure you were born in the Caribbean?"
"I don't know."
"And you have a sister named Estelita?"
"Had. She committed suicide."
"Where?"
"At Estelita's Leap. I mean Point Peter."
"When?"
"I can't remember."
"Were you an adult then?"
"I don't know. Am I an adult?"
There's silence, an eerie one.
"This is the most lucid he has been, Dr Defoe. We shouldn't overtire him. He hallucinates when we do," Gladys Knights whispers.
Stein nods. "Dr Defoe would like to raise something with you."
"Mr Cock Robin, your back is covered with disfiguring scars—"
"Disfiguring?"
"All right, let's just say lots of scars. How did this come about?" Defoe continues.
"Doctors, aren't you glad that I now know you're doctors?"
Dr Stein nods.
"Let's not talk about scars now. In any event my mind is too fuzzy to answer you. We'll need a long session for this, when I'm rested."
"Were you burned in a fire?"
"Yes, in the one that consumeth not, that cleanses not, but is just as hot. Now get out!"
"Gladys, give him a relaxant, oral."
"He's been refusing oral medication for the last few days."
"Mr Cock Robin, will you take a pill from Nurse Knights?"
"Anytime."
"See, he loves you."
"See," Cock Robin says, "I love you, but I won't marry you."
"Well, love is better than nothing, especially seeing that I lost my pips on that midnight train to Georgia."
They all laugh.

He hears noises. A familiar male voice says, "He's back to where he was when he was admitted."

Another, huskier voice says, "You think it's because I raised the issue of the scars?"

"We'll never know," the first voice replies.

"Shhh. I thinks he's coming awake," a familiar female voice whispers.

He opens his eyes and sees a strange tree. Dwarfed. A sculpture? It moves. It faces him. Green. Moss green. A bird on its bough. A bird without a beak. A bird with china-blue eyes, wingless, beakless. Featherless too, it seems. Skin coral pink. It blinks. A bird? It speaks.

"Good morning, Mr Cock Robin."

"Good morning, bird."

"Gladys. You know my name."

"A parrot it is. With a shaved tail." He laughs. "Frankenstein's your daddy? Admit it."

"What's a parrot?"

"You are. Without wings, without a beak, gave you no feathers. Removed your tail. Without a tail you no have par—Can you fly?"

The pared parrot is silent.

He begins to sing,

All things bright and beautiful,
All creatures, great and small,
All things wise and wonderful,
The Lord God made them all.

"But not this parrot without a tail. He didn't make me. I'm not wise nor wonderful. Who made you?" he asks.

No reply.

"Well he gave you a tongue. If you lose that you'll be an -ot. Own up! Your daddy's name is Frankenstein. Is it not?

"The tree exits, bearing on its bough its (par)rot.

He continues to sing—

"The purple-headed mountain,
The river running by,
The sunset and the morning

That brightens up the sky.
All things bright and beautiful . . .

"*The poor man in his castle,*
The rich man at his gate—
God made the high and lowly
And ordered their estate."

Then he hears a gust of wind and a sail flapping in his head, and he goes blank.

"*Buon Giorno,*" *says a man in a white coat. He slowly moves a ruler, first from left to right then from right to left in front of Cock Robin's eyes.*

Right-left! Left-right! Attention! At ease! Please!

The man's head is like a tulip—an oval just-about-to-open tulip—on a tulip-stalk neck. Cock Robin knows that head. He knows that neck. The man's hair is brown, his face elliptical, his eyes glassy grains of corn, his nose big, and his teeth bulging. A middle-aged bantam with a saddle belly rounding out the middle of his white coat. Cock Robin knows him, knows him better than he knows himself, but has trouble recalling his name. This man is not a parrot.

At the man's side is a massive woman, taller than the man. She's in a green top that angles out at the sides triangularly. She wears bark-brown slacks. She holds a tape recorder. Her eyes are china blue. Her face is pink. From the shoulders down she resembles a cone. Breasts and chest and stomach merge. Arms are two large frontward tucks. Her legs mere stumps for her cone of a body.

"*The parrot I dreamed of,*" *Cock Robin says, staring at the woman's second chin that seems like an opaque half drop at the tip of some dropper embedded in her jaw. He expects the drop to round out and fall.*

"*Hello, Hope,*" *Cock Robin calls out to her.*

"*I'm not Hope,*" *she answers, light switching on in her porcelain eyes.* "*I'm Gladys. We've been through all that already.*"

"*Well if you're not blue of Mary's colour, then you're Envy. Your eyes are blue but your blouse is green. You are not a parrot, right, put on a bough to sing in the harems of Byzantium—of who is past or passing or can't come?*"

There's no reply.

"*Answer me! Goddamit!*"

"*!Buenos dias!*" *the man in the white coat says, laughing.*

He's been practising it for this recital, Cock Robin thinks. "*!Con su madre¡ No hablo. Hablamos todos con todos al miso momento es la misma cosa para nosotros.*

¿Verdad?" Cock Robin replies and notes that everything in the room sways while he remains fixed. Time must be moving backwards, he thinks, and wonders where he is. He is sure he is dead. This is the beginning of eternity, the after-life. *"¿Dónde estamos, en España o en el inferno?"*

"¿Hablas espagnol?" the corn-eyed man asks. The room no longer sways.

"No. No tengo ninguna lengua. No soy hombre. Soy boy. Boy-hombre . There's gold in your eyes."

"¿Hablas inglés?"

"No tengo ninguna lengua! Dammit! Are you deaf?"

"What's your name?" The gold-eyed, white-coated man insists, sounding like a robot or as if addressing an idiot.

"Cock Robin," Cock Robin says and sighs with resignation. He recalls the man's name then. *"And you're Sparrow. In the land of the dead. With an improved pipe. Wind. From either end with the same smell."* He crosses himself and sings:

"'Who killed Cock Robin?'

'I,' said the Sparrow.

With my bow and arrow,

I killed Cock Robin.'"

He stops singing and stares intently at Sparrow before asking, *"Why'd you kill me?"* His hand goes to his nose; he traces his upper and lower jaw; he hits his chin several times. *"Oh! I still have them. They're not a sinkhole."*

"You're alive," Sparrow says.

Cock Robin sings:

"Alive, alive, oh!

Alive, alive oh.

Crying cockles and mussels,

Alive, alive, oh.

She died of a fever.

And no one could save her.

"That's what happened to sweet Molly Malone," he says softly, staring at the foot of the bed. In a loud voice, he asks, *"What happened to me? You must know. You control my destiny."*

"Your destiny!"

"My destiny," Cock Robin repeats and falls silent.

Sparrow seems perplexed, the woman beside him too.

"I didn't think hell was like this."

"You sing well. Where did you learn such songs?" Sparrow asks.

"I don't know. I learnt some of them from you," he answers, annoyed.

"*This isn't hell. It's a hospital. And who am I? You used to know my name: Dr Stein.*"

"*Sparrow. It's no surprise you're here. For the people you fooled, yes, but not me. So there's a hospital in hell! And you're what? Chief physician? Or a live white coat? You always hid in your clothes and behind your sermons. God, help us all.*"

For a while no one says anything.

"*The world's a hospital, Baudelaire said. Is Milton here? Blake said he would be.*"

"*Who's Milton?*"

"*Illiterate! You read nothing but da Baable. And magazines with big dicks, which you hid. Didn't know I knew, eh?*"

"*What's your name?*"

"*Cock Robin Caliban. Prospero's my father. I'm son of his Maxim gun. Peesheewww!*" *He imitates the shape of a gun with his right forefinger, aims it at Sparrow's crotch and laughs.* "*His had a silencer.*"

"*Are you Spanish? Italian? British? West Indian?*"

"*I'm nobody, but Homer's not my daddy. You should be Polyphemous. It rhymes with blasphemous.*"

"*Do you know who Columbus is?*"

"'*In 1492 he sailed the ocean blue,*' *but couldn't steal its hue. Poopoo! Poopoo! Poopoo!*" *He imitates the blowing of bubbles.*

"*What are you?*" *Sparrow asks.*

"*For sure, no scion of seduction. A live mixture of shit, compost, and dirt. And foul wind. In this gut.*"

"*What's your mother's name?*"

"*I don't know. First I had one. Then somewhere it became two. Then vaguely it was one. And then it was none. Bita is the only mother I care to acknowledge. But you said you were my uncle and later my father. Imagine! You!*"

A long silence.

Cock Robin stares at the ceiling. There's a pulsing pain in his left foot, and he tenses in anticipation of each throb. "*The past poisons the present; the present poisons the future,*" *he states to himself aloud.*

"*You speak in riddles. Are you a poet?*"

"*Are you kidding? They have their seasons of calm weather . . . Poetry's useless. Blood's what's needed. Homer, houngans, even Christians know it. Soucouyans too. You should too, Sparrow, 'cause you ain't never read nuffin' but the Baable. 'Ev'thang a body needs to know he gon fin' in there.' Except filthy jokes, dirty maga-zines, and sweetness. 'Here, come taste the whole heap o' sweetness in this-here* bowl.'" He laughs.

"What's sweetness?"

"Two turned-down bowls with a hole hoping for a pole. 'Nibble lil' bit on this-here sugar cane. Yeah! See? There's sweetness aplenty in there.'"

"Do you like sugar cane?" This from a husky voice.

Cock Robin cranes his neck towards the head of the bed to see who it is. It seems to be a Black man. "Do you?"

"I chewed a piece in the Caribbean once. It was alright," the Black man continues.

"Obviously you didn't swallow the chaff!"

"Where do you live?" Sparrow resumes.

"Ghosts have no addresses."

"You're not a ghost."

"Tell that to Plato."

"We're pretty sure you're from the West Indies. You speak with a sing-song."

"India's in the east. I'm not Indian."

Cock Robin grows silent, thoughtful.

"Gladys, give him a double shot of the usual. And let's call it a morning. We'll resume this afternoon," Sparrow says. "Mr—er—Cock Robin. I'll pay you a visit later. Try to have a nap in the meantime."

"I am asleep—dead. It's you all who're trying to resurrect me."

They stare at him and then at each other but say nothing.

Sometime later Cock Robin is staring blankly at the ceiling when Gladys enters, wearing a white smock, pushing a trolley ahead of her and moving as best she can with her seemingly nailed-on haunches.

"Mr Cock Robin, I have to change your dressings."

A ditty is playing in his head. "Here's a riddle for you to figure out," he tells her: "'Ought's an ought, and nought's a figure: wealth for the White man and crap for the nigger.'" . . . He giggles. "Did you ever have a tiger in your tank? Can your tank hold a tiger? Of course, it can. Two for that matter. But not Sparrow's. That I'm certain of."

Sparrow and the Black man enter then. Cock Robin stretches. "Sparrow," he says at the end of his stretching, "Sparrow, you remember hugging me, and saying you were my uncle and I was your son, and I was not to be afraid of you? You are a queer man, Sparrow. Was that why you walked into the Atlantic? Or did you hope to calm the whirlpool and walk on it?"

"My name's Dr Stein, not Sparrow."

"No wonder we're in hell. You liar!" Cock Robin watches him skeptically. "Is that your nom de plume? Let me see if you are lying. Are you related to Gertrude Stein?"

"I have a sister by that name."

"Have you read her books?"

Dr Stein does not answer.

"Did you meet Alice B Toklas?"

"My sister does not write."

"That's strange. Gertrude Stein does not write! Then you're not a doctor and I'm not in hell. Because there's only one Gertrude Stein—she would never stand for two—and she writes, let me tell you. Ah, you're just Sparrow, pretending to be Dr Stein. You've got worse. You never lied unless you had to. You sound smarter, though, learned good grammar, and hell's heat has deepened your voice. Now it's Satan who works in mysterious ways. What other wonders he performed on you?" He stops talking and scrutinizes Sparrow Stein. "Look at your corn eyes. Translucent gold. They're twinkling. Is that for me or Gladys Knights? It better be her." He pauses then asks pleadingly, "You're not going to hurt me again, are you?"

"Not at all. Where were you living before they found you?"

"They found me and handed me over to you? Sparrow Stein Prospero? Then I'm truly lost. Well fancy that! Even if I die a second time, I'll denounce you. You hear me? I'll denounce you."

"His name's not Prospero or Sparrow. He's Dr Stein."

"Shut up! What do you know? You're not Miranda, though. Now who's in denial, Sparrow?" He pauses. "And Caliban is mine. And Caliban does as Prospero bids. Not this time. I won't. I'll kill you first."

"Where do you live?"

"Here. In Hell," he replies and sings,

"This earth is not my home;
I'm just a-passing through.
The saints on every hand
Are shouting victory.
Their songs of sweetest praise
Drift back from heaven's shore
And I can't be at home in this world anymore.

"Be serious. The earth is our home while we're on it, and, I see now, when we're in it."

"*You sing well. Where did you learn such songs?*"

"*You taught me most o' them. The ladies loved to hit the tambourine when they belted them out. Now fancy meeting you in hell, where you've become Dr Stein. You cozener!*"

"*What's your name?*"

"*My name! Are you losing your memory? It's Cock Robin.*"

"*That's not a name. You've already told us it's not your name. What's your mother's name?*"

"*Which one? I had two besides Sycorax and Bita. One almost drowned me and the other altered me.*"

"*What's your father's name?*"

"*I never had one. Caliban's mother bore him for the earth. And the earth was her mother. And you, you did a fine job of being my father.*"

"*We're overtiring him,*" the Black man whispers.

"*We're leaving you to rest now,*" Sparrow says.

"*Good riddance!*" Cock Robin replies.

"*Good morning, Mr Cock Robin.*" The man speaking is Eurafrican. Café-au-lait complexion; tall, over six feet; and handsome with a powerful chest, a finely chiselled symmetrical face, a big roundish head capped with thick, tight, glistening curls. A fine blending of Africa and Europe. "*I'm Dr Defoe,*" he says extending his hand.

Cock Robin remembers him. He was with Dr Stein sometime before. "*Are you one of those Blacks who don't pronounce the th?*"

"*I said good morning, Mr Cock Robin.*"

"*And I asked if you are one of those Blacks who don't pronounce your th-s.*"

"*Are we at war, Mr Cock Robin?*"

"*These are the only arms I have.*" He waves his arms. "*I've never hit a body in my life.*"

"*Dr Stein thinks that you and I might get along fine.*"

"*Is that why he brought you with him the other day?*"

Defoe doesn't answer but his eyes light up.

"*Do you know Ham?*" Cock Robin asks.

"*Who is he?*"

"*Your ancestor.*"

"*Is he yours too?*"

Cock Robin nods.

"*Are you suggesting that you and me're related?*"

"All human beings are. Do you know Ham?"

"I eat them. I love the sugar-cured ones."

"You practise ancestor-eating too? Many cultures did. You mustn't let Dr Stein hear you say that," Cock Robin whispers. "He'll say you're atavistic."

"You're interesting," Dr Defoe murmurs and seems distracted by something outside the window.

"So are you. What are you looking at? The cold, frozen trees out there? They're so cold they've stopped waving. Do you talk to trees?"

"No."

"You should. Why am I interesting?"

"Guess."

Cock Robin stares at him and squints.

They are silent for over a minute. Cock Robin eventually begins to fidget. He breaks the silence. "Doctor, let's cut out the games. You know I'm here because I can't remember my name, don't know in which city I live, and only know that I have a past because you and your colleagues say I have one, and with your prodding it returns in snatches. And you have already told me that if I can't remember who I am, you'll turn me out into the street. But, doctor, I don't think I ever knew who I was."

"You are eloquent. We won't put you on the street. Would you like to work with me?"

"It doesn't matter. From experience I know it doesn't matter. All human beings possess the same vices and virtues distributed differently. What's rewarded grows. We should begin to reward virtue in the cradle, don't you think? Do you believe in a Manichean universe?"

"I can't."

"I can. This place is white in winter. I know it's green at other times, but don't know how I know that. The only thing white in another place I used to know are colonizers, flowers, and beaches. Funny I can't remember where that place is."

"I can't believe in Manicheism. Look at me."

"I've been doing that. I'd love to look like you."

"Black you mean?"

"Yes."

"It isn't a colour."

"But I know a place where black is a colour and a chasm."

"Where's that?"

"The place where my sister died."

"My parents are from Nova Scotia. Africville. It no longer exists."

"And one was White and the other Black, right?"

"No. They're both Black."

"And they produced you!"

"I told you, Black is not a matter of colour."

"Bartolome de las Casas didn't think so."

"Well you and I are not responsible for what he thought."

"But we are the products of his thoughts."

"Partly, I'll admit," his brow wrinkling. "You're astounding."

"It's the EC whatevers you people have been giving me. My memory hasn't ever been as good. My tongue's become a duck's ass. Such garrulity! I'll be ashamed of myself if I ever get released from this prison.

"You talk a lot but you say nothing that's useful for your cure."

"Doctor-The-Foe, this is no simple matter of the world as will and idea."

"Goes without saying. Why are you and I doing this?" He looks uncomfortable saying this, his brow is furrowed.

"It's what we niggers do when we meet each other," Cock Robin whispers. "We sound the depths of sickness in each other." He has trouble recognizing himself in what he's saying. He seems to be discovering an alien self contained in his other, fuzzy self.

"So you're Black?"

"I want to be. I hope I am."

"Is a white skin a problem?"

"Doctor, you don't have to become a lawyer. You are a healer. Lawyers are . . . Never mind."

"Weren't you a law student?"

"No. I had intentions of studying law. I never learned anything really worth knowing. Look, I can't even remember my name or where I last lived. Not even sure of my race. No, nothing useful to me, at any rate."

"What's worth knowing?"

Cock Robin is forced to contemplate the question: "How to destroy greed and end cruelty and—and stay sane."

"You sound like you want to be Christ."

"Not Christ." He slowly waves a forefinger for emphasis. "Buddha. You . . . people have a name for that . . . I can't remember. Christ has no monopoly over goodness. Becoming a Bodhisattva—that takes doing."

A sort-of hazed-over thoughtfulness comes over Defoe's face.

"A nickel for your thoughts, Dr Defoe?"

"They're worthless."

"Dr Defoe, have you read Robinson Crusoe*?"*

"No."

*"*The Tempest*?"*

"No."

"Seen it?"

"No."

"Have you heard of Caliban?"

"Yes. He's a monster of some sort, I think."

"Yes, included in those St George must slay. But you can tame him. Like Asians do elephants and Buddhists human nature. Elephants are without predators, you know, until we human beings enslave them. And we human beings are our own predators. We hunt each other, but not for food. Doctor, you don't need to know you're Caliban. Dr Stein knows you're Caliban but doesn't know he's Prospero."

Defoe doesn't respond.

"If Daniel Defoe could have written freely like today's writers can, you know how he'd have civilized Friday?"

Defoe is silent.

"Cut off his dick. That's because alterity, altering, and civilizing blend—like molecules making water."

Defoe says nothing but the trace of a smile plays on his face.

"Prospero had to bewitch Caliban. Everybody in Shakespeare's day knew that it was because Miranda was close by. Wasn't that something how that woman came even before she saw King Kong's whang!" He stops talking, fidgets with the bedsheet, then says, "We're such stuff as our conquerors' fears are made of."

Defoe is still silent.

"My goodness, Dr Defoe! Say something! They haven't lynched you yet."

Defoe laughs. "That's because you've lost me. I studied medicine, not literature."

"Freud was thoroughly versed in art and literature, and Jung even more so."

"You're aggressive."

"Is that a joke?" Cock Robin feels his head growing warm and a surge of memory flashing through him. He raises an arm, palm facing outward. He closes his eyes and shakes his head.

He is under his mother's bed lying on the rags that are his bedding. Bita lies beside him as she always does before he falls asleep. Next he is being baby-sat by Miss Bessie, who is saying to him, "All this Whiteness going to waste. Child, you need for raise by a White somebody." Then he is with Bita, who is teaching him to recite after her, "I made a boat/ I made a town/ I roamed the counties up and down/ And named them one and all.

"*Pussy cat, Pussy cat, where have you been?*
I've been to London to visit the Queen.
Pussy cat, Pussy cat, what you did there?
I frightened a little mouse under a chair."

"We should call it a day," Defoe's voice breaks his reverie. "I'll ask Nurse Knights to give you a sedative right away."

A smiling Gladys Knights gives him the pill. "We're so happy you're getting better, Mr Cock Robin."

He swallows the pill and the accompanying juice and does not answer. She leaves. He lies on his back waiting for the medication to take effect. And the reverie resumes.

Now he is a baby that has been thrown into a river and the water is carrying him away and he loves it. Then he's outside a hut and Bita is bathing him. He's playing with his tolo. Bita spanks his hand. He puts it back. It becomes a game. Bita threatens to end the bath if he does not stop. He says he will. Stops for a minute, then resumes. Bita begins to take him out of the basin. He pleads with her. She lets him stay.

BOOK TWO

Dialoguing with the Dead and Living

10

COME TO THINK OF IT, he has never wanted to make a return visit to Isabella Island.

He wonders what became of Amanda Blenkinsopp. Mrs Blenkinsopp invited him by often, and found every pretext to leave him alone with Amanda. She was an only child, two years older than him. A plump, pretty girl with pale-green eyes, straight teeth, long thin lips, and golden hair that she wore in bangs and a long plait. Everything about her—everything but her intellect—seemed perfect. She was good at knitting and embroidery · and played the piano moderately well. She hadn't gone beyond elementary school. The Blenkinsopps didn't even bother to play the White card to get her into a secondary school. Amanda smiled a lot, as did her mother, who received a lot of criticism from the planter wives for volunteering at the local clinic. She was a trained nurse when Blenkinsopp married her. They had only a hundred and fifty acres. "That one," Elaine Manchester said, "is hell-bent on increasing their acreage." At the card games, where Mrs Blenkinsopp was present only when Blenkinsopp came to be with the men, the wives said she probably had Black blood and was afraid to admit it. Only that could explain why she wanted "to dress nigger sores. She's of Portuguese stock, you know. And let me tell you, they are a mongrel breed. A lot of them won't pass muster in South Africa, never mind Australia."

"Blenkinsopp took up with her, you know, because with one hundred and fifty acres, nobody of substance wanted him for their daughter." This from Eloise Kevin. (It didn't help either that Blenkinsopp drove his own tractor, did his own ploughing as well as the repairs to his house. Mommy admired him for it. She said he was the only one among them who wasn't a parasite. But she would quickly add that she shouldn't be talking.) Mrs Kevin never invited the Blenkinsopps to her receptions, and she didn't attend theirs. "Tradition must be kept up," she insisted, "There was a time when everyone knew their place and stayed in it." She drew the line and it left out the Blenkinsopps.

Teasing Mommy once, Mrs Kevin asked, "How's your future daughter-in-law, Averill?"

Mrs Manchester took over. "From the look of things, Averill, you'll die without grandchildren." She spoke as if her throat were lined with sawdust. Privately Mommy called her the bell-cow. The other women blamed her—behind her back of course—for her husband's philandering: "Kissing her would be like sipping acid." They winked at one another whenever she held forth on anything, and pretty well allowed her to feel she'd won every argument.

Mrs Kevin grinned, showed her tobacco-stained, ratlike teeth, her pug nose (which, according to Mrs Manchester, was a definite sign of lower class origins) flaring as if sniffing. "My husband tells me that these days artificial insemination is the surest thing." She flicked the ashes from her cigarette into an ashtray beside her, already half full with her butts. Behind her back they called her "the chimney."

Apart from Mrs Blenkinsopp, Joshua liked none of them, but his dislike for Mrs Manchester topped the list, and it was not just because of her voice or her triangular face, its leathery skin wrinkled in spite of copious makeup. Her jaws tapered sharply into a dagger of a chin, under which folds of skin were visible on her storklike neck, folds her six strings of pearls never hid. These and diamond earrings, of which she had several pairs, were permanent features of her appearance. Her hair was cut short like a fellow's. Her breasts were small, almost invisible. Her arms and legs were thin, as was her entire body, which was close to six feet and had no buttocks or hips to speak of. She walked as if in a military parade. Horseback riding and target shooting were her hobbies.

What he disliked about her most was the tone she spoke in. Every word came out of her sandpapery throat with extra emphasis, with an imperiousness that said hers was the final word on every subject. Excepting Mrs Blenkinsopp, who didn't count, the planter wives never opposed her, except to raise their eyebrows or smile ironically at one another at some of her remarks. She was indeed their bell cow.

She was Manchester's second wife, and was from Bermuda, from a family that owned several hotels and golf courses. She was already in her early forties when he married her, ostensibly because he needed her money to escape bankruptcy.

One evening when Joshua was around fourteen—he was in the parlour, they were in the recreation room playing bridge—Mrs Manchester said, "My dear, dear Averill—oh you poor thing, can't you see that poor boy's left-handed?"

I am not left-handed. What's she talking about? he asked himself.

"Light-footed, as sure as my name is Eloise," Mrs Kevin said.

Some of the wives laughed. In his imagination he could see them tearing their eyes wide. For a moment they were more interested in him than in bridge.

At that moment Mommy, who must have known he was overhearing them, called to him and told him to go fetch her glasses. He spent a while looking for them but didn't find them, and when he returned Mommy was alone. The wives usually left around nine and it was just about eight. He asked her why they'd left so soon. She said something had come up, not very serious, but serious enough, and they had to leave. "Why're they talking about me like that?"

"They're jealous of you, that's what. One thing's certain: Mrs Kevin wouldn't say silly things about you if you were interested in her niece." Joshua smiled. That niece was Mrs Manley's only child. Mrs Manley herself was a widow as was Mrs Kevin, who was Pine Knot's daughter-in-law. Pine Knot was Mrs Manley's brother and the manager of her 600-acre plantation. Something was wrong with Mrs Manley's daughter and only child. She was twenty-five, less than three feet tall and looked like a globe on stumps. From the back she resembled two tops: a small one perched on top of a big one on stilts. Once when Pine-Knot wasn't with them, Manchester said she was a breadfruit just waiting for "a nigger man to roast it." A week later she choked to death on bread she was eating in bed. Within a few months Mrs Manley also died from generalized cancer, and Pine Knot inherited her 600 acres.

Mommy felt that the planter wives hated her. The exception was Mrs Blenkinsopp, with whom she sometimes played scrabble and to whom she gave books in exchange for the fascinating desserts she brought her. But they'd made her part of their circle and were bent on keeping her encircled. They dropped in on her without warning, sometimes alone, sometimes an entire family. "To check up on me, make sure I'm doing nothing that undermines their rule."

After Mommy's husband died, and without consulting her, they'd made her home their meeting place whenever they had to plan or strategize. "A woman needs the steadying hand of a man. She can't be left to bob about and drift on her own," Flingfoot had told her, probably with his hopes for his brother. Mommy on occasion said the wives hated her because she'd got one of their prized men. She'd laugh and shake her head. "If they only knew. My husband, you see, owned the third largest plantation on the island: 1000 acres of the flattest, most fertile prime sugar land on Isabella Island. It burned their hearts to see it go to an American, still does . . . 'A classless Yank! God knows what she does in bed! Puts on airs like she's royalty'—was how Mrs Kevin put it."

"And you're still friends with them!"

"*Friends* is the wrong word. Do I have a choice? We can't always choose whom we live among."

The fur flew regularly between Mrs Blenkinsopp and the bell cow. When they got so they weren't on speaking terms their husbands ordered them to make up.

Mommy visited all of them, all but her in-laws and the Amassers, who owned the largest plantation: 5000 acres (Manchester's was the second-largest but half of it was hilly land); they'd broken off all ties with Mommy's husband after the marriage. He'd jilted their daughter to marry Mommy, and they never forgave him. Mrs Amasser was also American, from a Louisiana plantation family. Mommy said she was insane and they sometimes locked her up at home to prevent her from running away, because one time some Black men had come upon her bathing naked in the river a few miles from her home. The Amassers didn't come to socials at Arcadia and Mommy didn't go to theirs. When the men met at Arcadia to plan strategy, Manchester consulted Amasser beforehand and reported his views. And when his presence was absolutely necessary, they met at his house, and reported their decisions to Mommy. They never asked for her opinion on anything and she never volunteered it. Mommy's three brothers-in-law (her husband had no acknowledged sisters) did not speak to her. Something to do with her husband's will, she said. Two of them were married to wives who'd inherited small, hilly plantations on the Caribbean coast; the third owned a hotel in southern Isabella Island.

Bita had never told him what happened to Mammy when Emmanuel Éclair caught her stealing his peas. An hour before sunset, the Wednesday exactly one week before he left for England, he borrowed Sparrow's car and drove along the road bordered by cane fields to *Petit Bordel*, where he was born: one of three Éclair squatter villages (this one had been around since slavery;

the villagers pronounced it Pity Bidel). It was located on the western edge of the estate on the first slope of *El Tigre* (which got its name, so his elementary school history text said, because Columbus upon sighting it had thought the peak, yellow in the sunset, looked like a sprinting cat).

His mother and two women he did not know sat on the bleaching stones at the front of her hut. They stopped talking when they saw him. When he was within a few feet of them, one said, "You have company, so I going."

The other woman got up and dusted off the backside of her dress and said, "Sis, me best be going too. Sonny liable for come any time now. And he is one man that don't skylark when his dinner not on the table. A hungry man is a angry man, yes. Me going catch up with you, Sis."

His mother still wore her hair in several braids as when he'd lived with her, except they were now grey and not as thick. Her eyes were deep sockets, her dark beige facial skin was furrowed and looked leathery and darker and lighter in places, as if scarred. Her facial bones were sharp and severe. For years he had not seen her up close. Fleetingly her eyes made contact with his.

"Good afternoon, Mammy."

She nodded and stared at the ground for a short while, then looked up and asked, "What can I do for you, Mr Éclair?

"Joshua is fine."

"Wghhun!" she grunted. "Le's go inside." She got up and for the first time it occurred to him how tiny and short she was. Less than a hundred pounds and under five feet.

She had enlarged the shack to twice its original size, replaced the mud and wattle with boards and the thatch with corrugated galvanized steel. The underside of the roof was visible: there was no ceiling. A naked light bulb dangled from one of the beams, replacing the oil lamp he vividly remembered once knocking over.

They were both still standing. He moved to a Morris chair and sat in it. Quickly his mind flashed over the comments he had been hearing at Arcadia about how uppity the hands were getting: "living better than you and me." A few of the Black politicians had cautiously pitted their power against the planters and had arranged for small interest-free housing improvement loans and limited rural electrification in constituencies where their support was shaky, even though the British Administrator (who wined and dined with the plantocracy—occasionally at Arcadia) had the right to veto—and sometimes vetoed—"legislation onerous to the taxpayers of the colony."

His mother sat down, clasped her hands, rested them in her lap, and looked straight ahead of her.

"Mammy, I'll be leaving for England next week to study. I've come to say good-bye and to ask you my father's name."

"Good luck with your studies. 'Bout your father, I close the book on that."

"Bita"—he didn't have to say Lita; she knew the name existed between them though she probably didn't know why—"once hinted that she knew who my father is—was—but she was afraid to tell." He deliberately exaggerated what Bita had told him to give her the impression that others knew.

"Well, go ask her. Try a seance. It have a man here that can wake the dead. Why you don't try him? Why she didn't tell you before she kill sheself? That is what you come here for? Chut! For turn my soul wrong-side out? When Mistress Éclair asked me to let she have you, I tell myself that is one book, chapter and verse, I happy to see close. And it close. You hear me? I not opening it."

He said nothing. He waited. And when the silence became too much for him, he said, "Do you have something to hide? Are you afraid I will judge you? I won't judge you, Mammy. I won't."

She chuckled. "Well, I be damned! Imagine? This is too much." But she fell silent again.

It got dark, suddenly, like it always does in the tropics, and briefly he stared at the fireflies, twinkling emeralds, outside the window. For a while the darkness stood palpably between them. Eventually she got up and turned on the yard light; its glare softened the darkness in the room but did not altogether dispel it. But she did not turn on the light in the room.

She sat back down, quiet as if holding a vigil beside a corpse.

"So you have decided not to tell me."

She said nothing.

"Do you still think of me as your son?"

"Was you ever my son?" Her tone was icy. Her voice like spikes of broken glass insensibly piercing their target.

"I thought, you know, that now I am big; now that I can make my own decisions about whom I want to associate with and don't have to do everything my adopted mother tells me to do—I mean do what I know is right for me—now you and I could try to have a normal mother and son relationship."

She laughed, a cackling scornful laugh, and then was silent for about thirty seconds. "I don' know what all them words mean. I didn' have no rich, White mother for send me to schools what cost thousands o' dollars. But I know that I done close the book on your father. And on you." He could see her folding and unfolding her arms in the grey light. "You is not my son; you never was. Let we leave it at that."

There was a brief silence, which she broke, humorously saying, "I can't be your mother. I is a coloured woman. You is a White man. Your talks, your looks, your clothes, your everything, mark you out as a White man."

"We can't *leave it at that*. I'll go crazy. I have to know who my father was."

"Sorry, Mr Éclair. I done work hard today on your mother estate. Work till my insides feel like gravel. You see this house here? Every cent I work for today going to pay for the lumber I buy on credit for build it. Your mother probably have shares in that store. They own every Jesus-Christ thing on Isabella Island. The day the shit in poor people bowels worth something they will own that too. So you see, sweetheart, I have more important things for worry 'bout than *who* your father is. Forget 'bout who your father is. Just praise God and count your blessings."

"Who is Aunt Stacey?"

"What you want with her?" Her voice was cross.

"Just tell me who she is."

"I don't know nobody by that name." The menacing, jagged piercing-glass tone again.

"I'm staying here until you answer my questions."

"Make yourself comfortable then. Your adopted mother can put me in the street any day she please, flatten this two-by-four I live in, even set fire to it, 'cause is estate land this, and no judge will dare to tell her she wrong. But I not answering your question, even if you and your mother chase me off o' here. Tell me something. You come here for give me a nervous break-down? Is that what you come here for? Is that what you come here for?" She was shouting.

He knew it was her desperate plea for him to leave. He got up, drained of will and energy. There was something his mother was hiding. Perhaps that she once slept with White men for what she could get. But what was the big deal? Many Black women were forced to do it, and raised the children that resulted, sometimes with money they were given in secret but mostly on their own; and, according to Manchester and even Rose, some were glad to have them, because light skin and soft hair opened doors that Blackness didn't. She didn't want him to get in touch with Aunt Stacey. She didn't want him to know the truth. Mommy must also know this; her reason for not telling him about his father was to avoid hurting him. But he vowed he would find out, even if the truth gave him another breakdown. He felt like shouting—*I will get to the bottom of this even if sets me crazy*—but he restrained himself.

He remained in the car for a few minutes to regain his composure before driving back to Arcadia. In his bed that night, calmer, he made a mental note to return to the village and ask the villagers themselves, probably on Sunday when everyone would be home. He was sure there were people there who could tell him the whereabouts of Aunt Stacey.

Four days later, on his way to the village, he gave a lift to a woman in her forties returning home from church, and she told him what he needed to know about Aunt Stacey. Anastasia Brown now lived in Trinidad. The woman thought she knew someone who might give her the address. She promised she'd go looking for it right away.

After dropping the woman off, he parked the car on the side of the main road that roughly followed the river's meanderings. He took a footpath flanked by elephant grass down to the river, a distance of about fifty feet from the road. At the mountain end, the stream, no more than a yard wide, tumbled some fifteen feet over a basalt ledge and created a green pool where it fell, a pool that looked sufficiently deep to cover him. A few yards away from where the water fell, the river widened and was not even knee-deep. Here, rising above the water's surface, were sud-stained stones on which the *Petit Bordel* women did their washing.

As river valleys go this one was shallow—enough to overflow its banks when the rains were unusually heavy. Gru-gru palms lined the banks with the odd mango, white cedar, galba, or plumrose tree, all forming an arbour for a mass of dark green vines, behind which were young canes that could not be seen from the riverbed.

He was alone at the river. He stared at the water, transparent—everything visible at the bottom, where there were no ripples—wondering where his mother had thrown him in. Bita didn't say if he'd cried. He must have, must have been frightened by the sound of the booming water. She didn't say what time of day, but it had to have been around dusk or later, when there was no one washing at the river. He pushed his hand into the water to test its temperature, and wondered whether it would have been cold enough to shock him into crying. Where he had been thrown or where the current had taken him must have been shallow enough for six-year-old Bita to enter and get him. He must have floated on his back, or Mammy must have left right away. He wouldn't have survived long face down.

Why did she want to kill him? Bita's cryptic remarks to him that last time she visited him at Camden School made him think that there was definitely some part of her life that Mammy wanted to forget and that he'd reminded her of. He hoped the woman would find Aunt Stacey's address. She would probably be more willing to answer some of his questions about his mother. She might even know his father's name. And he would be in contact with the woman who'd helped to save his life.

He removed his shoes and socks, put his feet in the swiftly moving water, and sat on the stone that was nearest the bank and began to reflect on the last six years of his life, wondering whether he would be able to leave the pain behind on Isabella Island just as his mother had solved her problem by letting Averill Éclair adopt him. That way she'd blotted out some mysterious but ugly chapter in her life. Would he find similar release in England?

Footsteps broke his reverie. It was the woman. She had the address for him.

Two hours later, the time it took him to get to the telegraph office in Hanovertown, he sent a cable to Anastasia Brown in which he mentioned the telephone number at Arcadia and promised to refund her for the cost of the call, for he needed to talk with her urgently. Anastasia Browne phoned him just before supper on Monday and told him that his father's name was George Emmanuel Éclair.

"Are you sure?" he asked her.

"Sure. George Emmanuel Éclair who lived in Arcadia Greathouse."

His knees trembled.

"Anything else you want for know?"

"Impossible!"

"Child, 'them is who hold the handle, and we hold the blade.' What else there is for know? Your mother was having a hard time, could not make ends meet at all. All o' we was having a hard time. But her ends was shorter than ours. Lita father did done speed off on the never-return. She did have for take care o' Lita. Child, people survive how they can. All of us use for thief from the estate: groundnuts, pineapple, peas—any thing fit for eat that we could o' get we hands 'pon. One evening Mr Éclair hide out and catch your mother. I think he did find out that the watchman used to let we off with a warning. Child, he gave your mother a choice that was no choice: a beating or a screw. She say beating. He crack his horse whip six times over her back and then he ordered her to take off her clothes." She swallowed loud and stopped talking briefly. "I is who take care o' she when she drag sheself home afterwards." She stopped talking for a few seconds. "Anything else you want to know? Joshua? You hearing me? You still there?

"And after that she couldn' eat peas. She couldn' even smell it cooking. Her body would get stiff like board, and is vomit she did have for vomit for come back to her normal self. Joshua, you still there? You is hearing me, child?"

He could not answer; his eyes grew dark. He sat down in the armchair beside the phone to prevent himself from falling and saw then that Mommy had been standing behind him.

"Who're you talking with? What's the matter with you? Joshua, what's the matter with you? Has Sparrow been bothering you?"

"Go! Leave me alone, please," he said when he was able to speak. For in that moment she was a monster, and had she said another word, he might have strangled her.

Two days later he left Isabella Island: August 14, 1965.

He'd left Aunt Stacey's address at Arcadia. The one person who might have helped him reconnect with his mother. But in those first years in Europe, he'd felt no need to. Distance from Isabella Island was what he'd needed, lots of distance.

The night before he left Arcadia he'd wanted to go back to see Mammy, to ask her pardon for the thoughts he'd secretly harboured of her. But he was too ashamed, too ashamed to let her know what he'd been thinking. Ashamed too that he'd allowed himself to think as well that Bita had got the idea of selling herself to the highest bidder from seeing Mammy whoring with White men.

The morning of his departure Dawn had sobbed when he went into the kitchen to tell the servants goodbye. "You is different from them-others; you is part of us," she said through her sobs. "I counting on you not to forget us. I start to work here when I fifteen and now I is fifty, without a penny to my name. Joshua, don' forget us."

"I promise," he told her, embracing her, crying too, touched by her truth—the truth and vulnerability of the class to which she, and his mother, belonged. Rose, uncomfortable, and Henry, nervously wiping his hand before extending it, had looked away, embarrassed by Dawn's naked honesty.

The evening before, at the going-away party Mommy had for him, he'd promised Amanda that he wouldn't forget her. She was sure he would. A woman had ways of sensing such things, she said. In England he wrote to her until she stopped answering his letters. It was a going-away laden with promises and expectations. None of which he'd fulfilled.

In England he discovered books by Blacks about Blacks—by Baldwin, Achebe, Wright, Malcolm X, Ellison, Lamming—and read them. Voraciously. Mr Morrison, his literature teacher at Expatriates, had mentioned some of these writers' names, but their books had not been available on Isabella Island. Fanon's *Black Skin White Masks* he struggled through in the original French (he has since reread it several times in translation), and it changed his perceptions forever—about the plantocracy and colonialism, and he understood why such books weren't allowed on Isabella Island. And he came close to despising every drop of European blood in his body. In 1966, in her second-to-last letter to him, Mommy had mentioned that in an attempt to curb Communist subversion the Isabellan legislature had passed an edict banning the importation of all "Black-power books and preventing all Black-power agitators from entering the island."

His mind returns to the present, his eyes registering the white walls of the room, the chair beside the bed, the night table; he hears the sounds of the patients a few rooms down.

Are these things he could tell psychiatrists? How does one piece them together, do justice to them, not lie on the characters in these dramas? How do you justly put people on trial after they're dead?

11

GOOD MORNING, MR ÉCLAIR. My, my! Aren't you spiffy this morning!" She is too. Hair curled and dyed auburn. Lipstick—she doesn't normally wear lipstick—barely visible: blushing-flesh. Dark green satin dress, not the drab slacks and sacklike tops.

"Good morning, Nurse Knights."

"We're happy to see you wearing your regular clothes again, Mr Éclair. Yesterday I saw you walking without your cane. You're progressing fast."

"You are here to take me to this mysterious meeting?"

"Yes. Dr Stein and Dr Defoe and Leroy and Moses are in the room wait-ing. Let's go."

They head to the conference room. Joshua has never been in it before. Sunlight streams into it. It has a plate glass window the entire width and height of the room. The brightness makes him blink. The walls are a verdant green and the floor is covered with imitation black granite ceramic tiles. There are brightly coloured floral couches against two walls. A large circular table able to seat at least a dozen is in the centre of the room. He knows everyone there well, except Moses. He is the cleaner: a well-covered, average-height, dougla man. His accent suggests he's Trinidadian. His only words to Joshua have been, "Good morning, sir. I have to clean this room. Don't let the noise bother you." The wheels on his mop bucket rattle and squeak like metal sleds on concrete, and his mop handle knocks against the furniture in the room as Moses moves it furiously across the floor madly rushing to get his work done. He snorts when he squeezes the mop and snorts a second time when he lets go the lever. *Who'll do his cleaning while he's here? They're exploiting him: therapist and cleaner—two for the price of one.* He feels like telling Moses, before the session gets underway, to demand the salary of a therapist. But he doesn't.

They are all seated around the table.

Stein, his elbows on the table, his fingers interlaced in his clasped hands, leads off like the alpha male he probably thinks he is: "Mr Eclair, Dr Defoe and I have decided that you might benefit from a little more group interac-tion." His eyes are riveted on Joshua's face.

Joshua turns to staring at the table's surface. It's of smoked oak and has a dull finish.

"Yes," Defoe takes over. "We think you can't go on being the introvert that you quite clearly are."

Joshua is half-amused and half-annoyed—*How can one not be what he is? You absurd asses!*—and now looks in turn at the faces of everyone. It's a round table all right, he muses, but no Arthur is here and certainly no Merlin in the background. He wonders what role Moses will play in his therapy. *Take me to the edge of the promised land, maybe?* It's not snobbery. He doesn't know anything about Moses and he doubts that Moses knows anything about him.

In the silence he thinks of all the games he could play with them, how he could turn them, literary ignoramuses, upside down. Gladys Knights could be Guenevere and Defoe Lancelot. They could search for the grail of sanity while Moses looks for the promised land. But the thought that he'd only end up hurting Moses keeps him silent.

The silence grows.

"Say something," Defoe says.

"Shhh!" he puts a finger on his lips "There's a foetus in Silence's womb. Don't abort it." And he vows to himself that from then on he'll just shake his head to any questions, even better than he had done decades before with the psychologist in New York.

The members of the group are fidgeting. Gladys Knights coughs.

Joshua gets up and returns to his room. When he sits down his forehead feels cold but sweat is trickling down his armpits.

About three minutes later Stein and Defoe come into his room. "Dr Defoe," Joshua says angrily, "don't you think the least you could have done—and I am saying this to you, Dr Defoe, because you are Black and until a short while ago you'd earned my trust—was to inform me that you intended to exhibit me like a circus monstrosity? I see now I was mistaken." He hears the anger in his voice and feels it rising in him. He knows that he must stop.

They tell him they did not intend to insult his intelligence, that it was all calculated to get to the source of his trouble, that it's because they're making no progress in the one-on-one conversations; he turns them into games of one-upmanship, and the ECTs they've done on him have had limited success. In any event he's no longer psychotic—at least they don't think he is. But they're at their wits' ends trying to get him to face, to express, to externalize what triggers his amnesia. They're getting ready to release him and they want him to leave with a better understanding of the root cause of his troubles. And in a way they're convincing.

"Folks," he says, "I know the root cause of my troubles. I studied literature but I also took several psychology courses—not for credit—just to get a finger on the pulse of human bullshit. I too would like to know what triggers my amnesia." He pauses. "You're going about this the wrong way, if you permit me. You have to be prepared to accept that there are things I won't tell you, and things I cannot tell you because I don't know them myself." To himself he mutters, "Shit." *Wrong thing. You're inciting them to make you talk.*

"Why's that?" Defoe asks.

"Why's what?"

"The things you're not willing to tell us," Stein answers for Defoe.

"Because I don't . . . because I can't find words for them. I don't know why."

"Like the scars on your back?"

"Like the scars on my back." He stares at Defoe hard. "You're obsessed with them, aren't you, Dr Defoe? They didn't come cheap, let me tell you."

"I know that."

"What else?" Stein asks.

He's a while answering.

A long silence ensues, in which he tells himself to calm down. When he feels calm enough, he says, "My father. My adopted relatives. Life. People. The whole world! When I was seventeen my adopted mother took me to see a psychologist in New York. It was a waste of time and money. A complete waste." He stops talking for a moment. "What you did this morning offends me."

"How's that?"

"Come on! Did you make them rehearse the questions? Nobody likes to be stripped in public, Doctor. It's rape."

"Rape!" this from Defoe. "It's well and good for you to decide not to tell us about yourself, but we can't accept that. Our duty is to make you well, to bring into your consciousness all that horror buried deep inside you; that's bludgeoning you into forgetting yourself. We want to help you exorcise it."

Joshua reflects on this for a while, registers Defoe's exaggerated self-confidence. *A well- intentioned waste of time.*

Eventually they leave.

Maybe it was a staged provocation, he thinks, a variation on shock therapy. They did get him to tell them things he hadn't mentioned before. *Let them go to hell.*

But his thoughts turn to Alexander Manchester, snuggling up behind him. Alexander felt—he said it once during the bull sessions they held on *Expatriates'* grounds under the willow and cedar trees—that there was no such thing as rape. You only had to convince a girl you'd give her a whale of a time. In the faces of the holdouts you wave a five-dollar bill. Let them know you could buy it and them too.

Forget about Alexander. Why am I thinking about him? But he doesn't forget. He occasionally went horseback riding with him and his brother Vincent, and sometimes just with him alone. They kept six thoroughbreds for that purpose. Their stepmother, the bell cow, stringy and hyperactive as ever, her hair roots a mix of brown and grey, tips blond and trimmed like a man's; her face plastered with makeup; her eyes hidden behind dark glasses; her breath a distillery—would look at him furtively. A few times he'd seen her smiling, grimacing was more like it, at him, and wondered if she was trying to figure out his paternity—to see whether her husband had done the job. It was a standard joke, and only a slight exaggeration, that Manchester had "fathered" one quarter of all the children in the North Atlantic constituency; not because of dollar bills waved in hungry, barefoot women's faces but for mere guarantees of year-round work.

She could have hardly had such thoughts, he now thinks, for once he'd been adopted, she'd have inquired around to find out which White man's seed he was. But he did not know that then.

He hears the sound of rustling fabric—Gladys Knights' green dress—and realizes that she's in the room. She has brought a sedative. He opens his mouth and swallows it and the orange juice accompanying it as if it were part of what he is recalling, as if she were a benign Mrs Manchester.

In London he had lived the first year in Lynden Hall, at Woodford, and commuted to campus by bus—a thirteen-mile journey. He liked the several acres of woodland around Woodford, especially the seasonal changes in the trees, even the fact that the leaves altered the sound of the wind, from tenor in summer to soprano in winter, from the sound of brisk-moving shallow water to a hiss and a whine. In winter, stripped of their leaves the trees became brooms frantically swaying in the wind, impatient to sweep the sky. On foggy days they were grey skeletons that seemed to be floating.

His taste adjusted to white bread, bland roast beef, tough, fried, dried-out mutton chops, boiled cabbage and potatoes, grey stew, and chicken rank enough to make him retch. After Rose's cooking it was an effort. But adjust he did.

The British students in residence were friendly with one another but imperially glacial or silent towards him. One tried to recruit him for the Young Conservatives. At the time the Conservatives in the House of Commons were supporting Ian Smith's UDI, and Enoch Powell was drawing large crowds wherever he went with his message that Britain must end non-White immigration and repatriate all non-Whites already there. The issue was ferociously debated in the Queen Mary College student paper, *The Cub*. Britannia's imperial waves had halted and were turned back onto its shores. The empire nipped at the emperor's heels. Colonial *children* flocked to meet their guardians and found them dowdy, doltish, and dull like most of humanity—not universally brilliant and omnipotent—and the dowdy, doltish, and dull resented the scrutiny of brown, Black heathens who some believed had tails that shrivelled at sunrise and returned at nights, tails, that Sam Selvon said, the English factory girls often asked to see.

In his second year he took a flat in Tower Hamlets on Morgan Street, a ten-minute walk from campus. He moved there largely because he felt he wasted too much time commuting; it was too much of a bother to get to Woodford from London on those evenings when he went to the theatre. The Underground had not yet been extended to Woodford. He arranged with an agency to send a charwoman to clean the Tower Hamlets flat on Monday and Thursday, a fact he kept secret because most of the students at Queen Mary lived on five hundred pounds annually.

Except for Paul, there was no one at Queen Mary College whom he could call a friend. Paul was from Guyana, New Amsterdam. He remembers Paul every time he smells lanolin or bergamot. He oiled his skin with lanolin-scented cocoa butter and used Bergamot-perfumed Afro Sheen to give his Afro a softness and glow it did not naturally have. He had a slender, short (about five-four), flexible body, no bottom to speak of, and matchstick legs. His voice was deep. He spoke with loud impatience, and stared at everyone with frank, inquisitive intensity. He laughed easily, always exposing his dark gums and slightly overlarge teeth with large natural gaps. Mischief abounded in his bright, froglike, bulging eyes. But for the fact that he had a slight, barely noticeable case of strabismus, he might have easily been mistaken for James Baldwin's twin. His eyelashes were uncommonly long and jet-black, and their fluttering prefigured trouble. He'd often begin cursing someone under his breath and finish by complimenting the person aloud. *"Haul your skunt!* But look how beautiful you look today!"

They'd met at the Dramsoc performance in the spring of '66. Paul's play hadn't won and he wanted to see what was so special about the ones that had. He made a few lewd jokes about Humphrey Hole, who was the lead actor in one of the winning plays. Hole's play dealt with the travails of being homosexual. Paul criticized Hole's performance, which Joshua thought had been outstanding, and then went on to speculate quite crudely what someone with a name like Hole could be expected to do. Joshua liked Humphrey. It was he who'd invited him to the Dramsoc. He never knew whether or not Humphrey (Hol(e)y Humphrey, Paul called him) was gay and was indifferent to whether or not he was.

About six months later Joshua found out that Paul was gay. "Josh," he asked, his eyelashes batting away, "bet you don't know what perspective is?"

Joshua shrugged his shoulders. He found the question stupid.

"That's cause you never had any. A hard Black dick! And I need one tonight." He paused, a big grin on his face, to let Joshua's shock dissipate. Then smiling and fluttering his long eyelashes, he added, "You not a candidate. Don't try even if your dick can get hard. One time I sleep with this nice-looking boy, nice no skunt—if you see that mother? Handsome for true, a kiss-me-ass model, I tell you. He couldn't get it up. Try all night. Waste my time no skunt. First I did want to box he skunt. Waste me damn night, but in the end, I did feel sorry for he. I tell he next time to eat a pound o' oysters before he try to screw."

"You're dotty." Inwardly Joshua smiled. *Maybe you didn't turn him on.*

The next day on campus, just outside the refectory, Paul told a lanky fellow who'd bumped into him but grinned instead of saying sorry, "Boy, watch where you going! Don't make me thump in your skunt." The fellow's friend—a close cropped, golden-haired tun, on salami-size legs—said, "Ignore the cock-eyed fool. Asinine bastard!" he hissed, hate glowing in his grey eyes. Paul replied with gunshot speed: "Cock-eyed, for sure—but not for your cock. You have one? *Bastard*: no, even if I never saw my father. *Ass-in-nine*: no. I'll enter a *nice* one before *you* could count two, forget about nine."

The lanky fellow grinned all the more, his lip condescendingly upcurled. His tubby friend's ears turned a cyanotic blue, and he began hitting his right balled fists against each other as if they were cymbals, before his lanky friend held his sleeve and pulled him in the direction of the library.

"I don't know why you say things like that," Joshua told Paul when the fellows were out of earshot. "You'll get beaten up."

"Because I live on my terms. I won't let any White somebody—or Black somebody—push me into any corner. I'm taking centre stage like everyone else, even if I have to knock out a few teeth to get there and stay there."

In the Britain they were in, it was more likely Paul's teeth that would have been knocked out. And taking Stephen Lawrence as an example, he wonders how different today's Britain is.

It was fashionable then for Blacks to state outright their hatred for Whites and White culture. Even bovine Queen Mary, where griping about parking spaces and inadequate student allowances was the main extracurricular activity, wasn't spared the turmoil of the sixties. There was the camp that defended colonial oppression as a fact of life and mourned each time the Union Jack got hauled down for the last time in some distant corner of the earth, and the camp that vigorously opposed it, and both sometimes clashed. Amnesty International (QMC) busied itself with political prisoners in Angola and Rhodesia. The Young Socialists invited Cheddi Jaggan to the campus, and it had been quite an event. There was even a rally against the Vietnam War. Malcolm X, Stokely Carmichael, and Martin Luther King were spoken of as often as Enoch Powell, Ted Heath, and Harold Wilson. There were few Blacks on campus but it was "hip" to be racist if you were Black.

And Paul's stories! One about Jesus and Peter:

"Jesus was walking by the Sea of Galilee, and he sees Peter.

"'Peter,' says he. 'What you bothering with them fish for? Go catch men.'

"So Peter does as Jesus tells him.

"When Jesus comes back to Galilee two weeks later he meets Peter waiting for him, vexed to rass! 'Master,' he shout out to Jesus. 'I catch a whole mess o' men but look! Nobody buying.'

"Jesus scratches his head. 'Peter,' he says, his finger-them shaking no rass, "do you sell all the fish you catch?'

"'No, master. Some o' them not fit to eat."

"'Then, Peter,' Jesus says, 'man, next time catch men people going want to eat.'"

"Why you're wasting your time in history? Why you're not out there pimping?" Joshua teased.

"And if was you alone in me stable, I would starve to rass."

One evening Paul and he were in a gay pub in Soho discreetly observing a Black guy who couldn't be more than twenty sitting on the lap of a man old enough to be his great-grandfather. He fed the old man sips of beer, after which he too would sip from the same mug. Periodically he licked the bits of froth the beer left around the old man's lips. Suddenly someone standing behind Paul said, "You handzome Black stud! Vhat is your name? I vant you to fuck me."

Conceited though he was, Paul knew he was neither.

"Hits is King Kong, but you von't have my vhang!" Paul replied with slow deliberate caricature.

The fellow, nearly seven feet tall and one shade darker than an albino, froze momentarily, then left the pub.

Halloween night, 1966, Paul suggested they go to a gay bar in disguise.

"Tell you what, Josh, I going put a dog collar 'pon you, see, and a leash and a tail, and I going carry a whip, and every time I hit you, you going say, 'Ruw! Ruw.'"

"And I have a better idea. I'll fit you with horns and a skirt with nothing underneath, and you will walk spreadeagled and bent forward, and every time I pull your balls you will go, 'Mooooo!'"

"Go fuck yourself!"

That Halloween night on their way back to Joshua's flat, where Paul was overnighting, they ran into one of Joshua's classmates, Suleyman, and another fellow at the Bethnal Green station. Joshua introduced Paul to Suleyman, and Suleyman introduced his friend, a chisel-faced, squat fellow called Akbhar, who said to Suleyman as soon as they turned away, "Your friends are throne rockers?"

"Throne rockers!" Paul called back to him. "What the hell's a throne rocker? Takes one to know one." Thereafter Suleyman avoided Joshua in class, in the cafeteria, and even at the Departmental Teas. A few months ago, listening to a CBC Ideas programme on Islam, Joshua learned the full significance of Akbhar's remark—shorthand for Mohammed's statement: "When a man mounts another man, the throne of God shakes."

He was uncomfortable with Paul's abrupt dismissal of anyone who differed from him and his use of obscenity to gain attention. He even stopped hearing Paul's most frequent outburst: "Haul your skunt." All things considered they got on well, *no rass*. Or is it, *to skunt?* Joshua laughs to himself.

Paul lived in North London with an aunt who was a State Registered Nurse and a fundamentalist Christian. "You should tell her your story about the Essequibo guy," Joshua told him after one of Paul's complaints about his aunt's fundamentalism.

"*Listen to this. It had this gay fellow who live in a lonely village somewhere out in the back o' Essequibo. Only thing a gay guy can do out there is listen to crickets while he jerking off. Then a day one o' these preachers that get you in the spirit and thing set up church in his village.*

"*Well, the preacher want for get the young girls them for join his church, so he preach straight to them: 'I say a good man is hard to find.'*

"*Oh, Lord, yes,' the girls-them reply, the gay man sitting up front right along with them. So the pastor hear him.*

"*Pastor to the man: 'Ain't a good man is hard to find, brother?'*

"*Man: 'You damn right he is.'*

"Pastor: 'Then put your life in Christ hands, brother.'
"Man: 'Me no want no dead man.'"

Other than Paul, Joshua invited no one to the flat, and not even Paul knew about the charwoman. Even so, Paul did on occasion ask him if his old man was shitting the stuff. To which he'd reply, "Yeah, man, gold turds the size o' ostrich eggs." And eventually, seriously, "My old man's dead."

"Death never stopped rich people from shitting," Paul retorted. "That's why they call the orders they leave behind wills."

"So you had plenty chances to fuck, then?" Paul continued.

"What do you mean?"

"The servant boys-them. Who else? That is what I mean. Don't pretend you don't know what does happen in rich White people houses. Rich White buller men back home fuck their chauffeur, their gardener, and the nephews and sons o' their servants. Don't pretend you don't know."

"I don't. I never did." He remembered the incident with Alexander but it was unlike what Paul was saying.

"And they didn' fraid o' people finding out, 'cause, as you well know, no Black somebody could go round the place accusing no rich White some-body o' bulling. So when a rich White man grab your dick, you enjoy it and keep your mouth shut, 'cause you don't want you or your family to lose their job. Or else if you don't have a job, you know he might be in a posi-tion to help you to find one, or even give you one. Besides, if he like what you got, he likely to treat you nice, especially if he got a wife. 'Cause he wants it to stay all-you special secret. And poor people can always use a few extra dollars and keep their mouth shut 'bout how they get it."

"You know a lot about it."

Paul stared at him intensely and nodded slowly. "Don't I? I can write two books about it." He raised two fingers and nodded slowly. Joshua wanted to hear more, but Paul was not about to reveal his past. He changed the subject.

They were sitting at the oak dining table in Joshua's flat. It was a grey, drizzly afternoon. Paul got up, pulled the curtain and looked out into the wet, deserted street, his back turned to Joshua, a slight odour of perspira-tion coming from him. Then he turned suddenly and said, "I ever introduce you to Kwesi?"

Joshua shook his head.

"Boy, that is the sweetest fuck in all o' London. Spice up with pepper and ginger and something else I don't remember."

"You lunatic!"

"*Lunatic?*" He came and sat back down at the table, his eyes bulging bright with mischief, his eyelashes batting, "Your parents ever catch you doing it?"

Joshua shook his head. He wasn't about to tell Paul or anybody about what had gone on between him and Sparrow.

"Well, Kwesi." He passed his tongue over both lips and swallowed while he stared straight into Joshua's eyes. "He from Ghana. He studying mathematics over at King's College. He say his father is a chief. But you know every African here say that. Anyhow, back in Ghana when he was around thirteen, somebody catch him fooling around with another boy, and man they put a mixture o' pepper and ginger and something else up his arsehole and hold him down so he couldn't go to the toilet and shit it out right away. Kwesi say that is what they do when they catch children playing with themselves or in sex play. He say it does work. But I think that ever since that day Kwesi always want something hot up his arse."

But he wasn't always this flippant. And Joshua suspected he too was running from something in the Caribbean. Out of the blue one late Saturday afternoon while they were walking east along Mile End Road, he said, "One thing I don't want to catch me is old age. I already have one strike against me. Gay reality not easy, you know. It's not easy. The only people crueller than gays were nineteenth-century capitalists."

"What's the strike?"

"Don't play you don't know."

"I don't."

"Even my mother wasn't afraid to tell me. You know what I tell her? 'Is you I take after.' Boy, she beat me until I almost passed out, but I felt good backchatting her." He paused, with eyes glazed over. "Boy, if I wasn't bright, crapaud would o' been smoking my pipe."

Joshua laughed at the unintended sexual pun.

Paul stopped walking. They were at the street corner near Bethnal Green station. A crowd was surging out of the station. Paul stared at them with bulging, unseeing eyes. No fluttering eyelashes.

"What did your mother tell you?"

"That I Black and ugly as sin."

"Your mother told you that?"

"Yes. What? You think I lying? I don't lie about serious things."

"And you believe that?"

"Yes!"

What am I to say, Joshua thought, suddenly feeling listless, distressed.

Paul continued. "I criticize my aunt who lives here, about her religion and all that. But I would give that woman a kidney if she ever needs one to save her life. That's how much I love her. My uncle was all set to carry me into the bush to be a pork knocker—and I only twelve. Imagine! When he propose it to my mother, you should see how her eyes glitter, with all the gold and diamonds she imagine I would find in the interior. But I wrote my aunt. And she sent me to school in Georgetown, and as soon as I wrote A Levels—she didn't even wait for the results—she brought me here." He stopped talking briefly.

"So now you know what the first strike is: ugliness. I'm not hanging around for strike two: old age. For old age to make me uglier? You crazy! As soon as I get to forty, I turning off the lights. In the meantime, I intend to fuck any Black guy that want to fuck me. I living to the full, and that means getting all the sex I can get, and still some."

In the clubs several White guys were attracted to Paul. They rarely were to Joshua. Yet Paul considered himself ugly. Joshua was puzzled. "Paul, White men stare at you in the bars and drool. They certainly find you attractive."

"*Attractive.* Yes. I attract. Because they want animal sex and think they can get if from anybody with a black skin. And the uglier the Black man the more he turn them on. They don't see us. They see their fantasies of big, Black cocks that can fuck whenever they want. You don't have that problem. And you better say thank God you don't. One time, one o' them showed me the length o' his arm, saying he want to get fucked with a dick like that, and asked me if I had one. 'Why, you don't try a donkey, or a table leg?' I told him. Their foreparents called us animals. Behind our backs these here call us monkeys, sometimes to our faces. I?" He pointed to his chest with his thumb. "You crazy! Fuck them? Never! I prefer to stay home and jerk off."

Joshua could say nothing. He'd heard H Rap Brown and Stokely Carmichael express similar anger, but felt that it had been staged for the reporters and TV cameras. He remembered the conversations the planters held when they came to Arcadia. "Let's go have a pint," he finally told Paul, hoping this would break the tension and change his mood. They walked to the nearby King's Arms, where they sipped lager in almost total silence.

Usually they would have gone to Soho, because it was a Saturday, but when they left the pub, Paul returned to his aunt's home in North London.

Among Joshua's professors, Killam, aka Snowman, stood out. A comic, middle-aged man whom Joshua associated with Wallace Stevens's "The Snowman." His first day of class he made them repeat his name twice. When they were finished he said, "Now that you killed and resurrected me, I'll survive." An average teacher who seemed drawn to foreign students. Joshua and Suleyman were the only non-Brits among the twenty-five freshers in English in the fall of '65. "Go have another scone, lad. Eat a do(u)zen if you can. They're calculated in your fees," he told Joshua and Suleyman a couple of times at the first of the departmental teas, which were held the third Thursday of every month in the Upper Refectory. Teas that began, wrote Quaint Mary-Mother-of-Cant (the name her disparagers gave her, for no one knew for certain who she was), by asking the Lord to prevent poisoning from what they were about to receive. Killam the buffoon, always in his grey, smelly tweeds. Killam punctuating his carefully cultivated Oxfordese with a nonstandard phrase or two whenever he wished to wake them up or take them down. "'Ow now, Misz Marshall, you be sinkin' in the marshes." And the nodding-off Miss Marshall, buxom, pigtailed, and blonde, now startled, becoming rose-red, her eyes blue bulges, would stare at Killam and stiffen as if suddenly manacled by her khaki-green sweater and her coral miniskirt that fell just below buttocks that could rival any Bantu woman's.

Once Suleyman asked Killam a question that involved the word bough, except that he pronounced it bo. In a cadenced, reverential tone Killam told him, "Laddie, that's bough like, I *allow, now* is the time to steal a *cow*, and when we're t-h-r-o-u-g-h, through"—his tone changed—"Oooh! Ooh! Ooh!"—his voice now two octaves higher—"no one will say booooo or we'll lock the bugger in the loo." He paused to let their giggling die down. "Laddie, you see," he threw back his arms like drapes parting, "English is a whore who keeps all her presents." Half the class applauded, the other half seemed shocked and offended.

Every student got it from Killam, even those who never spoke in class, but Suleyman, Ms Marshall, and Mose were his favourite targets. With a wink to Joshua at the first of those Thursday teas, he said to Suleyman, "On Monday," (the day of his lectures), "I saw ye, lad, abusing yourself when Misz Marshall bent over to pick up her pencil case. What were ye saying,

lad? At the 'eight o' things were ye saying, 'God is great! God is great?'"
Suleyman went pale, but Professor Killam did not notice. Instead he continued, "Cause bedlam in your harem, that Misz Marshall. Be careful, lad."

The following Monday in class, Suleyman attempted his second and very
last question, "Professor Killem—" but got no further.

"Laddie, Killam I am. Kill 'em I've never done. Not even me father's
chickens."

The class laughed.

When Killam was bored by his own lecturing, he turned on anyone he
fancied. Joshua's turn came one day while he was nodding off in class.
"Éclair, that's symmetry with an S, not a C as in the dump for dead bodies."
The class groaned but Killam continued, "For a moment there your light-
ning stopped flashing." To which Mose, an older student—a luggard of a
fellow, who captained the cricket team—who liked being chummy with
lecturers and tutors, said, "Impossible, *you* are thundering."

Briefly Killam stopped flashing. When he opened his eyes, he turned their
glare, magnified by his thick glasses, onto Mose and slowly said. "I see now
laddie why your trousers are worn at the knees. You may make it yet
beyond a BA-Failed, lad." The class roared. Mose wilted. "Don't scoff at it,
lad. In me young days, many a notary public adorned his shingle with BA-
Failed. Me Form I teacher was a BA-Failed. See, lad, in me days 'twas
respectable to be a BA-Failed." After that Mose stopped attending Killam's
lectures and attended only the class-related tutorials.

In the breaks between classes, Killam was always the subject of conversation. Rumours about him abounded. One that he was alcoholic. Whenever
he missed lectures, on average once every six weeks, Ms Marshall said she
was sure he was at home drying out. Mose said someone had told him
Killam was a defrocked Presbyterian minister. The day they discussed the
US Constitution in their world history course, Ms Marshall said, "That's
what's needed here: restraints on professors, checks and balances." The
lecturer, a tall, athletic, doctoral student, with thick, shoulder-length chestnut hair, who more than once caught Joshua staring at him in inappropriate
places, grinned in answer to Ms Marshall, probably looking forward to the
day when he could humiliate as he had been humiliated.

Then professors ridiculed their students and got away with it, and it was
the rare professor who was not patronising. In the classes he's been auditing in Montreal over the years to keep himself busy, professors dare not
humiliate their students. Now it's the professors who fear the students,

whose evaluations of their teaching may well determine whether they get tenured, promoted, or fired.

The week Killam declaimed the "Snowman," a group from King's College campus was performing Gilbert and Sullivan's *Gondolier* at QMC. "Popcorn," Killam called it. "Popcorn for plebs. Legions of leagues from the distilled tragedy that will keep 'The Snowman' erect in granite millennia hence"—his right arm extending upwards, perpendicular, the class giggling (he loved it when they did), for Killam venerated Freud. As if the university wanted to take him down a peg or two, they made him lecture in the Bow Extension, a converted warehouse that was every bit a warehouse. And their first day there, Killam, who played right along, said when he finished taking attendance, "From the bill o' lading I see a good deal o' the merchandise has gone missing."

12

JOSHUA WAS ALREADY LIVING in the Morgan Street flat when news of Mommy's death reached him. She was returning from Hanovertown, from a welcoming party for the new British governor, who was there to push Isabellans towards becoming an independent nation. She was in a car driven by "Horse Jaw" Langley. He lost control of the car and drove it over a precipice just before Point Peter, close to the cliffs where Bita had jumped into the Atlantic. They were both killed.

She was to be interred in Tallahassee, four years after she'd fled it for the third time. Sparrow wanted him to attend her funeral, but Joshua's memory of what he'd witnessed there was too graphic, and he did not go.

He felt a perverse pleasure in handing her her comeuppance: she'd prevented him from having any awareness of Bita's funeral, and she'd deliberately withheld from him the identity of his father. Did she know he was the product of a rape? Coming from Florida, and given his mother's race, perhaps she wouldn't have cared. But it would have been better if he had gone. The nightmares that followed, in which she hounded him, might have been avoided.

A copy of her will, a page from her journal, and a long letter she'd written him but could not bring herself to deliver while she was alive were mailed to him about three months after her death. From the letter's date,

July 15, 1963, she'd written it while he was attending the sessions with the psychologist in New York. There was no date on the journal entry, but it too was tied in with the US trip.

All three were in a sealed wallet that contained other papers, including the adoption certificate and a photograph of his "father." There were instructions on the wallet itself that was to be given to him unopened at her death.

He read the undated excerpt from her journal first.

Now back in Isabella Island, I am aware of the changes time has stamped me with; aware too of the games memory plays on me; of the games we White Americans play with ourselves. Marjorie tried in every way to humiliate me, to punish me for what she feels, I am sure, are advantages I have and she hasn't. That dance she did, every step a stumble, about Joshua's genesis came mighty near exhausting her. I cannot but wonder about what grand putdown she had planned for me. She'd had every intention of sweetening her dinner with my humiliation. Joshua and I would have been dessert—illicitly sweet! What a bitch! A school principal, huh!

"An' now y'all," I can imagine her saying, "le's drink a toast to Averill here and her Joshua. We gon celebrate the heights she done got to. Mighty high she's gotten. Oh, yes. High! Joshua, move over into the light so's ev'one can see you. Ain't he a beauty? Don't y'all agree? Them mulattoes in the Caribbeans is mighty beautiful. Comely. Now le's drink to Averill's success and to Joshua, her mulatto son." Oh what a bitch! Fancy, her telling me, "Now Averill I been living too long in the South to mistake a mulatto for a White man. You just be careful now the neighbours don' see him up close, 'cause we's all riled up over these niggers who think it's time they be treated like White people. I don' relish being charged o' being no innergrationist. 'Cause I ain't one. So you be careful now." What a bitch! She certainly had me where she wanted and loved every second of it. She was all primed to prove she's no "innergrationist," and Providence only knows what trauma she'd have inflicted on Joshua to prove it. To think that in a moment of frolic she'd have destroyed all I've done this past year to rebuild Joshua's confidence, and send me back to Isabella probably with Joshua again psychotic!

Her attacks on me personally I could have handled. Bilious Marjorie, bilious with envy. If you only knew the price it all comes with . . .

"Averill, you sure he . . ."

"What, Marjorie? What are you trying to say?"

"Ah know you tell me he your husband son"—her eyes, big and brown as a cow's, for a moment fixed on the floor before she raises them and turns their cruel glow on

me. "Ah won' judge you, Averill. Ah sure won't. He your husband son?"

"No, Marjorie, he's mine. My husband ran a whorehouse. No, I had him for . . . Oh, God, I don't know which one: the chauffeur, the gardener, the field hands; I did it with them all."

"Don't you be gittin' so upset. You was always a lib'ral woman 'n Ah jus' wanted to know the truth. Well, it's kin'o odd, you know, to show up in ma house wid a coloured kid 'n tryin' to pass him off for White. More'n enough to make a body suspicious. 'N seeing you was always lib'ral 'n ev'thang, well, Ah just had to clear that one up."

"And Marjorie, what if I'd married a Black man?"

"Sh! Sh!" her fingers on her lips. "Ma neighbours lakly to hear you. No need gittin' carried away. What's wrong? You a lil pale around the gills, Averill. You been away too long, Averill, and you done gone and got more lib'ral in the Caribbeans. Ah won' talk 'bout it no more 'cause I see where it be upsettin' you. Le's be lak in the good ole days when your ma was alive."

"There were no good old days, Marjorie."

"Sure there was. Course y'all didn' lak ma mother . . ."

So much in my birthplace stinks. While I lived there I had become accustomed. That's what it was. I had to leave and return in order to smell and see and remember. Oh Marjorie, I don't hate you. To do so would be to hate myself and a large part of humanity. I see, indeed only now do I see, why West Indians cannot smell the rot they mistake for normalcy. No wonder most, perhaps all, societies fear foreigners and move quickly to co-opt or restrict them. Oh, how we fear to be judged openly or secretly! And strangers see us as we are.

I guess I'm hard on Marjorie and on these Isabellan Whites, whom I dare not criticize, especially now that I know there's no quarter in the US south for me. People aren't so different, just blind to the evil in themselves while they obsess over the ugliness of others.

He was, therefore, glad he did not attend Mommy's funeral. So "Aunt Marge" had known for sure he was mixed. But he merely smiled upon finding this out. To him, she'd been no more than a comic character one might see in a film or on TV or read about in a Dickens novel. When did they have these conversations? Well, the good thing was that he now knew for sure that she'd known. He was glad Mommy didn't take the chance of exposing him to her friends' outright racism, or the veiled, crueller kind, where they turn you into a poodle.

But Mommy's letter to him was a completely different matter.

New York City
July 15, 1963

Dear Joshua,

I am distressed that the therapy sessions I arranged for you here have fallen short of my expectations. My dreams for you, Joshua, are many, but first I want you to go through life a healthy human being.

I lie in bed at nights reflecting on how and why I failed you. I know my first mistake was forcing you to deny the African part of yourself. Being Black is not a cancer that you surgically remove because it threatens your life. I know that now but I didn't then. I was certain at the time that race controls everything, and one is trapped, and sometimes doomed, if he or she is born into the wrong one. When I did what I thought I had to do, it was not like now. I truly believed that a Black person who had the opportunity to hide his Blackness would jump at the chance to do so and would be foolish not to. At Smith there was a very gifted girl named Martha, the valedictorian of our group. Initially we all thought she was White. We all kept pictures of our parents and spoke of them. She did not. In her senior year, just before the spring break ended, one of our cohort was out front and she saw a car driven by a Black man stop and Martha get out of it. Next she heard Martha arguing with the man about why he shouldn't come inside. The girl distinctly heard Martha call him daddy. Martha was later asked who the man was, and she said he was the family chauffeur. I remember too how the film "Imitation of Life" had moved me to tears. It's about a Eurafrican woman who disowns her Black mother.

I know you must wonder why I never speak to you about my husband, your father. Yes, it is he who is your father. I could not tell you this before. Here, for whatever reasons, planters don't own their illegitimate children. Your father never spoke about you except on his deathbed. I never knew what the relationship between him and your mother was, didn't even know that it had existed. On his deathbed he said you were his only child, and asked if I would be willing to adopt you, or, at the very least, see to it that you got a good education. You were two when he died. Before moving to adopt you, I waited to make sure you would not become a Negroid child. I know what you will think when you read this, but one thing you can be sure of is that now I love you like my own flesh and blood, as if I myself had birthed you.

I know now I should have never cut you off from your sister. I had known for a long time of your secret meetings. Marie never conned me on that one, but as long it was hidden from me I felt it was all right, until Mrs Manchester informed me that some of the surrounding planters knew about it and were upset by it. It was only then that I took action. I didn't before because I didn't want to hurt you. By the time your sister died, I had already convinced myself that you no longer wanted to be associated with your biological family, that going to school in Hanovertown had cured you of that. My unfortunate reaction at your sister's death came out of surprise, not malice. My mistake was interrupting you before you could tell me she was dead.

I married your father thinking that life in the Caribbean would be without the ever-present racial barriers everyone in the US lives behind. But the racism of West Indian plantocrats equals and sometimes exceeds that of Mississippi Whites. It took your breakdown—can you believe it?—for me to discover that I carried those barriers inside me. Racial barriers—and it's a sad comment on humanity—are not easily circumvented. In another setting I would have been able to throw away some of the racist baggage I carried. But the plantocracy polices its members. Upon my arrival it taught me its code and set about making sure I enforced it. A desire to please, fear of not sticking out, loneliness, and my own weak character, which I did not understand at the time, made me comply eventually.

Human beings are marvellous liars. We are especially good at lying to ourselves. Whole communities, whole nations, whole races lie and are forever ready to silence those who might accuse them. I have seen it in the race problem in the US, especially in our cowboy movies, and I see it among West Indian Whites who live off the labour of the very people they call lazy.

Your illness plunged me into a deep depression, for I saw then that the betrayal I had already committed against myself was being repeated in what I was doing to you. I had dreams once, Joshua, of becoming a writer. The glitz-and-glamour of a radio hostess was too much of a shallow existence for me. I wanted to plunge deep into my imagination: to write! I married your father thinking his wealth would give me the freedom, leisure, and security I needed to write. I realized quite soon that I did not love him and I despised all that he and his class represented. And soon after my marriage I knew I had sold myself to the highest bidder. It seems that while I waited for the right moment to end my marriage, a toxic lassitude, like lead or mercury leaching from the silver it's disguised in, filled my soul and blanked out my imagination. (We'll do well to inoculate ourselves against the ills of wealth.) And so the streams of my creativity dried up. Once I dreamed I was in a library and all the books began to jeer me, and as I tried to run, but couldn't, they leaped off the shelves and came after me. I needed no psychoanalyst to tell me what the dream meant. So it was no surprise, when your father died, that I found myself in a crisis. While trying to come out of it I saw that for a long time I too had become one of *those planter parasites, and in the process, my inner life, the place from which writing comes, had been choked to death, had been stifled into stillness. (Please forgive me, Joshua, for repeating myself.) It's true that sometimes I did speculate about returning to the US. Why didn't I? At first you know you are in a rut, and you think you are eager to get out of it. But you wait for the right moment, and while you are waiting you get distracted, and accustomed to being in it, and until something reminds you of your plight, you forget about it. In the end you resign yourself to it. When my mother died and I inherited her estate, I could have left. When I went to Tallahassee in 1946 to attend my mother's funeral, I was certain I wouldn't come back to Isabella Island. But two weeks in Tallahassee showed me that everywhere is a rut, that the rut is in us, in our psyches and in the psyches of those who force their wills on us. There is no escape; we are prisoners of society and ourselves. I came back and have been depending on my stoicism to take me to the end of my days. And sometimes stoicism fails me. And my dreams, in which I often discover that I'm a ghost, show me many things I dare not face while I'm awake. What a desert my soul has become! Arcadia is a fabulous place all right, where a woman must be Sheherazade to stay upright.*

Marriage had few compensations. Your father expected me, because I'm American, and because of the few brief encounters we'd had in New York, to be, in his words, "free from hang-ups." I would rather not get into what he meant by that. Unfortunately he'd never discussed any of this with me before we got married, and we were already married for more than a year when he revealed his special needs. Later he kept a mixed-race mistress in Hanovertown for that purpose, and must have compensated her well for her to endure so long. I accepted it all because I could not meet his needs. He never hid the fact of his mistress from me. He'd even suggested I get a lover, in one of the other islands, mind you, and on occasion get together with him there secretly.

I've known no one to get into a rage so easily and violently as he. He broke things when he got angry; whatever came into his hands he'd hurl against the wall. Then, regardless of the hour, he'd go riding. On his return it would be as if nothing had happened. I lived with this for fourteen years. Why? Was it because I came to understand, quite soon after marriage, what it means to be naked under our clothes? Almost everything we do, everything we acquire, is an attempt to hide that nakedness. Yet we never fully succeed. It is one reason so many take to alcohol.

But I should be fair to your father and let you know that he treated Gloria, his mistress of some twelve years, honorably. He left her enough insurance money to take care of her for a lifetime. In that way he was different from the lot that at times take over Arcadia. I found out after his death that his cronies used to tease him about her, but he had the honesty to admit that he needed her and the decency not to join with them and belittle the race she in part belongs to. Setting aside his sexual anomaly, I think he would have been a happy man in an egalitarian society. But he was not strong enough to oppose his class (few people are: I only know about three: Bertrand Russell, Leo Tolstoy, and Mahatma Gandhi), and your father's protest extended merely to marrying an American and maintaining a long-term, respectable, by West Indian standards, relationship with Gloria. Yet he was such a silent man! And so easily enraged!

I mustn't give you the impression that your father was a monster. Far from it. It was he who suggested that I give the servants a month's extra pay at Christmas and a ham. Of course they were not supposed to tell anyone about this. His fellow planters would not have been amused that he broke the ironclad agreement they have on wages. They were already angry enough with him for marrying me. He and I had a good Platonic relationship, so good that he'd at times tell me about his quarrels with Gloria. You no doubt have seen his collection of books about war in the bedroom adjoining mine, which became his after our intimate relations ceased. I'll confess I was never interested in them and could only listen politely when he shared his reading with me. He called my reading woman stuff, so I never spoke to him about my books. Just around the time his cancer was diagnosed, he was planning to sell the plantation, and we would have moved to some rural spot in Florida, somewhere that was within a short driving distance of Miami. But that was not to be; and after my last visit to Tallahassee, I'm glad it never happened, for I would not have been happy there. To Boston, maybe, but not Miami.

Since your father's death, I have felt like a ghost searching for its body to reconstruct its life. While he was alive my hatred for him, which I kept carefully hidden, propelled me. Even so, that went when he died. For a while I did wonder whether I would hate you, but the first time I observed you from afar, you melted my heart, and your coming to live at Arcadia gave me something to live for. I want your life to be different from mine. I want you to be true to yourself—as genuinely true to yourself as is humanly possible. I shall bequeath you your father's wealth and my own to protect you from the prostitution penury forces people into. Every penny of it! It's an inheritance I've paid for dearly. Your father, I suspect, would approve. (How he hated his class! That's why he married me. Can you believe it?) The Éclairs were firm believers in primogeniture. Wouldn't his brothers boil when it all comes to light!

Oh Joshua, I'm such a fake! I betrayed myself, betrayed my calling, committed the unpardonable sin against the Holy Ghost that Sparrow constantly prattles about but dimly understands. But I'm not a monster, Joshua. It would hurt me deeply were I to know you think me monstrous. I wouldn't be able to live with such knowledge.

I've often wished I could change the world I live in, but I cannot, and it is the only world there is for me to live in. I know no other and can invent no other. I know it's a world built on racist notions. We are questioning those notions now, but the world is founded on them, and I'm afraid the world is not in the business of dismantling.

Please bear with me. There are a couple of other things I must address, for when I set out to write this letter, I promised myself to be totally frank. This is the most difficult subject I have ever had to broach, even more so than the cause of my own barrenness—in every sense of the word—and one that I have never discussed with anyone, not even with my late husband, your father.

You remember my stopping you from going to church with Sparrow? Well, it was because I have always known about his inclinations. What I never suspected, could never have imagined, is that he might take advantage of you under my roof. I would not be exaggerating if I were to tell you that although he is not my brother, I have been as fond of him as you have been of Bita. He doesn't believe this; he even thinks I despise him, and sometimes I make him think I do. I asked him about it during your illness. He denied it. I think he is lying, but I told him I would be watching him. I'm still hoping that I'm wrong, that I'm accusing my cousin wrongly, and that is why I have not yet asked him to leave. Yet I'm afraid to find out that my suspicions might be true. I cannot bring myself to ask you, and I won't ask you while we're in the US. I think I'll give you this letter when we return to Isabella Island.

Another thing: Joshua, are you homosexual? Mrs Kevin and Mrs Manchester have been hinting that you are. I would prefer that you weren't, but I know that no one can turn a brown horse white. I want you to know that much as I would regret your being so, it would bother me only if it's bothering you. I'm sufficiently wise to know that a person doesn't choose which sex he is attracted to. All I want is for you to be frank with me about this, and for you to talk to me about it if it bothers you.

Joshua, in the package that's life, we get one or two things that we truly desire. But to have them we must endure the detested rest. I never thought I would live most of my life on a tiny Caribbean island with a population of just over a hundred thousand people. I laugh—bitterly—each time I remember that when I left Smith and went to work as a radio hostess in New York, I had thought cities the size of Boston too small for me.

I know that we cannot undo the wrongs we have done, but I would like to be able to make whatever amends I can. I would at least like you and me to talk candidly about these problems and the hurt they have caused.

Affectionately,
Mommy

In a different colour ink: blue—the New York part of the letter was in black ink—she'd scribbled an undated addendum, as if she'd reread her letter and found that it had left out something:

I belong, Joshua, to a race which, in its need to oppress, uses Blackness to designate subhumanity, much as the ancient Jews, themselves descendants of Canaanites—I'm part Jew—created the requisite myth to enslave the Canaanites. Necessity is indeed the mother of invention. I am sorry, Joshua—sorry. I have played by the rules of power. I'd hoped the books—those books again—I never wrote might have furthered the cause of human justice and dignity.

Joshua, I'm a coward. I know that even better than you who've seen my cowardice many times, seen me silent when I ought to tell that posse of parasites, liars, and thieves that time and again infest this house where to put their outhouse souls. How we clothe ourselves in lies—make them truth—to avoid, to circumvent, conceal our moral rot! I am digressing, perhaps because I'm afraid to say what I want to say, afraid that the filament of salvation that I want to believe is left in me may not be there. But I must clear my throat and say it. Joshua, I want to know, to know with certain certitude, before I die that you love me, without reserve, without qualification, the way a lamb loves its mother; with instinctive naturalness like leaves turning to light, like roots tending towards water. Oh, Joshua, if I could only feel, not necessarily hear, that you love me unconditionally, instinctively, I would feel redeemed, feel that in some small way my life has been worthwhile.

And the final passage, written with what seemed like a trembling hand at a later date:

I never gave you this letter. Why was I afraid that you'd turn it into a whip to flog me with? Why was I so afraid to let you into the darkness of my soul? Now that you are abroad I cannot send it, for it is useless unless I can register your reaction— be it hatred or forgiveness. Maybe when you return home on your summer holidays or when I make a trip to Britain. But perhaps having fled from me, you won't want to see me again while there's still breath in my body.

He was numb. He sat at the oak table he'd rented the flat with, and sentence after sentence of her letter replayed in his head. Later, a little calmer, he could visualize her writing the New York section, over several days, pulling at strands of her hair, then patting them back into place, getting up and pacing the hotel room and looking out the window—and whatever else she did whenever she was nervous. She would have had room service send her up a pitcher of lemonade, the way she would have asked Rose if she'd been at Arcadia. With that letter in her purse, they'd driven through the roadblocks the police had erected in Tallahassee that summer to prevent Blacks and their White supporters from integrating the city, and listened to her cousin spout her cracker liberalism. No wonder the trip ended six days early! What would her cousin have done if she'd found the letter? Used it to humiliate her? Would his life have been any different if he hadn't received this letter? It has added to his burdens. The last paragraph of the New York section always strikes him as cruel. It expresses so much lost potential.

Then there was her *"But one thing you can be sure of is that I love you like my own flesh and blood."* Yes to the point where she was too damn selfish to deal with the fallout a revelation of his father's identity would have caused, especially because she had given him the impression that she did not know. Whose certitude did she have in mind? Why was his opinion of no importance in such a matter? What was he? A dog or cat you took in and fed because its previous owner could not afford to? His trips to the psychologist's office in New York—were they trips to the vet? How did the Jim Crow milieu she grew up in explain her silence in such a crucial matter? With wealth she'd bribed her way out of the tortuous journey those who truly seek pardon must make. She'd have had his help through this journey— would she? Yes—and he would have had the occasion to see a genuine, perhaps altruistic side to her, and he was sure it would have burned away the bitterness that rooted in his psyche and grew. Maybe he might have convinced her to beg his mother's pardon on behalf of his father. His mother needed to have the hurt done to her acknowledged by the class responsible for it. That would have meant so much to him, and might have helped lessen the deep pain his mother most likely died with.

Instead Averill Éclair chose to ask her questions when she'd be no longer there to hear the answers, and left him with the burden of never answering. After her silence and deliberate deception, forgiveness was the last thing in the world that Averill Éclair Mann deserved.

Hindsight.

He remembers Paul's statement that death never prevented the wealthy from enforcing their will. He wonders if Paul fully understood the truth of his remark.

Seated on a bench beside Regents Canal a week after he'd read her letter, he wrote—

Power's

fortress

is stor(i) e (y)s of

bones. force and ideology guard

it. its music: the wails

and whimpers

of those it

wounds

starves

unclo

the

s

Was his assessment fair? At any rate it was written after her death, was triggered by her death, when he could no longer wound her, while she continued to wound him. Imagine, she'd let him have her letter when she would not have to deal with the issues it raised! *Yes, Averill, you were indeed weak—a very weak woman.*

By the time he got to Montreal, a few years later, his judgement had softened somewhat. He'd reflected on the iron-clad way in which she had made her will, and he was forced to admit that this was a woman who had cast aside the race bigotry she'd imbibed from her Tallahassee upbringing. Perhaps it was this that made her cousin Marjorie so spiteful. He saw why she'd resisted Ichabod's attempts—and he was sure there were others—to marry her after her husband's death. And she was astute even in the choice of her lawyer. A Black American married to an Isabellan MD was her attorney. She must have been aware that the local lawyers were beholden to the plantocracy and she couldn't trust them not to subvert the intentions of her will. Even so, he found it cruel that she'd left nothing for Dawn, Rose, or Henry. No doubt, she'd come to believe Mrs Manchester's assertion that Blacks can live on almost nothing. Yet she praised his father for his secret generosity. He promised he'd rectify this injustice but never did.

Our decisions are motivated by self-interest regardless of how they're clothed, he thinks now. Mommy did not give him that letter because she couldn't risk having her suspicions of Sparrow confirmed. Would he have told her the truth? No. He wouldn't have told her. He was so ashamed of himself then for what he'd been involved in. It was over before she wrote the letter, before his breakdown even. After the Mardi Gras night when Sparrow awakened with his bedsheet already ablaze. And Joshua had dared him to tell Mommy about the attempted fire. Two days later Sparrow placed bolts on the inside of both doors leading from his bedroom. In any event Mommy had probably come to the conclusion, unconsciously, that he would soon be away studying, and dismissing Sparrow, sending him back to the US, would have meant spending the rest of her life alone on Isabella Island without relatives, among her superficial, parasite planter "friends."

No. He wouldn't have told her. Those who give loincloths to naked emperors get hanged for too much sight and too little foresight.

And as to accepting his homosexuality, such information was useless after her death. It would have been beneficial when his character was still being moulded, when he needed to have his doubts allayed, when he needed to be told he was not a disease. At the very least he would have put the burden down when he was with her. And outside of home it would have been less difficult to carry for the simple fact that at home he hadn't borne it. *Mommy, why did you deprive me of that? Why? It would have helped to know there was one being who didn't think I was a disease. With your and Bita's acceptance the rest of the world could have gone to hell. Instead I felt loaded down in your presence, and even when I was asleep. Always some nightmare of being beaten by some man whose crotch I'd stared at. In one nightmare you walked away when I called out to you to help me.* In his only such nightmare in which Bita figured, she had walked in on him and Sparrow and had held Sparrow's own handgun to his temple. The next night Joshua decided to set Sparrow on fire in his bed.

Then he didn't think her death would break him. Not even when the nightmares began to come, but those came after the will and her letter. And it forever ended the ambivalence he'd felt about revealing his racial makeup. *The nightmares!* He hadn't attended Bita's funeral; so missing hers was no big deal. And those Florida relatives—that they, seething with bigotry, might embrace him was more than he could stand at the time. That, at least, was the reason he'd finally settled for: the one he had given Sparrow. After reading her letters he was glad he did not go. Marjorie would have probably told them to prevent him from entering the church.

Before her death he'd been afraid that she would judge him if he hadn't achieved and made her proud. In her way she laughed at the pretensions of the different planter families on the island. Had a little sympathy for Mrs Blenkinsopp and loved her independence, which was a great deal more than she had for any of the others. Not for Amanda though. "Better to marry poor and bright than dumb and rich." Beyond the price of sugar, arrowroot, coconuts, and cotton, she said, they knew nothing. Except in the rarest of cases, their children rode horses, sailed from island to island in their yachts, gave orders, played tennis, fornicated, drank, and despised all who couldn't or wouldn't do like them. The exceptions were a Manchester who'd studied medicine and went in the fifties to practise in Australia, probably because at the time Australia prohibited non-White immigration; and Ovid Sinclair, who'd as good as exploded a stink bomb in their shrine when he married a Eurafrican woman and took the son he'd had by one of the servants to live with him. And when the manager of the Plantocrats' Club—the same club where Mommy had bawled the doorkeeper out—refused to admit his son, Ovid broke the manager's jaw. For a while it looked as if they would chase Ovid into exile. But he was more than a match for them. She did not want Joshua to be like them. It did not matter to her what he studied, what he became, she said, as long as he liked it and went on to get as many degrees as he wanted in it. She herself had done a degree in English. Now she was dead, he didn't even have to get a single degree. And he didn't, for other reasons.

Can he forgive her? What is forgiveness? Is it when you no longer wish vengeance for a wrong you've suffered? Or is it when you pity the person who has wronged you? Were her decisions misguided? They were definitely determined in part by racism: that desire to consolidate and hold on to power on the basis of race or caste, and to perpetuate the inequality that makes the keeping of such power possible. And in part by the times she lived in. Still she left him with her several questions, and the undelivered answers are a burden.

Can someone be fed by injustice and be just? He cannot answer this question about her. Probably because it would force him to see where the sums he inherited from her and his father are invested. He would like to close the case but he has not forgiven her; and, on one level, he wonders whether what he deems her transgressions are not really transgressions in the overall human scheme of things.

In the case of his biological mother, the question of forgiveness ceased to be an issue. After Aunt Stacey's revelation, hating her would have been absurd—cruel. But he understood that she was a phenomenon he had to run from, the way he would run from a fire he could not put out. From the half million dollars that Mommy had left him in a flexible trust from her personal fortune, he arranged for land to be bought and a simple but comfortable house built for Mammy—with a kitchen, bathroom, living room and two bedrooms—and for an annual stipend of US$6, 000 to be paid to her in monthly remittances. But he made sure that no one on Isabella Island, apart from the attorney and Sparrow, could communicate with him.

He knows now that it was mostly his bad conscience over what had happened to Bita that had pushed him to do this. Many times when he should have been working on his assignments, or while on his solitary walks along the Regents Canal or the back streets of Tower Hamlets, he'd be thinking of how able he was now to have made a difference in Bita's life, and he would compose a picture of her from her mannerisms—her head cupped in her hands, contemplating the stretch of dreary years unrolling before her like infinity, her dignity and freedom like balls of crumpled paper in a rubbish bin, superfluous, stripped from her so that her body could be clothed and fed; her youth a pack horse pulling Skeeter's aged body; his whip cracking when she displeased him.

Now that she was no longer around, he was in a position to help her. She couldn't have known that one day he would be wealthy. Besides, in her eyes his being wealthy did not mean that he would relieve her poverty; in fact, it meant the exact opposite: being wealthy and White-skinned meant that he should have disowned her.

Even before he left Isabella Island, he'd been wondering whether his breakdown at her death had not been made worse because he'd felt ashamed of her—too ashamed to want to get close to her—after he'd understood why she had gone to live with Skeeter. He'd been too young to understand the flimsy basis on which he had judged her. And on top of that he'd had his own battles surviving within Sparrow's clutches—even after the Mardi Gras fire he'd always felt Sparrow was biding his time to resume—and bearing the burden of his homosexuality. He did not even know then who his father was and was afraid to find out lest it confirm his fear that his mother had been a whore.

It's the ways of humans—not God—that are past finding out. On that score the psalmist got it wrong. He has ordinary dreams about his biological mother, about Sparrow too, but never about Averill Éclair. A bizarre phenomenon. It wasn't she who'd tried to drown him. Given how Sparrow took advantage of his innocence, he doesn't understand why in the dreams in which Sparrow now figures he is usually in Sparrow's car being driven from one plantation squatter village to another.

Despite the nightmares, he'd settled down after her death and even socialized a little. Paul was especially good to him during December and January. Their friendship deepened as a result. He especially remembers one Sunday morning in May '67—Paul had slept over the Saturday night—when they walked along Regents Canal, beginning at Mile End Road, along the side of Victoria Park, through Clapton and into Islington. At New North Road, where the gardens at the back of the houses came all the way down to the water's edge, he and Paul spent a lot of time admiring the flowers. Near Angel Station, at Paul's insistence, they jumped over a shoulder-high fence and went to have coffee and scones in a nearby café.

By late '67 Joshua was expecting to get at least an upper second, and by spring 1968 he was sending out applications for admission to law school, including one to the newly opened law faculty at Queen Mary. The only cloud in his life was his discovery that he had to be whipped to have orgasms. It left him sleepless whenever he pondered it, for he feared that in some way it was linked to what Mommy had mysteriously called his father's sexual anomaly. It was while he was in the throes of this that news of Sparrow's death came.

His mind returns to the present. His hands are sweating. Nowadays whenever his thoughts turn to Sparrow, they're not easy to quell. He notes that it's 3:17 P.M.. Should he ask them for a tranquilizer, one that would knock him out? What if Defoe comes and begins to question him? He lifts his hands and examines them. Sweat's dripping off them. *Those things happened over thirty years ago. Why can't I bury them?*

13

IT IS A SPRINGLIKE DAY though it is only February 14. The February 14 fact is underscored because of the Valentine's Day fuss on the ward. They'd insisted that every patient come to the common room and share in something or the other—the handing out of chocolates probably. Hope it doesn't make too many of them psychotic. He stopped eating chocolate since he was fourteen because of what Sparrow had done with it. Now anything containing chocolate nauseates him.

He tells them he doesn't want to go. They go on and on about why he should go. You would think that in a psychiatric hospital they would understand the diversity of human personalities. But in the long run you realize that the whole business—and it's a business—of therapy and wellness is about some sort of banal, predictable conformity. If those who engineer society could have their way, we'd all be programmed like dolphins in an aquarium, all but the programmers. Not so long ago those who refused the bidding of the powerful classes were hitched to horses headed in opposite directions and pulled until they severed their limbs: quartering they called it. Crippling conformity. At the appointed time, 2:30, he makes sure that he's asleep, and Gladys Knights does not wake him. He couldn't fault her judgment in such things.

Shortly after the nurses change shifts at four, he decides to make use of his newly acquired privilege to take unescorted walks about the grounds. Before, he could only do so accompanied by Leroy, and he works days. The evening staff member assigned to him is also assigned to several other patients. Joshua prefers not to be herded outside or in one of the two common rooms with six or seven psychotic or semi-psychotic patients. Mr McKenna (he prefers to be called Percy but Joshua chooses to be formal with him), the nursing assistant assigned to him for the evening shift, is a gruff behemoth from Nova Scotia. He wheezes: loud when excited, a low whistle when calm. He sniffs and pulls his nose several times per minute when people are present. Away from people he neither sniffs nor pulls his nose. Alone or with others he chews his nails. He has glowing green eyes— as if all that's beautiful in him were concentrated there—in a tallowy moony face. The upper half of his right cheek is covered by a strawberry birthmark. He is the only member of staff who wears a white uniform so— Joshua thinks, and hates himself for the cruelty of the thought—he'd be distinguishable from the patients. He speaks like a slowed-down record except when he's disgruntled. Then his wheeze becomes a rattle, his voice a whistle, his speech a train at full throttle, and his twang a squawk. When he walks—a penguin strut—he swings his arms from left to right with a chopping motion. Something about him evokes fear in Joshua, and he wonders whether his revulsion has anything to do with the vague superstitions he had absorbed from Bita about people whose birthmarks and oddities endow them with evil powers. His unkind thoughts about McKenna fill him with guilt. He makes sure he's reading whenever McKenna rocks his unballasted self into his room to suggest some sort of group activity.

He decides to walk to the boardwalk along the river and back. The grounds at the front of the hospital are spacious too but, in their superabundance of trees, they're the exact opposite of the back. From their bark, height, and shape he thinks most of them are elms, oaks, and maples with some willows scattered among them. He tries to imagine what the front looks like in summer when the trees are in leaf and the ground is grass-covered. Must be quite a haven for birds too. Across from LaSalle Boulevard there is the river, lakelike in its expanse. He continues west and comes upon where the river flows swiftly and noisily. Elsewhere it's mostly clogged with ice. This must be what's called the Lachine Rapids. While watching it he thinks of downhill flows, roaring drunkenness, degradation, degeneracy, destruction, baseness, phlegmatism, flatness. An uphill struggle. Where there's no struggle, no struggle to scale heights, transcendence is missing and dissolution lurks. *I must not give up the struggle to get well. I must not.*

None of the possible nerve complications resulting from his amputated toes seem to have materialized. He no longer needs the cane. Maybe it has to do with the long walks he has been in the habit of taking up to Mount Royal on as many days as the weather permitted him. In winter it's usually along Sherbrooke Street to Parc LaFontaine. On exceptionally cold days he'd take the Metro back. He'd made George's acquaintance that way. He misses the walks since he has been cooped up here. He had undoubtedly gone for one such walk when the mysterious incident that landed him here took place. He wonders what it was, whether he would ever recall what he was doing immediately before his loss of memory.

He is surprised by how unseasonably comfortable it feels. There isn't the faintest hint of a breeze. The snow is banked high on both sides of the path that leads to the riverbank, and has the grey grimy colour of February snow. In his mind it's associated with old age, each fresh coat a temporary facelift or paintjob. There's nothing on Isabella Island he could compare winter to, not even the dry season, because things can and do grow there during the dry season and there is always some rain. The air now has a clean crisp smell that makes him think of ozone. Crows alight and fly off the ground.

His mind returns to a conversation with Leroy shortly after breakfast. He'd asked him if Gladys Knights has a boyfriend.

Leroy said that she is "spinstered."

Joshua laughed and asked him if it meant she hasn't been splintered.

"No."

"She should be a nun."

"She *was* a nun."

"Be serious! She wears lipstick and perfume."

Leroy nodded. "Maybe that is the reason she not a nun no more."

"Well, that doesn't mean she's a spinster. Besides she can't be, she is married to Jesus. The Catholic Church does not recognize divorce."

"Jesus don't want wife." Leroy put his hand to his mouth quickly, to unsay what he'd said. "Keep what I tell you to yourself. She don' like fee talk about it."

"And here I was thinking she had a boyfriend and a girlfriend, and they all live happily in a gingerbread house and sleep in the same king-size bed with a red counterpane."

Leroy's eyes squinted, his face grew taut. "You take your pills this morning?"

Joshua nodded. Leroy seemed unconvinced.

"Well Gladys Knights looks after my health and Christ looked after hers—for a while at any rate. Guess when nobody wants you, there's always Jesus. Leroy, why don't you help her out? You're a lot more substantial than the holy spirit. Offer her a little warmth. It would be a most Christian thing. 'Inasmuch as ye have done it unto one of these least my brethren ye have done it unto me.' That's Christ's commandment, Leroy. Never mind Blassingame and your church. Compassion is the greater virtue. Did you hear me, Leroy?"

"Hear what, Mr Éclair: your blasphemous talk?" He sucked his teeth with loud impatience.

Now his body feels overheated from the walk. He unzips his coat, moves apart the flaps, and lets the cold air reach his body.

There's something he has to consider. Tomorrow they want to inject him with drugs and subject him to some sort of chemical hypnosis.

"Why do you want to do this?" he asked Defoe.

"Because you prevent us from assembling the information we need to diagnose what brings on your amnesia. You were a good deal more honest before you became lucid."

Joshua pondered this but did not reply.

"You refuse to give us a next of kin, or a friend or someone we could turn to—somebody with power of attorney."

"Why do you need such a person?"

"To authorize your treatment."

"Why can't *I* authorize it?"

"Will you sign the forms then?"

"I don't think so. Not based on what you've told me."

"We could argue, you know, that you're incapable of making responsible decisions vis-a-vis your own treatment."

"And if I sue you afterwards? You've both said I'm not psychotic."

"We could . . ." Dr Defoe stopped.

"—change the diagnosis! Really, Dr Defoe! After this, I will never sign anything."

"Let's not be confrontational. It won't help your recovery. I expect you to sign the form tomorrow morning. Think about it before you go to bed tonight. Why're you smiling?"

"The way you talk, Dr Defoe, a stranger to this earth would think that I'm paid for your voyeuristic pleasure." He turned his head away. "After you've poked and probed and cracked open my psyche like an egg whose yolk you think holds some special secret, will I be privy to what you find?"

"No. And your psyche is no egg."

"I'm not entitled to know what's in *my* psyche, but you are! Get lost, Dr Defoe!"

"Well, we'll proceed against your wishes."

"And this evening I'll call my lawyer."

"Suppose we suspend your phone privileges."

"What do you mean?"

"Never mind. Just stop being so paranoid. You're not psychotic."

"You trust your own diagnoses? Under hypnosis are you going to order me to stop forgetting who I am?"

"We're not in Hollywood."

"Psychiatry is Hollywood. I have to see the questions you'll ask me."

"Sorry. We won't show them to you. You'll use them to play games with us."

"You mean I can't see the questions beforehand and strike out the ones I don't like? A friend—an acquaintance really—I once had here, a writer, used to ask journalists desirous of interviewing him to submit their questions beforehand. Questions he didn't like he crossed out, and questions he thought should be there he wrote in."

"What's the name of your acquaintance?"

"I knew you would ask me that. I invented him. One of those characters, you know, that people create when they talk about their problems in the third person." But he was lying. Or was he? It was during the brief period that he'd been thinking of creating fiction. In any event, invented or not, the acquaintance taught creative writing at Concordia. He'd graduated to telling journalists to imagine his answers. The radio and TV journalists said it wouldn't work. He suggested they get their colleagues to act his part. By the time his third novel was published, the message on his answering machine included, "If you are a journalist, don't leave your name and number. I'll call you." He ceased talking for a while, stared at Dr Defoe, and sensed a fellow feeling that he knew was bizarre. Perhaps because of the . . . —he couldn't find the word. To distract himself he said, "So, Dr Defoe, we patients are, for all intents and purposes, dolphins in the Douglas Aquarium? To crawl or not to crawl—is that the question, Dr Defoe?"

"No, that's not it."

"What's it then: crawl willingly or be starved?"

"Let's get back to the subject."

"Which is?"

"That if you want to get well you have to cooperate with us."

"Dr Defoe, you make me sick. . . sicker, I mean."

"Tomorrow, we'll be adding a new psychiatrist to the team. A Dr Blenheim."

"Is this Blenheim a man or a woman?"

"Why?"

"It matters."

Defoe frowned. "Meaning?"

"Men." He shrugs. "Bulldozers. Conquerors. Lovers of guns, tanks, missiles, bombs. Keepers of slaves and harems. Measuring success in rubble, corpses, theft, orgasms, penis size." He spoke with his face averted, glancing at Defoe's occasionally. "If you had your way women would be reduced to making babies, males mostly, future warriors. Men," he said with derision. "Tomcats on the prowl for territory and sex. I'm saying nothing that beer, car, and cigarette advertisers don't know."

Defoe seemed half amused but said nothing.

"Say something! Dammit! You have a tongue. One of flesh, at least."

"You exclude yourself from men?"

"I'm not a man, Dr Defoe. Certainly not according to you Hemingway he-men types. Did you know Hemingway never consented to having his voice recorded? That's right." He nodded slowly. "It was high-pitched and he hated it and did his best to hide it."

"There are three female psychiatrists on staff here, and nowadays nearly half of all the students in med school are women."

"Following a curriculum that turns them into menstruating men. Right? Men should stay away from psyches. They call orgasm death and death orgasm. Did you know that vagina is the Latin word for scabbard? Try asking a Frenchman to show you his bayonet."

"Let's get back to Dr Blenheim," he said, smiling in spite of himself.

"Is Blenheim male, female—or androgynous?"

He laughed. "Male. Not the fanciful kind you've been going on about. I rather suspect the two of you will get along. He is passionate about literature and mythology. We'll still be part of your treatment team."

"That's good. I want you to stay. I'm comfortable with you, even if you're a man. I might even cooperate with you when I'm able to. Will Blenheim help me net Proteus and keep him netted?"

Defoe smiled. "Sounds like you need a he-man therapist after all. You'll find out."

"Would Blenheim want Doctor Stein on the team? I'm just kidding. Stein's alright."

"But you won't mind if he leaves?"

"Or if he stays."

"Well, he alone will determine that."

"I know. Dr Defoe, you have a genius for saying the wrong thing."

"And you never miss a chance to notice it. See, we're on an equal footing." He extended an open palm, obviously expecting Joshua to slap it.

He never slaps palms with anyone, has always been suspicious of the solidarity it connotes—or the condescension it hides—but he slapped Defoe's, easily, gladly.

After Defoe left, he wondered why he'd ranted so much. Did he believe what he'd just said about men? And all the fuss to make him well? What is being well? Why all the anxiety—his own and others'? What is it? Why do we want to stay alive? This mystery we call life. Mammy had advised him to count his blessings and praise God and leave the unknown alone. Which part of her life did she consider blessed? *"Thank God for his sparing mercy, daughter, [son] thank Him"*—was an automatic part of the call-response daily greeting Petit Bordellians called out to another. Gratitude for being alive— they of all people.

So much of our lives is spent in a fog, he thinks. All uncertain answers.

Fog had fascinated him before he went to live at Arcadia. He'd imagined it was the blanket that *El Tigre* covered itself with before going to sleep. On days when *El Tigre* was uncovered, he stared at it, hoping that he would catch it unrolling and pulling on the blanket. He'd wondered what happened when it rained: whether *El Tigre* liked water the way fish did. It couldn't seek shelter, like goats and chickens, and he. It was fixed like the trees. Poor thing, it couldn't walk about. He never could make up his mind whether the trees liked rain and wind. They cried out aloud, it seemed to him, when wind and rain lashed them, and he had seen once where the wind broke off some of their branches and where sap was dripping from the wounds; he'd thought then that if he were left outside in it, the wind would blow off one or more of his limbs or his head, and he became afraid of the wind. But he never told Bita this. Bita said that trees loved the rain; her teacher had told her it was how they got their food. Bita was sure too that it was how they got their bath. If he didn't have his bath he'd stink like his kaka, Bita said. Would the trees stink if rain didn't fall? One time when it hadn't rained for about three days, he'd smelled the bark of the golden apple tree at Miss Boucher's gate. He could not make up his mind whether it was or wasn't stink.

In second grade he learned that the green colouring in the leaves along with the light of the sun and the things that roots suck out of the ground and send up to the leaves mixed together in some sort of way to become food for the trees. He'd asked his teacher, a very nice man who never flogged his pupils, if the leaves complained when the roots didn't do a good job. His classmates laughed. The teacher smiled and said he didn't know, but that maybe the leaves would be afraid to complain, that without the roots the leaves wouldn't be able to stay up in the air, off the ground. He'd thought then of the roots living in the ground, in darkness and doing the dirty work. He was sure they complained, like the servants at Arcadia did when they thought no one was listening.

He discussed it all with Mommy, except the servant bit. She beamed, her eyes got bright, and her cheeks carnation pink. Her face always became one big smile whenever he discussed his schoolwork with her. She taught him the words photosynthesis and chlorophyll then. He asked her how did humans know so much about trees seeing that trees couldn't talk, and she said there were machines that could measure the feelings of trees in the currents they gave off, and scientists could tell from that whether trees were happy or unhappy. "They are living things, and we must be kind to them."

"Is Henry kind to the flowers?" he asked her, seeing in his mind the clipping action of his shears, hearing the snip-snip of his cutting.

She'd thought for a while before saying yes, because dead leaves and dead flowers can cause plants to get sick. At some point she'd hugged him and said she was glad he asked questions and paid attention to what goes on in nature and around him.

El Tigre. When he first arrived at Arcadia, they told him that mountains weren't alive. He lost interest in *El Tigre* then. Later he had a picture book with real tigers, knew they had sharp teeth and loved meat. From Blake's "Tiger," which Elizabeth recited to him, he always understood "the burning bright in the forests of the night." He'd seen how cats' eyes looked when a torch was shone into them. She should have recited it to Mommy, he thinks now. Elizabeth didn't understand it. But undoubtedly Mommy could. Mommy would have understood too some of the stories Henry told him, especially the one about Sis Hen. He wonders whether she would have fired Henry after hearing it.

"*Master Joshua, Sis Hen and her little chicklets-them was grovelling in a field behind her house one time, and up comes Brother Mongoose. He says to Sis Hen,*

"*'You don't have no business grovelling here, and 'cause you is trespassing, I 's going to eat you.'*

"*'I is tired o' injustice. This field belongs to all of us,' Sis Hen tell him, thinking to sheself she should try to pick out Brother Mongoose eyes before he get a chance to harm her; meanwhile she forcing she wings so much to cover she chicklets-them that did done run under them when Brother Mongoose show up that they paining she. 'Brother Mongoose, I think we must settle this in a court o' law. The land belongs to all of us,'" she tell him, playing brave.*

"*Brother Mongoose agree.*

"*The day o' the trial Sis Hen show up in court, her feathers-them glistening. She was pretty, Sis Hen. In she mind she keep thinking 'bout what Brother Rooster tell her when she ask him to accompany her to the trial.*"

"*What did Brother Rooster tell her?*" Joshua asked.

"*I don't remember. Honestly, I don't.*

"*Well Sis Hen she was plenty surprised when she see that the judge was a Mongoose, and the jury so look like Brother Mongoose, they had to be his brothers and sisters. Same thing for the hangman; she suspect was his cousin.*

"*Sis Hen stated her case. She wasn' one that stumble and get mixed up easy. No sir. Except that while she talking she hear a noise coming from the jury bench, and she turn and see that the jury fall asleep and some o' them snoring.*

"His Honour Judge Mongoose hit the gavel and the jury wake up and shout, 'Guilty!'

"'Unjust. I going to appeal to . . .'

"But Brother Hangman Mongoose paws was already around she throat. He strangle her right there in the courthouse. They pick her feathers. They eat her flesh. They crack open she bones and suck the marrow."

Henry never said what became of her chicklets. *What had Brother Rooster told her?*

As he turns in the entrance to the hospital, his thoughts return to the writer with the egregious message on his answering machine, to the story's lack of verisimilitude. Could it be an attempt at fiction? A hallucination? The writer's own? His? What's hallucination and what's reality? He distinctly hears in his head, thirty-two years later, Professor Killam reading Wallace Stevens's "The Snowman." Killam's eyes behind lenses like liqueur glasses; his facial skin looking like pocked, centuries-old acid paper; his quavering, cracked, andropausal voice bringing the snow man to life. *". . . For the listener, who listens in the snow, / And nothing himself, beholds / Nothing that is not there and the nothing that is."*

He oscillates slowly and scans the acres of snow studded by the dark-grey, dark-brown cadavers of leafless trees that front the southern pavilions all the way to LaSalle Boulevard, as if he too expects to see *the nothing that is not there and the nothing that is.*

The nothing that is there and the nothing that is not. What is reality, he hears himself wondering for the umpteenth time. What is it? Where did it originate? How many of his own memories are hallucinations? Not the seeing-things-that-aren't-there hallucinations, rather the kind that are an unconscious rearrangement of the facts so they'll accord with his needs. Perhaps we are no more than protagonists—puppets where we have no agency—in someone else's unscripted drama. Which is he? The question comes before he can censor it. He must not try to answer it. But his mind is tyrannical. He tries to suppress it but instead wonders if this were Mommy recalling her life, how he'd be represented. Has he been fair to her? Has he been sitting in judgment over her? What does it mean to judge someone? We're fated to spend ourselves making judgments, failing which we'd die quite young. Could Jesus have been serious when he advised us not to judge others? Perhaps the confusion is in the translation: from Aramaic to Greek to Latin and eventually English. In the beginning was the word. A treacherous structure on a quicksand foundation. He feels eerily light-headed and panic-stricken as he opens the door of Douglas Hall and descends hurriedly into the tunnel that leads to Reed, the pavilion he is hospitalized in.

He returns just in time for supper. His left foot is pulsing with pain; he has overexerted himself. Bonita Ramon resents it that he eats supper in his room. Yesterday she asked him why he doesn't eat in the cafeteria like everyone else. In her tone he thought he heard, *Do you think you are special?* and he replied in kind: "Because I pay not to have to." *Do you begrudge me the services I pay for?*

An hour later Bonita Ramon arrived with two pink pills in a medicine cup. She swishes her hips and has full round breasts. Joshua had a strong temptation to pinch her buttocks, knowing he could get away with it here. Instead he told her, "I don't need them."

"It's the doctor's orders for you when you are upset."

"Are they? They are bootiful!" He mimicked an imaginary child. "Bootiful, bootiful, bootiful," he sang to the tune of *This is the way we brush our clothes . . . so early in the morning,* and watched her jaws clamping.

Her name tag reads Bonita Ramon, IL. "The last word on your name tag is misspelt. An L is missing."

"No, it's not." She has trouble pronouncing the English I. "It means 'infirmière licenciée.'"

"No, it means 'ill, licentiously ill.' Mais ça ne dérangera personne, si vous serez licenciée."

Her eyes narrowed, her forehead furrowed.

To mollify her, he continued in a sugary tone, "¿Eres mi bonita, mi amora? ¿Quieres ser mi esposa?"

He saw he had confused her. Here anything goes. You could metamorphose. An imprisonment and freedom not possible outside of madness, unless you're the fellow who lives in the apartment facing him.

"Don't be so smug, Nurse Ramon. The madness that's roaring in me is asleep in you. Had the dice rolled differently, you'd be me, and I'd be you."

As if to disarm him she nodded.

But he continued, "*You* are upset, Nurse Ramon, because I eat in my room. Take my pills, they'll calm you down."

"If you keep this up I will have to restrain you and give you a needle."

"Don't upset yourself, Nurse Ramon. Llamas Bonita. Debes ser bastante bonita en todo tiempo. ¿Verdad? You're too nice, too pretty to upset your patients. In nursing school they definitely taught you not to upset your patients. Where were you trained, Nurse Ramon? Here or in the Philippines?"

He watched her lower jaw fall, the tension leaving her face. Knew he had won. "You are all right, Nurse Ramon. We're all entitled to get upset: you probably because you're overworked, I because I've lost my freedom and my sanity."

He was relieved to see her leave.

Even here, he thinks to himself now, you have to walk a tightrope between preserving your dignity and brown-nosing.

He thinks of tomorrow. He knows they'll railroad him into hypnosis. Very little difference exists between himself and a quadriplegic: he and they are at the mercy of caregivers. He could give them shit but in their arsenal are the invincible syringe and diagnosis.

His anxiety is mounting. Maybe he should ask for the pills Bonita tried to give him the evening before. If the anxiety keeps up he'll have no choice.

When he falls asleep he dreams that Bita is visiting him. "You're only now coming to visit me? I have been sick for several weeks," he tells her. She is dressed in white like when she attended Sparrow's church, in the womanly shape she'd acquired by then.

"You didn't come to my funeral," she tells him.

"I wasn't allowed to."

Somewhere the dream gets mixed up. They are picnicking on one of Isabella Island's privately owned beaches. Randolph Kevin, staring away from the others and with his mouth half open as usual, Alexander Manchester and his brother Vincent are there along with several of the families who sometimes visited at Arcadia. Bita is there too, the only visibly Black person in the group. He wonders how's it she hadn't been stopped at the entrance to the beach. Alexander Manchester's hand is on one of Bita's breasts and she is giggling. Mrs Manchester is sitting just ahead of them. Joshua feels like killing both of them. He would like to accost Bita and call her a whore to her face. Then he remembers that once Alexander had snuggled up behind him with an erection and had come in his trousers. Oh God, he thinks, he'll give her AIDS. He'd better warn her. He tries to scream, "He's bisexual. He may have AIDS." But the sound sticks in his throat. Then there's vagueness followed by a loud scream. He turns around looking for Bita and she is nowhere to be seen. Just as it is dawning on him that the cry had something to do with her drowning, he awakens.

The dream perplexes him, especially the link that his unconscious has made with same-gender sexuality and AIDS.

The building makes a loud shiver, like a body coming out of a cold shower. It must have turned cold outside. His body has chased away sleep. He sits up and decides to read the latest copy of *Emerge*. Nowadays, accompanied by Leroy, he goes to his apartment once a week to collect his mail. This issue was in the last pile. He hopes the night nurse doesn't see the glare and come to turn off the light. He already feels his stomach knotting as he thinks of how he will argue with her, telling her that's why he's in a private room. Eventually she'd ignore his wishes because she has power and he does not. But no one disturbs him until the night supervisor, accompanied by the night nurse, does her morning rounds.

An article in *Emerge* making the case for Black reparations sets him thinking that such compensation would bankrupt the capitalist system. An academic exercise, he tells himself. First Blacks must have powerful armies, navies, and air forces equipped with nuclear weapons before their claims would be taken seriously. The platitudes the Occident spouts as it slowly starves Iraqis into submission don't fool him. The call for Reparations would be one more reason for the West to keep Africa weak. It has always been about who produces raw materials at slave wages and buys finished goods at extortionate prices. All talk about changing the model is legerdemain.

He thinks that Éclair Estate belonged to the hands who worked on it. He remembers the insults the servants traded when their frustrations became unbearable. Dawn sometimes told Rose, who dyed her hair—it was usually chocolate brown near the roots and black at the tips—that it wouldn't prevent people from knowing she had been a stowaway on the Ark.

Rose would answer that being on the Ark meant she was holy, but if Dawn wanted to talk about age, it was time she changed her name to Dusk. She'd go on to say that when Dawn began working at Arcadia she did not now even know she should wear drawers. "I taught you everything you know, even how to stay clean. What is my thanks? You strip the feathers off of the bird and throw them away, and want me for tell you what kind it is—giving me basket for carry water! Ungrateful bitch!" She spoke near-perfect English and was very proud of it, though it lapsed when she was cursing or gossiping. "Talk sense, you hear me?" she told Dawn once. "Eh-eh! You confounded. Don' tell me you been one o' those God strike at the Tower o' Babel!"

"I confounded but nobody certain if you is man or 'oman. You don' got children, you don' got a man, and your voice just like a man. What else your frock hiding that only man got?"

Joshua laughed. They took note of him and stopped.

Another time Dawn said that when Rose died they'd have to wrap her in lime and put her in a sealed lead coffin to prevent her from poisoning the earth.

"At least I will rot, but you won't need burial. They will keep you on show as the body that is too evil to rot."

Dawn digested that one for a while before countering, "And you, you not going dead. God done answer Satan prayer for have mercy on him and keep you outta hell."

When Rose ran out of comebacks, the veins on her craglike forehead would bulge and her left eye would twitch, and she would sing: "*Yield not to tempation, for yielding is sin. Each victory will help you some other to win . . .*" but would interrupt the singing as soon as she thought of something stinging to say.

On occasions when the tension mounted between them, Dawn would say, "Stop hegging me, else I will drop two words 'pon you, your drawers string will bruck—if you wearing drawers." Joshua would shake with laughter as he imagined this happening to Rose, Rose's mouth shocked open, her eyes like boiled eggs. They chased him from the kitchen area when they discovered him. At first he'd leave, but he soon knew servants were powerless (though he never said it, to them or to anyone) and ignored them.

He always sided with them in their complaints about how poorly they were paid. He must have linked them to Bita in some way. Pine Knot's bragging about emptying his revolver in his two attackers always left Joshua wishing the attackers had succeeded.

They didn't always take it out on themselves. They had a lot to say about *Bacra*.

"Them bad-mouth us, child; rob we and all kind o' thing. But when them want a good screw is who them turning to? Nigger 'oman! And is pointless to tell them no. Them take it."

Joshua was standing near the steps that led out of the kitchen. Rose was standing at the kitchen counter peeling carrots, her back partially turned to him. Dawn was out of his line of vision.

"Well, that's 'cause nigger tail sweet."

"You mean 'cause *Bacra* got the devil in them!"

"But the 'oman them don't does screw nigger men."

"Hah-hah-hah!" Rose laughed and grabbed her sides. "Give me that stool near you. Sit down too. Lemme tell you story. You know Hackshaw the druggist? He look White to you? He is Emmanuel Éclair brother, me dear. Born right here. In this very house. When that child born, Joseph Éclair beat his wife! He beat her. Beat her black and blue. Beat her so doctor had to come and attend her—even for long years afterward doctor had to attend her—for force her for tell him the father's name. Tiny woman with big, sad blue eyes that stare at you pitiful. Full lips, and dark brown hair. When she comb it out it come down to her waist. Quiet woman. Never give the servants trouble. I was a strip of a girl then. Of course, we did all know what been going on. Child, Averill Éclair know what she been doing when she tear down the servants' quarters. When Joseph Eclair in Bella sugar-bowl, the chauffeur use to be in here carrying his wife to all the places he couldn't take her. All the same, we didn't know if spite was in it, because one time Joseph Éclair did come in from somewhere on his horse and see the car out front all dirty, and he call the chauffeur and crack his horsewhip three times over his back, and leave him there without saying a word. A week after that child born the chauffeur light out o' here for Trinidad. He was family to Henry wife's people.

"She was smart though. She did know her husband would o' never been able for live down the scandal, that he had to hush it up. They pay Ma Hackshaw—she done dead and gone, before your time—for adopt the child. Child, Dr Hackshaw is Emmanuel Éclair brother. And Emmanuel Éclair got three more bastard brothers and a sister—from his father side—Bella's children.

"I agree with you *Bacra* women can't do it in the open 'cause they don't have the power for get away with it. But tricks got power that power don't know a damn thing about. Child, what eye no see heart no grieve. And pleasure sweet—Lord, it sweet—when you use tricks for get it."

She and Dawn laughed, a cackling laugh, and she turned and winked at Dawn. Dawn cackled a second time.

Dawn loved to get under Rose's skin, mostly in the lull between lunch and supper. At times Rose took the bait and other times she didn't.

"You always talking 'bout who the Éclairs-them screw, how come them never screw you?" Dawn asked her once.

"Rose is my name. I cover with briar *cashee* all over. Sharper than barbed wire. One of them-so touch me and is hedgehog them dealing with. Is blood I drawing."

"That going make it sweeter for them. And when them knock you down all the cashee fall down too. Say 'thank God' them never fancy you."

Rose stayed a long time responding to that. And Joshua suspected she knew it wasn't a compliment.

"Them ever screw you?"

"No, 'cause them see I have children and them know I have a man."

"Since when that stop them?"

"Tell me the truth, Rose. The two o' we is big 'oman. You won't would o' like for have a light-skin child with straight hair and half-blue eyes that could o' get work in the bank with collar and tie or pretty frock, else 'come manager on one o' the estate-them? And if the child bright, go way oversea and study and come back big doctor, big lawyer, big whatchamacall it, and make your head swell with pride?"

"No."

"Gal, you cover over with cashee for true. Plenty Black 'oman don' mind that kind o' thing."

"Yes and the children-them ashame o' them. A shame o' their mother 'cause they Black, 'cause for keep their job they had to go down 'pon their back. See that one that is here—especially how Mistress Éclair want him for think he White—him so wouldn't say howdy to his mother if he meet her out in the street. I see you nicing him up from the time he come here. I not doing that, no sir, 'cause the day he vex with me, ugly nigger is the first thing he will call me. Mixed-colour children, they worse than the White ones, 'cause them shame o' what they be—vex cause they got coffee in their milk."

He waited eagerly to hear Dawn's reply. But she said nothing. He hoped she didn't believe that, and he would have liked to tell her that he would never hurt her. He would have never said anything cruel to Rose. It hurt him to hear her say that he wouldn't speak to his mother. It wasn't his fault that he wasn't allowed to visit her. He might have visited her if Bita was with him. But Bita was living with Skeeter then, and he was ashamed of Bita. And he was sure that just by looking at him she would have known what he and Sparrow were doing. He always believed that Bita could look at him and instantly know everything about him.

With mischief in her voice, Dawn told Rose once, "So how come a time I dream I come into the kitchen and meet you bracing the kitchen counter and Horse-Jaw pumping you like a bicycle tyre?"

"Darling, don't put what in your own heart 'pon me. Like you want for

kill poor Horse-Jaw or what? So you dreaming White man fucking you?"
She laughed. "You better hurry up if is breed you want them for breed you.
How come you never offer yourself to Mr Éclair when he been alive?"

But Dawn did not answer.

"You listen to me. White people only notice you when you have something they want. The rest o' the time one plus one is still one."

"What you mean? You always saying things upside-down."

"Darling, if you see things the way they teach we in school, it mean we
is nothing and White people is everything. One plus one makes one. Since
you so damn stupid, I mean, in White people eyes we is nothing. Dawn, one
plus nought is still one."

When Joshua got older their conversations interested him less, but one
day he could not help overhearing their debate about men-women relationships. Henry had come by, had winked conspiratorially at Joshua, and had
listened to parts of their banter, at times pursing his lips, shaking his head,
or rolling his eyes. Dawn was telling Rose how upset she was that her older
daughter was "in the family way" for a boy two years older than she, "that
ain't working no where, and depend 'pon his mother for food, shelter,
clothes, and pocket money."

Rose replied, "Even if you vex, ain't a Jesus-Christ-thing you can do 'bout
it, 'cause is married man you had them two girls for. Thank God, I don't
have none for bring bastard give me. My mother had Mrs in front of her
name, and ugly as I be, no man will ride me unless he put a ring on this
finger, Mrs to my name, and have a house for put me in."

"You mean like a wattle-and-daub on somebody rent land?" Dawn teased.

Henry opened his eyes wide, wrinkling his forehead, and shook his
fingers with a "touché" gesture.

"Know your place, Dawn. That is your taste, child. I hear they got birds
where the male, if he ever hope for get a screw, does have for build the nest
first, and only after the female inspect it, and it to her liking she does move
in to share the nest. And I sure those female birds does look at all kinds o'
nests before they choose. But they have some females—I not calling
names," she cleared her throat, "them drop them drawers and breed for
man before them know them going support the children-them. Some
women—I not calling any names—don't have the brains some birds got."

Henry shook his hand again, looked at Joshua, and slowly bowed his
head, his face enveloped in a smile.

"You know me story, so don't pamperset on me 'cause I have my two girl children-them, and soon I will have grand."

"Grand you will have. More than you can feed. Mark my words. You started it off, dropping your drawers for married man without a thought o' what will happen. I will tell you something I never say to you yet. Listen good. I want you to take it all in. I have more respect for whores than I have for you, 'cause whores make men that always hunting for pokey pay for it, and only the stupid ones mongst them that breed. But women like you, who give it away—and to married men on top o' that, married men that done got their wife—you know what you is in my eyesight: a public toilet where horny men relieve themselves."

Henry slowly moved his head from right to left, silently saying *but this Rose here is something else.*

"How you tallawah so? Is 'cause no man bird never invite you into his nest or what? Or because you never hold a bird?" Dawn replied. "Big sister, 'cause that is how you is to me—a big sister—all me want from you is the little understanding one poor woman owe another. Me didn't ask you for trace and trample me in my distress. Rose, sister-mother, have pity!"

And then the back door of the kitchen opened and Rose came upon Henry and Joshua.

"Dawn, look out here and see this," Rose called.

Dawn pushed her head out the open door.

"Look at them two antipympym out here, listening to us worse than jack-abats looking for comess."

"What's a jackabat?" he asked Henry two days later.

"Master Joshua, you won' want to know. That Rose got a tongue on her that full o' acid. Don' ever get in her way, 'cause if she use it on you, you will carry the scars to your grave, Master Joshua."

Rose! Now he smells her kitchen each time he thinks of her. Once, walking past a restaurant in Madrid, not far from the royal palace, he smelled okras cooking for the first time since he left Arcadia and remembered her cou-cou. He'd suddenly longed for Henry, the mountains, the ocean, the birds twitting contentedly in the cherry trees or darting about or resting unmolested in the orchard. He loved okras. There was nothing that compared with the pleasure they gave as they slid down his throat. Mommy had Henry plant them for the only reason that he liked them, and she made Rose prepare cou-cou once a week because Joshua loved it. Cou-cou with kingfish or red snapper! Rose's kitchen! It was her kitchen—Dawn helped her when she wasn't house-cleaning, carrying out her orders mostly—and it smelt of meat cooking in curry, cardamon, cumin, rosemary, and basil; of cake batter or baking cakes effusing vanilla, almond essence, nutmeg, clove, and cinnamon. And her bread puddings! The recipe for which Mrs Manchester constantly asked but Rose never gave. Aromas that never quite sweetened her life or even the lives of those she served. But he wasn't aware of that then. She was.

He wondered whether they were aware of how the planters saw them. They must have. There was nothing they didn't seem to know. Rarely did the planters gather at Arcadia without talking about the threat servants and field hands represented. From 1962 on, after Jamaica and Trinidad became independent, their discussion focused on the independence Britain was granting her Caribbean colonies.

The day Jamaica got its independence, they'd met at Arcadia because for them it was a crisis. "This Titanic hit the iceberg while you've been sleeping and fucking," Pine Knot told them. "Strike up the orchestra. Never mind lifeboats. We were too damn sure of ourselves to bring any. Our young people know something we old fools forgot. Everywhere, from the Bahamas to Guyana, they're leaving in droves for Australia, New Zealand, and South Africa. If I was a sapling I'd be escaping too."

"Stop being so pessimistic. We're White men," Flingfoot said.

"What do you mean?"

"If it's one thing niggers know it's where we draw the line. See what happened to those Mau-Mau?" Horse Jaw said.

"Go on being foolish. It's a foolish luxury, I tell you. Giving them the vote was the thin edge o' the wedge. I always said so. Now it's independence—*independence!*—the British are offering those that want it. You know what that means? Control. Control over *our* lives and *our* property! We'll be dead in our beds before the British and the Americans come. They'll come all right: to bury us."

"Every night you must dream they're coming at you with their machetes," Blenkinsopp said with a chuckle.

"If you think they'll spare you because your wife dresses their sores and you work with your hands like a common nigger, think again. They'll cut your throat first," Pine Knot replied, "'cause it will be the easiest one to cut."

"Blenk's just humouring you." This from Manchester.

"You're counting on your bastards to protect you?"

"Come on, fellows, stop it," Flingfoot said, getting up and walking over to where Pine Knot and Manchester sat, opposite him. He reached for the whiskey bottle in the centre of the table and refilled Manchester's and Pine Knot's glasses and urged them to drink their fill in case "tonight's the night the angel of death passes."

His thoughts turn to how poorly the workers were paid. He'll have to do his own reparations, he thinks. What could he do? Something for sure for the Caribs, the Aboriginals of Isabella Island, whose land was stolen so he could eventually inherit it, but he does not know what. But for the descendants of those who worked on the plantations, he could use his money to build and endow a school on land that formerly belonged to Éclair Estate. The descendants of those whose parents and grandparents had worked on the estate would attend it cost-free. And there should be no age limit to who could attend it. He does a quick calculation and thinks that a year's earnings from his investment portfolio would be enough to build the facilities, a second year's earnings could equip it, and thereafter eighty to ninety percent of his investment earnings could be used to run it. There would still be more than enough left over for him to live on.

Massive wealth, he thinks, is always tainted by blood and suffering. Always. Whether from killing people in order to steal their lands and leaving the survivors to die of starvation and disease, or from overwork and underpay in capitalists' factories and fields. Always. And history glorifies the pillagers because pillagers endow the institutions that sponsor historians, who are loathe to bite the hand that feeds them. We should be ashamed, not proud, of wealth. On that score Shelley's absolutely right.

The idea of giving it back excites him until he realizes that it would necessitate his return to Isabella Island. He knows only too well that a board put in place to administer such a project would siphon off the money for its members' private ends. The Third World curse. He would definitely have to be on the spot. The thought of returning dampens his ardour.

Why has he never wanted to return? Why? He'd left just before he turned twenty and has never once returned, never even thought of it. If he likes Dr Blenheim, it's an issue he thinks he'll want to explore with him.

14

NINE O'CLOCK. HE HAS SHOWERED and dressed and is reading a copy of *Newsweek* but is unable to concentrate. *Why are they taking so long to come?* He reads on. His hands are sweating. He walks to the nursing station. Gladys Knights is on the telephone. She cups the receiver, then excuses herself, and tells the person she's speaking to that she'll call back.

"What can we do for you, Joshua?" Now she sometimes calls him Joshua, sometimes Mr Éclair.

"I thought Dr Blenheim would be by to see me already."

"Let's see." She phones, affects a smile, and tells him they'd be by to see him in fifteen minutes.

Returning to his room, he passes several of the patients in the main dorm because the corridor passes through it. Now he knows a few of them by sight and a couple of them by name. There's an older Black man among them. Joshua deliberately avoids them. Their psychosis frightens him. A long time ago—he was still in London, because he never kept a journal after that—he'd written: To be insane is to be helplessly caught among mountainous waves with compass, mast, and rudder gone.

He reenters his room, sits down in the armchair there and continues thinking how willy-nilly the vagaries of life toss us about, independent of our resisting stratagems; so much of what we do is geared to avoiding or lessening pain. What is it that suddenly sends torrents raging through his psyche, inundating memory and consciousness like mudslides flooding valleys? What gets silted up, shrunk, enlarged? What?

His thoughts go back to Horton. He and Jerome Quashee jockeyed for top spot in Joshua's cohort at Expatriates. He had to be the most handsome of them all: glowing amber eyes, palm-tree thighs, sculpted buttocks, muscled like a thoroughbred—a member of the soccer and rugby teams. What a way he went berserk that morning long ago in algebra class! Seeing it had taken Joshua back to the windows he'd broken at Arcadia, had shot paroxysms of fear through his body, and left his brain feeling like dry clay powdering between someone's fingers; and he had to be taken from class and medicated for five days.

It had taken every male staff member and some of the bigger boys to restrain Horton and keep him pinned to the ground until rope was found to tie his arms and legs—the instant sanity left he transmogrified into a beast that had to be bound—while they waited for the police and ambulance to come. The week before Joshua left for England, he went to see Horton at the Good Shepherd Asylum. "Horton, it's Joshua. Prufrock! Proufy! Don't you remember me? We were at Expatriates together." He pleaded for recognition and stared into Horton's vacant eyes. Horton mumbled to himself, turned away and grinned a scattered-yellow-tooth grin. The sunless indoors had leached the beige from his skin, like darkness whitening chlorophyll, and wrinkled it as if it had been immersed in soapy water; his thighs were now sapling-thin, his arms reedlike, his head shrunk, his eyes cavernous, his movements slow and arthritic. He smelt of urine and stale sweat. The super athlete-turned-raging-beast now turned ghost. Joshua tried to fit his memories of the sane Horton over the foul-smelling spectre with back and shoulders curved into a comma standing before him, but they would not match. Shocked by what Horton had become, shocked by what he Joshua could become, he left the ward praying silently, "Please, don't let me lose my sanity ever again, Lord. Let anything else happen to me in life, but do not let me ever again lose my sanity." He repeated the prayer out loud when he was once more in fresh air and sunshine. He believed in the Christian God then.

Each time he has been hospitalized, it always came as a relief when he was told he was no longer psychotic. He knows now the egotism and arrogance of that prayer—the difference between the naivety of twenty and the experience of fifty-one. But the fear is as chilling now as it was then, and now he is a lot less confident.

They arrive. It's as if he expected a fanfare. Four of them. Too many to stand comfortably in the room. Blenheim's eyes seem snipped from an Arctic sky. He is around forty-five, short: about five-five, with a bantam compactness. His face is elliptical, with a desert brownness to it, but acne has pitted it, making it look a limestone landscape. Below his hawkish nose there is a barely perceptible scar on his upper lip, suggesting a lip-splitting accident or a repaired harelip. His auburn hair is short and slicked close to his skull with a path on the left. He wears faint indistinct cologne. The collar of his sky-blue shirt shows above his white hospital smock. His pants are cocoa brown. His and Joshua's stares are locked.

Other than formal greetings they've said nothing to each other. Joshua senses that Blenheim is an intense, energetic person, someone he could easily like or hate.

Defoe speaks, "We are leaving you and Dr Blenheim to get acquainted."

Blenheim sits on the edge of Joshua's bed. He looks around the room and out the window. "You have a good view here. Needs more trees, though. So many of us have an uneasy relationship with trees."

"Like the earth," Joshua adds. "We're made of it, we feed off it, we're eventually buried in it, yet we vilify it."

"Early humanity didn't. Most traditional Africans and North-American Natives still consider it sacred."

Joshua disagrees. *Early humankind was afraid of it, felt the need to bribe it,* he silently answers Blenheim. But for Blenheim's statement alone, accurate or inaccurate, he thinks he'll like him.

"Mr Éclair, what would you say is your biggest worry?"

"I'm not sure there is one. There are many small worries. For one thing, happiness is something I've long ago bundled up and put on the garbage truck; and when I hear talk about it, I wonder if something's wrong with me. I suppose you could say I'd like to end the turbulence in me." He stops talking for a moment. "Vaguely there's something in me, something that has to be siphoned out. I don't know what, nor how." He pauses before adding, "I hope it isn't as real and unreal and . . . whatever, as . . . as original sin. And . . . That's it."

"And?"

"The ugliness of . . . who I am."

"Meaning?"

"Doctor, I'm even afraid to think about it."

"But you know you'll have to face it?"

Joshua nods.

"Do you consider yourself normal?"

"No. Not if you mean if my life and beliefs are similar to the average person's."

"Go on."

"Well the average North American gets up every day and goes off to a job he probably hates. But it's part of the maze society has put him in. Every society, I guess, has restrictions of this sort. I don't fall into that category."

He has never articulated this before.

"I understand that you are quite wealthy."

"Yes." He watches Blenheim warily, wondering if he's about to hear some updated version of *Go sell all thou hast and give it to the poor and come follow me.*

"How do you feel about your wealth; I imagine it's this that puts a wedge between you and the toiling masses."

"I don't know. I live simply, have chosen to live simply."

"Is that because you feel guilty about your wealth?"

"Maybe. But it's because I have learnt that wealth could be a burden. I give most of it to charity. Even so it's burden. I wonder at times how much of it is invested in mines where people are killed and factories where there's child labour and cancer-causing chemicals."

"I just wanted to get a feel of how you think about things. You've said that you would like to quiet the agony inside you. We'll try to work on that. Would you like to be discharged?"

"I'm not yet in control of my psyche."

"No one ever is. Fully that is."

"I mean my level of confidence. For example, when I'm normal I stutter."

"Did you always stutter?"

"No, it came after my first attack of amnesia at sixteen."

"And what if you regain your usual self but no longer stutter?"

"I'll have to see that to believe it."

"How frank are you going to be with me?"

"Why do you ask me that?"

"Because you haven't been frank with the staff here."

He thinks, wonders if he should say what he is thinking, and decides what the hell. "Doctor, it seems that from the time I was born, everyone saw me as plasticene they could mould and remould into the images they fancied—not always with bad intentions—but like plasticene each moulding left me a little more soiled. So I have come to value my privacy. I no longer let soiling hands reach into me. I won't let my being become sounds on a tape recorder or words in someone's dossier . . ."

"What if I promise not to do this?"

"You can't. The rules of your profession oblige you to keep a record of your interactions with me."

"You are correct. But the rules do not oblige me to share them with anyone."

Joshua wonders about this.

"Can you control the occurrence of your amnesic bouts?"

"No."

"But you would like to work towards preventing their recurrence?"

"Yes."

"Well, listen carefully to what I'm about to say. You and I cannot control a great deal in life. When we try to do so, we risk our health. Stop worrying about what gets put in your file. I guarantee you that if you give voice to what's inside you, you will gain a new perspective, deepen your understanding of yourself. I'll promise not to share your file with others, not to have student psychiatrists interrogating you, and am even prepared to let you see what I've written in your file. How does this sound so far?"

"How do I know I can trust you?"

"You do not, but you have to take it on faith, the same way you get on a plane and trust the pilot to get you to your destination."

"Pilot?"

"But I never guarantee a smooth landing. A couple of things: I would like you to begin keeping a journal about anything important that you've mused on."

Joshua thinks about this for a while. Eventually he nods.

"Good. Another thing. Your insurance provides for your own private nurse. You haven't been making use of this clause. I've been told that you get along well with Leroy."

Joshua laughs. "He's so good-heartedly naïve."

"We've checked with the company and it's all right to assign Leroy to you. Would you like that?"

"Maybe."

"Why the hesitation?"

"I don't want him always standing guard over me."

"Fine. But we would like you to resume doing the things you habitually did before your hospitalization here. You know, going to the museum, taking long walks. But if you relapse, and it is possible you will—in fact, I am certain you will—as you explore the painful areas of your past, we want someone to be on hand, someone you trust. How does that sound?"

"Complicated. But I could give it a try. One false move on your part though, and it will fall apart."

"I know that. Do we start today?"

"Fine with me."

"Leroy's at your disposal. Do whatever you want today. I'll be here to see you at nine tomorrow morning."

"I think I'll go to a West Indian restaurant for lunch. I long for a bowl of callaloo soup."

"Go right ahead."

While he waits for Leroy to come, he thinks about his promise to Blenheim to keep a journal and remembers that when he got to Madrid, he'd needed to express himself in images—not in words: they were corrupt, treacherous, ambiguous. He had an urge to paint. Perhaps all that ochre in the buildings and the tiles in the plazas, the immense green of the Bueno Retiro, the flowers spread along the earth's floor—not to mention the limbs of hope that took him there, or the trips to the Prado Museum—inspired him. An urge he'd never had in England, despite the purple and white blankets of crocuses and vast beds of sunshine daffodils (the only sunshine there was), despite the cherry, prune, and apple trees that metamorphosed from grey January gargoyles into bouquet trees, blossom-covered: white, pink, magenta; and instant perfume factories—a cadaverous landscape instantly come alive; an evanescent, mesmerizing Eden.

He bought a small supply of various paints and brushes and manilla paper, and thought eventually he would get a bookstore to order him manuals in English on painting. For days, before and after his Spanish language classes and his walks around the city and the occasional visit to the Prado, (a ten-minute walk from the hostel where he stayed), he painted what he told himself was an exploring "study": a life-size beige human figure on sheets of white manilla paper he'd scotch-taped together and laid out on a twelve-by-eight plastic sheet he'd bought to prevent soiling the floor tiles of his room. Before purchasing an easel, he wanted to see what he'd come up with. He got as far as putting large raven-black curls on the figure's head, but could not decide how he'd draw the face, the colour he'd give the eyes, whether the lips and nose would be Africoid or Caucasoid, how he'd dress it. Eventually he painted just a hint of a face veiled in deep twilight, and dressed the figure in dark-grey clothes denser than the twilight swirling in a storm around it. One evening, after his walk through the park, he drank half a litre of red wine and decided to colour all but the figure black and to superimpose on the whole a gridwork of white bars. Next day he hated it, ripped it up and promptly discarded the bits.

His second attempt was to paint, against the backdrop of the treed landscape, some of the couples he saw walking the trail towards the stadium at the centre of the Bueno Retiro, arm-in-arm, the women in their green, yellow, pink, blue, mirroring the flowers along the park road—scenes that brought back his drives with Sparrow on dirt roads between cane fields in the Isabellan countryside; of days with Henry in the garden watching the golden-and-brown-striped bees and yellow-and-brown polka-dot butterflies busily flying from flower to flower; of his own irresistible need to feel the silkiness of the petals of the blood-red tea roses, his nostrils lightly touching their petals as he inhaled deeply, hungry for their scent, until Henry told him that insects would crawl out of the flowers up into his nostrils, lodge in his skull and turn his brain to maggots, but when no one was looking, he'd continued to smell the cut flowers brought indoors; of the long periods he used to stand and watch the double gerbras, magenta, salmon, peach, lily-white, fuchsia, ochre, canary yellow, orange, especially after a light rain had washed and refreshed them and made them sturdy like sentinels, like miniature palms with petal fronds. They had no perfume to speak of and their petals weren't silken, but they put their all into a spectacular feast for the eyes; he wanted to grow his own garden, but Henry would not allow it.

"Master Joshua, your Mommy will fire me if she catch you soiling yourself in the earth alongside me."

The earth soils no one, Henry. It purifies even despots. Even they can't soil it. Mommy wouldn't have minded, but Mrs Manchester, Mrs Kevin, all but Mrs Blenkinsopp would, and you couldn't have known that Mommy was different.

So in Madrid he must have wanted to paint the flowers he couldn't cultivate at Arcadia. That painting too was ripped up, discarded, after he met Juan and sank into a crippling depression.

And now he wonders why he never wanted to paint again, has felt no need to express himself in images. Keeping a journal, he gave up on that since England, and the thought of writing for children when he got to Montreal remained just that, a thought. And music he never learned. Instead two to three times per year, he debrides, cauterizes, reduces what he can only call the psychic tumour within when it grows too large and begins to suffocate him.

Later, when he and Leroy are on the bus heading towards the Verdun metro station, Joshua asks, "Leroy, if I decide to take a trip to Isabella Island, do you think they'd let you accompany me?" Joshua is surprised by his own question.

"How you expect me fee know that, Mr Éclair?"

Too late, Joshua thinks. He'll report this. Then he thinks, well, maybe he himself should raise it with Dr Blenheim, test him to see how far his promises extend.

They are at the Verdun metro station. Joshua buys a copy of the *Montreal Gazette*. Lucien Bouchard is threatening Quebec's public sector unions with imposed legislation. He folds the paper and promises to read it when he returns to the ward.

Later that evening Nurse Ramon peeps in his door. She doesn't speak.

"Hello Nurse Ramon," he calls out to her.

She comes back. "Must I curtsey? I see where you are getting treated like royalty?"

"I could make you my queen. You could sit on the throne all day long."

"Which one? *All day long!* God help me!" She is laughing. That's what he wanted.

"I wanted to see you laugh. May I please, dearest Nurse Ramon, have some writing paper?"

Three minutes later, she returns with a bound notebook, and tells him Dr Blenheim had ordered it for him.

"I can kiss you for this?"

"My husband won't like it."

"No problem as long as you do."

"Stop flirting with me." She can hardly repress her giggle.

"You are wonderful, Nurse Ramon. I'm beginning to feel that the staff here is my family." It strikes him that what he has just said is true.

"That's not so good for you."

He knows that she is right too.

He writes: *I would like to return to Isabella Island for a visit. For one thing I would like to visit Bita's grave.* He stops and thinks that there's probably nothing marking it. Almost thirty-five years now. They've probably buried someone else in it, mingled her bones with someone else's. Does Bita have a grave? In the elegy he wrote in '64 and '65 he did not give her one. He doesn't remember hearing of her body being found. There was some sort of agreement, he suspects—probably on Mommy's orders—that no one was to raise the subject. And if there is one, how would he find it? He has never visited his mother's grave. Maybe going back would be one way of making peace with her. He hopes she died knowing he did not hate her. What would he say to Bita were he to find her grave?

He resumes writing: *Bita, I forgive you for offering your body to the highest bidder. I admire you for deciding to end it all when you saw your life becoming a dung heap getting stinkier by the minute. That market mammy who told me of your death—she was your aunt, come to think of it—must be dead.*

He pauses on the word *dead.* Death. *My father became humane on his deathbed, a luxury he could not afford while he was sure he'd live tomorrow, next week, next month, next year.*

Mommy was very evasive in the way she spoke about his sexuality. Did it have anything to do with how he raped my mother? And my own sexuality, does it have a genetic basis? His hands have begun to sweat. He must change these thoughts.

I'm sure I have relatives—my mother's relatives—on Isabella Island. There are of course the Éclairs, Mommy's in-laws. They would welcome me with poison . . .

I wonder if Horton is alive. Would I have the strength to visit him and not break down and cry?

He doesn't like what he is writing now and stops. His mind returns to his thoughts earlier that morning of wanting to build a school on what used to be the Éclair plantation. Why just a school? Why not a clinic too? *Because wealth is not infinite. You are not God, able to do everything.* That's probably it. He wants to play God. The wealthy, although they vehemently deny it, feel they're the gods of this earth, some of them as vengeful and tyrannical as Yahweh. "If salvation was a thing that money could buy/ . . . The rich would live and the poor would die," Sparrow's congregation often sang. Perhaps they did not associate him with Averill Éclair's wealth, otherwise it would be mockery. They were on to something. Salvation can't be bought; he could tell them so from personal experience. But, setting aside the human beings that nations sacrifice to the god of war, neither can it come through the shedding of another's blood. On that score they were wrong. It must be earned through pain, through the perpetual traversing of the fires in the psyche. Saint Paul got the metaphors right but got the process wrong. He rereads what he has written down, thinks for a while and adds, *We're all trying to reenter Eden and we must find scapegoats, someone to punish, for our failure to do so.* There's something, he admits, to putting your thoughts on paper, to rescuing them from the void in which they're uttered and instantly lost. Now he wonders if he will show them to Blenheim in the morning.

He thinks again about building a school. Yes, he'll have to give it up unless he undertakes to run it himself. The absurdity of the thought makes him laugh.

He's tired. It's not yet 9:00 P.M.. He's had a long day. Should he ask for a sedative? No, he'd get dependent on them. But he is a long time falling asleep. Thoughts of Horton return periodically, the look, and smell of the ward. The iron bars in the windows, they'd frightened him. Horton, if he's still alive, is human. We cannot cast aside the sick and infirm and remain humane. Now he really feels the need for a sedative but resists ringing the bell.

At eleven when the night nurse comes on duty, his mind is roaring like a cataract and he eventually asks for a sedative. The pills are different. The nurse tonight is a Black man, cold and indifferent, with none of Defoe's spontaneous warmth. He has a don't-trifle-with-me mien. Everything he says is razor-edged, not even the lilt of a Caribbean accent Joshua is unable to place softens what he says. Joshua reminds himself that the man has the right to be who he is. He is not a servant at Arcadia.

He tells Joshua the doctor has changed his prescription to Valium. "They'll leave you feeling less drowsy."

15

TONIGHT HE AND BITA are in a dark room, and Bita's voice, sounding hollow, is saying, "Talk, Joshua, talk. Hide nothing. Tell them about Sparrow, tell them why you have the scars on your back. If you want to get out of your prison, you have to tell them. Go down in the cellar, climb up into the attic; check everywhere for woodlice; overlook nothing—otherwise you'll be trapped forever in this dark prison without any light. I didn't lock you in and I don't have the key to get you out." Her voice goes and he awakens. He looks at his watch. It's 3 A.M. and he's wide awake. He knows it will be another sleepless morning. *"Tell them why you have the scars on your back."* Does he really know? *She means I must find out by winnowing what I already know.*

These dreams featuring Bita. As if she's some amulet, some password the heroes in fairy tales and romances had to touch, state, to move through, to escape from grave danger. The texts he'd read about African beliefs emphasize the responsibilities of the living to the dead. According to them he hadn't buried Bita. In West Africa the dead protect and advise the living. He ponders the advice Bita has just given him. And what he dreads, reflecting on what Sparrow did to him and the fracturing of his psyche that Sparrow's death triggered, takes over despite his desire to squelch the whole thing.

He learned of Sparrow's death in April 1968: a suicide disguised as an accident. He is sure now that Sparrow ended his life because he was gay, but he didn't think so in the beginning.

He'd been only vaguely aware of some monster on his trail after Averill Éclair's death. It caught him when Sparrow died, put him in penance—for himself, Averill, and Sparrow. A penance in which he examined each memory he could summon up, piece by piece, the way one sorts the things one discards before moving, for he knew that what he did not dump then he'd be forever sentenced to carry. But he found everything bound in ambiguity. And the threads he pulled and the strings he cut unstitched, undid, his very being. And soon he found himself trapped in languor, and the pouches he'd willed into place for garbage distended and broke and poisoned his sanity and mental being—like tubercular calculi exploding in a weak and malnourished body, releasing their bacilli to wreck those organs where they meet no resistance.

When the divine (fake or real) begins to rot, ordinary mortals had better run. Wise to bury yourself before you poison others. But before the fog of insanity had fully thickened, he glimpsed in Sparrow's demise a hint of what lurked for him in the tangle of tomorrows.

At some point long afterwards, he doesn't remember when, he decided that Sparrow had been the victim of religious and societal cruelty and of his own psyche. The advantage Sparrow had taken of him was a by-product of all that. He wished Sparrow had found peace. Who finds peace? He has certainly not found it.

Yet years later, reflecting on how insidiously it had all started, he could see that Sparrow had planned it. So innocently with Sparrow's telling him, long before the smutty jokes, "Ah bet you sneak into Averill's room when she ain't there. 'N Ah knows what you be doing in there. You be in there a tryin' on her bras 'n a wishin' you could wear her drawers."

He'd never had any such need or thought. "You're crazy," he told him.

"Know som'n," Sparrow replied, "Ahm gon catch you one o' these days before you take off them false boobs you be wearing 'n before you wipe that lipstick from yer lips." His eyes were glowing. "Lemme look at them-there fingers."

Joshua stretched out his fingers. Sparrow took each hand and inspected the nails.

"See, there's the evidence." He pointed to a red spot, a smudge left by a red ball point pen Joshua had been using earlier. "See, just lak Ah thought. Lord, have mercy. See? you been sneaking into Averill's bedroom and puttin' on her nail polish."

You lead-headed fool! Joshua said to himself, and aloud, "That's an ink smudge. Are you blind?" and he pulled away his hand angrily.

And one day Sparrow patted his bulging belly and said, "Ma gut's gittin' so big, it's mighty hard to see ma prick."

Yes, he'd been too naïve to sense what would follow a couple months later.

But he cannot believe that Sparrow had taken advantage of him because he was a pedophile. Even now he could not live with such a belief. He cannot believe we wilfully corrupt the things we love. No, Sparrow was a desperate homosexual with no other outlet for his sexuality. Is there a causal link between his peculiar sexuality and what had gone on between Sparrow and him? Sparrow had nothing to do with the origin of his homosexuality. Does Sparrow have anything to do with his *peculiar needs*? Once Joshua had threatened to denounce him to Mommy and to the members of his church. Sparrow said that Mommy wouldn't believe it, and even if she did, he had ways to keep her quiet. Then he looked away before adding, "N even if she was to go 'n do som'n foolish, she'd only bring scandal on her ownself 'cause I'll take me one o' these here firearms 'n blow ma brains out. I ain't no ways goin' ter allow maself to face that kind o' disgrace." His face turned sallow, his eyes shrank, beads of sweat stippled his forehead, and his knees shook. "You'd lak to see me humiliated some, won't yer?" his voice quavering. Joshua did not answer. Of course, he never told Mommy about it. He'd been bluffing anyway. And Sparrow kept on coming into his bed at night whispering, "It ain't so bad. Don't yer love it? Ah knows yer love it. Ah got me the answer right here. Stiffest prick Ah ever felt. You's on fire with desire."

He'd never associated Sparrow with physical pain. *I who'd been born of a rape in which my mother had been whipped. Was it possible for that sort of thing to be inherited?* Strange, very strange, he had truly liked Sparrow. What had he been? An older brother, a father, an uncle? All three—and he had been so comfortable with him until . . . . Perhaps society and religion were to blame. They had made his and Sparrow's needs illegal. And Sparrow was too weak to resist either.

He'd never thought of it as an incestuous act. Incest, as he understood it then, had to be consanguineous. His revulsion came when he discovered the horror Americans attach to what Sparrow had done to him. No such scruples obtained on Isabella Island. But Sparrow had done so with full knowledge of the implications—like today's First Worlders who globetrot to sate their needs in pediatric brothels.

Later, long afterwards, he admitted as much to Joshua, even telling him he had been selling his body to older men, "some of 'em in suit 'n ties," from as early as age thirteen; he'd been "precocious some." At thirteen he could look into his clients' eyes and tell what they wanted, and could give it. Funny, what he was saying was supposed to have been an apology.

Did race matter in what Sparrow had done to him? If he'd been caught fellating a Black pubescent 1950s-60s Florida youngster, would it have been worth the attention of the legal system? And even if the boy's parents knew, they'd have been powerless to act. That Éclair wealth had made Joshua White, he had no doubt. But southern American conditioning predominated in Sparrow's psyche. Besides, in 1950s and '60s Isabella Island, sex with minors was more normal than aberrant. Every year, in every hamlet, a couple—and sometimes more than a couple—of girls around age thirteen got pregnant from their teachers. The pupils left school quietly, the teachers stayed on, impregnating. Brother Harry, the headteacher of Petit Bordel School, the elementary school Joshua would have attended had he continued living with his biological mother, had married one of his students, a thirteen-year-old pregnant with his child. Giggling, Pine Knot had told his admiring cronies at Arcadia that Brother Harry (*Brother* because he was a Methodist lay preacher) knew his "nigger folks" well, their love of living pens. "Now that's live script—the word made flesh. His pen's not likely to run dry any time soon."

"If you ask me, their ink flows too freely. Watch out they don't scribble on your pages," Manchester said with a wink.

"No one writes as well as you—on *their* pages!" Horse-jaw intervened.

Everyone laughed, including Manchester, who erupted in a wheezing, choking cough.

"You write a mean script yourself," Manchester told him when his coughing subsided.

"We all do. Even Manny," Flingfoot said, glancing coyly at Mommy, who happened at that very moment to be bringing two bottles of whiskey to the table.

"But he only got one page," Manchester added.

On another occasion, Blenkinsopp said that too much sex had disjointed Manchester's back.

Ramcat, one of Manchester's "bastards" who was a petty overseer on his "father's" estate, raped young Black girls with impunity and bragged about it. A villager had stood up to him, had beaten him and left him unconscious in a cane field near the village of Compton. Manchester occupied himself with their mothers; their jobs depended on it. Their husbands, those who had them, knew better than to fight back and quietly took their anger out on their wives. He'd got most of this from Rose and Dawn's conversations, sitting at the part of the porch closest to the kitchen, where he could listen without being seen. Everyone with power to take and power to silence *took* sex.

The residents of the plantation villages made effigies of men who engaged in incest and zoophilia, put the effigies on trial, then hanged and burned them. But they did no such thing for those who had sex with minors.

No, it would be wrong to fault Sparrow outright. There were too many factors. But had he been able to, he suspects, he'd have been better off. In the long run there is only one thing he became certain of: how lonely, isolated and frightened Sparrow must have become. It made sense that he chose to end his life. In any event, he had been thinking about killing himself for quite a long time.

His response to Sparrow's death was first depression, followed by a complete shutting down of his psyche. Paul, visiting, found him psychotic and alerted the foreign students' advisor at Queen Mary College. He was taken to Mile End Hospital, and when his condition did not improve, he was transferred to the County Hospital.

At Mile End Hospital he'd been initially incontinent. He'd come to consciousness briefly one morning while the student nurse assigned to him was getting him out of bed to remove the clothing and linen he had soiled. First it had shocked and afterward depressed him. The student, a slender, innocent-looking, caring young man with grey sorrowful eyes, had spent a large part of his shift trying to reassure him. He wonders whether he was incontinent at the Douglas too. Now his hands are sweating profusely.

When they discharged him from the County Hospital he fled to Madrid, where he'd met Juan. That too ended in depression and a subsequent running away—to Paris. There he ended up at St Anne's Hospital. From there to Montreal. How could he tell Blenheim this? But he'll have to. And about his sexuality too. How would he tell them—*The scars on my back are the accumulations of roughly three decades of whippings. I stumbled on whipping accidentally during my third and final year in London.*

For the record, I sleep with men. Not frequently: about three experiences per year now. But not any kind of homosexual man. He must be a sadist. It was quite accidental, you know. From the time I got to puberty I desired sleeping with men. At twenty I went to London and a year later found that I could have homosexual sex without fear of persecution. I tell you I thought I'd stumbled into paradise. But no matter how long the sexual act lasted I could not come. One night a pickup asked me to be his slave. He pauses. He has never vocalized any of this before. *The long and short of it was that he strapped me to his bed and began to whip me. That night I had my first orgasm with another man in London. From then on whipping became an orgasmic precursor. But I hate pain. Isn't that strange? Above all else, I crave tenderness.*

He knows that what he has just thought out needs nuancing. *I should backtrack a little and say that during adolescence I did have orgasms. But I was not responsible for them.* He stops thinking out loud, asks himself if this is totally true. Sometimes he blames Sparrow but other times he tells himself that if it had been so bad, he wouldn't have got the erections and achieved the ejaculations, even though they left him feeling guilty, shameful, and angrier with himself than he was Sparrow.

He waits, expecting to hear a prompt. *Go on . . . How do you feel about whipping as a prelude to ejaculating and who was this someone else? Sparrow?* And realizes that he has resumed talking to himself, rehearsing as it were what he will say tomorrow, if he finds the courage to do so.

He stops the rehearsal but continues his train of thought. Jonathan and Joseph are the names he'd devised to use with his pickups. The idea not to tell his pickups his real name had come to him during the last months he spent in Madrid. He never as a rule asks for the names of those he picks up. If they volunteer the information he promptly forgets it. He doesn't remember ever knowing the name of the fellow who'd introduced him to masochism, though he recalls every detail of the encounter: how he'd stared at him, admiring his full green eyes, his mass of thick, black, glossy, hair, his blushing, symmetrical contrasting face, his athletic form, his large thighs especially—cycling was his hobby. He lived in a tiny flat on Buckingham Palace Road, and said he worked at the Tate Gallery. At the bar the fellow, his gaze burning, had said, "I'm a flag. Are you game?" And Joshua had thought he meant fag and had nodded. But he does not remember the fellow's name or for that matter if they'd ever told each other their names.

He met Juan during his second month in Madrid, on a very hot, end-of-July evening. He'd walked along the Prado, past Cybeles Fountain and had turned into one of the quieter side streets until he got to Cheuca, which he already knew was the gay district. He sat down at the plaza fronting the entrance to the Cheuca metro station and was daydreaming when Juan came to sit beside him, his face electrified and friendly. Joshua responded nervously. This was Franco's Spain and Juan could easily have been one of Franco's agents in plainclothes. He'd thought Joshua was Spanish. He was a reedlike fellow, with thin arms and legs and shoulders hunched slightly forward. In physique almost a replica of Vladimir . . . (David in Guiterrez's *Fresca y Chocolate*). He looked vulnerable. His chestnut hair covered his ears and was shoulder-length—imprudent in 1968 Spain because of the student uprisings taking place everywhere, but especially next door in France, and the Franco government's persecution of nonconformists. There was seduction in Juan's dark, moist eyes, and he turned out to be the gentlest, tenderest person in whose arms Joshua has ever found himself.

Juan lived in a rented room in an apartment that overlooked the Plaza Mayor. It was there that he took Joshua. It was early evening and the heat rose from the ochre bricks in the square below and stayed in the room. Joshua sweated, and Juan felt it was because he wasn't at ease. And when Joshua would not ejaculate, disappointment and failure coated Juan's voice, forcing Joshua to spend more than an hour in a lacing embrace, the sweat on their bodies feeling like glue; convincing him that it was all right, that it was probably because it was their first meeting. Juan had brightened at this point. He couldn't ask Juan to whip him, to become demonic. And it was an experience he wanted to remember without the pollution of pain. Juan wanted him to spend the night, but the gnawing inside him was already intense when he escaped to deal with the agony in his own room. After arranging to meet Juan at the same spot the next day—fully aware that he would not go—he left, taking a taxi back to his room on Atocha. At that hour, 10 P.M., he usually went strolling through the nearby train station, to watch people coming and going, and from there to the Bueno Retiro, where most people in that part of Madrid often walked or quietly sat relishing the relief the trees gave from the heat that had built up in their apartments. But that night he went nowhere and was indifferent to the painting spread out on the floor. Juan's concern for his partners, his open warmth and naked need for affection forced Joshua to look at a need he didn't want to know he had—the need for an affectionate, cuddly, dependable person to share his life with. For a while he cried. He stayed awake all night turning over his fears, examining them crease by crease, filament by filament, without understanding them, wondering if he should seek therapy, wondering if his orgasmic climaxes weren't the lowest stratum of sexual depravity. His fright intensified over several days and paralyzed his being as he focused on and found no answers for, and no way into, the mystery of his sexual needs.

Depression followed. He did not slip into amnesia or psychosis in Madrid, just a prolonged depression, worse than those he's had since coming to Montreal, in which he neglected and eventually stopped attending his Spanish language classes, and would not leave his room sometimes for an entire week.

He never allowed himself to meet anyone else over the next four months he remained in Madrid, but during his depression he came to the conclusion that to simplify his life he should give his masochist persona a name and that way contain it: prevent it from swallowing up, from becoming the matrix of his identity. He settled for Joseph. It wasn't the first time he'd undergone a name change of sorts. In London, everyone called him Josh. The student-playwright-actor Hole, whose name Paul punned crudely with, had started it, and others had followed suit. While it lasted Josh freed him a little from the many problems he'd not altogether left behind on Isabella Island, gave him something of a reconfigured self that put repressed parts of his being on stage and pushed others behind the curtains.

After his move from Madrid to Paris in November 1968, he gave his name as Joseph to those who introduced themselves in the sado-masochist bar he frequented while there. Once while he was strolling on the Champs-Elysée someone recognized him and called out to him. A sweat broke out all over his body and his hands began to tremble. He couldn't figure out what had upset him until he understood how the name Joseph functioned; it was to be restricted to a clearly defined space out of which it was not to travel. Like the barrier one keeps between cesspool and well. When, outside the bar, several people began identifying him as Joseph, the name became toxic, the barrier porous. And he saw that another strategy was needed to separate and keep pure the part of his identity that ensured sane functioning.

In Paris things eventually became worse than in Madrid. Towards the end he felt the separate strands of his psyche entangling, his will a helpless bystander, impotent just as it had been when he encountered the issues that landed him first at Mile End and later at the County Hospital. The breakdown in Paris was triggered, he knew, by the post-coital analysis his last pickup in France had made him listen to. A jeremiad about his father, an Eastern European, who whipped him on his bare buttocks and grinned.

He'd come to think, trapping himself in the process, that love was pain. It was what his analyst had told him, at any rate. He was a short, squat man with spindly legs; a spider-web pattern of blood vessels sullied his cheeks. He had to be in his late forties but said he was thirty; Joshua didn't wish to know his age or anything else about him. He'd had expectations of mutual whipping when he invited Joshua to his place, but he hadn't spelled them out, until Joshua, adjusting from the intensity of the pain, heard him say, *"C'est mon tour maintenant! Fouette-moi, férocement!"* to which Joshua could only shake his head. The man bawled: a loud, piercing wail. When he calmed down, he said that he had spent several years in therapy and that their affair had been the first since his last therapy session. *So much for analysis.*

They'd met on May Day, on the grounds of *Les Tuileries*, and between May 2 and May 26, when Joshua discovered that he was a patient at Hôpital Ste-Anne, he'd forgotten everything that had happened to him.

A few weeks after his release from Ste-Anne, he made up his mind to put Paris and Pigalle behind him, and made a mental note to never again listen to his pickups recount their sado-masochistic woes. He'd make sure too that he kept a physical space where he could cultivate the sentiment of being whole.

A desire to halt the London entanglement had caused him to flee to Spain. And fleeing to Paris had been because of what had occurred in Spain. So when he decided to abandon Paris for Montreal, he vowed that if in Montreal his psyche became burdensome, he'd dispose of it, container and all, for he'd had enough of running. Too many flights to escape from himself. And he knows it's what he'll do when he is discharged. No need to attempt it now, when he risks being caught and foiled.

In Montreal the depressions have been there, deepening or lessening commensurate with the angle of the sun's rays on the horizon and always affected by his latest sexual encounter. But for almost twenty-eight years he did not relapse into prolonged amnesia.

In Montreal he made a few basic decisions that he hoped would simplify his life. After all, in two years he'd had two amnesic episodes requiring hospitalization, and in between a depression that only the strongest exercise of will had dragged him out of.

He reflects on the fact that each of his moves was precipitated by a severe psychological crisis. Almost six years had intervened between the one he'd had on Isabella Island and his London breakdown. It had taken that long perhaps because the controls weren't in his hands, and he'd had GCE O and

A levels to prepare for. Will the present crisis cause him to move? To where? He's not now the shallow youth he was between ages sixteen and twenty-three. Each year has left its baggage, which he'll have to carry wherever he goes. Will he move? And what about the vow he'd made to dispose of his life rather than move again? He knows that he has been running away from his memories and himself, but has made it no further than amnesia. And the process of reconstructing his identity after each bout has always been something of a perilous adventure. Having a novel landscape to contemplate, finding lodgings, adjusting to something new, to distract him from the hell within—that's what running has been about.

He arrived in Montreal in late July 1969, two months before his twenty-fourth birthday. Considering that he is now fifty-one and that this is his first full-blown amnesic episode here, the measures he put in place upon his arrival must have worked well for a time, brief bouts of depression and amnesia notwithstanding. Until recently, the years between Paris and the breakdown that brought him to Douglas Hospital had flowed like clear unhindered water. Well, almost. The odd, contrary current occasionally came up from the bottom, but he'd accepted them the way we accept thunderstorms in summer. But silt had been building up, and it took just a heavier than usual downpour to cause a ravaging flood. He laughs. These attempts to shape the indefinable! He feels reassured somewhat. Unless the silt is cleared, the flooding will recur. *The flooding will recur.*

One of the things he had to settle when he got to Montreal was what to do with the fortune he'd inherited. Initially he'd thought of a winter house in Florida. Florida? Maybe one in the Mediterranean then.

He'd thought too of getting himself a companion. Together they could keep house and travel around the world. But a quick inventory of the qualities he needed in such a companion quickly convinced him that he'd sooner find the Sasquatch Monster. Was there someone who could be both Juan, to satisfy his greater need for affection, and the Tate Gallery worker, an infuriated flaying beast sated only by the orgasmic scream—catalyst for his own orgasm? Perhaps a different partner for each need. He did not doubt that in the sexual realm his money could procure him what he wanted—everything but sincerity. He foresaw the hospitalizations each broken affair would bring and convinced himself to stay single.

If anything, he moved to the opposite extreme: testing himself to see how long he could endure without human contact, and when he could no longer resist the need to hold the naked body of a man and to writhe under whipcracks on his buttocks and back, he goes to *Le Bar*. There are other spots where people with such needs meet, but he eschews them. The masks worn at *Le Bar* are few, negotiable, not the infinitely metamorphosing and impenetrable ones that had frustrated him in the London and Paris gay bars he'd frequented.

In the only well-lighted area of *Le Bar*: the foyer, where clients must identify themselves before they enter, there's a large poster of two naked men— one crouches on all fours; one stands with a whip horizontally extended in his right hand, like a freak tail, at the midpoint arc of promise. The whipper's biceps bulge, his face is contorted, his lips retracted, his teeth bared. Imagination supplies the snort and hiss. The poster is captioned "Felicitous Flagellation."

On a wall right beside the coat check is a large cork bulletin board under glass. There you could read the advertisements of sex workers offering their services. Even now he recalls some of them:

> *Satisfier of all tastes*
> *call: . . .*

> *Need a bear, wolf or sheep?*
> *I'm it.*
> *Money back guarantee . . .*

> *Always erect. Its your kum*
> *Rizunuble prize . . .*

> *No haste*
> *Great baste*

Some of the ads include penis length and girth to the nth millimetre. Each time he goes, he glances at the ad board and wonders who answers them. What percentage of people define themselves according to the number and intensity of their orgasms? Recently he learned there's an organisation like AA which deals with sex addicts. Delicious, delirious lust propelling some like rivers hastening into cataracts.

Now here, in the throes of insomnia, he thinks all male animals are sex-obsessed. Freudians say sex and aggression are the basic human drives. *Be careful about calling humans animals.* One night in a Pigalle bar, a fellow about six feet from Joshua had shattered a litre-size bottle of beer on another's head because the other had said he screwed like an animal. In the discussion that followed a few nights later some thought it was a compliment. *Where did I see someone slug another for trying to steal his pickup?* In London. Yes, with Paul present. "Lash in he skunt, to rass!" Paul exclaimed and clapped. "Damn right, man! Don't make nobody take steal your meat."

Yet the major religions teach that to see, taste, or even become God, we must shrivel our balls. And the Catholic Church removed the balls of young singers to create their castrati choirs—divine music for God's, and the castrati's, greater glory, they said. "What is man, that thou are mindful of him / and the son of man that thou visitest him? / Thou hast made him a little lower than the angels." *A little lower than the angels.*

Where was I?

Le Bar.

Le Bar is a membership club. With obsessive earnestness, the proprietor ensures that new members know what's expected of them. He reads them the rules—stuff like not revealing their names, exchanging telephone numbers with their pickups, stuff like that—his brown, beady eyes peering from time to time from behind his glasses; he makes them sign a sheet containing the rules—their agreement to abide by them—which he folds, slowly, methodically, and puts into an envelope of thick, high-quality linen bond paper and gives to them. Next he gives them a special handshake: a code to recognize but not reveal, and welcomes them into "the fraternity."

Inside, everyone quickly learns the conventions: on the ground floor sellers sit on one side, purchasers on the other. Those who are neither sit or stand around the imitation marble horseshoe bar counter, wreathed in a nimbus of cloudy green light with spirals and wisps of cigarette smoke here and there. The music's kept low, a mixture of current and older popular tunes. The second floor, painted an intense black and dimly lit, is where pickups sort out their contacts. Joshua's concerns are never more than two: one: avoiding pickups who'd go off on a bleeding funk once they get to the hotel (he keeps his apartment closed to the rest of humanity—and would neither soil nor become soiled in someone else's); and, two: ensuring he'll not be overpowered and buggered before the act is over, for buggery frightens him, ever since Sparrow had tried to penetrate him. Once he found himself musing that he might end up enslaved to it the way he had become addicted to masochism upon first try.

The manager at *le Bar* keeps an updated list of downtown hotels where his clients could trundle in and out no questions asked. In the tote bag—the French guys call it a *baise-en-ville*—Joshua takes to *le Bar* and eventually to the hotel, he packs a beach blanket along with his favourite whip, a beautiful one with an embossed sterling silver handle and plaited strands of fine Moroccan leather (it had cost him quite a sum at Les Plaisirs de la douleur, an S & M store tucked deep in the bowels of one of the warehouses fronting the Wellington Canal); iodine to forestall the wounds becoming septic; a hand mirror; and a couple of cotton swabs fixed to a foot-long skewer—his improvisation. He'd long debated carrying a switch blade to defend himself should his pickup try to rape him, but he soon saw the impracticality of this, not to mention the possibility of its being used on him. The hotel provides the security his own apartment could never provide, is a place where he could leave the bloodstains behind, though he takes every precaution not to leave any. And when the act is over he leaves with the memory only; he could not eat, sleep, and think in the same spot where his sexual agony is enacted.

In the early years he was invariably the youngest person on the purchaser side, about the same age as most of the sellers; none seemed older than thirty; some seemed as young as sixteen.

He'd chosen to use the name Jonathan there, just in case. But it has been quite unnecessary. In his twenties and up to thirty-five, he'd leave *le Bar* alone roughly one time in two, usually because the person he'd settled for turned out to be perturbing or because the men he preferred—the thirty-ish-looking ones whose faces did not look like canisters of acid—were absent or uninterested.

The morning after, and sometimes for three or four days, he'd feel wrapped in an elegiac mist, a postcoital blues web; and a couple of times he'd felt his sanity splutter like a candle struggling to burn past a defect in its wick.

Only his encounter with "Coetzee" stands out in his memory. Perhaps because he was one of two who refused payment, and the only one who'd ever paid the hotel bill. Perhaps because it was the Sunday Anita Hill inflamed White imagination over the size of Clarence Thomas's dick. Coetzee was quite an athletic fellow. He fixed Joshua with a hypnotic gaze the moment he entered Le Bar. Joshua noted his clearly defined biceps and triceps, narrow waist, thighs that filled his oversize jeans, and, when he turned away briefly, his discreetly bulging buttocks—and swallowed. When Coetzee walked over to the bar and the light fell on him, Joshua saw his luminous sky-blue eyes, as though he were on a sustained adrenalin rush, and his richly tanned skin, a few shades lighter than his thick mop of auburn hair. A health club, he could see, was his second home; someone with leisure enough to spend his days on physical workouts, and his nights on libidinal ones. Clasping a bottle of mineral water, he headed straight towards Joshua and extended his hand, not the usual gesture in such places. "Coetzee," he said, "but you don't have to break the rules and tell me your name. In any event it's a pseudonym I took on after reading *Waiting for the Barbarians*. Cool, eh? That book got me all upset, so it had to be good."

Joshua didn't say anything. He hadn't read it.

During the short walk to the hotel, Coetzee slapped him on the shoulder and said. "I get off on tanned crates, man. I really do."

"Crates!"

"Sure man! Crates for guts, and blood, and shit. We've got to take care of our carcasses. But let's not romanticize them."

In the hotel room. Teeth clenched. Knuckled hands and knees dug into the mattress. Rump in the air. The whip hissing as it furrowed his ass with blow-torch heat. And just as he thought he'd faint or besplatter the room with flesh and blood and bone, the crescendo came, and Coetzee's hiss and wail, enough to rattle the walls. *Waiting for the Barbarians*. He laughs.

On the odd occasion, he varied the routine and dropped in for an hour or so at Metamorphose, where female impersonators performed, before beginning his hunt at Le Bar. How those "women" didn't break their feet in those high heels that made them walk (some wobbled with arms extended for balance) with perpendicular feet. He went too infrequently to ever encounter the same acts. He remembers one in which a corpulent "woman" in green lamé and coppery hair that seemed ablaze went down on all fours and tried with her extended tongue to lick what must have been a 20-inch plastic phallus (black, of course) that another drag queen, dressed in Nazi regalia, had strapped onto "his" groin. "He" did a tantalizing dance about the other's tongue. Suddenly "she" stood up, whimpered like a dog in agony, and with the sounds of a saw encountering a knot, ripped off her laméd dress, turned her back to the audience, bent, showing the folds of her bare, crinkled buttocks and caterwauled, "Now fuck me!" at which point the lights went off. When they came on a few seconds later, her partner had shed his dick and Nazi clothes, was naked, except for a g-string, and had two full breasts that clearly showed she was a woman.

On another Wednesday, a couple, dressed in bath robes, one with curlers in her hair, holding a hand mirror while she dabbed cream on her face, did a Phillip-Elizabeth sketch in French Canadian English, every syllable accented:

Phillip: Lizzy dear, not'ing tonight.

Lizzy: Dat is what I get every night. (*Singing*) I get plenty of not'ing and I want more dan not'ing tonight.

Phillip: (*Pushes his hand in his bathrobe pocket*) Here's a mint, dear.

Elizabeth: (*Looks up at the ceiling and sighs, shakes her head and does not take it*). You are my subject, Phillip. I horder you to—

Phillip: Some t'ings don't hobey orders. Go to bed, dear . . .

Sometimes their acts burlesqued politics. When Reagan invaded Grenada, two actors played a scene of the Reagans in bed. When Reagan couldn't get things moving, he picked up the telephone and shouted into the receiver, "Henry, I must invade Grenada."

Most times the acts were light-hearted, other times raucous, with the actors even pulling the stuffing from their bras and throwing it into the audience, like brides tossing bouquets. When the acts went over the top the audience booed or threw pennies, but more often than not people would stand in front of the stage and offer them dollar bills.

He smiles, then gets goose bumps, as he sees himself recounting all this to Blenheim, Stein and Defoe. Later documented in his chart for all and sundry to read. Blenheim's less than honest about keeping what's in his file confidential.

To what extent is Sparrow responsible for what his life has been? Would he have been in this state if he'd never known Sparrow? Is Sparrow the cause of his amnesia? Why would anyone wish to erase his identity periodically? Why when his conscious self begins to re-emerge it behaves like an irresponsible child? The taped recordings Dr Defoe played for him of what he'd said as he emerged from confusion are the mere babblings of an incoherent toddler delighting in mischief.

What triggered this latest self-forgetting? So far his efforts to remember what happened to him immediately before this latest episode fizz out in sheer futility, resemble the dense grey smoke he felt enclosed in a few weeks before. There's never been a recognizable pattern to his remembering what triggers his amnesia. In London, it was only after he had resumed stuttering that he understood that Sparrow's death had brought on his breakdown. At Ste-Anne's in Paris, his consciousness had entered his head, sounding like galloping horses on a wooden bridge, before his stutter came and before he realized the Eastern European man's confession had overcharged his psyche and shut it down. Those horse-hoof sounds were still in his brain when he was asked in badly accented English, "What are you?" (Afterwards, when the sounds had left, he realized the doctor wanted to know his nationality.) But at the moment he'd answered, in French, "Flesh that shits, sweats, pisses, and stinks—humanity"—(*"De la chaire, frère. Elle pue, elle sue, elle pisse et elle shie—comme toute l'humanité."*) A shadow like a cloud had passed over the doctor's face.

There is no pattern really. Will he ever know what shut down his sanity this time? And if he never finds out? The thought is frightening. But he'll know when he is again himself: when his stutter returns, when people, when conversation become a burden.

Was it Sparrow's death alone or was it the fear it created in him as he contemplated his own sexuality—that and the guilt he felt for his mother's rape, the rape that made him a millionaire—that sparked the London breakdown?

He had been in Montreal a full year before deciding what to do about his fortune. Mommy's will instructed Sparrow to sell the plantation, all but Arcadia and its fenced-in three acres, and to invest the money; and that was what he did. Even before Joshua left Isabella Island cane-cutters had to be brought in from the neighbouring islands. As early as the 1960s the planters were worried.

Pine Knot had told them one Saturday night when they were all sitting around the dining table at Arcadia drinking. "Time was when they used to be begging for jobs. Now they're all heading off to England. In two years we'll be cutting our own canes."

"You swinging a machete!" Manchester told him. "That would be fun to watch."

"Yeah, watch him chop his legs off," Blenkinsopp said.

"True enough. Labour's a problem," Horse-jaw put in. "We should all support that Renfrew fellow in Antigua on that petition he plans to send to the House of Commons to put a stop to coloured immigration. He told me he sent it to every planter from the Bahamas to Guyana. I told him to point out that since Britain is offering the islands independence"—a few of them guffawed—"they should make West Indians stay home to develop their country."

"Excellent argument that," Pine Knot said.

The others nodded.

"I don't know about you, mates," he continued, "but I intend to oppose this independence thing with every drop of my blood. No oath of allegiance from me to nigger politicians with deep pockets. Never! But one battle at a time. First we must stop this mass migration."

The ban on Black immigration did come, a year or two later. Independence too, in 1971. He read about in the *Montreal Star*. The article had focused more on the fact that the prime minister had fought in the Canadian military during World War II and had studied political science at McGill. He wonders where the plantocrats and their relatives are now, whether most of them had moved to Australia and South Africa as they'd threatened to do rather than live as non-British citizens under Black governments.

The government bought Éclair Estates Ltd; and Sparrow, who knew nothing about investing money, had simply deposited the proceeds from the sale into three US bank accounts. In 1967, in fact until 1971, when Isabella Island became independent, inheritance taxes were unheard of. For although the planters were no longer being elected to the Legislative Council, their Black stooges needed their money; in return they eschewed policies inimical to the planters' interests. Keeping inheritance-tax legislation from passing was one such policy. Apart from legal fees, all Averill Éclair's wealth was passed to Joshua and Sparrow; and eventually all that Sparrow had, save a small endowment that he left his church, he bequeathed to Joshua.

To Joshua the sums seemed enormous. Even after the penalizing income tax deductions imposed on US nonresidents, he was left with an annual income of over one million US (now it's over four million). He concluded that he should hold on to it, if for no other reason than the freedom it would give him. "Blessed are the meek," Mommy was fond of saying "when wealth insures their meekness." Poverty bothered her, she said; and occasionally she speculated that, "in an ideal world, everybody would have just enough and no more. Socialism, if it could work, would be the thing"; but she must have added silently that she did not live in an ideal world and hoped she never would.

During his first year at Queen Mary, after he'd pulled away the screen set up by the plantocracy to hide reality, it had struck him that the beatitudes— *Blessed are the meek, . . . Blessed are the poor in spirit*—in fact three-quarters of the Bible, could have been written by a committee of plantocrats, one delighting in cruel irony.

Mommy's congregation at Saint Andrew's Presbyterian Church often sang, the organ a deep roll (a suffusing ethos they might have termed the holy ghost):

Almighty father, king of kings,
The lover of the meek,
Make me a friend of helpless things,
Defender of the weak.

Beneath his heaven
There's room for all.
He gives to all their meat
He sees the meanest sparrow fall
Unnoticed the street.

And now he wishes he'd had the awareness to challenge her to remake the hymn:

Almighty father, Tyrant supreme,
Created by the rich,
Make me the richest of the rich,
Pro-pri-e-tor of everything.

He gives to all their meat, so they were justified in paying starvation wages. And so that first year at Queen Mary, Yahweh became the capitalist's god much like Poseidon was the mariners'.

A month after he arrived in Montreal he got a financial brokerage house in New York, one with a Montreal branch office, to manage his fortune. But there would be no house in Florida or the Mediterranean, nor here either, and no partner or partners. If Bita were alive it would have been a different story. She and her children—if she had gone on to have children—could have lived with him or he could visit them, or they him. She never did have any. No surprise in that. Mammy had told her often enough what a burden she was. She wouldn't have wanted to have to say so to anyone. He had never for a minute thought about her having a husband. But Bita was not alive, at any rate, not in the flesh.

In an American literature course he audited at Sir George Williams University (it was not Concordia then) his first winter here, he had come upon Thoreau's *Walden* and Emerson's essays. Thoreau and Emerson answered his question about material possessions. "Things are in the saddle and ride mankind"—Emerson's words. They would not ride him. "*Simplify! Simplify!*" was Thoreau's clarion cry. And it was catalytic in making up his mind to keep an income of $40,000 for himself and give the rest to charitable organizations operating hospitals in Africa. His financial broker convinced him to make this a temporary agreement, renewable every year; and to always reinvest a third of all his earnings. Not quite how Thoreau would have done it, but Emerson would have approved. Cultivating his six feet of earth, though, as Thoreau advised, has been slow and, he sees now, futile.

He has always lived simply. Come to think of it, Mommy did too. Her receptions were the exception. Expensive clothes had never interested him. In Europe he bought clothes that kept him warm in winter and comfortable in summer, and merely ensured that he had enough to change until he got back those he had taken to the cleaners. He ate in very modest restaurants and cooked for himself sometimes: bland food mostly, for, after Rose's cooking, food became like petrol to a car. His only passion was going to the theatre and books. He bought a lot of books but always found them too heavy to carry whenever he moved, so he always left them behind, hoping they would get into the hands of someone who'd appreciate them, remembering and laughing about a set of outdated *Encyclopaedia Britannica* Mommy was discarding and that Dawn had begged for to prop up her bed which, she said, was sinking in the middle.

How, he asks himself again, is he going to be able to tell all this to Blenheim, Defoe, and Stein. But Bita has ordered him to do so. And he cannot disobey her.

16

AT NINE DR BLENHEIM ARRIVES but Joshua is drowsy.

"You look like a wet towel this morning," Blenheim tells him.

"I had Valium around eleven and I was wide awake by three, awakened by a dream, and my mind was as keen as a January wind until a couple hours ago."

"What was the dream?"

He tells him.

"Sounds to me like your sister gives you good advice."

Joshua looks at him with skepticism.

"How was your day out?"

"Okay. They didn't have callaloo soup so I settled for oxtail soup. A little too much pepper but otherwise quite good. Afterwards I had jerk pork. It burned the hell out of me. It was really Caribbean food, the way I imagine my biological mother would have cooked it. Though I don't usually care one way or the other how food tastes."

"Have you begun keeping your journal?"

"I wrote a few things in it. Let me read you what I wrote." He adjusts himself and pulls open the drawer of his night table and takes out the notebook and his reading glasses.

When he finishes reading and looks up, Dr Blenheim is nodding. "Good. There's a lot there to work with. A lot. You know what archetypes are?"

"More or less."

"I've been told that you know a great deal about Jung."

"A little." He is feeling anxious and wonders why. He puts the notebook and the glasses back into the night-table drawer. His back is itching him. He tries to scratch it without distracting Blenheim.

"According to the information in your file, you spoke a lot about Jung before you got around to controlling your thoughts, even lectured the staff on occasion." He smiles. "Do you see any parallels between the country where a person grows up and his mother?"

He wants Blenheim to leave so he could scratch his back properly. He wishes he could say so, but he forces himself to answer the question silently. Blenheim is on to something. On Isabella Island peasants bury the umbilical cord in a ceremony. And when people want to say they belong to a certain place they say their umbilical cord is buried there. He yawns, loud, uncontrollably. "Excuse me, doctor."

"I'm going to leave you to have a nap. Anything you think of, write it down, and we'll explore it tomorrow."

He scratches his back and falls asleep as soon as Dr Blenheim leaves. When he awakens and checks the clock it is 10:30. He feels rested now.

He sees Gladys peering in at the door. "Would you like some tea, Mr Éclair?"

"Yes. Thanks."

She returns with it, pours him a cup, puts it on the tray, and puts the tray on his night table. "Are you going out today?"

"I don't think so." He likes her perfume. It has a lily-of-the-valley fragrance with something acrid—like ashes—mixed in. It's different from her much stronger one, which is faintly cinnamon, but she is wearing those god-forsaken, bark-brown slacks and that awful green top that makes her look like the Montreal Expos mascot.

"Can I get Leroy to do something for me then?"

"Certainly."

The tea revives him and the nap has truly refreshed him. He decides to get out of bed and sit in the armchair. Otherwise he'd have trouble sleeping again tonight. Sleeplessness has plagued him for several years. It's the rare night that he isn't awake by two. Most times he spends it at his window looking out at the human traffic on Ste-Catherine Street. That's how he had become intrigued by the gay fellow whose apartment is across the hall from his, not that Joshua has ever spoken to him. He seems to change national-ity every day, as much as clothing and wigs permit. Some days he'll wear a kilt and a beret, some days a *bou-bou*, other days tucks and tails, dashikis, togas, and even leather stockings. His hair sometimes fools Joshua and he would listen, only to hear him opening the door. Eventually he'd recognize him by his gait. His Caucasian wigs range from platinum blond to raven black, some with pigtails, others with bangs and still others with huge curls. But when he dons dreadlocks, or braids, or his gollywog Afro, he is indeed a sight.

He must be hot stuff because he scores most nights. Between three and three-thirty, without fail, he returns each morning, rarely alone. If Joshua did not see him enter, he would hear the key turning in the door and the indecipherable words he and his pickup exchange. He doesn't seem to have a job, unless it's as a waiter in the bar where he meets his lovers. Joshua wonders if, like him, he lives off an inheritance.

Initially the fellow's need to metamorphose perturbed Joshua. Were the fellow to write his memoirs, he once mused, he would be among the first to buy a copy. In flesh-and-blood mode he'd never want the fellow to know how much his life intrigues him. He read somewhere that often people with unsalvageable childhoods invent identities that are easier to live with, and sometimes multiple identities with fatal results. How, he wonders, could someone take his clothes off night after night and share his body with strange men. Yet it's precisely because of the fellow's oddity, he knows, that he has paid attention to him. He would be hard pressed to identify anyone else who lives in his building, even the janitor.

Once the fellow had winked at him. It was an early summer evening a few years back. The fellow had just entered the main entrance. He was dressed in leather and cowboy boots and carrying a riding crop. Joshua was just behind him. A gaunt woman in a grey two-piece suit with an iguana-green scarf loosely thrown over one shoulder was coming down the stairs from the mezzanine level. She gasped when she saw the fellow. They fixed each other with their eyes. Suddenly the woman became something of a granite perch for her iguana, as if the fellow had Medusan power. When the fellow unlocked his gaze he turned around to Joshua, winked, then bounded up the stairs, two at a time, flicking his whip. In the meantime the woman regained motion and left.

Stop thinking about him, he tells himself. But his mind will not let the fellow go. He remembers Germaine Greer's moving defence of her father when she uncovered the identity he'd created for class purposes; and there was Grey Owl, an Englishman who'd come to Canada and re-invented himself as a Mohawk. *I don't even know the fellow's name.* His nameplate on the building's directory reads "Occupé." *Perhaps he changes his name to fit the clothes he's wearing.*

Of course there'll be those who'd say—and he was one of them at first—that these are mere masks, which, if stripped away, might expose emptiness. Like Mommy says, and as Mrs Blenkinsopp once told Mrs Manchester, under our clothes we're all naked. Now he believes that, worn over the banality of most people's reality, his own included, a complex mask might make a person more interesting. There'd be trouble though if the person became his mask; we do not need Jung to tell us that.

He wonders if he hasn't been living a big part of his life vicariously, via this fellow who daily gives the finger to those who, like himself, drift along in a don't-disturb-the-waters conformity. There is vitality and variety, he seems to be saying, outside the predictable centre. He remembers those nights following Reverend Ealing's murder when he hadn't seen or heard him enter and had worried about his safety.

Promiscuity has always bothered Joshua. He wonders whether his fear of it is not just another of the barricades he has tried all his life to build to wall out what frightens him, to stave off the chaos inside and outside himself. But this fellow suggests that it's better to become Proteus than to bind him.

Perhaps, too, in his sexual sampling, he finds home and hearth, and freedom in fluidity. Even that bugle of Victorian conformity, Tennyson, heard Homer's false note, knew that the adventurous prefer Sibyls, one or two in every port; that hearths can constrict, can be for some the eighth deadly sin. *And perhaps no Penelopes or Sibyls when the ports of call are in the soul.*

This fellow. Deviant, sorcerer, heretic, abominator: he'd have been any of these not so long ago (would be still in some societies and still is in segments of our own), and would have been summarily lynched, burned, quartered, or stoned.

He's no help for me. I belong to the fixed centre.

Perhaps he should talk to the fellow, introduce himself. Yes, when he gets out of here he'll do it. Let him know he enjoys watching his ever-changing personas. But he has always had difficulty striking up conversations with others.

The semester he began auditing courses at Sir George Williams University, he saw a leaflet inviting Isabellans to join the Isabellan Association of Montreal. "The next best thing to being home is to be with those from home," the leaflet advised. But Joshua had fled from home without it ever looking as if he'd done so. There was a phone number for its president, Max Sinclair (whose father, Ovid Sinclair, had caused a stink at the Plantocrats' Club). Joshua was intent on joining the Association, largely because Max was its president, but he never got around to doing so, and never once did he run into Max.

In the raucous seventies he felt an urge to join one or other of the many militant Black organizations that sprang up in Montreal. He even considered wearing an Afro wig. Then his hair was sable, now it's eighty percent grey. He bought *Black-Is-Beautiful*, *Free-Angela* (Davis) and *Free-Huey* (Newton) buttons. Two Black female students, in sparkling green-and-gold dashikis, their arms, ankles, and necks indefatigable cowry-shell orchestras, sold them in the foyer of the Hall building. But he never wore them. The young women, their cowry shells percussing (or protesting their exile from West Africa), addressed the Black students as brothers and sisters, harangued them to read the books they were peddling, to seize their heritage, and "expunge the man's beliefs and abominations." Not one of the pamphlets or spiels they routinely gave to Blacks who passed by did they give to him, and it was too humiliating to beg to be noticed. *Whatever you think, Dr Defoe, black is a colour.*

One of them especially attracted him. Her round, oak-brown face dimpled when she smiled. Her every movement was an effortless glide, a subtle dance that set her dashiki rustling and the cowry shells trilling; she seemed complete, a nation unto herself, with parliament, army, air force, and navy. He'd have renamed her *Together*, the word then for today's *cool*, could he have done so. In her speech he heard the rustle of the breeze as it gently undulated the fields of green, growing canes that stretched for miles on the flat fields north of Arcadia, and in her placidity he saw quiet confidence: the confidence of the Caribbean Sea. Her friends going to and from the escalators called to her and greeted her as Sis.

Her companion Hilda, who rarely got greetings, made him think of a steep hill culminating in a cliff. Her voice was sharp, high-pitched, flagellant; her elliptical mahogany face already etched with frown lines; her skeleton meagre, with just enough flesh to bind it; her movements and gestures slicing. In her he saw Medusa, a deeply wounded human being.

Yet those were appearances that most likely belied their private lives. Public images: the faces we don in public to conceal our private, barely-held-together lives. Faces for the societal stage we're trained to act on—faces of blissful fictional lives that shroud the unpleasant that's beyond the sound, sight, and smell of others. But sometimes we fail, are more than the automatons society wants—and it is a good thing—even when we're punished for it.

He had gone by their stand at least six times and stared at them rather than at the identity trinkets they were peddling, so they must have remarked him, and must have had their own assessments of him. They must have known too that he wanted to converse with them. But they were from the Caribbean, their memory tinctured, even scarred, by the slights and the silent and not-so-silent insults of West Indian "mulattoes"—the venom too of those "mulattoes" left empty, bitter and turning rancid after independence swallowed up their space and stripped them of the perquisites of being beige. "*If you're White you're right. If you're Brown hang around. If you're Black move back.*" "Mulattoes" who no longer had first pick of what Whites did not need, "mulattoes" unwanted in Australia, New Zealand, and South Africa, who had to meet the requirements like everyone else and stand in line rather than head the line of would-be immigrants to Canada and the US, where they promptly discovered they too were niggers. In the Caribbean, Hilda and Sis would have responded to his gesture, and mocked him probably after he'd left. But such conditioning was superfluous in

Montreal. The baggage should be too, but our past contains our present and its threads bind our psyche, even when they are threads of hate and pain.

Unconsciously something in him must have been crying out for belonging, for loneliness isn't something he's conscious of. Belonging. But relinquishing control comes with belonging. These are things he has never allowed himself to think through. Why? And so he settled for human spaces he could enter and leave at will. Spaces like Le Bar and Metamorphose, Concordia's classrooms and George's. For relationships require that we numb parts of our being. Honesty cedes to the lies and flattery that lubricate the axles and pivots of relationships. We become auxiliaries in our own relationships. Much as Mommy's was swallowed up by her marriage; even when marriage became a corpse she felt unauthorized to bury.

On one of those days he happened to be in the foyer of the Hall building when the Quebec Board of Black Educators was having a recruitment session in the auditorium. The meeting got bellicose, and spilled into the foyer, and name-calling eventually gave way to fisticuffs. Suppose he hadn't been there that morning, would he have worn the wig, joined an organization or two, and stayed, for how long? Years later, when CSIS and the RCMP publicly sniped at each other in their battles for turf, he learned about *agents provocateurs*: their spies planted to sow dissension in groups they deemed subversive. Their *provocateur* for QBBE turned out to be a Black American, who later told journalists what he'd been hired to do and how well he'd done it; he sued the RCMP for firing him. Joshua wonders what became of the lawsuit.

No belonging for him. Instead he has been drifting along from day to day and year to year, in limited channels, here and there recognizing the odd Isabellan and saying hello until the alterations of time made him and them no longer recognizable. Reduced to watching his neighbour enter with his pickups, then reading until seven-thirty before falling asleep again, to remain in bed until ten. In the afternoon or evening, if there were courses he was auditing at Concordia, he headed there. And before or after class, weather permitting, he'd take a long walk. Each year he'd go to see a few plays and the art exhibits in the museums. That's the sum of his Montreal existence.

Now he recalls something that had been discussed in a political science class devoted entirely to the works of Rousseau. He remembers a pink-skinned, burly boy resisting the professor's attempt to disqualify Rousseau's fatherland-identity argument: when one "has ceased to have a fatherland, he no longer exists; and if he is not dead, he is worse than dead." Joshua sided with the professor, but even then he knew it was because he was afraid of the personal implications of Rousseau's statement.

None of this is worth writing down, he thinks, but he gets up and pulls open the drawer of his night table and removes the notebook and his reading glasses. Now he realizes that to write comfortably he needs a desk and there is none in the room. He writes for a while as best he can and somehow an echo of the Apostle Paul comes to mind, no doubt one he'd heard in Sparrow's church. And he adds his thoughts to those he has already written down.

This envelope Paul or King James's translators call the mortal coil holds so much that's enemy to physical and psychical stability—shit we imbibed and never expunged when we emerged from the primordial sluice. Not just the seeds of death, much else that finds food in our ill health. That omniscient God that primitive and not-so-primitive religions credit with creation every day appears more and more incompetent.

Gladys Knights comes into the room. "Oh, you're writing. There's a desk belonging to this room. Where did we put it?"

She heads back to the nursing station. Ten minutes later Leroy brings the desk. It's just a twenty- by thirty-six-inch plank with supports, barely enough to write on. But it beats being propped up in bed writing in a notebook resting on his knees. He sits down, thinking he has lots more to write but finds that each time a thought begins to coalesce, it's as if something, a hand or a net, comes forward and snatches it. After trying for fifteen minutes and experiencing only blanks, he gives up.

He turns the radio on. The spring weather of the last couple of days has ended. Winter's brief holiday is over. It has rarely ever been too cold for him to take an hour-long walk, sometimes a two-hour walk. In all but the coldest months, he'd go up to Mount Royal—"the Mountain"—daily, carrying an umbrella if necessary, wearing a raincoat when it was wet and windy.

In fall, when the summit is one giant sunset glow with dashes of russet and oxblood, and Michaelmas daisies, gentian and white, rise a foot or two above the leaf-strewn ground. Later, when the still-falling leaves swirl around him, and his footsteps crush those the wind strews on the steps to the summit. Eventually the naked trees, silently mourning their lost clothing, sun-cursed and sun-sentenced to periodic whippings by glacial winds, their naked grey bodies against an azure sky, or beaten by cold wind and rain, their branches and twigs arms and fingers extended in futile pleading to the indifferent canopy of ash-grey sky. Here and there a lone hemlock, rocketlike, green, resists winter's fluid, icy fingers. In blossoming spring, when the translucent leaves hurrying to maturity tint the slopes avocado green with splotches here and there of apple blossom pink, and the air is full of fragrances. And, of course, summer, when the chestnuts, maples, walnuts, willows, oaks, beeches, poplars, elms, and birches that clothe, shelter, feed—birds especially—seem invincible; harmonize with the air and make music. Trees, trapped like us in the cycles of time, conforming to the sun's vagaries, smiling at us perhaps, knowing that we, for whom they're fuel today, will be their fuel tomorrow.

But in winter he dares not scale the Mountain, knows he's from the tropics. He abandons it to the skiers, snowshoers, and tobaggoners. *And for good reason, he now sees. The one time he did so was in mad oblivion, and he had to be rescued half-buried from the snow, and he lost two of his toes.* Instead, except on days when the ice crackles under foot or denies him a foothold, he walks all the way to La Fontaine Park, pausing on his return to warm up in the same café, George's, whose owner is also called George. There he buys a bran muffin and coffee, George getting to know his order so well that he merely asks, probably without listening, *"Comme d'habitude?"* two minutes later bringing him a reheated bran muffin, a gob of butter, and a cup of coffee.

Usually the café is empty, and he and George exchange banalities, about the weather mostly. The second winter George seemed happy to see him and wanted to know if he'd been ill or out of the country, and Joshua had explained, while George wiped the tables and paused briefly every minute or so to make eye contact, that in the warmer weather he prefers to walk up on the Mountain. George straightened, stared hard at him, and brought his bushy, black eyebrows closer in a deep frown, but said nothing. Only when Joshua read a few years later about police raids on the Mountain in areas where gays congregate to have sex, did he understand the meaning of George's gesture. In winter George could hardly think that his walk that ends at La Fontaine Park is for that purpose. The day following George's puzzling reaction, he asked Joshua, *"Comment tu gagnes ta vie?"* Joshua was tempted to translate it literally—"How do you win (earn) your life?"—and answer, "One minute at a time." *(Today he would have answered, "On ne gagne pas sa vie, on la perd, souffle par souffle.")* Instead he lied, told George he works at night as a security guard. At that moment George came over, in a gesture of solidarity, and topped up Joshua's cup, and a certain guarded tenseness that had been in his face earlier dissolved.

When George is turned away from him he is usually frowning. It has etched deep frown lines in his forehead, just above his thick eyebrows that join in a thin line at his nose. His eyes are dark, and at a certain angle, his brows, eyelashes, and eyes seem to merge into two circular dark masses. His hair is black (without a strand of grey although he is around Joshua's age), plentiful, and bristly like the hair on a pig's tail. He told Joshua he has two boys. Disappointments both. "Bums." When Joshua did not volunteer any information about himself, he asked if Joshua has children. Joshua avoids asking George about his children, fearing that it would be an invitation for George to ask him questions he has no answers for or that he does not wish to answer. Instead winter after winter he watches George furtively as he moves among the tables, wiping them even when no one has used them, his round belly pushing out his white apron further and further, his shoulders broad and sturdy. He measures about five-seven and has, like so many men in northern cities, a torso disproportionate to his legs. Joshua feels drawn to him but would not want him to know this. George is probably wondering what has become of him. If he is discharged before spring, he'll have to concoct a story for George. Nothing about illness or death but something that won't make George think he's lying.

Joshua has often wondered if he's Spanish, has heard sounds like the Spanish "ou" instead of the French "u" in his pronunciation, and has been tempted once or twice to call him Jorge, but remembers that some immigrants prefer to blend into the host society, and bristle at the slightest reminder that they originated elsewhere.

And suddenly he remembers December 22. He was lucid on December 22. He took a Christmas card for George that day. The first time he'd given a card to anyone in North America. George had stiffened a bit when Joshua handed him the card, but later came and topped up his coffee cup without Joshua asking him to. He'd forgotten that. So between December 22 and January 6, when they took him to the Douglas, he'd been in a mental void.

He writes none of this down.

His thoughts return to his immediate need: finding something to fill his time. What books are there to read? He'd rather do something physical. He remembers hearing someone mention a swimming pool. He'd occasionally gone swimming to distract himself from the dreariness of the London winter months, even when he lived at Woodford. Observing the London skyline from the campus at Mile End, he'd noted in his sporadically kept journal: *Day after dreary day, a million chimneys from a million coal-consuming*

bowels perpetually fart their foetid fumes. Even the trees weep. Wordsworth, your
"great heart" envenoms blood and scorches lungs.

And yet he has to admit that on some Montreal winter days—no question here of London smog; large chunks of Cree homeland are under water to prevent that—the cold and wind race with blood-curdling hisses off Mount Royal's face, easily piercing clothes and skin. He preferred the much drier air of Madrid, though not its broiling summer. He has no vivid memories of Paris's winter, though he recalls that it was damp. But he remembers its silver-blue spring sky and its mathematical, rational, arrogant architecture, venerating man's instinct to debase nature and exalt reason. Their differences hardly matter; he lost his sanity in all three. Lost it before then too, in the land of his birth, and now here. Place does not ensure sanity. It comes from within. *It has to come from within.*

He thinks again it might be a good idea to go swimming. He never did swim in Montreal, though once he was tempted to join the YMCA for exactly that reason. The walks seem to have satisfied his need for exercise. But he won't walk today.

He goes to the nursing station. You have to reserve, Gladys Knights tells him. Besides, each ward has its day and hour. But she phones anyway. And since it would be he alone—Leroy won't be swimming—it's okay. Then he remembers he doesn't have trunks. Leroy offers to go into Verdun and buy him a pair. It makes Joshua feel guilty, reminds him of the privilege of money. He lets Leroy keep the change.

17

HE'S IN MIST AND FLOATING. He lifts an arm. It's limp. He brings it down and it falls with a plop. Yes, he's definitely in bed. There's a vague light in the room. Dimmed by fog, it seems. His head is pulsing. He can hear every single heartbeat. "Where am I?" The question is to himself.

A gruff voice he recognizes but cannot place says, "In ya bed."

He is falling through thick fog and then he is blank.

He awakens suddenly with an explosive headache. He can feel the pulsation of each heartbeat in his eyes. He remembers that he should have gone swimming. Did he go? His lips are parched and his throat's dry. He sees an IV pole. He's on an IV drip. He turns his head. The rails are up on the right side of his bed. He looks to the left. They are up there too.

"You wake up?"

It's Leroy's voice. Joshua discerns his upright figure moving towards the bed.

"Glad fee see you awake, man. Tough going a while back there."

"What you mean?" He has trouble talking. His throat is so dry.

"The doctor else the nurse going tell you."

"My throat's on fire. May I have a glass of water?"

Leroy leaves to get it. Joshua smells feces and realizes that he is wet. It registers. He has had a relapse. That's what the fog was all about.

Leroy returns with the water, helps Joshua into a sitting position, props him up with pillows, and Joshua slowly drinks.

"Can you get me some cyanide, Leroy?"

"Nurse Knights on her way to see you; ask her for some."

She's in the room before Leroy even finishes the sentence.

"Good morning, Mr Éclair."

He does not answer.

"Good morning, Joshua."

"What's good about it?"

"First, let's get you comfortable, then you'll feel better." She disconnects the IV and lowers the rails on the bed. She holds his legs, Leroy his torso, and they have him sitting up with his feet dangling on the side of the bed, Leroy's steadying hand keeping him upright.

Through the half-open door a linen trolley is visible. Nurse Knights puts on gloves, removes Joshua's hospital gown. He has no recollection of ever putting it on. Leroy puts a hospital robe over him and supports him to the bathroom. In there he is made to sit on a chair while Leroy runs a frothy, perfumed bath. Leroy deftly sits Joshua on the rim of the tub before easing him into it. He's about to wash Joshua with a rag but Joshua takes the rag from him. *I can do that at least*, he tells himself. Leroy moves to shampoo Joshua's hair. He shakes his head. *Not in fecal water*, he thinks. "Afterwards."

He has been soaking for about five minutes. "How long I've been out, Leroy?"

"Three days. Nurse Knights else the doctor going tell you 'bout it."

"That bad?"

"Kind o' violent too."

"Who was the person in the room before you came?"

"McKenna."

"Oh!"

Leroy chuckles—an involuntary chuckle, which he moves quickly to suppress.

"The other day I heard him ordering that Black man—"

"Boysie?"

"Yes—about, shouting at him *'Move it, man! I ain't got all evenin'!'*"

"Don' surprise me one bit. Him is from Halifax. He not going bother you: monkey always know what tree him can climb 'pon, who him can piss on and whose fleas he got to pick."

They fall silent. The bath makes him alert, the ache in his head is less acute, and he is thinking he has regressed. *Rub-a-dub-dub, two men in a tub. I've regressed.* With his big toe he undoes the cork. "Now I can shampoo." He reaches for the bottle. Leroy helps him get up and adjusts the water for a rinsing shower.

He's now back in bed with a dull headache. The IV pole's no longer in the room. The window is open a crack. The wind whistles through, a veritable siren seeking to enlarge the sliver. The linen is all fresh. The room's been sprayed with air freshener. Leroy is sitting in the armchair. Joshua smells roses, and turns to see a beautiful bouquet on his windowsill. Two double peach gerberas stand out from the remaining flowers. He wonders who sent them. They take him back to Arcadia, to Henry manuring the flower beds, cutting off the dead blooms with the shears attached to a second belt; to Dawn meeting him at the gate the day Bita died; to the windows he broke before blanking out that first time. He feels a deep sense of loss, a deep awareness of how cut off he is from his past, the breadth of his aloneness.

Suddenly he begins recalling his last dream—a nightmare really.

He's in a forest and can't find his way out. The trees are thick; no light pierces the overhead canopy; his feet are caught in lianas. Where's Bita? She would know how to get him out of here. His mother's voice answers: "This time you will have to do it by yourself. Don't you think it's time you grow up? And let me tell you something: Bita is your sister, not your wife, if you know what I mean."

He wants to say something sarcastic and hurtful to her. Imagine, lecturing him! Where was she when he needed her? He hears her laughter: a jackal's mocking laughter, in the distance.

Hissing follows. It gets closer, louder: a frenetic whiplash. He wants to look behind him, but the lianas binding his feet have extended to his torso and hold his head in a vise. A snake! The hissing's now directly in his ear and becomes a thundering heartbeat interspersed with Sparrow's loud, high-pitched laughter. He wants to scream but is afraid of Sparrow, bound as he is. "Don't hurt me, please! Don't hurt me!"

His body is covered in icy sweat.

"Who is hurting you?" the voice is Gladys Knights'. "Were you dreaming?"

But at that point the hissing resumes, joined by the drumming heartbeat and laughter. Amid it all he hears Gladys Knights speaking, other voices too, but cannot discern what they're saying. He's screaming and when he stops he hears footsteps running and he remembers no more.

"I've brought you a pot of tea and some cookies," a smiling Gladys Knights says. He almost weaves her into the nightmare he is recalling. She hands the tray to Leroy, who holds it while she pours a cup of tea from a cafeteria-type stainless steel teapot.

"Who sent the flowers?"

"The woman you asked to marry you. You see, I'm not even jealous, though I have every reason to be. Nurse Ramon. Didn't you propose to her? Her husband brought them while you were having your bath."

It touches him. He tells himself he must give her a thank-you card. He places the cup on the hospital trolley tray overhanging his abdomen. You need friends and relatives to do things like send you flowers when you're sick. All his years in Montreal he'd never thought of these things in serious ways. One Christmas day—1985, he believes—he'd deviated from his usual path and had walked to Verdun. It was raining heavily. Must have been around two-three in the afternoon. It wasn't yet dark. Along the way, his attention was caught by the number of people getting out of cars, heading off to family Christmas dinners, their arms laden with presents. He'd felt he needed no such thing. Rationalizations. Protection from the painful fact that he knows nothing of such family communion. On Christmas Day and New Year's Day he eats leftovers, in protest, he tells himself, but has never bothered to identify what he is protesting. Christmas at Arcadia used to be a simple affair within the *family*. There were no servants on hand. The cooking was done the day before. He and Sparrow did the cleaning up. Mommy used to make a thick chocolate sauce for a white cake that she herself baked. It used to be his delight until he became revolted by chocolate because of what Sparrow once did with it. The act had made him want to vomit, but in England he discovered that it's a common practice in the gay world and even has a name. She stopped making it after he no longer ate it.

He knows he is trying to get at something in himself. But the pieces aren't converging, stay scattered across his psyche. He thinks of reaching for the notebook to write, but although his thoughts are clear—the tangled branches and lianas in his head earlier are gone—his muscles are limp.

He turns his head to the window. It's snowing outside. He looks at the flowers again, admires them, and is reminded of the need for relatives and friends.

An image of the mud hut he was born in fills his head. *Pity would be no more, if we did not make somebody poor.* He admires Blake's idealism, always did from the time he discovered Mommy's copy of *Songs of Innocence and Experience.*

Leroy is dozing.

Joshua wants to talk to him—about injustice, about poverty, about Bita, about his mother, about his being rich (and poor) because his father, a White man possessing power and property, had raped his mother. But Leroy's religion sings, "Wash me in the blood of the lamb and I shall be whiter than snow." And Leroy is Jamaican, knows this reality, and would be annoyed with him for talking about it. But Joshua needs to talk.

"Leroy, money stinks. They deodorize it. But it stinks. Your master Christ was right. Buddhists feel the same way about it. Run from money lest it taints you. No use using it to buy crutches. They're no substitute for legs. Blood redeems you, Leroy, but money blights me."

Leroy looks up at him but does not answer, and it makes Joshua uneasy. His religion probably tells him to be like Job, that he's of the Elect, and stands a good chance of dying rich. *Change the subject.* "Leroy, can you find out if Dr Blenheim is coming to see me today?"

"I have fee use your bell."

"Oh!" *I'm under twenty-four-hour, round-the-clock surveillance.*

They awaken him for lunch. Dr Blenheim will be by to see him at 1:30, Leroy tells him. He has no appetite for the dried-out lamb chop, mashed potato, and string beans, so he drinks the barley soup and eats the custard, and while doing so wonders how he'll face Blenheim. He's almost blaming Blenheim for his relapse. Is Blenheim blaming him? What caused it? Would they now say he's psychotic and perform whatever procedure they please?

Blenheim arrives accompanied by Defoe. They get over the greetings quickly and then there's an awkward pause.

Joshua remembers a funny line from Toni Morrison's *Song of Solomon*, modifies it to—*if you ain't the dumbest unhung nigger!* ... but stops short of saying so to Defoe. "Why are you both so silent?" he asks and stares at the wall near the foot of his bed.

"Good question. You couldn't ask that yesterday, nor the day before—"

"Nor even the day before the day before," Defoe completes Blenheim's sentence.

"You've come to tell me I'm psychotic, right? That you've changed my diagnosis to—"

"No. We want to let you know," Defoe answers, "that this is to be expected."

"That's why we assigned Leroy to you."

"Will it recur?" he asks, hoping they won't hear the fright in his tremulous voice.

"Quite possible," Blenheim says, then pauses before adding, "a few times even."

"What we don't want is for you to return to zero," Defoe takes over. "If you see your relapses like your body falling asleep when it's tired, you'll worry about it less. Let's see, where were we? Do you remember?"

Joshua does not. He looks at the night table.

Blenheim nods. Joshua pulls the drawer out, reaches for his reading glasses and reads them what he has written there.

"Good, now I want you to take it from there. Have as many setbacks as you must have but you must return to the point where you were and keep doing so until the setbacks end," Defoe says.

"Then you would have removed one obstacle," Blenheim intervenes, "and be ready to tackle the next. Ever seen a newborn calf trying to stand?"

It sounds simplistic to Joshua—he knows that's not how psychological processes work—nevertheless he nods and is relieved.

18

A WEEK HAS PASSED since his relapse. He's almost himself again. The psychotropics they give him let him sleep through the night now. First time in twenty-odd years. His memory of the person who watches over him at nights is a blur. He no longer knows when the morning nurse makes her rounds. When he's awake he's chronically thirsty, and his lips are cracking, but it's a small price to pay for such welcome sleep.

Earlier today Blenheim removed him from twenty-four hour surveillance, largely, Joshua initially felt, because McKenna's evening presence is distressing. Two days ago McKenna ordered him to come with him for a walk and they had quarrelled, and Bonita Ramon had to intervene.

After that McKenna grew lobster-red, out-of-breath, his strawberry birthmark no longer distinct, pulled his nose and sniffled in between chewing the quick of his nails. For the rest of the shift his breathing remained abnormal, and Joshua could hear him turning constantly in the chair he sat on just inside the door. Joshua read in bed with his back turned to him.

After supper, McKenna left the tray in the room. When Nurse Ramon came at eight it was she who removed it. When the shift ended McKenna told him, his voice rasping, "I don't wanna be assigned to you tomorrow. The only thing you people that got lots o' money know to do is rub shit in people's faces. I'd rather scavenge in garbage bins than look after you."

But McKenna was assigned to him yesterday, and they did not speak to each other. Joshua knew he should have apologized, put him at ease; say that he didn't know why things got out of hand, that he doesn't like to hurt people. But he didn't, and they spent a tense evening in which they both fidgeted, each waiting for the other to take the first step towards breaking down the barrier.

So this morning, when Blenheim made his rounds, Joshua told him that McKenna's and his personalities grate, and it would be better to snip such irritants before they explode.

"McKenna isn't what you think. He has his problems, like all of us, but they aren't what you think. If you'd tried to get to know him, you'd find he has a great sense o' humour and a sizeable intellect."

"Well, he checks them at the door when he comes to work."

Blenheim didn't answer right away. "That's cruel. He's just a little too overcareful, that's all. You're just the sort of person likely to make him feel awkward. He has his problems but he's not a bigot."

"Why does he chew his nails till they bleed?"

"Why do you have bouts of amnesia? And why do you lose your self-confidence when they occur? Leave the man alone. In any event, I'm taking you off 24-hour surveillance today."

Lying on his back now, alone for the first time in a week, he feels as if a too-tight skin has cracked and fallen off. Regression. No one likes to slide help-lessly back down the hill he's already laboriously climbed. Normalcy. You don't think about it unless you've lost it. A banal truth. A laborious strug-gle. *Brent Lockwood.* Never played sports. Wore baggy trousers, almost as full as skirts, of the same grey wool their trousers were made of, but his were specially made. It made them curious. Brent met their curiosity with a grin. The same grin day after day, perfected by use. He rarely wandered far from the teachers. He did very poorly in his schoolwork, and when he thought others weren't looking, his eyes glazed over and his jaws tightened. When Joshua returned to Expatriates after his breakdown, Brent was not there. A classmate told him that Brent's baggy trousers had been designed to hide a urine bag he wore strapped to his thigh; that Brent had lost his bladder, and his ureters were connected to a tube that emptied into the bag on his leg. "Bull" Breton, captain of the rugby team, had surprised him emptying the bag in the toilet and jovially asked him if it was a sanitary napkin. Bull was incapable of cruelty. Brent took a walk on the beach late that same afternoon, ate manchineel, and crawled into a clump of seaside grapes. He was dead when they found him. Horton, Brent, himself—the casualties. Maybe there have been others since. *Normalcy.* If you don't have it . . . *If you don't have it.* He clenches his fists tightly. Slowly he unclenches them. Of course, if you're like his unconventional neighbour, you could toss mud at it, rattle it. *Occupé.* Out of context, it means so much. Yes, he'll definitely ask him his name and tell him he admires his attires.

Nurse Ramon enters the room and interrupts his thinking. She tells him that whatever McKenna's problems are, he's not a racist. She sounds cross. "His life might've been simpler if he was," she adds as an afterthought. He sees it as an invitation to question her.

"Meaning?"

"He was married to a Micmaq woman. It didn't work out. He's doing his best to hold his life together. He raises his two children with help from his sister. She's also a divorcee. They share a house. He works evenings; she works nights, on another ward here. That way one of them is always there for the children."

"Did he have a psychotic breakdown?"

Nurse Ramon squints, is silent for a while. "I've been indiscreet enough already. I won't tell you anything more."

"Have you told Leroy this?"

"Only that Percy has two children and he loves them a lot. Leroy came to work here a year ago when the ward he was working on closed down. You don't expect us to go around broadcasting the man's problems. I'm telling you now, because, with all that that man is going through, I don't think you'll want to complicate his life any further. He's in the dumps as it is. I assigned him to you the last seven days to give him a break from this ward that's been roaring with patients out of control. His job and his children are all he has to cling to. Please don't undermine his self-confidence. Oh, and by the way, not a word of this to anybody, not to Leroy and certainly not to McKenna. Is that clear?"

She leaves and he feels foolish. He admits that he was unnecessarily wilful and judgmental. He must try to chat with McKenna. About Nova Scotia. About fishing. The sea. What else? Getting electricity from the tides in the Bay of Fundy. The Sable Island Gas Project. So that's the origin of the penguin strut and the fidgeting! It's from stiffness of the joints and an inability to remain still: side-effects from the phenothiazines he's taking; a trifle aggravated perhaps by his obesity. He doesn't drool but he swallows his saliva frequently. His imperative style is probably a loss of savoir-faire. He remembers again how he'd turned his back to him, and McKenna's parting angry words, which he'd had to swallow the next day.

The least he expects from others is that they be kind, respectful and considerate. *Where's the reciprocity?* True, much about the man repels him. *Life gave it and life shapes us. We'd all select the best if given the choice.* Is it wealth that makes him gallop over such things? Is he indifferent to the feelings of others? Is he callous? Is it because he too is not normal? *Have I ever been normal? Normal? I couldn't be and be here. Still nothing excuses cruelty.*

For a while he thinks about wounding and healing. The horns we wear invisibly, our buried tusks, the claws hidden in the words that roll off our tongues are there and elude our best governance. Some cruel need we all have in varying degrees is gratified when we puncture others' egos and put dents in their dignity. We understand it best in the theatre: we enjoy Shylock's demise or the make-believe woe in *A Midsummer's Night Dream*. There we can unmask collectively, revel in and unleash our cruelty.

Early societies have always known this, and provided scapegoats for it. At puberty he'd realized he would have been among those stoned to death had he lived in the biblical state. Sparrow too, he had on occasion thought and laughed, envisaging the shower of falling stones, until he realized they'd be raining down on him too. *Love thy neighbour as thyself. And as ye would that men should do unto you, do ye also unto them likewise.* An impossible necessity.

He wonders what his mother had in mind when she named him Joshua. What was she thinking of? Was she able to think? Awareness now feels like a hammer and memory the nails it relentlessly drives. I'd better, he says out loud, write some of this down.

19

TWO WEEKS HAVE PASSED, and he's in Blenheim's office.

"You look very distinguished in your own clothes."

Joshua looks down at his clothes. He sees nothing unusual. He's wearing grey cotton slacks, a thick navy blue cotton sweater, and brown, loose, comfortable kid leather shoes. Convention requires that he say thanks to Blenheim but he doesn't.

"Joshua, from the entries in your journal, your dreams, and stray comments I've deduced that you're missing something important in your life."

No kidding.

"How long have you been away from Isabella Island?"

"I left the August before I was twenty: almost thirty-two years."

"Have you ever returned?"

"No."

"Ever wished to return?"

"I've thought about it only since I've been admitted here. I got a crazy idea about going back there and building a school, but I've since changed my mind. It was what *you* would call it a . . . *a delusion of grandeur.*"

There's silence. Joshua knows Blenheim wants him to talk. That's how they do it; they start off like a waterspout, start you gushing too, and then shut off and let you flow.

"How do you feel when you hear people talking about their family reunions?"

I'm never around that many people. He shrugs his shoulders. "The issue never arises."

"Shouldn't it?"

"Oh doctor, there you go again with your normalcy talk."

"No, Joshua. Everyone's sense of reality is shaped . . . everyone's nourished throughout childhood, in some place, unless he's had a roving childhood. Our roots are in such places. That's why it's easy for people to die for their country."

Blenheim's right. He feels stumped. "Are you implying, Doctor, that my indifference to Isabella Island reflects some sort of pathology?"

"A colleague of mine does research exclusively with psychotic émigrés. Many of them, he concludes, feel broken and disconnected; they feel that in emigrating they committed sacrilege."

"What does he prescribe for them?"

"A return visit . . . to regain perspective."

Joshua smiles. "When would you like *me* to return to Isabella Island?"

"As soon as you are ready to." Blenheim stares Joshua in the eyes as he says this, then looks away. When he looks at him again he says, "But before you do so, I would prefer to see a little of Isabella Island come to you." He pauses then resumes very slowly, "Is there someone in the Caribbean—not your sister, *someone who's still alive*—whom you'd like to see?"

"Anastasia Browne. But she's probably dead."

"Who's she?"

"A woman who took my mother through the trauma of my conception, and ensured that she did not murder me during the crackup she suffered at my birth." He is staring out the window at the snow covering the hospital grounds all the way to Champlain Boulevard. He takes several deep breaths and continues. "Doctor, you have got me onto a subject I don't like to talk about: the circumstances of my birth."

He recounts what he'd learned from Bita and adds, "In fleeting moments I admire my mother for not going completely mad. I don't know how she could have regained her sanity. To keep it she had to place a barrier between herself and me. I think her need to care for Bita kept her sane. Luckily for me, I've never known my father. Shocking as it might sound, his deathbed wish—that I should be cared for—made him a great deal better than most plantation owners, who raped their workers or screwed them in exchange for year-round work." He is trembling slightly.

Blenheim seems moved too. His teeth are clamped.

"I *hate* the Isabellan planter class, Dr Blenheim. I hate it!"

"Let's focus on someone you love. This Anastasia Browne, would you like to see her?"

He takes a deep breath and answers, "I'd exchange my wealth for it."

"How's that?"

"I've never told her thanks. And she left Isabella Island before I could remember what she looks like."

"You've wanted to thank her?"

"Not before I got here."

"Why's that?"

"Doctor, you know why."

"I want to hear you say it yourself."

"All right then: because I didn't think it was such a wonderful idea for me to be alive."

"So now you want to thank her?"

He sees the trap. "You psychiatrists! You should be lawyers. I left her address on Isabella Island. And once I left there I lost all desire to want to be associated with Petit Bordel."

"Petit Bordel?"

Joshua nods. "It's the name the original plantation owner gave the village I was born in."

Blenheim whistles. "How old is your Aunt Stacey?"

"I don't think she's my aunt; my mother's sister, I mean. I don't even know if they were blood relatives. I have no idea what her age is. Probably around my mother's."

"How old's your mother?"

"*Would have been.* I think she died in 1982."

"How do you know that?"

"I'd arranged for a stipend to be paid to her. It wasn't paid after early 1982."

Blenheim's nodding. "Yeah, your mother's age?"

"I'm not sure. In 1965, which was when I last saw her, she looked like she was in her fifties. But that could have probably been because of malnutrition and hard work."

"So if she and your Aunt Stacey were the same age, they'd be, let's say, somewhere in their eighties."

"Something like that."

"Are you absolutely sure you'd like to see her again?"

"Doctor, I mean it when I say I would give half my fortune to do so. But she's probably dead."

"Earlier you were prepared to give your *entire* fortune. But half's all right. Yes, it's a real possibility that she's dead. Any friends from school days?"

He shakes his head.

"Your adopted mother's friends and relatives?"

"Are you kidding?"

"Your own?"

He shakes his head.

"If I let you return to your room and I give you a mild sedative and let you rest, and we resume, let's say around three, will you tell me the facts about Sparrow?"

He thinks about the question, purses his lips. He feels good about the discussion they've just had. Talking about Sparrow would spoil it, but he says, "Yes. What I'm allowed to remember."

"Allowed?"

"When I begin to talk about painful facts something clamps my memory and opens up the nonsense valves."

"I see. I hope I remember this in your exact words."

"Dr Blenheim"—he hears the pleading note in his own voice—"promise me I won't go psychotic again."

"I'll do my best."

He returns to his room. A few minutes later Gladys comes, gives him his sedative and leaves.

It's two when he awakens. They've let him sleep through lunch. They bring a special tray for him. He is touched, surprised a little by his feelings and cannot find the appropriate English word. He settles for the French *compatiser*. It strikes him that Stein no longer comes with them, has probably left the team.

A few minutes before Blenheim arrives Joshua gets fidgety. His feelings for Sparrow are fuzzy, unlike those for his mother. Those have clean edges, definite shapes. Where Sparrow's are concerned the business of culpability is still unsettled. He hopes he'd be fair to Sparrow. Sometimes he thinks he bears Sparrow's burdens, unnecessarily.

Blenheim arrives. He brings a tape recorder this time. A faux pas. When he was a toddler, older Blacks opposed being photographed. Bita had told him so. Looking at Blenheim holding the tape recorder, he thinks he understands why. They felt that anyone possessing their image could use it to harm them. His speech is his breath, his spirit. To capture that in fixed form! He feels himself tensing.

"Had a good sleep?"

"Yep."

"All ready to go?"

He does not answer and looks away from Blenheim.

"Is something wrong?"

"That machine you're holding. I won't allow you to tape-record what I say. You've won my confidence, Doctor, but I won't let you tape-record what I say."

"That's final?"

"Yes."

"You're a difficult man."

"Yes. In this world you have to be difficult to have a little space for yourself, away from all the garbage others constantly toss onto you and force into you."

"All right. It's off. And so that you don't think I want to trick you, I'm putting it right here beside you."

First he tells of the quarrel that Sparrow and Mommy had. When he finishes he adds, "My homosexual urges at thirteen and fourteen were excruciating, Doctor. To watch a classmate and feel myself getting an erection and helpless to prevent it . . .

"Sparrow struck around the time I was wondering whether he could help me hide all the embarrassing evidence—and, believe me, all my classmates knew; I was so helplessly and visibly queer. He came into the bathroom one evening while I was in there—the bathroom he and I used was located between our bedrooms and could be entered from either bedroom—and the rest, as we say, is history. I must have registered disapproval for he said to me—

"'No need o' actin' like you surprise. I been told all 'bout yer. Everybody knows you's queer som'n awful. Everybody's that got eyes to see, that is. Wanna know som'n? I'm queer too. Just don' show it. So you's queer, I'm queer, we's both queer 'n ev'body hates queers, so let's just keep it to ourselves 'n have us a lil' fun in the meantime. See, Ah know Ah's right. Your eyes aglowing 'n you's a-whirling yer tongue 'n a-wagging yer tail just lak the snake did when Eve bit into that apple. Holy Jesus!'"

Blenheim laughs.

"And with that Sparrow was down on his knees and had taken my penis into his mouth. Against my will I got an erection and against my will I ejaculated.

"'Ain't you gonna do the same for me?' he asked, and I complied.

"'See, ain't nothing dirty 'bout it. Whole lotta fun too, if we jus' keep it to ourselves.'

"And so it started, Doctor, and so it continued. And so began the cycles of guilt. I on occasion would resist him. One time especially. He'd said to me 'Them buns o' your'n, Lawd help me. They been suckin' in the sun since they see light. They be som'n sweet. It gon be glory hallelujah, sweet honey Jesus, the day Ah explode in 'em.'

"'And afterwards, when you're asleep, I'll come into your room and slice off your prick,' I said. He blanched and his eyes grew small, and for two weeks he did not bother me.

"On occasion he admitted that our act was wrong, and on occasion that he thought it was all right. One time he said the Bible was against it. Another time that 'God takes care o' what's goin' on in heaven and that ought to keep Him mighty busy. We's to take care o' what's on earth.'

"'What if Mommy finds out?' I sometimes asked him.

"'Then she gonna know you're queer. Right now she don' wanna know 'bout it.'

"'And what about you? If she finds out?'

"'I can deny anything's going on 'tween us. She knows 'bout my being queer already. But I get 'way with it 'cause I look like a man. Ma voice kind o' off a lil' bit, kind o' the wrong register, I'll be the first to say, oth'wise I'm kosher. You can't say the same for yourself. You walk and swish som'n awful, lak you be invitin' a body to come right 'long 'n taste you. 'N them-there beautiful buns—Negro buns—mmmm! I'm a-dyin' to get into 'em. But you done threaten to cut off ma prick if Ah does.'"

"Are you always this good at imitating people?" Blenheim interrupts him.

"It's not difficult at all. His language, its quaintness and rhythms, fascinated me, and I had a lot of fun trying to reproduce it, sometimes to his face. But that was when I'd felt we were buddies. I liked him a whole lot, Doctor. From the time he came, up to when I turned thirteen, he gave me the affection no one else thought I needed.

"One night the whole thing became overbearing for me: what we were doing, society's and the Bible's condemnation of it. I thought long and hard about killing myself. It would have been easy. All I had to do was walk into the whirlpool in the sea just a half-mile from Arcadia—the same one he walked into—the Atlantic currents would have done the rest. I'd resolved to go that very night but I fell asleep before getting up to dress. The sexual encounters stopped when a couple of months before my first breakdown—

which you already know about—I went into his room one night and set his bed on fire while he was asleep in it. It was after a dream I had in which Bita came upon us having sex and she held Sparrrow's own loaded shotgun, which he kept in a drawer of his night table, to his temple." He stops speaking.

"What happened?"

"He woke before the fire took fully, and we made something of a silent pact not to let anyone know about it.

"A month before I left Isabella Island to study in England, he and I spoke about what had gone on between us. He acknowledged his guilt, even called himself 'a abomination in the sight of the Lawd.' But he was sure it didn't interfere with his bringing souls to God: the instrument was one thing, what it was used for was quite another. I don't remember his exact words on the subject.

"'This was three years after my breakdown; three years after he'd stopped molesting me. We'd not spoken about it in the interim. I think he believed that sex with him was a causal factor in my breakdown. 'Joshua, let's me 'n you get one thang straight: you been a minor 'n Ah been the adult. Ah should o' never taken advantage o' yer innocence, even if my innocence was abused som'n awful too. Gawd, He goin' judge me severely for it. He's a-gonna judge me, oh yes. It's certain. He's a-gonna judge me. Ah tremble fer to think on it. But I'd kindo' like for to go to my grave knowing *you* done forgive me.' He stared at me sheepishly, then tears welled up in his eyes and he wiped them on his shirtsleeves before he resumed talking. Now he looked away from me as he spoke, his tone as if talking to himself, as if I were a mere eavesdropper. 'I had me a few relationships all right in Florida. I started kind o' young, first year o' high school. That urge was som'n mighty powerful. Mighty powerful. Had me kind o' hitched and just drug me along. Try's Ah might jus' couldn' unhitch. When Ah got older, Ah went sometimes in my truck out on the highway stops 'n study the men a-comin' 'n a-goin'. Sometimes Ah got lucky. But Ah always knew 'twas wrong. 'Course, Gawd would o' consume me with fire if I'd o' lived in the time o' Sodom 'n Gomorra, 'n Leviticus says Ah should be killed. 'Course, Ah can't question that now, 'cause that's Gawd's word. A body's got no business pickin' 'n choosin' what parts o' the Baable he gon' ter b'lieve.

"'After I had me my fun, I'd get depressed som'n awful for a spell. For a whole heap o' days. Sometimes Ah'd push ma hands down ma throat 'n vomit; other tayms I'd take me a whole heap o' laxatives to purge ma insides, or I would go for days 'thout eatin', but the filth 'twas in ma soul, see. Ah prayed 'n prayed a whole heap 'bout it. I been to see all kinds o' healers—a whole heap of 'em, I tell you—but 'twas no good, see. That desire stayed in me som'n powerful and got worse. After a while I just gived up, 'n ma worry's been 'bout being caught by the police or bein' picked up by the wrong kind o' fellow. Still it bothered me som'n powerful 'cause I worry I be on ma way to hell.'"

Joshua pauses for a long while, trying to recall what he said to Sparrow that late afternoon. "Doctor, I listened to him attentively. I wanted to hear if he would tell me any of the information I already knew from his quarrel with Mommy. When he didn't I knew that he was merely saying what he felt comfortable saying.

"Doctor, he and I held this conversation sitting on the back porch. The sun was setting. The mosquitoes were particularly vicious that July. I remember constantly slapping the ones that had settled on my arms and neck, but I cannot recall a single word of my reply to Sparrow.

"His statements came back to me, word for word, when I learned of his death, and since then they've replayed several times in my head. When he died his words made me examine myself as only the death of someone close can, especially someone for whom our feelings are ambivalent. My own sexuality suddenly overwhelmed me; it had been less than a year since I'd discovered masochism. At his death a lot that I had been trying to suppress forced its way out and sank me into darkness. But not before I had seen with utmost clarity that Sparrow had no place to go but into the sea. At fifty he wouldn't have had much success finding sex at rest stops on Florida's or any other highways. Attempts to find homosexual sex on Isabella Island carried the risk of physical beatings, humiliating court trials, disgrace, ostracism, ongoing verbal harassment, and extortion. For his church's sake he could not risk it. To Isabellan plantocrats, he ministered to the unwashed and mingled with the dehumanized and was therefore *persona non grata*. Doctor Blenheim, his life had washed up long before his body did. In his suicide I saw what was waiting for me down the years. I peered, you might say, too far into the darkness and I fell in."

Blenheim is silent for a long time after Joshua has stopped speaking. "Do you still hold what he did to you against him?"

"Sometimes I do and sometimes I don't. When it gets mixed up with race, it's then that I do. When I separate it from race, I pity him."

"And what do you feel for yourself?"

"Meaning?"

"In regard to *your* sexuality."

"I would rather not be a masochist. That's for sure. You won't believe it, Doctor, I *hate* pain. I indulge only when a tension in me needs to be released and I can contain it no more. You know, the feeling that if you don't do it you would explode or something, or some force within you would expand and cause you to burst?"

"What do you think you have to be punished for?"

"Doctor, that's as wide as the ocean and as unfathomable as original sin. I don't know. All I know is that periodically I must get flogged or go crazy.

"I have wondered: Is it because of the way I was conceived? Is it because of the pain I caused my mother? Is it because I haven't lived up to Mommy's expectations? Is it because I sometimes enjoyed what Sparrow did to me? Is it something I inherited from my father? Is it because I didn't denounce Sparrow? I couldn't and have Mommy send him back to America. After doing so, she would have turned on me with a vengeance. He was a source of needed penance for her: a constant reminder of the abortion she'd had. I have often thought it's because I don't deserve to be alive. Afterwards I'd think of my mother's inability to feed Bita and suddenly finding herself having to feed me as well. And now, having inherited my father's wealth, I'm part of the system that raped her."

"A part of all you've said is part of the truth. But why the melding of sex and pain? I mean do you feel you must be punished for what you enjoy?"

"There's no enjoyment in it, Doctor, just release. I don't know. I understand self-hate. That is about as much as I know. I doubt I'll ever be able to have a regular homosexual relationship ever again."

When Blenheim does not respond, Joshua prods, "Probably not. On the sexual score my psyche is as good as callused. But that's not my immediate problem."

"I want you to feel deserving of life and love and happiness," Blenheim interrupts him. "As unconditional gifts. Not as things you pay for or suffer for. After that many important pieces would fall into place. But tell me, was there no one you could have discussed your problem with Sparrow with— while it was going on or since?"

"Are you kidding, Doctor? I didn't want anyone to know about it. It was bad enough to be fingered as a latent homosexual. It could mean literal death to be confirmed as one."

Blenheim shakes his head skeptically and purses his lips. It's the big difference between him and Stein, whose face is a mask. It makes him so much more natural, human, caring, involved, and makes it easier for Joshua to converse with him. "In your earlier hospitalizations, how much of this did you reveal?"

Joshua ponders the question. "I don't know. I truly don't. I don't know what I said when I was out of control, but I'm certain I told them nothing when I was in control."

"Why was that?"

"Are you off your rails, too, Doctor? I don't want anybody's pity or scorn. That's what the world reserves for homosexuals, those they don't kill off like vermin. I wouldn't even discuss my experiences with other homosexuals. You know why? Because deep down they too believe what heterosexuals say about them. Don't take my word for it; go to a couple of queer drag shows and you'll wince at the self-hate masked as humour. You won't believe the pecking order among gays! The bisexuals, especially those with children, are at the summit and scorn all those *below* them. Next in line are the macho-looking guys; covertly and overtly they mock those who're *effeminate*. Even the so-called effeminate mock themselves and others who are." He remembers a put-down he often heard among London's gay guys: "'Stop wasting me time, sis. I'm not into lesbians.' It's a complex hierarchy, full of self-contempt. Suffice it to say that at the very bottom are the effeminates and queers with small dicks."

"You're saying *they*."

He didn't realize he was. "It's easier to talk about it in the third person."

For a while neither speaks.

"Pity, scorn, extermination—those are the circles we're penned in. We create gay ghettoes to minimize the extermination but still hear about it from reports about fags killed because the Bible or the Koran authorizes it, or because all fags are pedophiles, or because fags are degenerates—for reasons those who hate us invent. I'm telling you nothing you do not know. But no ghetto can protect us from the pity and scorn of heterosexuals and other homosexuals." He stops talking briefly. "I couldn't divulge my early experiences to anyone. That would only fuel the pity and scorn they already feel for people like me."

"And yourself—have you pitied and scorned other gays?"

He doesn't appreciate this question and doesn't want to answer.

Blenheim repeats the question.

"Since you insist, yes. What! Do you think I escaped the defining?" His mind drifts to the man he'd slept with just before his breakdown in Paris. Yes, he'd been angry with him for the jeremiad he'd subjected him to, and he blamed it for the breakdown that followed. A simplistic rationalization, he must have known from the very beginning. He looks up at Blenheim and smiles. "Yes, I've definitely internalized the definitions. But I don't feel like talking about it."

His mind drifts to Paul, to Paul's exaggerated story about rich White Caribbean homosexuals being able to command all the sex they want. Even then he knew it was Paul's attempt to take their friendship to a level where they might confidentially speak about their pasts. Paul as it were had begun by taking the first step into that forest, made it in a tree or two deep, but Joshua had not followed.

"How do you feel about externalizing all this for the first time?"

"In a dream my sister told me I should. It's as simple as that."

Blenheim compresses his lips, wrinkles his brow and nods complictly. "You must be tired now. Tomorrow or the day after, if you're not too bruised from today's sessions, I would like us to talk about your memories of Arcadia, those who visited there, who lived there, what was in the house, and your own feelings about what went on there."

"I'll try. But back to something you said. You know, Doctor, so-called primitive societies never saw the blessings of life as unconditional gifts. From Mexico to the Andes, the Bight of Benin to Cape Horn, they thought otherwise."

Blenheim does not answer.

When Joshua returns to his room, his mind revisits what he's just said about his sexuality, and he wonders at what point unconventional sexuality becomes pathology. He's sure many sado-masochists are happy. Happy? At the very least lead guilt-free lives. Although, overhearing their joyous expostulations and exclamations over things some of them do or have done to them—body burns, piercings, penetrations with wrist-size objects—he wonders. In a Pigalle bar, a humungous fellow, a White King Kong, his deep blue eyes glowing in his pink face framed by his carrot hair and beard as if they were a wimple, had taken off his shirt and showed them his back polka-dotted with scars, and had gone on to tell them that he'd asked four guys to tie him up and use their cigarette lighters to burn his back. He'd wanted to test his pain endurance threshold. He was proud to say that that it was the burners who'd panicked and stopped. He had intended to continue until he passed out. But when they'd all screwed him afterwards it was the best orgasm he'd ever had, and one he'd like to repeat. *"Vous autres, ça ne vous tente pas?"* There was among them too a club of card players. The losers carried out the winners' orders. They'd asked him to join, but he said no, and they said he was dull and couldn't tell the difference between fun and a block of ice. He agreed with them for he couldn't see the fun in their fun-filled games. Yet he knows that the brutality that they and he need is foreign to most sadomasochists who merely dally with pain but don't actually inflict it. Even so the stories he'd overheard from the habitués in the SM bar he frequented in Pigalle made him think that most of even those who need to administer or receive pain take their sexuality in stride; embrace it free from moral taint, like plain (or adventurous), like any form of pleasurable, stress-relieving sex. That was how, he thinks, the raven-haired, emerald-eyed fellow who'd introduced him to it went about it. And it was for the adventure—the adventure of the moment—that he'd consented, though if he'd understood the meaning of *flag*, he would have never gone to the fellow's flat.

Why is that whatever's coupled with danger excites us? Jung notes that societies experience a collective high in the early heady days of war. Why? The rest of the time our sports teams are our armies, filling us to explosion with their victories, explosions that sometimes make us break windows, damage cars, and attack police officers. Some mysterious desire for adventuring, exploring, enduring pain, and privation, and triumphing. Scandinavians consider icebaths a tonic. Religionists endure long bouts of hunger to induce hallucinatory visions. Some walk on flaming coals. Some pour hot pepper into their vaginas. Others battle (sometimes succumb to) thirst and hunger in deserts alone. We eschew pain and yet reinsert it, masked by ritual, or desire, into our lives. Inscrutable needs limned in the darkness of prehistory, indelibly encrypted in the psyches we've been bequeathed.

Why are we so different from other species, whose every act is predictable? We need novelty, we hate routine.

Enough of that. Tomorrow Blenheim wants to hear about Arcadia. Where will he begin? Mommy had organized her household simply. But he did not know that then. Each Saturday the butcher brought meat. Some cattle were raised on the plantation, since there was a lot of grazing land on the two hundreds acres given over to coconuts, but they were sold to butchers wholesale. Rose was both cook and steward. Mommy trusted her totally. She informed Mommy of whatever was in short supply and Mommy would give her a grocery list every two weeks to take to Robinson's Grocery, where Ichabod Crane, who'd wanted to marry Mommy, was the manager. Whenever the local fishermen caught red snappers they reserved the best one for Arcadia. Mommy loved red snapper and had taught both Dawn and Rose to prepare it the Florida way: blackened and served with a black bean sauce. She came to supper eagerly whenever there was red snapper. When it was particularly good, she complimented Rose profusely. Dawn and Rose liked their fish fried, and Mommy would let them have a few slices to themselves.

They were the only family he had, and when he left them, he did not know how to make friends at a deeper level. He talks to George in the winter, and then for eight months does not see him. *There's a limit to what money can procure you. And what you haven't cultivated you cannot harvest, unless you are a thief or parasite.*

Has he shunned people because he prefers to remain unseen? He fancied at one time that women considered him physically handsome. Until they heard his voice, noted his gestures, realized he wasn't John Wayne. Sylvia Plath felt that every woman loves a fascist. *Near to you, people smell what they cannot see.*

What has become of Amanda? He hopes she found a husband, at any rate that she leads a meaningful life, with or without a husband.

Whenever Mommy, Sparrow, and he interacted it occurred in the family room, which was separate from the parlour and less formal. It was a large room, at least thirty by twenty feet. Three years after he went to live at Arcadia, Mommy replaced the original flooring of balata wood with dark brown ceramic tiles because termites had invaded the wood. The piano was in there. Occasionally Mommy played it. Whenever Amanda visited she played it. Elizabeth had tried to teach him to play but stopped after Mommy took over one day to prove to her that she didn't know music. Above the piano was the family's coat of arms encased in a glass-and-mahogany picture frame. It was brought from Haiti in 1793, where, Mommy told him, it had been taken when Louis IV granted a lesser son of the Éclair family (his father had been one of Louis's courtiers) a plantation there. The whole was on a field of what must have once been green velvet but was now somewhere between dirty yellow and green. At its centre was a Latin cross. Suspended above the cross was a crown. On the left was a gilded lion standing upright and biting three spears. One of its front paws supported the pole of a spear bearing the blue-red-white French flag; the other supported the cross. Slightly above and to the left side of the lion was an eagle with outstretched wings, open beak, and extended talons. On the right side was a bridled horse standing on its hind legs. Both front legs supported the pole of a spear that flew a blue flag inscribed with three white fleur-de-lys. Stencilled scroll-like in gold lettering, at the very bottom, below a pelvic-shaped base in silver that had turned black, was the motto *Compos Sui*. The eagle and spear-biting lion were replicated on the gate to Arcadia.

Three glass-and-mahogany cabinets in the recreation room contained the family's heirlooms. One of them was full of hollow silverware, a few pieces of which had been brought by the founding Éclair patriarch when he fled Haiti in 1793. On rainy days Henry was sometimes in there removing the tarnish. In another, always locked, cabinet, also of mahogany but no glass, were several firearms, most of them from the nineteenth century. Apart from the danger they represented he had no interest in them. Sparrow and Mommy each kept a handgun and several clips of ammunition in their night tables.

During his first year in high school Mommy had pestered him about taking shooting lessons. But he said no. He'd asked her if she wanted him to become a hunter, knowing that hunting was something they both abhorred. She'd fished for words until she found "target shooting. It's a *bona fide* sport. Something right for you. You're not interested in sports." But he'd remembered the riots and had known that fear was her real reason. "Why don't you just say it," he'd asked, fixing her with a stare: "that I should keep a gun for self-defence in case there's another uprising? Well, I won't be killing anybody—Black, White, or Brown." Hurt, she had turned pale.

The southern wall, without windows or doors, displayed six large portraits of five generations of first-born Éclair sons, the earlier ones in oil, the later ones in daguerreotype. The first, who'd fled the slave rebellion in Haiti, was almost lost in a glossy blackness, all but his face. His son, Emmanuel's great-grandfather, was there, with narrow features that made him look delicate and sickly; he wore a dandyish white ruff, waistcoat, baggy tunics, knee breeches, and knee-high boots, his right hand on the hilt of a partly drawn sword. One in oil of Emmanuel's grandfather with a frightened look in his too-bright blue eyes, in military uniform, standing beside a horse. One in daguerreotype of Emmanuel's father sitting in a rocking chair and wearing a burgundy smoking jacket. A daguerreotype of

Joshua's father in military regalia; an oil portrait of him too, on a horse, his right arm partly outstretched and raised, the taut whip taking up considerable space, as if the painter had wanted to make the whip the focus of the painting. The strict primogeniture the family practised was evident even in the size of the portraits and the space accorded to first-born Éclair males.

On the northern wall, in the spaces between the windows, were the smaller portraits of the Éclair matriarchs with their families. Éclair aristocratic lineage made them something special to Whites across the Caribbean and so the family was spread out over the Caribbean and even in Bermuda; the lesser sons had married, when they could, women heiresses in families where there were no male heirs, and some of the daughters had married plantation owners; the few who didn't had remained spinsters. There was one such great-aunt, a woman in her nineties, living with the Éclair who was a hotelier, but Joshua never met her. In New York, Mommy had taken him to a photographer's studio to have his portrait made but she never did put it up on any of the walls. He himself had not thought of taking any of his photographs to London, and there are no photographs of him as a baby. His mother was too poor to pay for photographs. It's possible that the photos taken of him after he went to Arcadia were in Sparrow's belongings, among Mommy's personal items that he'd kept. The lawyer settling Sparrow's estate had asked him to come back to Isabella Island to claim the items he wanted, but it was around the time he was getting ready to go to Madrid. He told him to give away what he could and to dump the rest. He hadn't thought about the photographs.

It was in the rec room that Mommy's female "friends" socialized and gossiped. Every Tuesday was bridge and every Thursday backgammon. Each week a different woman hosted. The men got together less often, and for some reason always sat around the dining table—only rarely in the parlour—and spent their time drinking, teasing one another, or running down their workers and whichever politicians happened to be in power. Seated a little way from the women with a book while they played bridge or backgammon, he'd listen to their games of one-upmanship or putdowns of the absent ones. Mrs Kevin was often talking about the trip she was planning to Scotland or the one she had just returned from. Her maiden name was Anderson, and it seemed that she was forever attending gatherings of her clan. Her great-grandmother had been governess to a Scottish laird, she told her friends. "A chambermaid," Mrs Manchester said when Mrs Kevin left the room, "taken on to put down everything that came up. I'll wager they're all from a line of bastards." Mrs Manchester was of Scottish ancestry too. She had been a Cameron. She wore her tartan on special occasions but never focused on what her ancestors had put up or down, taken or touched. They said Mrs Robinson's great-grandmother had been a harlot who'd married a wealthy Welshman and promptly poisoned him after she'd got him to make his will, before he had time to find out what she was. It was that money that had bought the plantation. It had come to her because she was an only child. Her husband, Flingfoot, was a second son, which meant he'd had no plantation of his own.

Mrs Kevin and Mrs Manchester were sometimes asked by the others about some sort of genealogy project they were working on. Mrs Blenkinsopp—she was never present with the other wives except when the husbands and wives came together, on average four times per year—told Mommy in one of her frequent solo visits that Mrs Kevin and Mrs Robinson were hoping to discover nobility in their lineage. In the last years they never said much about it, and eventually they said they'd dropped it. It was too difficult to trace the different branches of the family. The others opined that they didn't like what they were finding.

Their favourite subject was whose clothes were bought off the rack, even down to who was wearing false titties. Mrs Manley, who had lost her breasts to cancer, still sported two very full ones, and out of Mrs Manley's earshot, Mrs Kevin once said that cancer had its blessings.

"You shouldn't say things like that," Mommy told her.

"It's true," she insisted. "She's never had lovelier tits."

"Get serious! No prosthesis can replace a woman's real breasts."

Even Bell Cow Mrs Manchester felt Mrs Kevin had taken that joke too far.

Occasionally they differed on how strongly the reins should be applied to the labouring class. On such occasions Mommy—this went on until his late adolescence—made feeble protests, and Mrs Kevin or Mrs Manchester would accuse her of wanting to run with the hares and hunt with the hounds. Mommy would say, "Believe me, they are hardly different from hunted hares," meaning the field hands. Mrs Manchester once looked around the room and told her in her sawdust, militaristic voice that if she wanted to live like a queen, somebody had to pay for it; and she took Mommy's hand, raised the finger with a diamond on it for all to see, and said, "Averill, dear, there's a lot here that glitters and is first rate. The money to pay for it has to come from somewhere, while you sit in your armchair crocheting. For Christ sake, Averill, stop worrying about Ham's dscendants.

They are content with the lot God predestined for them, more satisfied than all of us."

"Illusions Elaine! Illusions and delusions," Mommy retorted, and quickly brought her hand up to her mouth, tensing for the shake down she was sure would follow.

"Let me tell you," Mrs Kevin intervened, "the life of leisure you lead has to be paid for by someone. Look at all those books you read. You are a lady of leisure, my dear. Ladies of leisure must have servants. Do you want rough hands and cracked nails, my dear? Of course not. So you see, dear, *they* have to do the domestic tasks. Mr Kevin says it's how the conquered are made to know their place. The Roman and Greek wives had slaves for their domestic chores. But maybe in America you do things differently. After all these years, you're still uncomfortable with leisure, Averill dear?"

To which Mrs Manchester added, "My dear Averill, it's what we've been trying to show you for years. But you're such a bleeding heart, bourgeois liberal. Start being overgenerous to your servants and watch the liberties they'll take with you. Darling, they are Black. They know how to make ends meet on little. God made them so that their wants are few. We are different. We are *White* people. Our needs are imperial."

"We should have our paws on the wheel then," Mommy said in a half mumble.

"Speak up, Averill! Paws on what? Pause as in p-a-u-s-e?"

"That too," Mommy replied. "Forget it. It's not important." She picked up her cards. "It's your turn to play, Millicent."

And they returned to their bridge game.

In the library at QMC, a few years later, he came upon a book with photographs of Egyptian art and saw the figure of Nemesis with its paw on the wheel of fortune and realized that it was to Nemesis that Mommy had been referring.

On some occasions the gatherings became the sites for power games, usually involving Mrs Blenkinsopp—and indirectly Mommy, since they were friends. They'd expected Mommy to show her loyalty to them by filling the place acreage had given her in the pecking order and by exercising the prerogatives that came with it. Mrs Manchester was Bell Cow for that reason, but if Mrs Amasser had been there and wanted the role, it would have been automatically hers. Mommy's preferential friendship for Mrs Blenkinsopp, who'd taught her embroidery and crocheting and with whom she exchanged books, was in their eyes problematic. Mrs Blenkinsopp met them halfway by being absent when only the wives got together; they saw it as her tacit acknowledgement that she didn't quite belong. But it was because she knew them better than they knew themselves. In intelligence she was the opposite of Amanda. Occasionally they did go to her house, even the Amassers—all but the Kevins—but that was because Blenkinsopp made her receive them. Usually after a quarrel the husbands of the women would show up with their wives and order them to make up. Horse Jaw went as far as slapping Millicent once when she refused to take Mrs Manchester's hand (this information he got from Mommy). They'd say things like the links in the chain mustn't be broken, and they loved the old cliché, "We'll survive collectively or hang separately."

One of their worst verbal clawings occurred a mere six weeks before he left for England, on an evening when Mrs Blenkinsopp laughed sarcastically while Mrs Manchester, just returned from a trip to England, was describing the jewels worn by her widowed millionaire aunt at some function in some London hotel.

"What do you find so funny?"

For a reply, Mrs Blenkinsopp laughed a second time.

Smirking throughout, Mrs Manchester said, "Class, how some people lack it! It's something you're born into, dear. *You* couldn't tell a diamond from a rhinestone anyhow, let alone own one. Left up to me alone, my dear, the likes of you and me would never be in the same room."

"The likes of me, the likes of you," Mrs Blenkinsopp said in a dusting off way. "Take off your clothes sometimes before death undresses you. We'll all be housed the same way in the long run: in dirt. Without feathers and hides carcasses are just carcasses. Take off your makeup for God's sake: your Black boys, older than you, trimming your flowers, mowing your lawns, tending your horses; your butler; your cook; your retinue—they're dresses, lipstick, face powder. Take them off sometimes, for God's sake, and let the wrinkles show."

"Well, those who have it flaunt it."

(Mrs Blenkinsopp had no permanent servants. She hired temporary help when she was entertaining the plantocracy.)

"Flaunt what? Greedy foolishness? It's not glittering dresses that heal wounds. A million-dollar hospital gown won't cure sickness. Evil decked out in diamonds is only evil glittering brightly."

Mrs Robinson cleared her throat, crossed herself and said, "That was quite a sermon, Reverend Blenkinsopp. Let's all sing the doxology." She got as far as "Praise God from whom all blessings flow . . ." when Mrs Manchester exclaimed:

"Doxology! If I get my hands on this bitch, *she* won't *glitter, she* will *bleed.*"

The others bristled with excitement.

"This has gone too far. Control yourselves, please," Mommy interjected.

"You shut up!" Mrs Manchester turned on Mommy. "You probably put her up to it! You Yankee nobody! Not because I'm in your house—it's not even yours; it's Emmanuel Éclair's—you let this church mouse, this two-bit slut, insult me. When did I come to this?" She picked up her glittering shawl, quickly draped it over her shoulders, grabbed her purse and headed out the room, the heels of her shoes a quick syncopation of clicks on the ceramic floor, opened the door—the wind slammed it shut after her—then the vroom and lights of her car. She didn't even tell her husband, who was in the dining room drinking with the others, that she was leaving. Outside the wind gusted, inside there was a tomblike silence. Up to the time Joshua left for England the breach had not been healed.

Mommy could go only so far in opposing them. She needed their company. They were her fence against fear, and they fenced her in. To Joshua, whom she'd made into something of a confidant by then, she protested their invading her house, but if three days went by and she didn't see any of them she fidgeted and worried that she had in some way offended them, and would be on the phone to them.

Perhaps she'd been born a generation too early. It's people of his generation who've had the courage to convict Byron de la Beckwith for the murder of civil rights leader Medgar Evers and who've reopened the files on the many Blacks and Whites murdered during the US civil rights campaign. One, the niece of one of the bombers of the 16th Street Baptist Church in Birmingham, turned her uncle in. Mommy might have had the courage to revolt if she'd been of his generation. Idle speculation. But the thought lets him think, as he often does, of how little we control the forces that shape our lives, of our enslavement to the groups we're a part of and the times we're born into—never mind our needs.

He wonders again what became of the household things. All that heritage! He chuckles. Were they included in the sale of the house? It was sold while he was in Madrid to an English merchant, a relative of the Langleys.

How should he feel about Arcadia? He had a deep fondness for Dawn and loved Henry's company in the early years. Rose was acidic. She shouted at him when he was little and said little more than good morning or good evening when he got bigger. He once overheard her telling Dawn she would rather whore than work for coloured (meaning biracial) people, and "worse yet for Black people. Nobody with my colour will show off on me or boss me around." She probably resented serving him because he was a bastard Éclair. He wonders if they're still alive.

His mind returns to Sparrow, to what he's just told Blenheim about him, and it's as if he expects Sparrow to appear and challenge everything he said about him.

When Nurse Ramon comes on duty an hour later, he barely returns her greeting. Normally he likes it when she's on duty. He likes her frankness, her concern for others. This afternoon he's indifferent to her presence. She senses a problem and assigns someone to stay in his room, and administers whatever it is the doctor has prescribed for him on such occasions. It's not long before he knows that he's fallen over the edge again, though he remains semi-lucid.

"*Joshua,* Joshua! *Where are you? Hiding from me? Ha-ha- ha!*
"*Jo-shuaaa! You should be commanding the sun to stand still. You spineless fool! Imagine, going to get whipped! I sent you to Templeton's Academy because I did* not want you to grow up thinking it's right to flog or be flogged. *But who knows? You're probably overflowing with your father's depravity.*
"*Why didn't you come to my funeral? I have loved you, Joshua, loved you. And that is how you thanked me: refusing to come to my funeral? I despised your father, was glad he died on his own, that I didn't have to kill him. Are you listening?*"
He covers his ears but her voice intensifies. He feels the sweat dripping off his body and is aware that someone is mopping his brow.
"*But you, his son, conceived in foulness, I have loved and still love. You ingrate! When you had the one chance to show you love me, you refused. My comeuppance, as you style it! Psshaw. Shame on you! I'd have understood if you'd said that at fifteen. For crying out loud, you were past twenty-one!*
"*I will haunt you. Be warned—unless you make amends. I have not been the mother you wanted or even needed, but I was the only mother you had. I loved you. And you know it.*
"*Another thing: your father's wealth that you've been giving away. Oh that beast writhes in his grave. What sort of a fool are you? A fool and his money soon depart!*

What's the problem, Joshua? Didn't I raise you right? I thought I drilled it into you that without money in this world we get nowhere. Money is filthy and, God knows, it's always blood-stained, but there's no substitute. None.

"You're so silent. Aren't you hearing me? Or are you playing one of those dumb tricks you play when you turn your face from reality?

"What have you to show for the many years you've lived? You are fifty-one! If they are nothing else, the years are a strainer to trap and hold on to the little sense there is in this ocean of nonsense.

"You will continue to be whipped for your own foolishness. You don't settle scores with the dead, shadowboxing fool!

"Listen to me. There's a way to throw away the whip: come visit me in Tallahassee and tell me you forgive me for my folly. Tell Marjorie to fuck-off if you like. I'm waiting for you in Tallahassee."

"Ah-ah-ah—ahgggggh!" he hears himself screaming stertorously and realizes that he is thrashing the bed. The voice goes and his head clears. Blenheim, Nurse Ramon, and someone else are in the room.

"Are you hearing us, Joshua?"

"Yes," he says faintly.

"Are the voices gone?"

"Yes."

"We'll start an IV and keep you sedated. It will keep away the voices."

Within minutes after the IV has been inserted he feels himself sinking into sleep.

In his sleep the voice returns but this time it's far away, like a ventriloquist projecting sounds onto his dummy.

"All right then, I'll start all over. I will hound you till you get it right."

At some point he opens his eyes. The room is pitch black and it is as if she is now a bodiless voice hovering over him, whispering in his ear. *"Unless you start doing the learning for yourself. You're so damn passive!"*—here the voice was coming out of him—*"I'll force-feed it to you. Because you are my son and I won't let you destroy yourself."*

He's suddenly lucid, feels cold, and realizes that the clothes he has on as well as the bed sheets are soaked through with sweat. He wants to get up and turn on the lights, maybe even call the night nurse, but his body is catatonic. He remains like this for what seems like an hour during which the voice does not bother him. Slowly he feels pins and needles tingling his flesh as his muscles unlock.

His thoughts clear up.

He had gloated that she'd had her comeuppance for preventing him from attending Bita's funeral. He could have gone to hers. The Michaelmas term ended the same day he got the news. Wilson Pickett's, "The Midnight Hour," topping the charts then, was on his phonograph when the telegram was delivered. Her burial was on December 27, which would have given him ample time to return for exams and the beginning of the spring term. Any comeuppance you mete out to the dead, he's now wise enough to know, and she has just reminded him, has to be borne by your living self. You become castigator and castigated.

He remains awake, afraid to fall asleep. The person left to watch over him has fallen asleep too. When the night supervisor makes her final rounds he's still awake, but pretends to be asleep because he does not want to have to answer any of her questions, although he would have liked to get up and change his sweaty clothes. She checks the IV and injects more sedative into it, and within minutes he is yawning.

20

THE RADIO IS ON. Michael Enright is refereeing two Caribbean writers in A slug-out over whether Canada is or isn't the greatest country on earth. One of them, a novelist from Barbados, says that depending on who selects the criteria every country can argue that it is. The other, a poet from Trinidad, says Canada's greatness is in part the chance it gives immigrants to escape a painful past.

The novelist says that some immigrants encounter greater pain here than what they leave behind.

"*Some immigrants*! You mean Blacks, my friend. When you folks stop griping and start striving, you'll move ahead . . ."

Even Enright sounds shocked. Struggling to keep the emotion out of his voice, he quickly changes the subject to immigrants from Bosnia.

Joshua reaches over and turns the radio off.

You've been hiding in Canada.
Hiding?
Yes.

From whom?
That's for you to admit.
Who's looking for me?
Your heritage.

His armpits feel damp. His hands are moist with sweat. He'd better quell
these thoughts now, otherwise it will be a long night. He presses the bell.
Nurse Ramon comes, leaves, and returns with the sedative he has
requested. He swallows it, feeling like a deserter making a chemical escape.
He impatiently waits for the drowsiness to descend like a blanket on him.
Grateful for this small amount of control.

For a long time he's floating inside an enormous cloud. Sometimes it
disperses, and he sees vague surreal figures with strange postures, as much
as twelve feet tall, attached to disembodied voices, and moving about in
contorted motion.

Then he falls asleep. At some point he dreams that he is moving through
space and two turquoise stars are in his trajectory. They give off no heat. He
is sure he has learnt that stars are balls of fire several times the earth's size,
but these are heatless. He is surprised to see them blink as if they were
Christmas tree lights. He is so close, why not reach out and touch them?
They're smooth, not roiling lakes of fire. But as his hand moves towards
them he hears a piercing scream. It's a movie, he thinks. The floating
through space are special effects. *King Kong II.* Yes, and that's someone playing Fay Wray coming in King Kong's arms. Woman ejaculating upon touch
of apeman lover. That, he thinks, would make a good subtitle. What's his
part? It better not be King Kong!

He really does awaken and feels completely listless. There's an IV tube in
his arm. *It has happened again.* The movie. Just a dream. Leroy is in the
room. He's reading.

"You 'wake?"

"Yes."

"Good. You feel like eating?"

"What time is it?"

"Heading for three o'clock."

"I'm not hungry . . . Did you say three o'clock?"

"Yeah. You sleep all night and . . ."

"And what?"

Leroy pretends not to hear the question.

They're silent for a while. When they resume talking Joshua discovers that his movie dream wasn't a dream. A McGill student had been in the room, and he had tried to push his fingers in her eyes.

Funny, he thinks. I don't look like King Kong. "Leroy, did I tell her I'm King Kong?"

"You sure did and make for she eyes."

"That's not how I remember the dream. What was she doing here? You know if she had Dr Blenheim's permission?"

"He not on duty this afternoon. When he come for see you this morning you was snoring away. I going call Gladys right now fee tell she you 'wake."

Gladys Knights arrives with a tray containing a bowl of watery barley soup. He drinks it listlessly. The warmth sharpens his faculties.

"Dr Blenheim," she tells him, "says you mustn't worry. It's all part of your getting better. He'll be here tomorrow and Dr Defoe will see you in a minute."

She disconnects the IV and takes the pole with her.

Defoe and she cross paths at the door. Joshua notes the concentrated look on his face.

Leroy leaves the room. He always does when the doctors come, but stays when it's the nurse. Part of protocol, Joshua supposes.

"Feeling alright?"

"Okay enough, given the circumstances."

"You'll be alright. I'm not worried. In fact, I am encouraged. Have you gone through any thing like this before?"

"No."

"Well, I think you won't regret it. I had an aunt who, every year, come November, she'd have a breakdown, but would be well by Christmas. My mother even joked that she got better so's not to miss out on the Christmas turkey. Year after year they admitted her to hospital. The last time she broke down my mother decided she shouldn't be hospitalized. She looked after her in her home and forced her to say why she always had her breakdowns in November. She confessed that she'd been raped one October in a home where she was in service and in November she found out she was pregnant and had had an abortion. She died from uremia twenty-one years after her confession but she never had another breakdown after my mother got her to say what was wrong. I suspect that if you bring into consciousness what's corroding your psyche, you'd be firmly on the road to recovery. There's probably something you need to make peace with."

Maybe. Now he knows why he likes Defoe. He's the way he imagines he'd have liked a brother to be if he'd had one. The professional and the humane blend easily in him. In Blenheim too, come to think of it. He likes that.

When Defoe leaves, Leroy returns to the room and informs him that he'll be spending the next shift with him. They couldn't find somebody for the evening shift and they'd asked him to work overtime.

Joshua is thirsty. He sits up in bed. At first he feels dizzy. He drinks two glasses of water and now he realizes that he must head to the bathroom. Leroy gives him a hand.

The trip gets his circulation going and clears his head even more. He decides to have a shower. When he returns to his bed he sees that Leroy has changed the bed linen. Again in bed, he thinks of his brotherly feeling for Defoe and wonders how different his life would have been if he'd been raised with brothers and sisters, a blood mother and maybe even a father. He does not know what any of this is, nor can he imagine it. He'd so wanted Henry to bring André to Arcadia so they could play together, but Henry never did. Couldn't. After his friendship with Maurice was squished by Mommy and Maurice's mother, he must have become, without knowing it, full of distrust.

"Leroy, do you have brothers and sisters?"

"Four brothers and three sisters."

"All of them still living?"

"Yes, Mr Éclair. Them is all alive."

"Did you all grow up together?"

"Yes man. All o' we. In the country. In the parish o' Trelawny. In a place call Lime Tree District. Never go hungry a day yet. Me father was a hardworking man. And strict, you hear, sir. Man when I tell you strict, is so him did strict. You think we could o' pass a man or a woman in the road and no' greet him! No sir, not unless we did want for get the belt. Love him children. And love him church, you hear sir. Love him children and him church. Every Sunday he go. Methodist, sir. Him couldn' read but not a soul been know that. Not even we till we come big."

"What about your mother?"

"She die in childbirth when I eleven. Me father was thirty-eight and he never married again. No woman coming in him house, him say, for 'cause ruction 'mongst him and him children. Me eldest sister, the first child, was sixteen when Mama die. It come like she was we mother. She been the apple o' Papa eye. She been good too, and hintelligent, you hear, sir! She go to England when she nearly thirty years old and go back to school and come a nurse. Sir, is big matron in a Jamaica hospital she did done come before she retire last month. Everybody say she take after our mother, that is so we mother head been light."

"Your other brothers and sisters, Leroy, where are they?"

"Scatter, Mr Éclair. Them all over the world. Two in England. Two in America. One is in Germany working for the Jamaica Tourist Board. And me got a brother what is a university professor in Mexico. Them did got plenty more ambition than me. Me did like the young gals-them can't done," he grins. "But after me soul save me give that up."

"And your children, Leroy? Are you as good as your father?"

"Oh, Mr Éclair—"

"Why don't you call me Joshua?"

"Mr Joshua, them break me heart. Them skip school, them word off the teacher, and create 'ruction all 'bout the place. Mr Joshua, you bring children you no' bring them mind. Them no' interested in none church. All them want is for sing and dance and watch foolishness 'pon television. Easy life. But I tell them, life not easy. Them will find out." His voice is full of regret and resignation.

"All of them?"

"Two o' them is okay, doing well in high school. But me not getting me hopes up too high 'cause me did think so 'bout me second boy what use for be 'pon principal honour roll; but, Mr Joshua, when him hit college and the gal-them pounce 'pon him, and him discover how 'oman sweet—sin always sweet, Mr Joshua, always—him drop him book-them in the bush. Now all him do is perfume up himself of a evening and go meet de young gal-them. Him stop college. Stop! Not even looking for a job and expect me for feed and clothes him and buy him the latest fashion and give him money for buy sinful music. And me does do it. God know me does it. 'Cause if me don' do it and him go and thief and them put him in jail, I not going able for forgive meself, Mr Joshua. Oh, Mr Joshua, sir, you bring the pickney-them but you no' bring them mind."

"You're right about that."

Silence follows. He wishes Leroy would ask him about himself. But it is clear that Leroy's approach is the servant-employer relationship.

"Leroy?"

"Yes, Mr Joshua."

"Cut out the Mister. We are the same age. We're not in Jamaica."

Leroy laughs. "If you say so, sah. But fee call you by your naked name, sah, it don' feel right. And you is a important man, sah. Me have for put the handle to your name."

He notes the *fee* and harshening of the vowels sounds: the conscious use of dialect, and wonders whether Leroy is mocking him. Deference by the servants at Arcadia was sometimes masked mockery, sometimes hate. After that Joshua does not feel like continuing the conversation. But he forces himself to. "It's a while since I have seen McKenna."

"Him off sick."

"What with?"

"I don' know. I hear him off for a month."

I hope it has nothing to do with the way I treated him.

As if hearing Joshua's thought, Leroy says, "Him does be absent regular."

Sometime after supper he falls asleep and dreams that he's in a bed on a large stage. On his right Bita appears. About ten feet from the foot of the bed three persons are standing together. Someone else is standing a little apart to their left.

"Bita, who are those people?"

"Sh-sh!" she says with her right forefinger on her lips; she places the finger on his lips.

Complete darkness envelops the stage for a couple of seconds. Two spotlights come on and shine on the four at the foot of the bed. In the threesome, a tall man stands in the middle. To his left is Mommy. To his right Mammy. Anger rises in Joshua as he realizes the man in the middle is his father. The man apart, on the far left, is Sparrow. His head is bowed. Joshua's anger is now mixed with fear and anxiety. The spotlights go off and the entire stage floods with light. The four are still there.

Bita takes Joshua's chin in her left hand, fixes him with a stare, and with her right hand she gestures that she wants no nonsense from him. Now she raises her head and looks in the direction of the foursome. She lets go his chin. Joshua quickly glances back and forth between her and the four in the distance.

Bita beckons. Mommy looks at her expectantly. Bita nods. Mommy comes and stands on the right side of the bed. Next Bita beckons to Mr Éclair. He hesitates. Bita turns to Joshua gives him a stern stare and a watch-it-no-nonsense-from-you wagging of her finger. Joshua's resistance dissolves and Mr Éclair comes to stand on Mommy's right. Now she beckons to Mammy, who goes to stand on Mr Éclair's left. Next Bita beckons to Sparrow, whose eyes constantly shift in focus from Bita to Joshua while he vigorously shakes his head.

"Joshua! Jo-shaaw!" Bita shouts reprovingly while she beckons to Sparrow.

Sparrow comes forward, his steps unsure, his head bowed. He goes to stand on the left side of the bed, opposite Bita, Mommy, Mammy, and Mr Éclair.

With her right forefinger, Bita traces an arc, indicating the side of the bed where they are all standing.

Sparrow obeys and moves to the right side of the bed.

Bita takes Joshua's left hand and places it into Sparrow's right. Each of them holds the hand next to their own. Bita closes the chain when she holds Joshua's left hand.

"Now say after me, Joshua: 'I have forgiven you all from the bottom of my heart.' Are you ready, Joshua?"

He nods in spite of himself.

He repeats the words. The scene dissolves. His eyes open. It's totally dark.

For a long while he remains thinking, wondering about the significance of this dream. Mommy's words, the entire page on which they were written, come alive in his memory: *"Joshua, in the package that's life, there are one or two things that we truly desire. But to have them we must endure the detested rest."*

When he falls asleep again, Bita reappears and tells him, "Now you must come home and bury us. You won't find peace until you bury us. Say yes to me, Joshua."

"Yes," he says without thinking.

"Not like that. Say it because you mean it."

"Yes, Bita. I will."

She disappears.

21

IT'S A WEEK LATER. Dr Blenheim comes into his room. He's without his doctor's smock and it is 7 A.M., two hours before Blenheim ever sees his patients.

Joshua is eager to find out what has brought Blenheim here so early. For the first few moments Blenheim's face is a mask and he does not look directly at Joshua, who therefore cannot read anything in his eyes.

"Why are you here so early, Dr Blenheim?"

"Because I have some excellent news for you. But I won't divulge it before nine o'clock."

"Not even a hint?"

"It's someone who wants to see you."

"Name?"

"I'm not telling. Not one of your ex-boyfriends, but close."

Who could it be? It couldn't be Aunt Stacey. We've only spoken about her a week ago. Not enough time to track her down and bring her here. Joshua, stop torturing yourself; you'll find out soon enough.

At nine he enters a small room adjoining Dr Blenheim's office. A woman is sitting in it. She stands and seems to straighten totally when he enters the room, and she inspects him scrupulously. She is of brown complexion, with Carib-like facial features—circular face and protuberant cheek bones—and Afro-Carib hair bulging out from under her straw hat bedecked with plastic red and yellow roses. She is wearing a two-piece canary yellow suit that reminds him of the stolid matrons who attended the Camden Presbyterian Church, matrons whom he used to watch heading penitentially to and from the communion rail, decked out in carnival colours, never in anything drab or remorseful, the flounces in their dresses rustling, their perfumes the odours of roses, lilies, ladies of the evening, lavender. The woman now looking at him could well be headed there. She is daisies, saffron, buttercups, sunflowers, sunlight.

A smile invests her face, slowly, from inside out, it seems. Something about her face is familiar. She raises her right arm and rubs her forehead, which is the colour of baked bread. He has seen every detail of that movement before. He could have predicted its every aspect.

He moves towards her, extends his hand, "Joshua Éclair."

"Anastasia Brown."

"Aunt Stacey?"

"In the flesh. No one else."

"How did they find you? When did you arrive?" But he has fallen into her arms and is probably embracing her too forcefully for her to answer. He slackens his hug. She does too and raises her hand to wipe a tear.

He doesn't cry but he's forced to sit, in a chair facing hers. His hands have begun to sweat. He studies her. She looks like sixty but he knows she must be older. After all he's almost fifty-two. She was an adult when he was born. She too is watching him closely.

He hears Blenheim saying, "You two have a great deal to catch up on, so I'm leaving you alone for the next hour. If you want me I'll be in my office next door."

Joshua sees his mother's cheekbones in her face. Her gestures are definitely his mother's. Something too about the expression in her eyes, something close to, but not quite, a cynical squint.

He continues to stare into the face of the woman who'd stood in for the midwife, who'd knotted his umbilical cord, who'd slapped him on the ass to trigger the birth cry and force the mucus out of his lungs, and supplied the milk his mother had denied him. And here she is again, after a lapse of almost fifty-two years, to help him regain his sanity. His eyes well with tears.

She pulls up her chair and holds his hands, then asks, "How long you been sick?"

"A long time, off and on."

"Why you didn't come back home?"

"I don't know." *Why didn't I?* He knows the answers he's given himself before.

"Aunt Stacey, weren't you supposed to be living in Trinidad?"

"In 1980, my sister have a stroke and I go back home to take care o' she."

"How was Dr Blenheim able to contact you?"

"Is so long since you leave, you forget the place is small? If you check the phone book for Anastasia Brown, you will find only one name. It's not hard at all.

"When Dr Blenheim ask me if I know one Joshua Éclair, I tell him it's I self that give him the name Joshua. I give you that name 'cause is Joshua that take the Israelites to the promised land." She smiles. "But Moses should come before Joshua. But don't mind my foolish talk. When the doctor tell me that you sick and he think I can help for make you well, that me is the person you want for see, I say praise God, 'cause for years and years I been wondering what become of you, since that day I set you straight 'bout your father. So I go straight to the bank and take the couple o' dollars that I have there and buy my plane ticket."

"I didn't know you have a sister on Isabella Island. Did she live in Petit Bordel?"

Aunt Stacey stares at him and shakes her head in disbelief. "Boy, what's the matter with you? I talking 'bout your mother! You is my nephew. Me and your mother is one father children. Is true we all carry we mother name. But that don't change nothing."

Suddenly a lot becomes clear to him. "So it's my mother you went home to look after?"

She nods.

"I see now why you saved my life."

She shakes her head very slowly, deliberately. "I would o' do it even for a stranger. God know I not lying when I say that I can't count the number o' children I help mind. A woman in Trinidad whose children would o' go hungry if I didn't feed them did tell another woman, 'I hope that mule'— she did mean me—'not feeding my children in the hopes that them will servant for she in she old age.' Joshua, my child, I live for see she die in the poor house in Trinidad. Her children neither servant for she nor for me. But plenty others remember kindness. I get three-four letter every month from the States and Canada, all o' them with money orders from the men and women I help mind when they was little children in Trinidad. I always believe that if you don't sow you can't expect for reap."

He listens to her, knowing it isn't boasting, knowing too that she could have sown kindness and reaped cruelty.

"Is one o' them same children I staying with here. And one in Toronto done plan to come and get me and take me to Toronto Saturday."

Now it sounds like bragging, bragging that can be forgiven.

She talks on and on about trivial and not so trivial things: about whom he resembles, the family lineage, everything but his illness. She is a talker and Joshua wonders if he could live in the same house with someone like her. He wonders too why he has this thought: Is he thinking of returning to Isabella Island? He refuses to answer the question, remembers his promise made in a dream to Bita, and knows that not only must he answer it but answer it soon.

When Dr Blenheim returns, he asks Joshua to return to his room. Leroy is already posted there. Joshua smiles. *Not this time, folks. Not this time.*

Accompanied by Blenheim, Aunt Stacey comes to say good-bye fifteen minutes later. Blenheim tells him that she has the freedom to visit any time.

Joshua wonders what they had to talk about that they did not want him to hear. But he's happy. *I am happy. I cannot believe it. I am happy.*

But he later realizes that it's happiness that has come with conditions. He wonders now what his real motives for wanting to see Aunt Stacey were. Was it just a need to pin a face to her name? A chance to see the woman who'd ensured his survival? Did he think that she could in any way help him get cured? One thing is sure: Blenheim has expectations. Notions that she would be able to mother him back to health. For sure, the ship's about to sail and without realizing what he was doing, he'd booked passage. It's too much for him, to the point where he requests a sedative but it's a long time before he falls asleep.

His sleep is fitful. He awakens every half hour. Around one-thirty he asks Leroy to accompany him down to the boardwalk. He ignores Leroy's presence all the way. A question haunts him: Does he want to return to Isabella Island? Can he again go to the place where the cruel acts that impaired his sanity happened? Blenheim thinks that the best cure for guilty immigrants is a trip back to their birthplace. What about those who'd fled, willingly, gratefully from cruelty? To leave, as the Trinidadian poet was saying recently on CBC, a painful reality behind? Did he leave gratefully? *Yes.* Has he found health outside? *No.* What sort of life has he led?

"You in deep thought, Mr Joshua. How your visit this morning go?" Leroy interrupts.

"Wonderful."

His mind flashes across the years and he sees that his life here has amounted to little more than a long hibernation with brief interruptions. Like bears leaving their dens to shit, if bears do so. His bowels are psychic though. What if he becomes totally psychotic when he returns to Isabella Island? *Not that, please.* He remembers Horton. *No, not that. No!*

When he returns from the waterfront, he undresses and crawls into bed, and the same thoughts play over and over in his head. Gladys Knights asks him if he thinks he'll need supervision.

"Why?"

"Because you're distraught."

"Leroy, you want to work overtime?" Joshua asks.

"I have a important church meeting for attend."

"If it won't be Leroy, I prefer to be alone."

"You're sure now?"

"Yes. If I go berserk, you'll know."

"That won't help me. It would be too late then to get somebody to work."

"Do as you like."

She leaves.

At four a young man, a student nurse, comes to sit him. Joshua turns his back to him and pursues his thoughts. Around 4.30 Bonita Ramon spends fifteen minutes with him. He tries to be cheerful. Since their first show-down he has had nothing but respect for her, respect that intensified after she set him straight about McKenna. He asks her about McKenna.

"He's all right, getting over a little stress, that's all," she tells him. "How did your visit go?"

"Wonderful, but, as you can see, I'm exhausted."

She squeezes his hand gently. "You worry too much. After a house has been badly damaged, it takes time to repair it. Sometimes you have to reshape it. You'll be all right. Believe me, you will be. We're all counting on you not to disappoint us. And you won't, right?" She squeezes his hand a little harder and looks at him with a concentrated stare that reminds him of Bita. He feels privileged to have her looking after him.

"I'll do my best. I'll try not to disappoint you. You are a truly wonderful human being. I appreciate you. There are some incredibly good people working here. I shouldn't say it, but I think you're the greatest of them all."

"Oh, be quiet!" she says with a big smile and leaves.

There is screaming all over the ward throughout the evening. No sooner it dies down in one spot than it starts up again in another. It keeps Bonita busy. He doesn't see her again until she's about to leave at eleven. She comes to wish him good night.

Another male student nurse replaces the evening fellow. He brings his schoolbooks in a backpack and looks at Joshua guiltily.

"Go right ahead. I don't really need supervision. They just wanted to be sure there's someone here in the event I go berserk. I only go berserk when Leroy's here because then I can do so safely. Go ahead and do your studying. Don't make the supervisor catch you though. She comes around two and again at five. If you can manage it, catch a few winks in between."

The night nurse brings him his sedative. She's Trinidadian, British trained, full of precision, smiles, and professionalism. A patient listener. Jet-black, tall, with a lithe body. Would undoubtedly have made a fine model. She works only two nights per week. She is an MSN student at McGill and has two boys, one four and one six, she told him a while back.

"I'll go right off to sleep. I'll do anything for a wonderful person like you."

"You'd better not give me cause to come to your room then," she says with a wink.

"You have it on my honour."

"OK, then. After that, if I have to spend time with you, I'll know it's not your fault. Good night, Mr Éclair." She leaves.

He dreams he's sitting on a riverbank similar to the one below Petit Bordel. His mother appears in front of him holding a white lily in one hand and a calabash in the other. She offers him the lily but he refuses it. She continues to extend it to him and he persists in refusing it.

Two men arrive, one dressed in purple robes, the other, younger, in black. On the younger man's head is a bundle of wood; in one hand he holds a rope to which a goat is tethered. All four of them stare at Joshua angrily for refusing to take the lily. His mother drops it at his feet.

The man in black arranges all but one log of the wood in a pyre and lights it. Next he and the man in purple immobilize the goat, and, using the spared log as a support, the man in black slits the goat's throat. His mother catches the blood in the calabash. The man in black arranges the goat's carcass on the pyre. His mother stands facing Joshua and empties the blood onto him. Then the three of them bend in unison and kiss the ground three times, each time saying, "Forgive our abominations, Yaa." When they rise the third time, the carcass flames, sizzles loudly, and incinerates totally. The drama awakens him. Instantly he touches his scalp, expecting to find his hair matted and viscous with blood. It's damp. He smells his finger. It's sweat. The student put there to watch him is fast asleep, his textbook open on his lap, the flashlight he brought for reading casting its beam on the bed.

When Joshua falls asleep again, he dreams that he's journeying somewhere on foot. The destination is unclear and he's entangled in twigs and branches and struggling desperately to free himself. Momentarily he clears himself only to find Mammy and Bita blocking his path. They refuse to move. Both look morose and both are silent. "Let me pass," he tells them. They shake their heads slowly, in perfect unison, from side to side.

"You're both dead, please leave me alone!"

They laugh, hideous barking laughter, still shaking their heads.

"What do you want?" he screams at them.

They turn to stare at each other, nod mockingly, and laugh out loud, before again turning their stare onto him, with a so-well-timed deliberation it could have been choreographed.

Then, as if this were a stage trick, they disappear and Averill Éclair takes their place.

"Not you again!"

"What? You expect to put me down like that? I'm your past, Joshua. He-he-he-he. See. You can't put me down. You'll carry me uphill and downhill, into valleys and up mountains, to your grave even. Memories don't rot, Joshua, unless those who have them are rotting too. But venom kills. You're toxic. He-he-he-he!"

He attempts to answer, but before he can speak, she disappears, and Bita and Mammy take her place. "We'll rot even if she doesn't," they say in unison. "Bury us. We want to be buried. This is the last warning. Act or we're gone—for good."

If Bita has turned on me, what hope do I have?

"None!" both heads chorus and begin to recite:

Put it down! Oh, Joshua, put it down!
Why carry it?
Why hate the dead?
Hatred is not bread, Joshua:
It's tons of lead.
Love your flesh, Joshua.

Why feed it to the dead?

End the torture, Joshua,
You're no more wicked than another.

The voices increase. Mommy and Sparrow appear and sing with them, call-response:

He's not more wicked?
No! No! No!
Not more wicked ?
No! No! No!

"All right," Averill Éclair says. "Let him come and bury me too." She stares at him sternly. "Now that's an order!"

He begins to cry. When he awakens he discovers that his pillow is wet. In the brief interval that he remains awake, he is aware that he must begin making arrangements to return to Isabella Island.

Yet again he dreams. This time Bita comes alone. "You're almost better. Put away the whips. Yes, go back to Isabella Island. Let Aunt Stacey put you through the hoops you've skipped. And don't forget to come and bury us. You and we need concrete gestures. Don't leave anything out." Now she wags her finger at him. "All or nothing, Joshua. No half measures."

When he awakens he wonders about these dreams. The faces were the faces of his sister and mother but the language they spoke sounded more like his own, like Mommy's language, like the plantocracy's. He wants to distrust them, but knows that only by following their orders will he know whether it's true.

He's still thinking of the implications of his dreams the night before, when Blenheim enters the room. First they talk in bits and pieces about yesterday. Then Blenheim asks him if he thinks he's ready to leave. He tells him yes but adds: "Can I prove to myself that I am ready?"

"How?"

"I'd like to be left to manage on my own for a while—a week let's say."

They agree on a plan by which he would do so, but he must return to sleep at the hospital and he must phone the ward at least twice during his absence to let the hospital know he is fine. In the meantime, his drugs would be diminished. "We might have to reinstate the dosage if your body reacts negatively," Blenheim cautions with a stare so intense his lips pucker. "I don't want you to have any surprises."

In the afternoon he takes the bus and the metro downtown, drops in at his flat, and from there heads up to Sherbrooke Street to begin his walk towards Lafontaine Park. He turns back halfway there, before he gets to George's; not from fatigue but because he knows he shouldn't overtire himself. Even so he walks for a little more than hour.

When he returns to his flat, Aunt Stacey is there in the company of the woman she's staying with. He phones the ward and then turns to devouring the Caribbean goodies Aunt Stacey has brought him: eddoe soup, roast breadfruit, codfish cakes, and the most delicious almond cake he has ever eaten—food he hasn't tasted in more than thirty years. It brings back memories of Union Island, of Bita offering him, in his pre-Arcadian days, bite-size pieces of golden apple. "You must teach me how to cook like this," he tells Aunt Stacey. She grins, her Carib cheeks bundling, her eyes brightening behind her glasses (she wasn't wearing them yesterday).

While on the bus going back to the hospital, he thinks that he should resume the habit he had in London of keeping a daily journal. He sets about writing it as soon as he gets to the ward. He sleeps undisturbed by dreams that night, and when he wakes he thinks it's a good sign.

His routine continues for seven more days, his walk taking him to Lafontaine Park, and on two days when there is no wind, he walks back as well. He does not drop in to see George, largely because he doesn't want to explain his absence. Some days he meets Aunt Stacey at his flat, where he goes to phone the hospital and to shower. On the fifth day, he skipped supper at the hospital, took Aunt Stacey to a restaurant, later sent her back home in a taxi, after which he went to see a film at the Park Cinema.

By the end of the week he is sure he has never felt so good. But his stutter has not returned and he still does not know what brought on his last breakdown. Blenheim tells him that since he has had no adverse reaction to his decreased drugs, it means that his body is glad to be rid of them, and he stops them. So when they offer to discharge him he says yes. But they cannot decide whether he should remain for a while in Montreal or whether he should return to Isabella Island right away in Aunt Stacey's company. Blenheim prefers that he wait a month. Defoe thinks he should go right away.

BOOK THREE

Return to Arcadia

22

I T IS JULY 20, 1998, sixteen months since his return to Isabella Island. Today he changes the habitual route of his walk. Instead of going towards the foothills of El Tigre, he heads to the coast. Today he needs to return to Arcadia, to take a close-up look at it. He'd sold it while in Spain as part of his efforts at unburdening. Mommy probably wanted him to keep it, as his home perhaps. Since his return he has glimpsed it from a distance: a dome-like mass of tangled foliage.

And while seeing Arcadia he might as well have a look at the spot where Sparrow exited.

Walking slowly, more slowly than usual in the grey light, he recalls what he has so far encountered since his return. On March 19, 1997 he was discharged into Aunt Stacey's care. Everyone except Defoe was skeptical about what she had planned for him. But Defoe told him when the others weren't around: "Listen, we have an African past and we must listen to it when it speaks to us. Your sister is like an amulet you carry inside you. Listen to what she tells you."

So with two suitcases, books in one, clothes in the other, he returned in Aunt Stacey's company to Isabella Island. Healer André, a Spiritual leader she had contacted before leaving Canada, met them at the airport. He took Joshua to a temple in Éclair's Pasture and explained in the barest of details what would follow.

André is in his forties, is dark-skinned, of medium height; has deep-set, very bright eyes; generous lips; broad shoulders; deep chest; and large callused, gritty hands. He smells of wood smoke tinged with mint and sweat that has the odour of newly ploughed earth. He told Joshua that first evening, "You have to journey into your soul and make peace with it and with the universe. Give yourself to life. Become one with the wind and the rivers and the trees and the rocks and the sky and the sun. What more can

I tell you 'bout it. You will have to trust me and try. Anybody here that you did wrong to that you can beg for forgiveness or make restitution to?"

Joshua shook his head.

"Anybody in Canada or anywhere else?"

He thought of the men he'd paid to whip him. "Not really."

"If you ready, tomorrow we set out on the journey. If you can't go tomorrow, you going have to wait for a month or two 'cause I done plan for lots o' other things in the coming weeks and I not going be able to fit this in. Two more things: first, I not promising you a single thing. If you looking to heal yourself you will find what you need, not in one shot, but you will find it. All I can do is start you off and point out the road far away, up on the mountain and deep down in the valley and on the plains in the distance. After that you going have to walk it by yourself. Second, if you get better you have to promise me that for the rest of your life you will give up some of your time to help ease some o' the suffering in this world."

It sounded mysterious. But he was already in. He couldn't get out now. And what was the alternative? It frightened him just to think of it. *Tomorrow? Why so soon?* But he said yes.

He needed comfortable clothes, a gym suit, and sneakers. And a change of clothing for when he came back and a backpack to carry them. He had them.

Tired, waiting to fall asleep, he wondered how he was going to deal with the religious gobbledy-gook over the upcoming days. Only an insane man would obey promises he'd made in a dream. He'd turned his back on churches as soon as he arrived in England. It was in the heady days when the British parliament decriminalized homosexuality. The Christians who'd opposed it had instantly turned the Bible into a chastity belt for gays. Muslims sneered at the legislation, saw it as irrefutable proof that Western civilization was rotten through and through, and bragged about Koran death sentences for homosexuals. So he'd sidestepped the race by Western Blacks to convert to Islam, leaving it to those needing the bonds of religion. Later, he'd softened somewhat when he came upon Freud's observation that God is a human invention, and a necessary one. Now here he was, slipping on the chains.

That night he slept on a cot in a tiny room at the back of the temple in Éclair Pasture. Healer André woke him from a deep sleep at 4 A.M., so they could do a good part of the journey before the sun got hot. He handed Joshua a machete, saying it was all he needed besides his clothes.

Other than as a scout he'd never used a machete. What for, he wondered.

By four-thirty they set out, both of them carrying machetes and back-packs. Where was the goat? Maybe goats were available in the mountains. Oh, but the goat was in his dream. Healer André never said anything about goats.

By dawn they were well beyond the foothills of the mountains and were still ascending. Joshua's leg muscles were sore. He was very aware of the difference his missing toes made as he mounted the steep slopes. They paused often for him to rest. The temptation to call it off was strong. Occasionally Healer André asked him if he was sure he wanted to go on. Nine o'clock came and they were still ascending. By ten they had passed all signs of human frequentation. Now Healer André walked ahead of him to cut a path with his machete because there was no road. He mumbled some-thing each time he lifted the machete. They continued like this until noon. Joshua was hungry, tired, and slightly dizzy. Healer André handed him two slices of bread, a mango, and a banana and got him a tin cup of water from a nearby stream, to which he mumbled something before he dipped it.

The path-clearing continued. Sometimes they circled boulders; some-times they descended to beds of streams, some too wide to jump over; sometimes along the edges of precipices, steadying themselves by holding on to the branches above them or the saplings growing out of the sides of the rock—until they got to the base of a towering cliff that looked like a gigantic grey forehead crowned with trees and giant ferns. It capped the top of a summit that fronted another summit. Between the summits was a steep, narrow valley, almost a gorge. They were on the gentler part of its slopes. A mere sixty feet over from them a waterfall thunderously roared. "This is the place," Healer André told him; and the rocks around repeated, "This is the place."

The wind gusted through the valley; each gust bringing a perfume of lilies, lime, and gommier intermixed. Between gusts the smell of humus rose up from the earth, reminding him of the smell of decomposing leaves on the forest floor on Mount Royal on warm, windless November days. Hoots and tenor sounds stretched out in a wail came from the opposite summit and were answered from his side of the valley, interspersed with and overlapped by tweeting and chirping that sent multiplying echoes up and down the valley, making it a stage with its own orchestra led by a pipiree, the only sound he could identify with certainty.

Where would he and Healer André sleep? How long would they stay?

Mosquitoes swarmed about, landed on him, buzzed in his ears. He raised his hand to kill them. Healer André tapped his arm and told him, shaking his head, not to kill them.

"What if I catch malaria?"

"Malaria rare on Isabella Island. You could lose a little blood. You won't miss it. Think of all the things we take from animals and trees without the least bit of gratitude."

He was not amused. "I'm allergic to mosquito bites."

"I'll see to it that you don't die."

"Next you'll be asking me to make crickets sing."

André smiled, a big smile that put furrows in his cheeks. "First get your soul to sing. As to making crickets sing, you're going have to take on that yourself." He turned and looked at a huge clump of bamboos, raising his head to assess their height. Some were well over a hundred feet. "Let's get to work while we still have light. See that bamboo root over there? It offering us shelter. I will cut and shape the bamboo pieces. Those roots over there, you see them?" He pointed to some trees on his right covered with lianas—epiphytes. "You go over there to cut some *mahoe* vines to tie the bamboo in place. Cut the ones smaller than your little finger in strips 'bout the length o' your arm. Take my knife out o' the backpack. What you will say to the vines-them?"

"Say?"

"Say after me, 'Vines, I thank you for letting me make use of you. I won' take mo' than I need.' A prayer for everything you take a piece of, that you touch, that you use."

Bizarre. But he had nothing to lose.

By 6 P.M., Healer André with a little help from Joshua had built a lean-to roofed with split bamboo. The walls were of leaves supported by bamboo tied with epiphytes. The floor too was layered with bamboo overspread with branches. Joshua itched; in various places his skin was swollen from mosquito bites. As evening approached the mosquitoes quadrupled and the forest hummed with sound. He wanted to ask Healer André if there were scorpions here. What would happen if they bit him? But he kept his fear unvoiced.

Healer André told him to start a fire. "Remember to thank the trees for the wood. The smoke will drive 'way the mosquitoes. I going to look for supper."

Even as a scout Joshua had never made a wood fire by himself. He knew he needed dry twigs. He searched for them on the forest floor but it was damp. Before he could find dry twigs, a thin, faintly rank fog settled on the valley. It lifted only long enough for him to find some dry twigs in the lower dead branches of a nearby tree. He grabbed them with relief, remembering only afterwards that he'd forgotten to say thanks. He broke off as many of the dead branches as he could manage. He remembered then the machete and went to get it, but the fog had returned, and he knew it was unwise to use a machete in fog. He picked up the twigs he'd collected, this time remembering to say thanks. He used up the entire box of matches but did not start the fire. He realized then that the ground was damp and should have been coated with dry straw or leaves. Nothing to be done but endure the mosquito bites until Healer André returned.

By now sunset was in its dying moments. At ground level all was grey. In places the peaks were veiled, in others incandescent; and night's throats began to hum and throb and peal in every pitch and variation, from the summits down and from the valley floor up. The ground, the water, the rocks became ghostly, a fluid, live vocality. The fog got denser each time it descended. Finally a gust off the brow of the cliff dropped an opaque curtain and wrapped the bronze summit in the distance and everything else in oblivion. It stayed, settled in for the night.

Foregrounded in his mind, as he awaited the return of Healer André, were stories of people who had lost their way in the fog, who'd tumbled over precipices or had been swallowed by incoming tides—like a third-grade poem, one he'd memorized with Mommy's help: "*O Mary, go and call the cattle home/ and call the cattle home/ Across the sands o' Dee,*" in which the mist had caught Mary and she had drowned.

This was followed by Jack London's story "To Build a Fire." No, his situation wasn't as dire. But his thoughts returned to where he'd left off the night before. What the hell was he doing here? Why had he given the controls of his life to a 75-year-old woman he did not know? And she'd promptly handed them to a man younger than he, a man he knew nothing about. This required the sort of faith he could never have, could never cultivate, for it was stuff, he felt, invented for the credulous. But a frozen man will dive into excrement if he thinks it will thaw him out.

A blanket of darkness twinkling with green luminescent fireflies covered everything by the time Healer André reappeared, bringing a fish, half-dozen ripe guavas, and a *bobass* yam. He was silent about the unlit fire. From his backpack in the lean-to he took a cigarette lighter (he did not smoke) and a penlight. With the light he searched for dry leaves to start the fire. Within fifteen minutes a fire roared. The yam and fish were cooking in the open flame. The flame comforted, the smoke drove away the mosquitoes, the warmth reassured. Into this oasis of light the forest moths came in dozens to incinerate themselves. Outside the lighted perimeter, nature pulsed, hummed, screeched, hooted, sang. Below them the waterfall roared. Above them the wind serenaded the summit. Beside him Healer André sat cross-legged, his eyes closed, his hands crossed in his lap in a Buddha pose.

Later they ate and crawled into the lean-to. Within minutes Healer André was asleep. Joshua itched and scratched for a long time. When Healer André awakened him, he was sure he had just fallen asleep.

His need to urinate suddenly seemed a crisis. "Go over there." Healer André directed him to a spot in the forest about a hundred feet away. "Carry the cutlass with you, and while you're at it, dig a hole 'bout two feet deep for your waste. Leave the sand and a heap o' leaves 'round it for burying. What you going to say before you stick the machete in?"

"You said living things!"

"So you think the earth is dead?" His eyes squinted, exasperation in his voice. "You live off the earth, you're food for the earth, and you don't think the earth is alive? Whatever you do, just remember for thank it for 'lowing you to put your filth into it. Beg its pardon too. When you finish we have to go look for breakfast. You're not yet ready to live off your own fat."

Live off your own fat?

Healer André with a fishing line, he with a machete, they headed off down the steep bank, steadying themselves upright by clutching the lower branches and the trunks of saplings, a thin fog merging with the dew-drenched vegetation limiting their visibility; his leg and arm muscles stiff and painful from mosquito bites and the longest walk he'd ever had. At Arcadia he'd never slept outside a mosquito net. He was breathless. A tremor was present in both of his legs, but he merely noted it. He could not help registering the contrast between the present and his hospital room of a few days before. Shock for sure. Therapy? That remained to be seen.

Healer André pointed out a yam vine, a thin string Joshua would not have recognized in the fog's vapour. "Say the prayer o' thanks," Healer André reminded him, as if certain Joshua would forget. Together they did, following which Healer André stuck the machete into the ground and showed him how to dig the yam out. "When you finish, go up the hill over there." He indicated the spot. "You will find raspberries up there. Pick just a handful."

Healer André left him to finish digging out the yam and went off in the direction of the waterfall. Joshua scaled the hill to look for raspberries but discovered, when he got where the raspberries were supposed to be, that he did not know what to look for, and while he wondered the fog thickened and he could not distinguish one piece of undergrowth from another.

He returned to the path they'd made coming down the bank, an abutting, mushroom-shaped rock beside it orienting him. Healer André met him there. He brought a fish. Joshua had the yam. They mounted the slope to their camp, relit the fire, prepared their breakfast, ate it, and washed it down with water from the stream.

Joshua wondered when diarrhoea would begin. This water had to be contaminated. He hadn't brought his emergency psychotropic drugs either. This disquieted him far more than catching diarrhoea.

"I forgot to bring my medication."

"What they for?"

"To calm my nerves."

"Plenty things here in the forest to do that. Calm nerves, cure fever— even life." He winked at Joshua. "I want you to drink a cup o' water every couple o' hours till sunset."

He remembered Wade Davis's and Zora Neale Hurston's claims that Voodoo priests are connoisseurs of nature's poisons and cures. What was Healer André's relationship to Voodoo?

As if overhearing his thoughts, Healer André said, "I not doing nothing 'bout your mosquito bites; that's part o' what you have to cope with. You know why you here?"

"Up to a point."

"Good. You will discover the rest the way an unfolding bud discover the sun. You won't lose your mind, I promise you that. Instead, if you lucky, you will get a glimpse into it." By then, the sunlight was reflecting off the green leaves on the other side of the valley. It did not yet touch them because they were in the cliff's shadow. "Now we ha' to get to work before the fog come back"; and he continued as if speaking to himself. "Day. Night. Fog. Life. Need fog and night for appreciate light and learn for see in darkness; to bring us to the edge o' our limits." He paused for a while, seemed in deep concentration. Then he said, "Now you ha' to scour up there for firewood." He pointed to what looked like a terrace twenty or so feet above the lean-to. "Pile it on a bamboo platform and cover the pile with balisier bush."

Joshua frowned.

"Come, lemme show you how."

They headed to the bamboo root and repeated the mantra. Joshua felled a tall bamboo. His hand was blistered before he'd finished.

"Cut it up in lengths o' three feet, the length o' your arm 'bout. The general idea is you want three layers o' bamboo off the ground so if it rain heavy, the water will run under the wood."

Next they went in search of balisier leaves that grew in abundance on the banks of the stream a short distance in from where the waterfall started. Healer André cut five stakes, always after saying the mantra, and showed Joshua how to stack the wood in relationship to the four corner stakes and the centre stake to create a pyramid. And he showed him how to place the balisier leaves—overlapping, shingle-style, so that water would not get under them—and reminded him to use stakes to keep the leaves in place, and not to forget to layer the corners. Then he moved off down the slope, leaving Joshua to cut, gather, and pile the firewood.

His stomach felt empty long before he finished. But there was nothing to eat and Healer André wasn't there. He sat on some leftover balisier leaves and studied a pipiree in a tree not far from him. He tried to guess the number of seconds between each of its notes. They had invaded its territory. It moved away, shrieked, came near, looked and saw that he was still there. Then it flew to a safe distance and shrieked hauntingly. Its nest must have been nearby. Unconsciously he heard himself apologizing to it. A large brown bird, about the size of a seagull—definitely not a hawk: he could tell from its beak, and certainly not a parrot—flew into a gommier tree about twenty feet from the lean-to. It flapped its wings insistently for periods of up to a minute, enormous things that sounded like loose sails in the wind. Soon another joined it, which did not flap its wings. They flew away and then returned. He thought the wing flapping was its plea to him to leave its habitat and let it live peacefully. He apologized to it too, told it that they would do it no harm, that they would soon leave it to live in peace.

Two hours later, Healer André returned with the inevitable yam and fish and six guavas. He rekindled the embers of the morning fire and set about preparing lunch.

Joshua smelled his own sweat and his anus felt blistered, partly because of the leaves he'd been using. His last bath had been in Canada. It struck him that even if he bathed he'd have no clean clothes to change into. *Bathe? I don't even have soap.*

"I need a bath. I stink," he informed Healer André.

"If you stink but you not rotting, it's all right. But if you rottening and not stinking, God help us. Go take a bath if you like. Don't forget to thank the river. As for soap, plenty leaves here can clean you just as good. Come, lemme show you."

Joshua pulled off the leaves. "You didn't thank the plant. Throw down those leaves. Go have your bath without them. Reverence and gratitude to nature is the first rule of sanity. Get in the habit o' appreciating the earth now, so when you yourself about for come food for it, you won't be unhappy."

It began raining suddenly around the time the sun would have been at its zenith, around twelve-thirty probably, and it didn't let up all afternoon and evening. The lean-to stayed dry. The bamboo flooring was effective; the water ran under it. Around them the forest moaned, and the trees swayed amidst the dense sheets of rapidly moving fog and rain. They went to bed supperless, Healer André falling asleep almost immediately. Joshua's stomach churned and grunted and ached, but he fell asleep.

When they awakened next morning the rain was still falling. Healer André went out into it empty-handed. Totally drenched, the drops hanging like rhinestones from his eyelids, he returned with guavas and a handful of raspberries about an hour later. These they ate for breakfast. Now his gut felt like it had been tautly wound around some bobbin.

Around ten the rain stopped. Healer André lit a fire. He took a quart-size, home-made clay pot—the only cooking implement he'd brought—and put it on the fire, went a little way into the forest and returned with leaves which he dropped into the boiling water. He gave the mixture to Joshua to sip. "If anything like fever developing in you, this will nip it in the bud. Good for the cramps in your stomach too." Joshua hadn't told him about them.

Whatever the leaves contained, they quieted his stomach. Drowsiness came on and he soon fell asleep. He awakened to the smell of roasting meat. Healer André told him it was an agouti. He roasted it over the open flame, and then poured a sort of herbal tea over the meat. It tasted like nothing Joshua knew.

He asked Healer André how he had caught it.

"I make a trap with twigs. You have for find out what they like for eat and set it for them. After today no fish and meat, just tea for you. You will lie in here and think for three days. When you start seeing things tell me. If you think you losing your mind, tell me. I will stop it."

"Funny, I was wondering what would happen if we run out of food."

"Not here. All sort's o' things here to eat. I'm keeping your diet spare for a purpose: to ease you into fasting. Is in these mountains runaway slaves use to live. The yams we been eating come from pieces they drop all over the place. All sorts o' wild animals up here. A banana root not far from here, and further down in the valley I see a tall breadfruit tree with a girth o' over fifteen feet. That got planted before slavery end. Dasheen and eddoes growing by the waterside. They been growing there ever since escaped slaves bring them up here."

He looked at Joshua and smiled lightly, causing his eyes to contract and brighten. Then the smile became a laugh of short, staccato sounds.

"Why're you laughing?"

"My father talk 'bout you all the time. 'The lad the Éclair woman raise.' I think is because he forgot your name."

"Your father is Henry?"

"Yep."

There was a short pause, a thoughtful one.

"He never brought you to Arcadia. I wanted him to."

"Mrs Éclair never allowed the servants to bring their children to Arcadia."

Exactly what he'd thought. He remembered how eagerly he'd awaited Henry's coming to work day after day for weeks, thinking that would be the day he would bring André, only to be told, "Not today, Master Joshua, not today, maybe another time."

He studied Healer André's face for bitterness. He couldn't harbour bitterness for such things and be engaged in the work he was doing.

He continued to stare at his face. This time to see what resemblances there were between him and Henry. His shoulders seemed twice as large as his father's and were straight; his lips were thicker, his face rounder, his head more spherical; Henry's nose was more sharply etched, but Healer André had his father's eyes, although they expressed confidence, were bolder; his gestures and the coffee-bean complexion were similar too, as were his white, even teeth.

He'd noted, as Healer André walked ahead of him the day before, that his legs were slightly bowed. Now he tried to envisage the three-year old André squealing with glee; running around the lawn or on the porch at Arcadia on stubby, fat bowed legs; being tickled by him and vice-versa; he playing the role Bita had played with him, telling André stories, watching his eyes grow big with wonder. He was sure they would have had a lot of fun.

"*Mrs Éclair never allowed the servants to bring their children to Arcadia.'*
André might have been the brother I never had.

Maurice, the friend I'd desperately wanted—what has become of Maurice?

Cruelty, fear, folly. Mommy, however much you tried to separate yourself from
the plantocracy you were no better than they. Maurice had all the makings of a fine
human being but I couldn't be his friend. All you'd had to do was tell Maurice's
mother it was all right for us to be friends. But you had to please the planter lot. You
forced me to go to get-togethers and outings with Alexander and Vincent, who called
me mongrel to my face, and behind my back God knows what but forbade my friend-
ship with Maurice. What has become of Maurice?

"Le's focus on your cure," Healer André interrupted his thoughts.

But his mind turned to Henry. Henry called him Master Joshua and
sometimes Master Éclair, but he never knew Henry's last name, had been
conditioned not to. The servants were Rose, Dawn, Marie, Henry. On
Isabella Island it was rude to call someone other than a close friend or an
age-mate by his or her first name, but servants were never addressed by
their family names.

Pointer André did not indulge him, told him there was a lot of time to
inquire into such things.

Fasting turned out differently from what he'd expected. Maybe because of
the tea Healer André made him drink every couple of hours. Over the first
two days he didn't feel hungry, only dizzy each time he got up to void. On
the morning of the afternoon of the second day he saw Bita sitting beside
him. Later Mommy came, followed by Mammy. The last to come was
Emmanuel Éclair. Joshua waited for Sparrow but he didn't come. "Why
isn't Sparrow here?" he asked Mommy.

"I told him to stay away. Joshua, I am pleased to see you here." She
smiled. "So important, so important"—she looked around her, seeking Bita
and Mammy's assent; they were nodding their agreement; his father merely
looked on—"Joshua, this is wonderful."

Then they vanished.

He sat up. "Mommy? Where are you? Mommy!"

"Who?" the voice was Healer André's.

"Mommy, Mammy, Bita, and my father were just here. Where did they
go?"

"What did they tell you?"

"Mommy complimented me for being here."

"Good. Now you ready for begin the second stage. I going put a blindfold on you for you to see what's inside you."

He put on the blindfold and Joshua spent the time dozing off and awakening. At one point he was flying. He wondered where the blindfold went. But he saw clearly and he felt himself rise out of the lean-to up into the air above the mountain. His heart thumped rapidly but other than that he was calm. Then he felt the need to defecate. He could not hold it back. He let it go, and saw two pieces of feces, one white the other black, heading towards his face. He veered to avoid them but they veered too and headed right into his face. The encounter shocked him into consciousness. Slowly the blindfold registered, the place, his reason for being there.

Next he was on the shore of the Atlantic, the waves crashing against a large boulder on shore, striking the shore with gravel as they detonated, then scraping up the gravel and retreating to gather momentum for the next charge. Two arms of water stretched out of the Atlantic to embrace him. He tried to scream but he was choking. He got fully conscious then because of a bilious taste in his mouth. He had vomited, and Healer André was using leaves and a wet rag to clean him. Above them the wind whistled ferociously off the summit.

"You doing all right," Healer André said as he replaced the soiled leaves with fresh ones.

Cinnamon and sage leaves were mixed in among them. Their aroma calmed him. He sank down into them and later floated about a meter off the ground and stared at two pellets, one white one brown, pellets that suddenly became rats looking up at him with bared fangs. He worried that he would fall and be bitten and poisoned. Then they scampered off down the valley and leaped over a precipice.

"Joshua."

He recognized Healer André's voice.

"Joshua, how're you feeling?"

It was a while before he was sufficiently collected to speak. "It's horrible. I'm dreaming of brown and white feces that turn into live rats."

"Good." Healer André fell silent.

"What am I to make of that?"

"What you will."

Living shit. White and brown shit. Prevent it from diseasing you. Compost. You can't compost living shit. South Asians and tigers coexist. Tigers are not shit. Both are dangerous. Both? All three, you mean? All four. There's also you. Something's

still missing here. Guilt. Metamorphosing. Quiescent. Corrosive, sleeps a long time.
Awakens. Hungry. Guilt. Must I sacrifice myself to save myself? Absurd.

At one point he is ascending a steep summit, barren on all sides, the soil a dark grey except where the crystals reflect the sunlight pouring down from a cloudless sky. He is awash with sweat. It is stinging his eyes but for some unknown reason, he cannot use his hands. And he is out of breath; and each step he takes upward he slides back, as if he's walking on glass. And he asks himself, "Am I going to die here? He knows his life depends on his scaling the summit. "Look back," a voice whispers to him. "No. I won't. Lot's wife did and she became a pillar of salt." But he realizes why he cannot use his hands. He is pulling something heavy. Slowly, so he does not fall or get pulled downhill, he turns his head, but the cables he holds are taut, and any wrong move he makes will pull him back downhill. "Let them go," the voice says. I can't, he thinks. "Why?" the voice protests. "Because I can't." But the salt is stinging his eyes so badly that instinctively he lets go the right cable to wipe them and finds himself being dragged downhill. This time the voice screams, "Let it go, dammit!" And he does. "Look!" the voice says. "Look at what you've been dragging." He turns his head hesitantly and looks down the slope. In the distance he sees a cement platform, almost the size of a football field with clusters of people on it. In one cluster the plantocracy women are playing bridge; in another there's Mammy facing his father in saddle on a thoroughbred, his riding crop raised high above her in the act of beating her; in another the plantocrats are palavering; even Bita and Skeeter and the raven-haired fellow are on it. "See," the voice says, "you're a damn fool. Here's a little secret. Keep it to yourself. Always refuse to carry anything you aren't supposed to. Now keep going." But the mountain was no longer there and he did not know what do. He awakened then, drenched in sweat.

When he fell asleep again, six naked women holding dildos: two White, two Black, one Chinese, one South Asian—surround him. "See," they tell him, wagging their fingers at him, "it's because of you we do this. You are useless. Can't even fuck us." One magically produces a bottle, screws off the cap, and hands him the bottle. "Drink it. It will make you a woman."

"I don't want to be a woman."

"Then fuck us," they chorally respond, putting their hands on their vulvas and moaning like heat-crazed cats.

He realizes then that he is naked. One of the white women moves forward and raises his limp penis with her right forefinger.

"What say you sisters, shall we cut it off?" They nod and laugh. "And these?" She squeezes his balls. "Get rid of them. Afterwards you'll know who you are."

"Now, this is what you need," they say and fade out as if as if this were the end of a live-theatre scene.

He hears Sparrow's voice, "You love pain. Here is lovely pain." Then he is bound to a scaffold with his legs spread apart, and he sees Sparrow, naked, approaching with an erect penis the size of a forearm; and he screams.

"What is it?" The voice is Healer André's.

Joshua's heart thumped away; his breathing was loud and choking. Healer André placed his hands above Joshua's chest and simulated regular breathing until Joshua eventually calmed down.

Sometime later he is sure he's dead, is sure he's in a coffin with a glass lid, feels himself lowered into a grave, which turns out to be water. The dream changes. He's still dead but now the coffin is put on a lighted pyre and he becomes a cloud of smoke that rises higher and higher into the sky, so high he sees nothing below.

Next he's walking barefoot on a rubbish pile over a hundred feet high. He stumbles and rolls in it. And can't get up. He thinks about his clothes and is about to panic, when he realizes that there's nothing on him that water would not wash off.

What am I doing here anyway? Am I dead or alive?

"Both dead and alive. Contemplating your refuse. We're responsible for our filth and the filth we inherit. It poisons us if we ignore it." The voice is his but comes from another, invisible being.

Out of nowhere Mommy, Mammy, and Bita flank him, then hold his arms, and pull him to his feet, and arm-in-arm they descend from the rubbish mount.

"That's enough," Mommy sternly tells him.

Mammy nods.

Bita squeezes his hand and says, "Joshua, you are better."

He awakened. Had he come to the end of his ordeal? He was uneasy. He hadn't found any answers. After a long period of wondering, he concluded that perhaps he had to look for answers in order to find there were no definite ones. He sat up and called to Healer André.

Healer André answered in the distance, the rocks echoing both call and answer. He arrived in less than a minute.

Joshua recounted his last vision.

"Good. Now you can start to get back your strength." He removed the blindfold.

The brightness of the light forced Joshua to close his eyes, to keep closing and opening them periodically to readjust them.

"Is it over?"

"This part of it. The rest will last as long as your life. It's like the house you live in. You must clean it and repair it. See what you been through here as a single repair job."

Healer André left the lean-to and returned about five minutes later with the clay pot. It contained soup. Joshua drank half of it and lay back down. An hour later he drank the other half.

Healer André left him in the lean-to and went off in search of food, returning with two yams, other root tubers unfamiliar to Joshua, and two fish, a breadfruit, and a hand of ripe bananas. For the first time since arriving on the mountain, Joshua could eat all he wanted, but his stomach had shrunk.

That night he dreams he's wandering in a forest. Water laps over the stones of a nearby stream, the wind whistles in several octaves through the leaves of massive, centuries-old maples, poplars, cedars, and elms, and his feet rise and sink on the spongy leaves of the forest floor; and he knows it's an orchestra he belongs to. Eventually the sounds of the night merge with the dream and it becomes a cosmic symphony. And he has an urge to look behind him, and standing there's a man the exact replica of himself. "Love it all. It's beautiful. Embrace the joy and the sorrow. Dissolve into nature," his image tells him. Its arms stretch out to embrace Joshua and Joshua stretches his, and they move towards each other, and become one being. And at that moment the forest becomes one jubilant peal, and he become aware that the trees and the wind and the stream and all the creatures humming, hooting, and whistling have been effecting and are now celebrating his healing. Then he is alone in treeless space, and the pipiree and the unrecognizable brown bird and its mate, whose habitat his coming had disturbed, fly onto the ground a few yards in front of him. He stretches out his hands to them, and they come; the brown birds perch on his right shoulder, brushing his face with their silken feathers, the pipiree alights onto the palm of his outstretched right hand.

Next morning he felt rested and at peace within himself, and he knew that his dream was signalling to him that health lay in a deeper communion with the earth. He recounted the dream to Healer André, who listened, his face placid, his eyes fixed on Joshua. When Joshua finished, a pleasant smile spread over Healer André's face, and he nodded.

Next day he was allowed to move around and to eat until he felt stuffed.

"Tomorrow, we're going to make the journey part way back to the village. How you feel?"

"Like staying here a few more days," he said in jest.

"That's 'cause it only rained a couple o' days. If it did rain to wash away everything, you wouldn't be wanting to stay on. One time when I was fasting up here it rained so hard the stream reached halfway up the bank."

"All weather is good for something," Joshua replied.

Healer André reached over and tapped him. "Good statement that."

He wondered whether Healer André knew about his sexuality. He'd not thought about it before. What did Healer André think of homosexuality? It didn't matter. Homosexuality wasn't his problem. Guilt was.

While these thoughts filled his head, a thin young man, somewhere in his early twenties, showed up at their encampment. He greeted Healer André and nodded to Joshua. It was evident that Healer André knew why he'd come. "Everything will be ready for tomorrow night," he told the young man, who nodded and left.

Joshua and Healer André set out around 3 P.M. the next day. They walked for about three hours, by which time they were on the main road and darkness was falling quickly. They turned off the main road to a path that led up a hillside and into a thick grove, at the centre of which was a peristyle built around a living breadfruit tree. Two burrow-shaped rooms abutted from the central circular structure at sixty-degree angles, creating a triangle of yard space between them. Light streamed from one of the rooms. Before they entered the yard of the peristyle they heard women's voices.

"Here's where we going to pass the next couple o' days," Healer André told him.

He was taken to one of the adjoining rooms. It was dark in there and smelt of dried mud. He heard the groping sounds of Healer André's hands, followed by the striking of a match. Healer André lighted a candle that sat on a small table about the size of a classroom desk. A cot and a simple stool were the only other furniture in the room. Healer André told him to remain there until they came to get him for his bath. The inner walls of the room were of mud into which straw had been mixed; it was smoothed but unpainted. The floor was of pressed clay. It brought back memories of his pre-Arcadian childhood.

After about forty-five minutes Healer André returned and led him to what Joshua named the ablutions room. Three women, two of them probably in their fifties and one definitely older, wearing pecan-brown shifts and tartan headscarves, tended a zinc tub of herbal tea. Healer André turned him over to them. He undressed and they bathed him silently in the tea, then dried him and dressed him in a leaf-green toga. The oldest of the women took him to another room at the back. He realized then that there were three, not two, rooms adjoining the peristyle. This one was the kitchen. Against one wall there was a wood fireplace containing the still live coals of a fire. On it was a homemade clay pot. Wood was stacked under the fireplace. Against the opposite wall was a long table, half of which was taken up by clay pots, jars, and calabashes. The room had the commingled smell of saffron, basil, mint, and ginger. A young woman, wearing an ordinary floral dress and no headdress—not one of the three who'd bathed him—came into the room then. The woman who'd conducted him there left while the new one dished a calabashful of fish and vegetable stew for Joshua, laid it on the uncluttered half of the table, reached under the table, and pulled out a wooden stool. "Here's your supper," she told him. She removed the rest of the stew from the fire, stirred the fire and placed a log on it. In a large open clay jar she dipped a few gourds of water, which she poured into a clay kettle. From other small jars she took leaves that she threw into the water. He was impressed by the fact that each of her acts was preceded by the prayerful pause. Before Joshua had finished eating she put a cup of tea beside his plate. He ate all his food.

"Want more?"

"No, thanks. It's good."

She smiled.

She picked up the plate and stood waiting for him to finish his tea. While she waited, Healer André came to accompany him back to the sleeping room.

He spent two more days like this, but was allowed to walk around outside. He saw that the entire design was circular: a line drawn around all three abutments would have yielded a perfect circle. The small part of the peristyle that enclosed the breadfruit trunk was cylindrical. The centre of the peristyle was off limits, was "sacred space and only for those who get the call to enter it." Joshua's was a healing case.

"We going to travel from here into Éclair Pasture on Saturday. From there we'll go to the cemetery to make peace with the dead. After that you will have one thing left to do." He did not say what it was.

Saturday, two nights later, just before midnight they set off from the village temple for the cemetery, about a mile from the village. Seven of them: Aunt Stacey; the four temple women, three of them dressed as Joshua had earlier seen them; the fourth, the sister who'd served him dinner, was now wearing a white toga and a mauve head scarf the ends of which were draped over her right shoulder. She carried a large canvas bag. Healer André, wearing ordinary, everyday clothes, held the rope of a goat that trotted along behind him. Based on the dream Joshua had had in Montreal, he realized that he already had a notion of how this was going to end. It seemed to him that he had read about all this somewhere, probably in books about West African rituals. At the cemetery Aunt Stacey, using a flashlight, showed them Bita's and Mammy's graves—his first confirmation that Bita's body had been retrieved from the Atlantic—and left.

The sister carrrying the canvas bag took out of it a wood block, a blade somewhere between a knife and a machete, and a calabash. No surprise. Healer André blessed the instruments, put his hand on the goat's head, blessed it, and thanked it for the health its sacrifice would bring. Next, three of the sisters immobilized the goat. One pressed its head against the block. The sister wearing the black scarf caught the blood in the calabash. Healer André kept his hand on the goat's head until it died. When the goat was dead, the bending sisters rose. Into the calabash, which the sister held cupped in her palms, Healer André dipped both hands; he sprinkled a few drops to the cardinal points, the sisters and he repeating all the while: "Let our transgressions be forgiven; let the ancestors and we the living live peacefully. May you our forefathers and foremothers continue to teach and protect us, for without your guidance and wisdom we shall perish, and we will have no new wisdom to pass on to the next generation." Next he scooped up blood and sprinkled it on Mammy's grave. They moved to Bita's grave and did the same.

Healer André prayed. "Estelita Johnson and Rosalinda Johnson, we beg you both to pardon Joshua for his faults. Let the forgiveness his soul craves and healing reconciliation come to pass. Let him be whole again in mind and body, visit him in his dreams, counsel him how to live. You who now know the secrets o' life teach him how to live a healthy life."

"Sisters, dear ancestors, we beseech you!" the sisters responded.

"Joshua repeat after me: 'Mammy and Bita, I ask both o' you to pardon me for all the wrong things I did to you both willfully and unwillfully. And to accept this offering as a sign of my repentance. I thank you for the favours you done show and will welcome what other teachings you see fit to impart to me. Amen.'"

Next, it was Joshua's turn to sprinkle blood on the graves.

This done, Healer André took the bowl from the Sister holding it and poured the remainder of the blood onto Joshua's head. He held Joshua's right hand. The sister with the scarf held his left. The remaining three sisters joined in; they formed a circle and sang:

> *I am delivered.*
> *Praise our Lord!*
> *I am delivered.*
> *Glory to our Lord!*
> *I was loaded with guilt*
> *and broken by hate.*
> *Now I am delivered.*
> *Praise our Lord!*

They sang it three times, by which point he had learned the words—he already knew the tune—and was singing along with them.

"You feel delivered, Joshua?"

"Yes." He had no reason to say no.

"Praise the Lord!" the sisters chorused.

From her bag the young sister took two candles and a box of matches. She handed the matches to Joshua. He lit the first candle. She handed the lit candle to him. Instinctively he knew he should put it on Mammy's grave. They moved to Bita's grave, lit the other candle and put it there.

At that moment a man came out from the darkness. "Brother Bill," the young sister said, "see it over there." And Brother Bill went to where the body of the goat was, lifted it, and left the cemetery quietly.

Their solemnity ended as soon as they left the cemetery. The oldest sister began to tease the youngest one. "Sister Bernice, I see where you nearly drop that calabash." The others, including Healer André, laughed. They talked easily and teased each other.

"And you, Joshua, how come it take you so long for get the words-them to the song right? Like you didn' want to sing it or what?"

Healer André's arms encircled Joshua. "She's just saying that it's time for relax. The ceremony is over."

"Good thing Brother Bill come for that goat else Sister Bernice would o' come back here tonight," the oldest sister said.

"And you would o' come banging 'pon me door to beg for half," Sister Bernice—the young sister—retorted. She added, "In case you wondering, Brother Joshua, Brother Bill going prepare the meat and we will eat in rejoicing this evening."

While they journeyed back to the village he realized he hadn't been introduced to them. Perhaps they'd left it up to him to find out their names. "So you are Sister Bernice and you are?" he asked the oldest sister.

"Marian."

"And the Sister here," he asked the one at the end, "what is your name?"

"Melda."

"And the other Sister?"

"Pauline."

The name sounded familiar, but his mind turned to how old habits die hard. He still had the manners he'd insidiously absorbed at Arcadia. Why hadn't he asked them their names when he first met them? Had he responded to them as if they were servants? He must monitor himself. "I would love to visit your father, Healer André."

"He will love it. If you don't visit him, he will visit you. The other day he been wondering if Aunt Stacey will marry him."

The sisters laughed. Mother Marian's sounded like an explosion.

"So you don't remember me?" Pauline asked.

"No," he said after he couldn't summon up any memories.

"Did you ever learn to spin top?"

"You are Pauline who was with me at Camden School?"

"Same one."

The eel-thin, feisty dougla girl had become a portly woman and healer. He laughed.

"Share the joke, nuh," Pauline said.

"You remember:

"'Mammy say White man no' got pistle.'"

"'Well how them does make pickney?'"

"'Them does go by the hospital and the doctor does make the pickney for them.'"

Everyone laughed.

Then he'd been the emblem of privilege; now he was a broken man she was helping to mend. He was full to bursting with gratitude. "Thanks," he said. "Thanks, I will ask you at some point, not tonight, to tell me what became of my classmates." He paused. "And who knows? I may yet learn to spin top."

They laughed.

Back at the temple, after a herbal bath and an anointing with coconut oil perfumed with nutmegs, cloves, and cinnamon, he was left to sleep in the temple room. That night he dreamed that he flew—over Isabella Island, over London, over Madrid, over Montreal, over the world. Later he swam effortlessly, dived into transparent water, rose up through mountainous waves and rode them.

When he awakened he felt totally rested. Around 9 A.M., Healer André accompanied him to Aunt Stacey's place. At two he met with the community at the temple to celebrate the first phase of his recovery. The temple was full to capacity, and lots of people were on the grounds outside. They stated the blessings, set aside portions of food for the ancestors, and sang, and ate, and celebrated the earth's health-giving goodness.

23

HE HAS NOW REACHED the Coast Road. The Atlantic is boisterous today. He can hear it and see its waves, at least six feet high, as well as the waving fronds, tinted gold by the rising sun, of the coconut palms bordering it; he smells the surf, always strongest at this time of day, tastes it as he passes his tongue over his lips, and feels the heaviness of the moist salt air entering his lungs. Gratitude surges through him. Now upon rising in the morning, upon seeing a beautiful landscape, or sunrise, or sunset, or at the beginning of a rain shower, he instinctively says thanks and feels gratitude.

Traffic is heavy. In his childhood about ten vehicles passed along this road in an entire day. Now there are hundreds in an hour. Up until two or three years before he left for England this road had not been paved. He's at the track that leads through fat-pork bushes to the beach itself, which is all lighted up now from the newly risen sun. He sees that the beach has changed. During childhood the sand used to be dark grey with blond grains mixed in. Now it's streaked blond in places, unevenly mixed in others, some parts mainly grey, others blond. He remembers the mornings he would come here while he was recovering from his first breakdown. Looking inland at sunrise, where the Éclair and Manchester plantations joined, he'd see green fields of young canes, stretching for miles to the foothills of the mountains, and rising smoke (the shacks were not visible from here) in those nooks where the workers' squatter villages were. Now those fields have been turned into villages that emit no smoke, and he has to look towards the mountains for the fields of undulating green, not of canes but bananas, which their growers have trouble selling.

Healer André refused payment for his services, and Joshua was obliged to find out the reason. He and Henry live in a two-room wooden house painted grey in the centre of the village, in the seaward direction—the opposite end from Aunt Stacey—a little in from the main road. There's no road to the house. To get to it Joshua must cross through two yards and wend his way around a pigpen and a chicken coop. On his first visit Henry and Healer André were seated at a simple table with two chairs and having supper.

Instinctively Joshua stood outside. The polite thing was to wait there until they'd finished. The neighbours' television sets blared away. Somebody's radio was at jukebox high.

Healer André invited him in and showed him a seat in one of the two armchairs in the room and, before resuming his seat at the table, turned on the naked light bulb that dangled from the ceiling. The only other furniture in the room was a small bookshelf containing about twenty volumes. The room was small, less than a hundred square feet. Joshua scrutinized Henry, whose face was turned to him. He was eating what seemed like stew with a spoon. He made those involuntary sounds toothless people make as they try to masticate food with their gums. Henry's hair, as he'd expected, was completely grey but it was still quite thick. His face seemed even narrower, skeletal, and with all his even, white teeth gone, his jaws seemed hollow. His gaze that used to be pointed in the rare times he stared at his listener was now dispersed.

"Who it be, André?"

"Finish your supper, Papa. You will find out just now."

Healer André took the dirty plates to the outside room that was the kitchen. He returned with a small basin of water, in which his father washed his hands. He dried them with a handtowel slung over his shoulder. Henry got up without any help and came a trifle shaky to where Joshua was.

Joshua stood up and faced him, noting how much his height had diminished. Self-conscious about calling him Henry, he got around it by saying, "Well, it's so good to see you after all these years."

"You is who?"

"Joshua. Joshua Éclair."

"Ah Rosalinda Johnson boy. Come shake me hand. Yes, I hear you come home and I hear my boy did good work on you. I thank God every day for my son. I trying to see if I can make you out, but the cataracts in the eye preventing me. I cut one but it didn' do no good so I not letting them tamper with the other eye. How long you is staying with us?"

"I don't know yet. You are going strong."

"I praise God I not laid up. The eyes is my biggest problem. That and a little bladder trouble."

Healer André reentered then. He pulled up one of the dining chairs. They formed a circle of three.

"Healer André, I didn't get a chance to thank you like I wanted to for the healing you put me through."

"Just call me André. Is the people that pin the Healer to it. 'Bout your healing, nothing there to thank me for. I only doing what I promise I will do. It's my duty. I rejoice when I see people find peace in their soul."

"Aunt Stacey told me that you don't take money for your work."

"Aunt Stacey told you right."

"But the labourer is worthy of his hire."

"True enough. But that's not what I promise the forces that guide me. I don't need the money. I have more than I need. It's pay enough when I see people put their life back in order. As I tell you, any payment you have to make is to society, not me. How you feeling now?"

"Fine."

"If you run into any difficulty, don' feel afraid to come and see me."

"Only if you accept to be paid."

"All right, if you feel you must pay for everything you get, give it to the temple. Lot's o' people do that. We use it for building and helping out those in need. But don't mix up health and money. Spiritual healing come about when people come together and help one another get over their travails. Money keep people apart and frightened o' one another. If you understand how free the air you breathe is, you will understand what I telling you."

"But you spend so much time healing, how do you earn a living?"

"I work ten acres of land. It give me food and enough money to look after Papa's needs and my own. And it even leave me with some to give away. I live simple. See?" He made a sweep with his hand. "I have pipe water but is because of Papa, when he need it for his bath. I don' usually spend as much time with the sick like I spend with you. But I don't begrudge myself the time I spend with you. Nobody 'round here will refuse Aunt Stacey anything she ask. She is a mother to everybody. She minister to humankind in another way. If you ask me, in her own way, she is a better healer than me. Papa did already tell me a lot 'bout you, so I had a good idea what kind o' troubles you was likely to have, the troubles rich people that still have a conscience have. Complicated by your birth and so on. So I know those were the things I had to address. I know that it would take plenty time. I got Brother Bill to take care o' my cow, and Mother Marian takes care o' Papa when I can't do it." He paused for a while. "Most o' the healing I do don' take so much time. It's on weekend and between working on my land that I do it, sometimes in stages. The worse cases I work on out in the Grove Temple. Your case is the third one I take up in the mountains."

"When I hear," Henry interrupted the conversation, "that was you Master Joshua, Rosalinda's boy, that did need help, I tell him go right ahead and help that boy. Ain't I said so, André?"

Healer André smiled. "Yes, Papa."

"Just like I been seeing you in front o' me chatting away while I cut the grass or pick up eggs, the gentleman you was at Arcadia. You used for spend time with me . . . until your Uncle Sparrow come. Until your Uncle Sparrow come. Your Uncle Sparrow."

"Never mind that, Papa."

"Master Joshua, how soon you planning to go back?"

"Not right now. My big problem is that I've been away from here for so long, I don't know anyone."

"Friends, you mean?" Healer André asked.

Joshua nodded.

"It's not so bad. People are people. Everybody has some of you in them and you have some of them in you. So all you have to do is talk to people," Healer André said.

Easily said. He didn't have friends in Montreal either. Probably traumatized by how his friendship with Maurice had ended; probably because he'd lost confidence in himself as a result of his breakdowns; probably because he was afraid people would reject him.

An awkward silence grew between them then. It ended when Healer

André told him that if he felt like talking to someone he could come by. "I not a educated man like you, but such as I can discuss with you, I will. If you feel like you want to talk I will listen. I love to listen. And if I don't understand I will tell you."

"And I be here of a days. Don' have nowhere to go. Jus' for my walk. You can come and keep me company," Henry added.

You are both very kind. Very kind. "Thanks," he replied, unsure that he would ever take up their offer. He removed an envelope from his shirt pocket and handed it to Healer André.

"Money?"

"Yes."

"Give it to Mother Marian. She is the one that handles donations."

"Papa. Can I call you Papa?" he asked Henry.

"Sure, my son."

"What sort of settlement did Sparrow give the workers when he sold the plantation?"

"Not one penny."

"Nothing?"

"Not a red cent. One day we was working and the next day we was out of a job. When Mr Sparrow drown they come and lock up the house. That been all that left. The whole estate did done sell. Only Dawn and me was there. They tell we to take we things and when the lawyer settle we will get we pay. I still waiting for that last month pay. And Dawn where she is in poor home still waiting too."

"Poor home?"

"Yes, son. Poor home."

"What became of Dawn's children?" He'd met them at Sparrow's church. They and Dawn had attended once; out of curiosity, he was sure.

"Two daughters. They was both maids in Carriacou. The same Christmas after we lose we job at Arcadia, them girls was coming home for Christmas and the boat that was bringing them sink. Dawn walk into the whirlpool when she get the news, but two men did suspect what she was up to and follow her down there and pull her out before the current suck her in. She spend two months in the mental asylum after that. She was never sheself after that. I does go see she when I can. Her memory still good. But she all the time crying. 'What I do in this world to suffer so? Henry, why God give me so much for bear, and don' give none to them what can bear it?' That is what she always saying to me."

In a subsequent visit Joshua learned that Rose died three months after he'd left for England. She'd collapsed in the kitchen at Arcadia and the doctor pronounced her dead when he got there: a heart attack. Why hadn't Mommy mentioned it? Marie died in 1986 but her husband was still alive.

Six weeks after that first visit to Healer André, Henry and Dawn received their first pension cheques. Marie's husband received one a month later. It was then that he learned their family names. Henry's is Lyons.

He has gone with Healer André about a dozen times to his farm. Healer André showed him how to milk a cow and let him milk his cow once.

The third or fourth time he went, Healer André was sorting tannia slips while he sang for Joshua a song he'd learned in childhood from Percy Buckram, whose father used to lead a group of people to offer sacrifices to the spirit of the Ayahuna Falls. Later when the Falls were altered for hydro electricity they offered apologies.

Bacra and Black use for be buddy—
Use for be buddy

Bacra steal his buddy property—
Steal his buddy property

Then Bacra frighten and wonder wha' for do—
Wha' for do

Bacra invent a gun—
Invent a gun

Bacra man say, "Run, Buddy, run!"
Buddy no' run

Bacra man shoot and shoot—
Oh, 'im shoot

Buddy don' fall down—
Don' fall down . . .

"Yeah. Percy Buckram. Tall boy, chest the size of a tea chest. He's a Spiritual Pointer now. Lives down the coast. Following in his father's footsteps. Rich baritone voice. Used to sing the lead and we used to sing the chorus.

"'Where you learn that song?' Papa asked me after I sang it for him. We was on our way home from Arcadia. I used to wait for him outside the gate. He had to work late that day and it was already dark. He had his flashlight with him. He ordered me to sit down, right there on the side o' the road, tall canes on both sides o' us. He was silent a long time before he explain to me that if White people hear me singing that song they likely to send somebody for burn down our house. 'Percy can sing song like that 'cause Percy father live on him own land and his church feeding him. Mark you, they did burn down his church twice. And before you born they did arrest and take him to the courthouse and try to beat all sense out o' him because he told people not to vote for the planters.

"When we get home, he told me the story 'bout Sis Hen."

"He told me that one too."

"He did! Papa told you that story! He must o' liked you a lot. Papa only tells stories to people he feels close to. Still and all he was taking a chance."

"But he didn't tell me what Brother Rooster told Sis Hen."

Healer André laughed. "The first rule a good storyteller learn is you alter the story to suit your audience."

"Tell me something: you must have known that I had been crazy when you took me up into the mountains?"

Healer André shrugged his shoulders.

"Didn't you think it was risky taking me straight from a psychiatric hospital on such a long journey up into the mountains? If I'd known how long that walk was going to be, I wouldn't have gone."

Healer André smiled. "If you did get off the plane wheezing and wobbly, I wouldn't o' done it, for sure. But I took one look at your legs and see that they stronger than mine, and I listen to your breathing and figure out your heart and lungs in top form; and about your going beserk, I was sure that wouldn't o' happen; and if did happen they have leaves up there I would o' coax you to chew and chants I would o' do to ease your anxiety. Anyhow I asked Aunt Stacey all sorts o' questions over the phone 'bout your health, and I talked with Dr Defoe, and he and Aunt Stacey told me you love to take long walks."

"That Defoe!" He said it with admiration.

He was curious to know how Healer André became a healer. But he was too awed by his larger-than-life aura to broach the subject with him. So he asked

Henry on a day that Healer André wasn't here.

"A long story. I better start from the beginning. André mother—she name was Betty—and me move in together when we been both seventeen. She been a fine woman, Master Joshua—a fine woman. Master Joshua, women don't come like that nowadays. We begin life together on this self-same spot in a wattle-n-daub house. Betty mother did have plenty mountain land. Betty use for work piece of her mother land, and you knows I was the yard-boy at Arcadia. For a long time we didn't have children. And suddenly when we was both thirty-four we had André.

"Master Joshua, I never see a child like André. He uses for be still, and is the only baby I know that never used to cry a lot. He spend his time watch-ing things. Everything. A child o' few words. You see his eyes moving and coming back and stopping and going over everything. Could o' sit down in the same place for a long time and don't get restless. Soon as André could walk he would take off his clothes and go out in the rain. It wasn't no use spanking him. I tell his mother for leave him to do it. By the time he five he use to sneak 'way from home and go up in the valleys, all on the riverbank-them; take my flashlight and gone into the caves by the seashore and up in the hills. Mr Joshua, we spank him, we reason with him, we punish him, but he still go. One day—he was round eight—I give him six lashes with my belt 'cause he did disobey his mother and spend the whole day up in the moun-tain. When I finish, André, his eyes-them full-up o' water, say to me, 'Papa, you and Mamma don't understand. Something out there in the forest and in the mountain and rivers-them calling me to them. I have to go to them. Even if you beat me, I still have to go. Papa, please, don't beat me for going.'

"I say to him, 'Son, what is the something that calling you?'

"'Papa I don't know. All I know is that I have to go.'

"'You sure you not crazy? What you saying don't sound normal to me. A child your age suppose for like to play with children and should 'fraid for be alone in places like that. You not 'fraid ghosts going lead you away?'

"'No, Papa. Those places is like my friends-them. I like for be there and think and think 'bout all sorts of things. I love for hear the animals-them in the woods. You know how the pipiree sound Papa?'

"And forthwith I hear a pipiree song coming out that boy throat. He do a frog, he do a wild parrot, he do a plover, he do rain-without-wind, he do rain-with-wind, he do the sea when it rough and when it calm, the whistling sound the coconut branch-them make when the wind toss them. I can't remember all the sound-them that he did. I sit down there listening to him, spellbound and frighten.

"Then he say to me, 'Papa, I know you understand. I can read it in your face. You just don't want to say yes 'cause you don't want to go 'gainst Mama. But Papa I have to do this.'

"Master Joshua, I see no way I could o' win, so I set 'bout winning over Betty. Reluctantly we give in to him.

"André been ten years old when Betty get pregnant again. The child take her life. Oh, Master Joshua, I can't put in words what that did to me. Your adopted mother did give me two days off to bury Betty and twenty dollars to help with the expenses. Your adopted mother, Averill Éclair."

Joshua recalled none of this. He would have been around fifteen or sixteen, going to school in Hanovertown but coming back to Arcadia in the afternoons. Perhaps he wasn't as close to the servants as he'd like to think. Perhaps it was during the July-August holidays when he was in either Puerto Rico or Martinique practising his Spanish or French. Or during his breakdown.

"I not blaming her. I did love my work. Those flowers was pretty. Pretty too much, Master Joshua. I use for take pleasure seeing how that lawn green. And the roses-them, and gerbras-them, and the hydrangeas-them! Beautiful, Master Joshua. Flowers is beautiful things, Master Joshua. Wish I did have land here to grow some. But I thankful for what I have. Thankful in every way. What a blessing my son is! And every day I beg God for pour blessings 'pon him."

After the death of Henry's wife, Marian, her cousin, took over André's care. She was a spinster. "From the first go, Marian used for say to me, 'Give that boy his freedom. He got a gift. Leave him for develop it.' She send him off to school in the morning. But André was no trouble for nobody. He used for come and wait for me outside the gate of a' evening and the two of us walk back together, and he tell me what he do in school that day, and where he been after school, and what he see.

"Master Joshua, I did want for send André to secondary school. I did want to. I is a big one for schooling. I not criticizing your adopted mother. She was better than most of the other Bacra—especially when she first come. Before them others take she in hand and teach her their ways. I live here all my life. I know how the White people 'round here operate. No, I not criticizing she at all. 'Cause was not her fault. André go on to school until he fifteen, and I ask him what he want for be. And he tell me, 'I want for heal people. People greedy and selfish and it make them cruel, and I want for show them they're like that because they can't find peace in their soul. Nature have the answer to some o' their problems.'

"Betty mother had ten acres o' mountain land, and when she died she left it for Betty. At fifteen André say he want to work it. He going make his living from it. He did done already start to visit all the Spiritual Baptist pointers all over the island and questioning them. He visit the obeahman-them too. He keep what he find to himself. After that he used for go off and spend two-three days alone deep in the mountains. When he twenty-two he said to me, 'Papa I ready to start trying for heal people. I sure now that is my calling.'

"I say to him, 'Son, the Lord will be done.' I give him my blessing. Is all I could o' do, Master Joshua, 'cause I know he been preparing for it since he born, and is a gift he born with.

"He answer me, 'I don' know if is the Lord will, Papa. I don't know. Is just a deep urge in me. Something tell me I know now how for help people find peace in their soul. I not interested in curing things like cancer and all that. Let the doctors-them do that. That is not my work.'

"And is so it started, Master Joshua. All sorts of people who he help come together and build the temple here and they buy the land for the one in Pleasant Valley where the Grove Temple is. They would o' build that one with mortar too, but André insist that he want it build out of earth. People from all over encourage the work. Them build the temples with they money and they own hands. The Spiritual Baptist Pointers round here— Pointer Hodge been one o' them—them get André for agree for let them build a soul-searching room under the temples. So sometimes the pointer does be there guiding people. André don't belong to no church. I think he does hear God voice in the wind and in the waves, but is not something he will ever talk 'bout. All he believe in is helping people for find peace in them heart, for make peace inside them soul, peace with their neighbours and peace with the dead, peace with the world, peace with life. He think every religion that teach peace good.

"Sometimes I wonder if he not lonely. He don't interested in a wife and he don't talk 'bout children. Now when I see the good care he does take o' me, I wonder who going take care o' him. But when I ask him 'bout that, he does say to me, 'Papa, the earth will take care of me. I know how to be happy wheresover I am and in whatsoever state I am, even in pain. My life too full now for me to worry 'bout my old age.'

"Master Joshua, my boy is special, a blessing to a whole host o' people.

And I is proud o' my son. You hear me, Master Joshua? Proud!"

There's a group of about sixty young people on the beach. From the four older people supervising them, he sees it's a youth camp. No one is in the water. It's too rough for that. More humanity than he ever meets in his walk up the mountain valley. He stands gazing at the ocean: at its fluidity, its frothing, detonating, its rippling yield to the wind, in contrast to the fixed mountains in the distance at his back.

By June, two months after his return to Isabella Island—after the end of his healing, his days acquired a routine. By then he had no doubt that he was well, well in a way that he had never been before. Ten days after the Saturday night cemetery offering he'd decided to give himself a structured day but one that allowed him time to reflect on the direction he wanted the rest of his life to take. One thing he had to do was resume his daily walks. The insomnia he suffered from in Montreal was not happening here. By 9 P.M. he was asleep, and awake by 5 A.M.. A two-hour, meditative walk, each morning, even when it was raining, was what he settled for.

His usual route leads through a gradually ascending mountain valley cultivated from end to end with bananas. He walks until he gets to where clumps of forest begin to be more numerous. Mostly he walks alone, listening to the breeze moving through the contours of the valley, the shallow river water noisily rushing to the sea, and inhaling the commingled aroma of dew, ploughed earth, river lilies, fruit trees in bloom or laden with ripe fruit—mangoes especially. Occasionally someone going to look after livestock or an early worker walks along with him. Once he tells them his biological mother's name they know who he is. Usually they fall silent after that: intimidated, he thinks. He doesn't know how to put them at ease. Initially he worried about it but has now given up.

When he returns home Aunt Stacey usually has a hot breakfast waiting for him, sometimes of fish, plantain, oranges; sometimes johnny cakes and buljohl; sometimes freshly baked bread onto which he pours spoonfuls of stewed guava. When the sun leaves the front porch around eleven he reads out there, and in the evening under the porch light he writes his journal. Aunt Stacey's friends come and go, saying hello, but never much more. Two of them in whose company she attends the meetings of the Methodist Women's League are frequently at the house. One of them, Zelda, helps her cook on Fridays, when Aunt Stacey prefers to serve cou-cou, which she says Zelda is expert at. Then he smells the okras that on occasion remind him of Rose and Madrid and Juan. He wonders what became of Juan and of all those people he'd been involved with. Where are they now? Paul, Humphrey Hole, Misz Marshal, Mose, Suleyman. *Throne-rockers*. As good as saying they should be put to death. Suleyman had shunned him after that encounter with Paul.

Shortly after Joshua began sitting out on the porch, a man of about thirty, wiry, with rough skin, close-cropped, uncombed hair, a spotty beard and side-burns, and premature furrows on his forehead—a coarsely handsome fellow—would wave to him each time he passed along the road. Aunt Stacey's house is about ten feet in from the back road of the village. Other persons passing by wave perfunctorily. But there was a certain insistence in the way this man waved. Sometimes two girls, aged about seven and five, were with him. His children, no doubt. He would insist that they too wave to Joshua, would turn it into a mini performance.

Some three weeks after he began his morning walks Joshua met him standing at the roadside about a mile from the village. He was grinning. Joshua bowed slightly, said good morning and walked on.

"Why you's in such a hurry, Mr Joshua?" the man called out from behind him. "We's going the same place. I's here to keep you company."

"I'm not in a hurry at all. It's the pace at which I walk." Joshua slowed down, his antennae extended.

The man caught up with him. "I is Zagga," he said and extended his hand.

Joshua shook it. "You already know my name."

They walked on for about another half mile in silence, Joshua waiting to hear why this man had come to meet him outside the village.

"Do you farm up here, Zagga?"

Zagga shook his head. "For tell you the truth I been wanting for ask you something, but I didn't know how to come out with it."

"About what?"

"It kind o' complicated."

Joshua stopped walking, turned and stared Zagga in the face. "What exactly is it?"

"Never mind." Now it was Zagga who quickened his pace, quickly increasing the distance between them until he disappeared onto a branch road.

After this, Zagga's hellos became as perfunctory as everyone else's, and

Joshua ceased to be preoccupied by him. Then at the forty-night rejoicing—forty nights after the ritual in the cemetery—where the community came and feasted the end of the fifteen-year delay (the final send-off for his mother's wandering spirit was how the villagers put it), Zagga came up to him and stretched out his hand to be shaken. When Joshua took it, Zagga tickled his palm and stared Joshua straight in the eyes, nodded and said, "That is what I been wanting to tell you."

Joshua said nothing.

That night for the first time since he began sleeping at Aunt Stacey's, ten o'clock came and found him sleepless despite the fact that he should have been exhausted by the hundreds of people he'd had to move among and listen to for some two hours. Zagga wanted to sleep with him. His mind roved over all sorts of possibilities and dangers. Only the week before there was the story of a male bank employee who'd committed suicide after the bank discovered he'd bilked it of $60,000. His suicide note explained that the money had been used to buy the silence of a man he'd slept with. That was the second suicide. A few months before a teenager, unable to live with the taunts of "buller," "anti-pym-pym" and "anti-man" shouted at him through his window and on the street, had hanged himself. Many callers to the talk shows suggested that all bullers should follow his example. On one of those shows a member of the government, only recently demoted from attorney general because of financial embezzlement, was the in-studio guest. He opined that he would like to see the law courts enforce the ten-year jail term for homosexual acts. "That is a project I hope the new attorney general will work on." Beads of sweat broke out on his forehead as he listened to the callers. On Isabella Island, attitudes to homosexuality were worse than in the Britain of Oscar Wilde or when EM Foster wrote *Maurice*.

Do I like him?

Not particularly.

If I accepted to sleep with him, how open would it be?

It can't be. Buju Banton's and Shabba Ranks's songs advocating death for homosexuals are popular with the young. Minute by minute, day after day, their boomboxes strapped to their bodies blare out Buju's and Shabba's threats.

Next morning, Zagga was waiting for him a short distance outside the village. "You think I been going give up so easy, eh?"

Joshua composed his reply carefully before he spoke. "Last night, I thought about your message to me. I'm not interested. You're okay but I don't want to get involved with anyone at the moment."

"Why so, Mr Joshua?"

"Forget the mister. If I stay here, I'll be open about my sex life," he lied.

"Mr Joshua! You going be crazy for do that! Them will harass you 'pon the street, call you buller and all sort o' bad name, and beat you up too."

"It won't bother me."

"It will when the worthless boys-them 'round here waylay you, and bull you without grease, then beat you, and even stone your house."

"Have they beaten you?"

"No, 'cause I careful." He paused for a short while, looked away and smiled. "The five o' we in the village who I certain 'bout careful. Three o' we have girlfriends and children, so nobody can suspect we is *so*. The fourth one is a preacher man." He laughed. "He bulling his assistant steady though. And he too love it. He got his wife, so nobody suspect anything, and the assistant Pastor getting married next month." The grin left his face. His forehead rippled. "'Bout three years ago, Mr Joshua, we beat up a fellow call Danny in the village here 'cause he wasn't careful. He didn't hide his business like he should o' done. People use to see a certain young man visiting him. And one night they set up and catch them in the act. The man what was bulling him get 'way. Them beat Danny and would o' kill him if somebody didn't run and get Healer André for stop them. When Danny come out o' hospital he walk with a limp and he have a big scar on his top lip. One o' the blows did split it open. He move 'way from the village 'cause he couldn't walk through it in peace after that."

"You said *we*. Were you involved in the beating?"

"Yeah. I give him couple kicks 'cause we was all expected to."

"Are you homosexual?" Joshua asked him, astonished, his eyes fixed on his face.

"You mean if me is a faggot, a buller, Mr Joshua?"

"Yes, if those are the terms you use."

He shook his head and compressed his lips. "Them is people what walk and wind up them waist and swing them ass from country to town, and talk and carry on like 'oman, Mr Joshua. I not like that." He did the limp-wrist gesture and raised his voice to a screech. "I is a hundred percent he-man with two children; my girlfriend making a third child. I is no' half-man, man-woman. I can pump dick in any woman and keep she coming back for more."

"And into men too, I suppose?"

"You can say that again. Why *you* don't try me? We can do it up there."

He pointed to a field of bananas sloping up the hillside. "I bring a little vase-line just in case you 'gree right away." He placed his hand on his fly to draw attention to the erection already occurring.

Joshua smiled inwardly, visualized himself on all fours, undoubtedly the position Zagga would want him in—or would it be roast-duck?—Zagga greasing him up. He felt excited and thought he felt a slight throb in his groin, but he knew his answer. He looked at Zagga's lips, saw that they were cracked; next at his elbows and saw that they were ashen. "Zagga, put some o' that vaseline on your lips and elbows." As an afterthought, he added, "I bet you're too much of a he-man to have brought a condom," and regret-ted saying so because of the impression it would leave.

They walked on in silence for about another hundred yards, to the top of the hill at whose base they had been standing.

"Mr Joshua, can I ask you something?" They now stood under the umbrella of a mango tree that grew out of the bank above the road.

Joshua nodded.

Zagga looked at him, looked away, stared at the ground and said, "I don' know how to say this 'cause I don't want you to take it the wrong way." He stopped talking for a while and stared down the slope, at the stream flow-ing at the bottom of the valley. "As you see, Mr Joshua, I don't does work nowhere and I hear you is a man with money." He paused, looked into Joshua's eyes and then away from him and back down at the stream bed. "You think you can give me a little something for help me out with me chil-dren-them?" This he said with his stare fixed to the ground.

I knew it would come down to that.

As if he'd overheard Joshua's thought, he said, "Don't get me wrong. I don't charge all the time, but if the man old and nobody want him I expect him to give me a little change."

Joshua felt the goose bumps rising. He was about to say I don't pay men for sex but realized the untruth of this. *No longer pay. But why bother?* "Zagga, I'm at least twenty, twenty-five years older than you. I'm not interested. I did not come back here and undergo all I've gone through so I could hide in the bushes to have sex with men who expect to be paid for the sex they deny having."

"You not so old, Mr Joshua. And you is a good-looking White man. Is only White men I go with 'cause they know how to keep their mouth shut; that way Black people don' get into my business."

Business indeed.

Since then Zagga has left him alone. Victim of whatever—it doesn't matter—there's no need for him to pass judgment on Zagga, he needs to remind himself.

In May '97 he renewed his Montreal lease, just in case he were to return there. He was aware then that he was definitely more at ease with people than he has ever been at any time before. Periodically he thinks of his Montreal neighbour, thinks he misses the early morning entrances. It's enough to remind him that in the last five years he spent in Montreal, he knew no one, spoke to no one, outside of the banal exchanges with George in the winter and the professors of the courses he audited at Concordia. It's inhuman to live like that. It's easier to make friends here—and enemies.

In June last year, he spent some time travelling around Isabella Island. He revisited Expatriates Academy (it was already Hanovertown Secondary when he graduated but some still call it "Expatriates"). He goes to the library in Hanovertown once a week to read the foreign newspapers and check out the odd book. The cinema houses are in Hanovertown but there are no films advertised so far that he has wanted to see. He read *The English Patient* and liked it, but had no desire to see the film. Art films do not get to this part of the world. The library doesn't have a single documentary film. Can he survive here? is a question he has been frequently asking.

Last July was particularly difficult, heatwise. This one is just as unbearable. Sitting on the porch, he'd watched clouds of ochre dust periodically lift off the brown ground and shroud the village in a misty beige that turned the sunlight bronze. The rains had been loath to come. Aunt Stacey's banging pots in the kitchen while she exulted no doubt in her role of mother to other people's children would momentarily gain his focus. More than at any other time since his return, Isabella Island felt tight, like a garment he'd outgrown. At fifty-two he saw that he hadn't yet been weaned. Not once had he earned the food he'd eaten. The closest he'd ever come to it was milking Healer André's cow, and earning himself a pint of milk. He'd escaped the dark, escaped being alone in it at any rate, but the price had become tutelage.

It was one thing to be back in the country he'd been born in, so he could stare down the horrors that had made him escape and kept him away; it was quite another to feel himself emotionally dependent on the woman who for all intents and purposes delivered him into the world, nursed him as an infant, and has resumed nursing him as an adult. Had he become a child again? He'd thought of those who are nonfunctional: the chronically insane, the mentally handicapped, for whom tutelage must be constricting. He wondered how they cope with it in moments when they desire their independence. Was it really that? Or had he skipped, as Bita (whose advice, he now knows, was a projection of his own mind) had told him in a dream, some vital stages in his maturation? Was he like a poorly rooted tree whose foliage had brought it crashing to the ground? Is he such a tree righted again by external props? Had he been thrown into the sea of adulthood without first having learned to swim and is now being carried along by those who can?

His first month back on Isabella Island had passed like a carpet someone else was steadily unrolling. He'd had very little to do with it. The second month he'd spent letting his raw spots heal, like a pruned tree slowly growing bark over areas from which sap had bled. It was like this that the first months passed. Sometimes he was certain he wanted to stay on Isabella Island, sometimes not. By August he told himself he would have to make up his mind soon.

On October 31 he and Aunt Stacey and her Women League friends went to the cemetery and weeded the graves of loved ones. On November 1, they returned to light candles for them. The exercise made him feel good, like it was the right thing to do. For the first time he did not subject this act to interminable analysis. It was while he was at the cemetery that evening, enraptured by the thousands of candles lit by the living in memory of the dead, that it occurred to him that if he was going to stay on Isabella Island he should think of finding a suitable property to begin creating his own home.

He was sitting on the balcony next day thinking about this when a car stopped at the gate and a White man and a Black woman got out of it and entered the yard. The man, displaying the corpulence of middle age, was dressed in a beige bush jacket and matching trousers. He wore glasses and his still thick hair was completely white. He called out, "Hold your dog." Joshua beckoned to the couple to come on in.

The man and woman came onto the porch. The man stood in front of Joshua and stared at him intensely. The woman, who was about the same height as the man, smiled gently, showing dimples in her roundish, deep-brown, very youthful face.

"You are not soul catchers, American fundamentalist missionaries, I hope?"

The woman laughed.

The man said, "Yeah. Ah is. An' Ah is just 'bout to hurl yer dern soul into the pit o' damnation but I is can't find the formula." Then he broke into a laugh. "Randolph," he said, and stretched out his hand.

"Randolph Kevin?" Joshua asked skeptically.

"Yep. And my soulmate, Oya." He placed an arm around her as he said so, and she placed one around him.

"You are Randolph Kevin! Pine Knot Kevin's grandson—"

"Who used to ride in the same taxi with you to *Expatriates Academy*. I heard you're here and I could not let you leave without seeing you. Oya can tell you that I wonder often what became of you. After you left we haven't had any news of you."

There were three other chairs on the porch. He offered them seats. He stared at Randolph and Oya and then away from them. He wanted to question Randolph, to sate his curiosity. But he was afraid he'd come across as impolite, so he turned to Mrs Kevin. "Oya, that means you're Yoruba."

She nodded.

"Where did you two meet?"

Randolph looked at Oya, and they smiled conspiratorially, then he turned to Joshua and said, "Go ahead and ask. I know you're eager to find out how all this came about."

"Why don't you just fill me in? Things around here must have altered radically."

"For a few of us, yes. Time brings changes, some of it good."

In the questions and answers that followed while they sipped lemonade that Aunt Stacey brought as soon as she was aware of the visitors, Joshua and Randolph informed each other of their past. At age 25, Randolph Kevin got restless and decided to pursue a degree in management at Birmingham University, but when he got there he switched to history. He'd gone on to get a master's degree, with a thesis on the introduction of universal primary education in the British West Indian colonies, partly because his grandfather and father had always groused about it and he was sure that what he was told had been filtered by race. But he'd already begun to think that when he returned to Isabella Island he would want to be an educator. His father passed away during his second year at Birmingham and five years later, just as he'd begun a PhD, his mother was diagnosed with generalized cancer and he'd had to return to Isabella Island. Since he was the only surviving child, he inherited the plantation. (His sister, the "playwright" who'd made Joshua beg for *nyam*, had died two years after moving to Australia with her Australian husband.) He promptly sold it, returned to

England to marry Oya, and while they were on their honeymoon, he decided that he should build a secondary school on Isabella Island. Since then he and Oya have been teaching in it and managing it.

You wouldn't have dared to marry Oya while your mother was alive. She must be frothing in her grave. "Tradition must be kept up. Time was when everyone knew their place and stayed in it," her acerbic tone echoed across the years. If Pine Knot were alive, he'd have probably shot you both and turned the gun on himself.

"I am humbled," Joshua said out loud. "Humbled and impressed. Does the plantocracy still speak to you?"

Oya smiled.

"The plantocracy. It's no longer like when you and I were little. People, you know, will only work for slave wages if they're compelled to. Most of the plantocracy have emigrated. All the major plantations around here have been carved up and sold to small cultivators. It's only the Langleys who are bucking the trend."

"So you got out while you could"—that wasn't how he'd wanted the statement to come out. "I mean the school isn't altogether altruistic."

"We make no money off it, that's for sure, and that was never our intention," Oya said. "It's altruistic enough, believe me. When we finish paying our bills we take what's left, and sometimes that's nothing."

A week later he had dinner at their place, a modest three-bedroom house, simply furnished, on about an acre of land with scattered trees and flowering shrubs, located a couple of miles from Hanovertown. There were no servants. He'd wondered if it was because it was Sunday, but they don't keep servants. He couldn't get accustomed to seeing Randolph Kevin, wearing a dungaree apron over his dress clothes, opening an oven and sticking a knife into a cake then holding it up to see if it was baked, then setting the table while Oya cut the vegetables for a salad.

There was one other guest, Calvin Simmons, who was a mathematics lecturer at the Isabella Island Teachers Training College. Joshua had no trouble figuring out who he was. He saw the resemblance right away, and remembered Mrs Manchester's oft-repeated story. "Where's your father, now?" Joshua asked him.

"You know my father?"

"Of course I do, and I bet your middle name is Knox."

"Are you my godfather or something?"

Joshua shook his head. "Your father admired Calvin and Knox." He decided not to tell him how he knew, but said he used to attend St. Andrews

Presbyterian Church in Camden.

"My father died in 1978 from peritonitis caused by a perforated ulcer. I was twelve at the time. Because of her job, mother stayed on here. She's still alive. She's now the organist at St Andrews."

Joshua remembered that she occasionally filled in for the regular organist.

"Calvin," Oya said, "has no use for Knox or Calvin."

"Or any religious hawker. My father was enough of a theological fool for both us. This earth is my heaven, and hell."

Later, during their conversation, he learned that Alexander Manchester had married Amanda of all people. He understood then why she'd stopped writing. The story was not clear how it had come about; the parents had decided it, it seemed, had given him some sort of ultimatum. But three months after the wedding, the marriage was annulled and Alexander left hastily for England and Amanda for the US. What Randolph now knows for a fact is that Alexander owns a gay bar in London. He'd visited it.

When he recovered from the surprising and not-so-surprising news, Joshua smiled and thought of mentioning what had happened the Saturday Alexander and he had gone fishing, but decided not to; it would look like he was gossiping. He consciously repressed his smile as he remembered Alexander's sex boasts on the grounds of Expatriates, and Mrs Manchester's statement about the Blenkinsopps seeking to increase their acreage. The thought occurred to him that he should tell them he too was gay, but instead he asked Randolph how he'd found out about his return to Isabella Island.

Healer André had told him. "We have a comparative religions course at the school and we bring him in a few times per year to discuss with the students the relationship between nature and the soul. He told me that he thought you and I knew each other, and he was sure you would be happy to see me. That's it."

His head filled with images of quiet Randolph, almost always with his head turned away from the crowd. He'd never heard him put anyone down; he'd always seemed indifferent to the games of one-upmanship others played; but Joshua could have never suspected it was because he was questioning the values being foisted upon him and doing his best not to comply. He's two years or so older than Joshua.

A month after meeting Randolph and his wife, Joshua contacted a real estate agent. If Randolph Kevin could marry a Black woman and use his inheritance to educate Black children, he could at least live on Isabella

Island. Randolph was proof that things can radically change. He began looking for a very modest house on a half acre of land, close enough to the highway in southern Isabella Island. But the houses an agent showed him over the next few weeks were too big.

In mid-December Defoe phoned to say he'd be attending a conference in St Vincent during the first week in January, and Joshua invited him to visit neighbouring Isabella Island. In January, while an ice storm paralyzed Montreal, Defoe came and Joshua rented a chauffeured car and gave him a tour of the island. Randolph and Oya had them by, and Randolph used the occasion to try to persuade Joshua to come and teach at the People's Academy. And Defoe said it was the best thing that Joshua could do. But he said no. He could not make that sort of commitment but he promised sincerely that he would think about it.

He also took Defoe on a day cruise of the Grenadines and they overnighted on Union Island, his first visit back since age eleven. The only person there whose surname he remembered was Mr Stewart and he was now dead. The Anchorage Hotel now occupies the property where the Éclair holiday house used to be and he was surprised to see how far up the summits the houses now extended. He'd forgotten the scorched-earth stark-ness—the grey and brown hues with specks of cactus green—that Union Island assumed during the dry season.

In a corner of a drab, almost empty Clifton restaurant, fireflies flitting outside the screened window, coloured lights outlining the Palm Island shoreline across from Clifton harbour, he and Defoe talked and ate a meal of red snapper cooked in coconut milk and served with red beans and rice. He learned then that Defoe's first name was Maurice—and could not help making the connection to the Maurice of his childhood—and that Defoe's only brother by another father was not only gay, but also a masochist who was in and out of prison. That was how he'd so easily deduced the origin of the scars on Joshua's back. He advised Joshua to let an aesthetic surgeon remove the scars that are removable. But Joshua feels he could live with them. In his final vision up in the mountains he'd learned that one has to manage his own shit and avoid being poisoned by other people's. Defoe advised him strongly to remain on Isabella Island, especially seeing that there were people there like Healer André, Randolph, and Oya with whom he could form close bonds. Joshua told him of his encounters with Zagga, to point out some of the difficulties.

"I thought you said you're prepared to live with shit."

"My own, yes."

"Other people's too. They live with yours. I'd have been happier to hear you'd slept with him, guilt-free and enjoyed it, even if you'd paid him. No whipping, mind you." He winked.

And he and Defoe made a deal: when Joshua needs a break, he can come to Montreal and stay at Defoe's place and when Defoe needs a Caribbean holiday he can come and stay with Joshua. "And when you're here and want to talk, pick up the phone. *You can afford it.* I'm sure you've changed your mind about giving away your inheritance. No one can do that, if you follow what I mean. *That's part of the shit we learn to live with and draw strength from.* Be sensible. Use what you need to stay healthy and independent. Get rid of what's burdensome. And don't worry about other breakdowns. If they recur, and you let me know, I'll try to be here on the first plane. But you won't have them. I know you won't have them. Remember what I told you about my aunt? And if you're bored, go teach for free at the People's Academy."

He knew Defoe was promising more than he could deliver, but he understood and appreciated the generosity implicit in the promise.

"Why do you care so much?" he asked Defoe with earnest seriousness.

"Why do I? Do I? I don't know?" He grinned. It made him look boyish, bashful. "I never knew my father. He's still alive, they tell me. Lives in Halifax." He stopped talking, compressed his lips for a few seconds and then resumed. "A lot of aunts and uncles, few of them blood relatives—Baptist Church people—raised me. They tried with my brother too, but they lost him to delinquency quite young. That's how it is for a lot of Black people. I have to care. We all have to care what happens to one another—and I don't just mean Black people. I mean everyone, regardless of race. Our only hope as people is to care for one another, and if we forget that we'll all be damned. That's all the religion I have."

He said he wanted to meet Healer André, and insisted that for most Black people Healer André was better than any psychiatrist. Then, staring at Joshua, he stated slowly, "Your sister Bita restored your sanity. She gave you a Black worldview. Without her Healer André wouldn't have been able to help you. Those planter folk wouldo' sealed your fate. Trust the ancestors. They have a lot to teach us. The Ghanaians call it Sankofa, and they're holding on to something solid." Then he looked away with an intensive stare. "As long as Sankofa doesn't become a trap, a racist ideology. At this banquet table that's life—this banquet table—we must not only eat what we like but also what's healthy." His hand cupped his forehead, "Since when did I become a preacher?"

Two months later Joshua wrote to inform his landlord he'd not be renewing his lease, and he asked Defoe to put his books and bookshelves in storage.

Three weeks ago, around 3 P.M., he got the directions to Pauline's house and walked to it, about a half-mile from Aunt Stacey's place. Only when he neared her home did he think he might have phoned. But she was home. Her house is set back from the road, about twenty feet. Three flame trees covered in blooms stand in a line in front of it. To the side where her banana field begins there are pink oleanders and pink and white queen of flowers. Her house is about the size of Aunt Stacey's and it too is on land that was once part of the Éclair Estate. She was sitting on her porch and chatting with a woman who was breastfeeding a baby. Smoke blew to the front around the side of the house. Its smell told him she was roasting a breadfruit on an open wood fire back there. The girlhood triangular face is swallowed up in a jolly roundness; her longish semistraight hair is thinner now and all grey. She had it in canerow braids. She wore a green print dress imprinted with red roses, and beach thongs. "I see now why I stub my big toe this morning," she told him by way of a greeting. "What wind blow you this way? Come sit down." She pointed to a green plastic chair on her right. "I surprise you come see poor me." She introduced him to the other woman and then they fell into conversation easily. Within a few minutes the woman left. Pauline told him that the Maurice of their childhood went sailing. Nobody ever heard from him after he left, and nobody could contact him when his mother died. When she spoke about Fred, her eyes, still a clear brown, brightened. He now operates a bakery in Toronto. "You might see him. He come back home almost every year and he does drop in to see me." Brenda is a nurse in England. As they went back and forth from the porch to the wood fire at the back, so she could periodically turn the breadfruit and stoke the fire, she mentioned several other names that he vaguely remembered or did not remember at all. She herself is a farmer. When the government acquired most of the estates and parcelled them out to small farmers, she had leased twelve acres. They are now paid for, and apart from the spot containing her house, the rest is planted in bananas and food crops. Her son and only child is a computer analyst in New York. "Thanks to Healer André, I work my land and I serve my God; and, Joshua, I am a contented woman. I used to wonder what I will do if my husband leave me.

And when he leave me for a teenager, I find out, to my surprise, that I didn't need him. Strange, eh!"

She was as forthright as he remembered her in school. She questioned him about what his life had been, and he told her about the breakdowns he'd had, but not about his sexuality. As he suspected, she knew all about the details of his birth and wasn't bashful to state them. They conversed as if they were still on the school grounds in Camden but without the oneupmanship. She asked him whether he thought the ceremonies he'd undergone had healed him.

She invited him to share her "poor-people supper." He loved breadfruit. At Arcadia it was Henry's responsibility to roast the breadfruit on a wood fire outside. Mommy had once suggested that Rose roast it in the oven, but Rose told her (the story came from Mommy), "Mistress Éclair, I don't tell you how to stitch your embroidery; please don't come tell me how to cook the food I been cooking since I born." Mommy admired her for standing up for her rights. "Have you told her?" Joshua asked. "Are you crazy? You can't let servants know they're right, even when you know they're right. You just don't insist. Let them think you don't think the issue is worth arguing over. Good servants are hard to find. Rose was here long before I came from America."

Rose used to slice the roasted breadfruit into thin slivers and fry them a crisp brown in butter. But Aunt Stacey serves hers with the steam rising from it with buljohl (a salad of salted codfish), which he loves just as much. He accepted to taste Pauline's supper and explained that Aunt Stacey would not like it if her supper went to waste, and he made her promise to invite him for supper soon.

When he left her house the sky behind the mountains was deep amber and dusk was already settling in over the Atlantic.

The news about Maurice shocked him, and while he walked back to Aunt Stacey's his thoughts spun around it. Had he idealized Maurice? Why did he sever his family links? West Indians who abandon their relatives are not easily forgiven. What rancour had caused him to cut himself off from home and family? He was his mother's only child. If he's still alive, what does he now look like? He was so moral, so sincere! At least he was when he was nine or ten. He too must have left Isabella Island full of hurt. He was sensitive, the kind that easily registers hurt.

An explosion of joyous howls breaks into his thoughts. They're coming

from a group of teenagers playing volleyball on the beach. He hadn't paid
any attention to them. The howls are from the winning team.

He continues his walk, climbs the rock above the whirlpool and looks down
at it: swirling, whooshing, menacing, its watery arms like poison tentacles,
like adder fangs. He thinks quickly of Sparrow who ended his life here, of
himself who wanted to, and of Dawn who was lassoed out before the
currents took her. *". . . Listen! you hear the grating roar/ Of pebbles which the
waves draw back and fling, / At their return up the high strand, / Begin, and cease,
and then again begin/ With tremulous cadence slow/ And bring the eternal note of
sadness in . . . the turbid ebb and flow of human misery . . ."* More than sadness.
The hiss, snarl, and roar of a caged carnivore baring and testing its force
against the barricading shore. Existential discontent. Captivated, he stares
on and thinks of Bita's death at Point Peter, a sorrow akin to Antigonne's,
rooted in a world of fixed, oppressive traditions. They pulled Dawn out
from here alive. Did what they had to do. Does she now thank or curse
them? Would have pulled out Sparrow too, if they'd known. Further down
the coast, at Point Peter, Bita had been too quick for them. Undefeatable
Bita. Did life defeat her or did she defeat life? A moot point. *The turbid ebb
and flow . . .*

24

HE LEAVES THE SHORE and takes the shortest road to Arcadia. He walks
around it before halting at the gate. Both halves of the gate are arbours for
the omnipresent vines—an intense green. At the top of each half of the
now open gate, he sees in his imagination the two brass plaques that clicked
into place to form the spear-biting lion with an eagle perched to the side a
little above it, spelling out *Arcadia* in embossed lettering when the wrought
iron gate was closed. He goes forward, stands on tiptoe, pulls apart the
leaves and sees that they are still there, green now, as if they too had
become foliage. The coat of arms is indecipherable; the lettering invisible.
Rubbed with a little Brasso, he thinks, the shine would reappear. *The shine
would reappear but the gates are warped: this* Arcadia *can never again click into
place.* A sign staked just outside the gate proclaims in bleached red on a
white field that trespassers will be prosecuted. Many gaps are visible in the

chain-link fence that once separated the property from canefields. The fence used to be painted regularly to protect it from the corrosive salt air of the Atlantic. Behind this fence Bita had resumed contact with him. A road now encircles it. On the other side are the huge houses of emigrants who've repatriated. He has to battle a mass of weeds and shrubs to reach what was once the front porch. No rush of feeling, painful or pleasant, which he'd feared before coming, happens. From the absence of paths it's clear that not even children are interested in the cherries there on what is now a mass of thick, mostly self-sown trees. It's a mini haven for birds, now disturbed by his presence. The orchard is carpeted with a dense undergrowth.

No Trespassers! He wonders if the relatives of the Langleys still own it. Is he trespassing on his past? The house walls, those that are of cement and brick—most of the wood having dissolved to humus—now support a tangled mass of tropical vines whose weight and tendrils have dislodged some of the bricks of the rear wall. That wall dates back to the original eighteenth-century house—built in 1794. He thinks of crumbling mausoleums, of extinct civilizations, of remnants of a Knights Templar palace he'd seen in Spain, of Shelley's "Ozymandias." Arcadia's existence is now memory. Sometime down the road its present or future owner will incorporate its remains into the foundation for another structure that will house the cruelty and kindness of its new occupants. He stares intently at the mass of tangled vines, thinks of the supporting wreck beneath them; and how the beams of his own psyche, honey-combed by guilt, had crashed. But for the people who'd intervened, all according to their lights, he too would have been forever wrecked.

But suddenly his emotions change and a shiver goes through him as he contemplates the rubble and the mass of green for which it is now arbour and food. Not quite the collapse of an empire, he thinks. Arcadia never dies. He chuckles to himself as he recalls why Aunt Stacey named him Joshua, a name she'd picked from myths of colonization and racial supremacy she hadn't the dimmest understanding of. He nods. All this rubble. It's not here alone, but across the Caribbean, that the plantocracy has collapsed, so he cannot take credit for the collapse of Arcadia. Or sustenance from it. Rubble was what he'd become, or almost become, and he sees his kinship with the vines and saplings. What money shatters it may not mend.

His thoughts return to the collapse of the plantocracy and what has replaced it; to women still wearing maids' bonnets and aprons in restaurants, hotel rooms, and trinket shops, still smiling (or sneering) at

Europeans and Americans who, for a glorious, cancer-causing tan, come here to splurge the pennies they've scrimped to accumulate out of their menial salaries for menial jobs—their holiday from labour, their taste of the life of their "betters," their dance to the advertiser- puppeteers who pull their strings, their voyage to Arcadia.

And the men, liveried now, far from cane blades, blazing noonday sun, and perpetual thirst, lounge around the foyers of hotels, keeping the unwanted out, luring the wanted in; or in skimpy shorts, on beaches and in special clubs, advertise the size of their penises to those fuelled by myths of a carnal sort: another of Arcadia's farcical faces.

Arcadia, from time immemorial, you've enthralled us. We invented you. Now you invent us.

He leaves with an-after-the-funeral finality. And with a calmness—without the faintest rancour or desire for vengeance, with the proof in himself that he has truly forgiven all those who'd soiled his psyche, that he has put the burdens of guilt and hate and vengeance down—that surprises and pleases him. He'd not thought he needed further proof that he was whole again, but this return to Arcadia turns out to be exactly that.

It's sixteen months since his return, he thinks, as he walks back. In that time he has resolved more than he has done in all his adult life, thanks to Aunt Stacey's mothering and Healer André's intervention and the patience and concern of all who'd cared for him earlier at Douglas Hospital. He is delighted about the decisions Randolph made. How many more, he wonders, would have made them if cowardice and fear of class reprisals hadn't held them back. People need to be encouraged to make the right decisions, to be good. Unaided, so few of us can be idealists; so few can shed their communal clothes.

He reenters the village and stands for a while looking down its only paved, unnamed main street. This village that was once Éclair pastureland, that grew from the squatter village of about a hundred mud huts that existed on its border. Some of Sparrow's church people lived there, and he had accompanied Sparrow a couple of times when he was visiting them. They still call the expanded village Éclair Pasture.

What do they think of their lives? Rose gave hers to Arcadia. Mommy had never bothered to tell him of her death. He doesn't understand why she hadn't told him. Dawn's still alive, in the asylum for the indigent aged. Fate shattered her sanity. Her indigence is all he can remedy. She was fifteen when she began working at Arcadia, without drawers, according to Rose. And paid wages that might have left her without any. She was fifty when he left for England. She'd asked him not to forget them. But he had and the choice had not been altogether his.

Pigsties and chicken coops are appended to wooden or cement shacks randomly built on plots, most of which are no bigger than 1,200 square feet. It's 10 A.M. and already sweltering. By 2 P.M., when the heat is most intense, vapour from the sties and coops, decaying rubbish heaps, pit latrines, and stagnant waste water weaves a stink-steamy veil over the village, turning the sky leaden, refracting all distant objects, and driving swarms of flies indoors where they alight on everything and everyone.

Aunt Stacey's house is on a back lot some six hundred feet from the main road. There the plots are bigger, on average five thousand square feet, and grassier. There the livestock owners let loose their animals at 3 and 4 A.M.. It's no haven from village noise either. The air stinks there as well but without the intensity and pungent acidity of the village centre; and a shortage of water in the dry season makes the indoor toilets useless.

There are telephones in the homes of those employed and TV antennae on every house and hut. Aunt Stacey's days are organized around the afternoon soaps. The TV sound and glare constitute a third, live presence that shouts Chicago bargains all day and offers Isabellans a world trimmed, squeezed, and flavoured for US consumption.

So different from his childhood! Wood smoke, spiralling high into the sky when there was no wind, its smell identifying the wood being burnt, characterized the mornings, middays, and evenings of his pre-Arcadian childhood. Woodsmoke, dry mudwalls, the dry goat skin and pee-stained rags that were his bed, and the vapours from the soil he slept on—these were the first smells imprinted in his memory. Natural gas stoves burning fuel at ten times its North-American cost now replace firewood. He wonders how they're paid for. Half the village is unemployed, and half of the other half underemployed. Isabella Island has long ceased to be a plantation economy. And is not quite a tourism-based economy. Aunt Stacey says it's a drug economy run by drugged politicians.

And there's barbed cruelty here—everywhere on the island in fact: on buses, in the market, in the street, across fences. Renaming others and belittling them on the basis of their handicaps! Jemmoth, a teenage boy whose left leg is shorter than his right, lives in the house on Aunt Stacey's right. The villagers have renamed him Cripple. When he angers his mother she threatens to break his good leg.

And the ritual of daily beatings on children!

And men striking down women in the middle of the road, or screeching women's cries from such beatings indoors. He'd seen a man whack a woman across the shoulders with a broomstick; seen her stagger and fall; two women hurrying out of their yards onto the street to pick her up; the man staring at them briefly then strolling off. It seemed scripted, everything done from invisible cues—from long practice perhaps. It had made him shiver. The next day, a mere fifty feet from the same spot, a woman had run out of a rum shop, her man pursuing then catching up with her, then slapping her twice, resonantly setting her head pivoting clockwise and counter-clockwise. It's a rare day that he doesn't see human brutality or hear it borne in on the wind. Cruelty garbed in its own self-righteousness: curious wealth in a penury of self-esteem. The other societies he'd lived in— Franco's Spain, especially—seemed better able to bridle and unbridle their bullies.

Even so Éclair Pasture, it comes to him like a flash, is far more luxurious than the Petit Bordel he'd been born in. How do such communities nurture humanity like Aunt Stacey's, produce a Healer André? Understanding reality requires humility. We pierce its mask occasionally and what we find mostly confounds our understanding. Yes, humanity here has to be like humanity everywhere: empty, ordinary, conformist, bloated, pretentious— here, humanity without the institutions that rein in brutal excesses—and generous, forgiving, compassionate, sharing. His next challenge, he knows, is learning to appreciate this paradox in his species, to see himself as part of it. For hatred of humanity is self-hatred.

25

AND SO HE HAS MADE up his mind to remain on Isabella Island, its tyrannical conformity notwithstanding. "The end of all our exploring," Eliot tells us, "will be to arrive where we started/ and know the place for the first time."

And he's ready, he feels, to wean himself from Aunt Stacey's mothering. A child, even one almost fifty-three, seeks to be an adult. He's confident he has found a compromise: two acres of land on a gently sloping hillside in the south of Isabella Island, a mile from Oya and Randolph. He has already examined it and made a formal offer to purchase. It's naked, uncultivated land, located just above the coastal highway, four miles from Hanovertown. A sizable stream forms its northern boundary. He thinks he would build a simple two-bedroom house on it—his bedroom and a bedroom for Aunt Stacey when she visits, that Defoe can use when he visits; he hopes Defoe's sincere—with a living room with enough space for his books. And spend the next few years reading, contemplating, and gardening. He'll begin with a half-acre of trees between his house and the highway, and use the stream for irrigation in the dry season. His eyes flickering, his face beaming, Healer André asked him why he wanted so many trees. Joshua thought of those he'd so often contemplated on Mount Royal.

"They're good for the soul" was all he could say.

"Yes, trees are a lesson in humbleness, if we take the time to study all the things they do for us that we can't do for ourselves." He paused. "I would help you select and plant them but on one condition: most o' them must be fruit trees that the children around will have access to."

It wasn't a thought he would have had. In fact, he's now sure he'd conceived of the trees as a wall between himself and the outside world. But in the instant he'd agreed with some discomfort. And now he understands; it's reaching out and sharing that he needs to do. The healthy food in Defoe's banquet.

He mounts the four steps to the house, opens the door. Aunt Stacey is out. He eats the breakfast she has left him—fried plantain and scrambled eggs, and reheats the water to make a cup of tea.

He heads out to the porch, and from a side table just inside the main door, picks up the notebook he uses for a journal and the pen habitually clasped to it and goes to sit on the porch. *I'm still astonished that a mere ten days after my psyche was held together by chemicals I undertook the longest walk ever up into the forest, sometimes along the edges of precipices—I who used to be afraid of heights. To me this was the most shocking of shock therapies.*

He opens the journals and leafs through it without looking for anything in particular. On a blank page he writes:

What essential thing did I encounter up there that was the catalyst for my unburdening? I'm still not sure what role Healer André played. Did the reveries reveal to me the essence of life? I've known, since my second year at Queen Mary College, that psychic health requires an uncompromising and sometimes brutal encounter with the self, and have tried to do it. Even so self became more and more burdensome, insidiously so, until it shut its own self down.

He stops writing and begins turning the pages absentmindedly but continues thinking: *Defoe asked me if I felt secure here, and I told him yes.*

"Are you at peace with yourself?"

"I think I am. Yes, I am."

"That's what sanity is. Now it's your duty to maintain it."

His mind turns to Zagga, and he resumes writing: *Not sure I handled Zagga's situation well. Get him to help you plant those trees and pay him generously. He did say he isn't working. No question of his being my gardener or yardboy. (Wouldn't Paul love to play on this one! I should get in touch with the QMC Alumni Association and see if I can track him down. Maturity probably cured him of his fear of aging and his hatred—or was it fear?—of White people. What did he go on to do? When I left for Madrid, he'd already got his results—an upper second in history—and was already accepted into graduate school. I hope AIDS didn't get him. That's not news I'll want to get.) Together Zagga and I would dig the holes and do whatever's to be done. It will give us ample time to breakdown the rich/poor, lower class/upper class, pale-skinned/dark-skinned, giver/receiver barriers. Fences, however useful, trap us in our suspicions and false constructs of one another. I must make it so that in future Zagga or others like or unlike him can come to my place and share tea or lemonade with me for no other reason than the inherent goodness of human camaraderie.* He closes the journal, clips the pen onto it, and drops it onto the floor beside him.

Healer André—he crosses his fingers—is becoming the brother and friend he'd never been able to have. And already he feels there's a friendship between Randolph and Oya and himself.

Like his stutter, his guilt is gone. He knows he has cast it aside like an outgrown shirt, the way he'd once thought he would throw off his life if ever it got too burdensome. And now his feelings about his delights and disgusts have intensified. Never again will he whip himself, he thinks, for real, imaginary, his own, or other people's wrongs.

When he is settled he'll reconsider reapportioning the revenue generated by his inheritance. He'll have to think of some facility that would serve the villages of Éclair Pasture and Petit Bordel, perhaps a library and community centre: construct it and endow it with enough resources to educate people to have empathy for others and to resist deriving pleasure from inflicting pain. Something for the Hanovertown Ecumenical Centre against Spousal Violence, which, according to the letters in the press, men see as "setting our women against us." Something too for the disabled, People's Academy, and the Caribs whose stolen land is the basis of his wealth. At some point he'll also volunteer his labour somewhere—he has every intention of fulfilling that promise—more than likely at the Asylum for the Indigent Aged, where, many, like Dawn, have been put to die in poverty after a life spent serving the wealthy. And who knows, he may even turn to inventing characters for children or adults. But for the moment he must focus on building *his house* and cultivating *his garden.*

He bends down and picks up his journal and writes: *Humanity is as humanity has always been. At some level, we're all fools on the road to death, toting the dead and trying to revive the comatose parts of ourselves. How easily I understand this now! And how easily I accept it! Suffering humbles us.*

All that remains is the journey to Tallahassee, to tell Averill Éclair that she is understood and forgiven. She made a Pygmalion foul-up of my life. But Pygmalianism is endemic to humanity. Her life and life in her home are my best examples of human unhappiness and lives founded and foundered on lies. When I visit her grave, I think I'll recite:

Nature's first green is gold,
Her hardest hue to hold.
Her early leaf's a flower,
But only so an hour.
Then leaf subsides to leaf.
So Eden sank to grief,
So dawn goes down to day.
Nothing gold can stay.

And if I too cry while reciting it, it would be all right.

Acknowledgements

I'm grateful to my former employer, Université Laval, for encouraging and rewarding my creative writing and availing me the time each year from May to August to indulge my creative passions.

There are several persons to whom I'm indebted in the writing of this novel. Some of them are relatives and close family friends who, during my childhood told their stories about working for the plantocracy in St Vincent and the Grenadines. Even though *Return to Arcadia* is totally a work of fiction, i.e., comprised of invented characters, it's their stories that comprise its inspirational nucleus.

A significant amount of research was necessary to write this novel. Anselme Nye, librarian at Queen Mary College: University of London, directed me to the archival material for the period that *Return to Arcadia* covers; later he mailed me photocopies of relevant material that I had missed; my brother Oliver Sandy and his then wife Elrah Jack housed and fed me for the three weeks I stayed in London; my cousins Gloria Cyrus and Doreen McDowall and my friend Irma James went out of their way to make my stay in Britain an unforgettably enjoyable one. During the actual writing, fellow writers Nalini Warriar, George Elliott Clarke, Cecil Foster, Pam Mordecai, Afua Cooper, and Horace Goddard offered encouragement during moments of deep doubt. Thomas Glave, professor and fellow writer, took time from his busy schedule to read and comment on the manuscript. Fellow writer and friend Malcolm Reid and his spouse Rejeanne Cyr read an early draft of the manuscript and offered their candid comments.

Of course, there is my publisher Nurjehan Aziz. I am grateful for the faith she continues to have in my creative vision and for the thorough editing to which she subjects my books. Last, but definitely not least, is Troy Cunningham, who ably performs many functions at TSAR Publications.

A point of clarification—Caribbean readers of my books sometimes assume that Isabella Island, the fictional site for my works set in the Caribbean, is St Vincent. However much Isabella Island's villages and capital may resemble St Vincent's, Isabella Island is not St Vincent-only its fictional neighbour. Isabella Island is an invented Caribbean island inspired by St Vincent, St Lucia, Dominica, Grenada, Jamaica, and the various other Caribbean islands I have visited.

H NIGEL THOMAS was born in St Vincent. He has been a teacher with the Protestant School Board of Greater Montreal, and professor of American literature at Université Laval. He resides in the Montreal suburb of Greenfield Park. He is the author of: *Spirits in the Dark* (novel), which was a finalist for the QWF Prize, *Behind the Face of Winter* (novel), *Moving through Darkness* (poetry), and *Why We Write: Conversations with African Canadian Poets and Novelists* (criticism).